Susan Arnout Smith is a third generation Alaskan now living in California. Winner of the Stanley Drama Award, she has written television movies that have been aired in the United States and other countries. She has been a playwright at the National Playwrights Conference, Eugene O'Neill Theater Center, and an essayist for National Public Radio. She is the author of *The Timer Game*.

OUT AT NIGHT

Professor Bartholomew lies dying in a field of GM crops, the victim of a brutal attack. He has just enough time to spell out a message — a name. That name is Grace Descanso, CSI Detective Grace Descanso. While she knows of the professor, Grace can't understand why she has been dragged into this horrific crime. But the FBI leave her with no choice — join the investigation or become a suspect . . .

Books by Susan Arnout Smith
Published by The House of Ulverscroft:

THE TIMER GAME

SUSAN ARNOUT SMITH

OUT AT NIGHT

Complete and Unabridged

CHARNWOOD
Leicester

First published in Great Britain in 2009 by
HarperPress
An imprint of
HarperCollins*Publishers*
London

First Charnwood Edition
published 2010
by arrangement with
HarperCollins*Publishers*
London

British Library CIP Data

Smith, Susan Arnout.
    Out at night.
    1. Women detectives- -Fiction.
    2. Criminal investigation- -Fiction.
    3. Suspense fiction.
    4. Large type books.
    I. Title
    813.6–dc22

ISBN 978–1–44480–471–3

Published by
F. A. Thorpe (Publishing)
Anstey, Leicestershire

Set by Words & Graphics Ltd.
Anstey, Leicestershire
Printed and bound in Great Britain by
T. J. International Ltd., Padstow, Cornwall

This book is printed on acid-free paper

For my father
    Ernest Weschenfelder
    who taught me to love mountains

and my mother
    Florence Weschenfelder Johnson
    who showed me how to move them

                    rest in peace, Dad

The use of recombinant DNA could potentially alter man and his environment, for better or worse, by intention or accidentally. Therein lies the promise and danger of this new technology.

— Testimony at HEW hearings on recombinant DNA (1978)

All the predators come out at night.

— TOUR GUIDE, *Palm Springs wind farm*

1

Wednesday

'She'll call the police if I don't come home.'

Professor Thaddeus Bartholomew kept his hands on the wheel the way he'd been directed, his eyes straight ahead. Actually it was a desperate gamble, his last. His wife had been dead over two years.

'Shut up and drive.' The man in the seat next to him pressed the snout of the revolver against Bartholomew's thigh and he tensed involuntarily and felt the gun nose him hard.

In the headlights, giant windmills whirred against the night sky. They'd been driving toward Palm Springs for almost half an hour and they were getting close.

Bartholomew had spent the entire time searching his mind for a way out and finding none. He was a scholar, at home in the tranquil world of old wars and settled battles; the voices that called to him were the ones that lived on the page and in polite debates on the History Channel. He realized in that instant he could speak so confidently about history because it was done.

It wasn't sitting next to him reeking with sweat, crazed with some plan to maim and kill a substantial part of the world's population.

A plan Bartholomew feared had every chance of working.

Bartholomew rubbed his hands on the wheel and tried again. 'Maybe I'm wrong. Maybe you could talk to me about it again. Make me see.' His voice held a tremor he didn't like.

'Turn left here.' The gun jabbed him again.

'Careful with the gun.' Bartholomew instinctively jerked the wheel toward the dark dirt road leading between the high fields of soy. He slowed to avoid a sudden dip in the road.

He thought despairingly of how he'd almost made it to the car when the man had emerged from the shadows of the parking garage. He could admit it now; why lie, what was the point? He'd been flattered, more than happy to stand there a few moments listening. Relieved to postpone going home to an empty house and his solitary meal.

They'd talked before; or more precisely, he'd listened to him rant. Bartholomew wasn't a man given to snap criticisms, but this man scared him.

At least he did now.

There'd been enough signs.

Documented. Why hadn't he ever documented what the man was saying?

Ironic, when he thought about it. His lifework had been spent painstakingly resurrecting those marginalized, forgotten ones history had relegated to footnotes: the dispossessed, disenfranchised, the lost. Yet here was one of that very number whose words Bartholomew hadn't thought to record. And the ingenious plan the man proposed had made him recoil in horror. The very next instant, it seemed, he'd found a gun pressing into his side.

Fast. It had happened so fast.

He wasn't going to make it out of this.

Not alive.

'Stop right here.'

They were in a small dirt parking lot next to a four-acre plot of soy contained by a barbwire fence. On the fence was a sign:

USDA EXPERIMENTAL SOY PROJECT 3627
DO NOT ENTER
VIOLATORS WILL BE PROSECUTED

'Turn off the engine.'

Bartholomew shivered, his head bowed. The man reached over and switched the engine off, yanking out the keys.

'Move.'

'Where?' His lips were numb.

He'd left the headlights on and in the wash of light, barbwire hung in strands where it had been cut, revealing a hole large enough for a man to crawl into the dark rows of soy.

'I'm giving you to the count of ten.' His voice was flat.

Bartholomew lurched off the seat and scrambled toward the gaping hole, his heart hammering.

'One.'

He clawed through the fence break, his jacket catching on the barbwire, and plunged into the soy. A cloying, sweet smell bit his nostrils. The ground was uneven and the darkness almost impenetrable. He stumbled and went down hard on his knee, feeling the dark cold earth and the

3

familiar odor of mulch. Pain shot through his knee.

'Two.'

The voice was coming from the outside perimeter of the fence.

Bartholomew whimpered and immediately cut it off, swallowing the metallic taste of fear that was flooding his mouth. He grasped a sturdy plank of soy and heaved himself up. The stalks upended under his weight, the roots leaking clots of dirt. He took a staggering step and regained his balance. The pain was volcanic, roaring up his thigh into his groin.

'Three.'

He thrashed farther into the thicket and felt the stalks give way, sending him sprawling into a cultivated field. He panted shallowly, getting his bearings. In the dim moonlight, he could see the soy laid out in neat, bristling rows. He scanned the field and spotted another place along the fence where the soy seemed to be growing wild. He limped toward it, gripping his thigh above his injured knee to brace himself.

Dimly, he'd been hearing numbers.

'Eight,' his attacker said, his voice still distant.

Bartholomew wormed his way as far as possible back into the dense undergrowth and slid down, gripping his knees to his chest, making himself as small as possible.

His cell phone.

'Nine. I lied. Any last words?'

The voice was dead-sounding, clearly coming now from somewhere inside the fence, and most alarming, seemed to be turned straight toward him.

His attacker couldn't possibly see him. Bartholomew yanked the cell phone free and dialed the familiar number, his hands shaking so badly he balanced the phone on his good knee to find the numbers. His phone was an old model, the kind nobody made anymore. The keys sounded unnaturally loud. He waited for the voicemail to kick in.

He had to focus now, figure out what to say and how to say it. He peered at the small electronic keyboard in his hand, lit with the comforting green light. His fingers moved carefully across the keys.

'Okay, then.' The man's voice was closer.

The air seemed to shiver and in the next instant, a piercing pain slammed into Bartholomew's chest. The velocity of it crashed him backward and sent the cell phone flying from his grasp.

At first all he felt was stunned disbelief coupled with a roaring pain, and then he realized something was lodged in his chest. A stick.

An arrow.

He couldn't breathe. No, he could breathe, but not deeply; he couldn't move, he was pinned to the ground. It was getting warm under him now, and that was a comfort. He touched the arrow and wondered if he could risk yanking it up. The soy above him parted and he stared up at his attacker's face. It was blank as an insect's. The man was holding aloft the cell phone.

Goggles, Bartholomew thought wonderingly. Why was he wearing goggles?

Wordlessly, the attacker shifted the crossbow

in his grasp. He reached down and grasped the arrow and — *God no!* — yanked it with all his might and then tipped it back and forth as if trying to work it free and a fresh wave of pain engulfed Bartholomew.

He cried out in terror and pain, his voice an incoherent tumble of words pleading and thank God it stopped, stopped and his attacker pulled a water bottle from his jacket.

Bartholomew's field of vision was narrowing, the edges fuzzy and gray. He fought to stay conscious. His attacker unscrewed the bottle and tipped it over him and for a brief instant, Bartholomew thought, Water, he's going to grant me that, at least. He caught the sudden sharp odor of gasoline. Through an agony of pain, he peered up and saw the attacker light a match, the sharp tiny prick of flame a bright cold thing, the burning match falling, falling like a small meteorite through the black night.

Flames boiled up his body and the last thing he heard was a crackling noise, close to his face, and the attacker retreating into a haze of orange. And then the orange window narrowed to a pinhole and Bartholomew eased into it and was gone.

2

Thursday

'Let me get this straight.' Mac McGuire shifted on the blanket, digging his feet into the sand. 'You've come all the way from San Diego, down through Florida, on to the island of Eleuthera in the Bahamas, so you can take our five-year-old swimming on a beach that's covered with razor-sharp coral.'

'First of all, it's not covered with coral, just that one side.' Grace Descanso squirted a dollop of sunscreen directly onto his back and smoothed it in. 'And secondly, she's wearing beach shoes. She's fine.'

A warm wind gusted across the waves, creating a froth of white that enveloped Katie in foam. She twisted her arms out like a windmill, the turquoise water sparkling around her chest, floating the ruffles of her hot pink swimsuit. Her hair was wet, the golden curls darker than usual.

Katie saw them watching and beamed. 'Hi, Daddy Daddy Daddy.'

And Mommy Mommy Mommy, Grace thought sourly.

'Hi, sweetheart, I'll be back out in a minute.'

Grace could tell by the sound of Mac's voice that he had a sappy look on his face.

He kept talking, his voice dropping down into the reasoned, considered tone he used on air. He was a CNN health reporter, responsible for filing two stories each week and available for live reports. He was also the face of the unit, on air every week-night introducing stories researched and prepared by producers behind the scenes. When viewers turned on CNN, they often thought of Mac. At least that's the way they spun it in promos.

'I know she's fine, I just thought it might be nice to take her someplace amazing. Both of you,' he amended.

Grace worked the sunscreen into his muscles a little too vigorously. He smelled like a tropical fruit drink. She'd already slathered Katie again, until her daughter was slippery as a baby seal and just as quickly had slid out of Grace's grasp into the water. Then it had been Mac's turn with Grace, his fingers strong, his touch lingering. The mating dance of the tropics.

Now his skin glowed hot under her fingers; he'd arrived in the Bahamas the day before, and the sun had already streaked his hair with gold. Grace shifted position and kept working. Over his shoulder she could see part of his dark green swimming trunks. A fine pink scar ran up his left arm, still new. She felt a twinge. She'd put that scar there, and if it had happened the other way around, she doubted she'd be letting Mac anywhere near her body, no matter how good his fingers felt.

'I mean, it's *interesting* the place you rented,' Mac continued. 'But I would have opted at least for a real bathroom.'

'It's ecofriendly.'

'It's a compost heap, Grace, with a wooden throne that sits behind a curtain. How in the world did you find that place?'

'A Portuguese cousin in the travel business. Remind me to kill her when I get home.'

In truth, the bed-and-breakfast was a little more primitive than she'd expected; the promised gourmet lunches had turned out to be leftover mac and cheese wrapped in crinkled aluminum foil and cut into cold wedges, served with hamburger buns studded with raisins accompanied by a vat of peanut butter; and the beach billed as remote was an inaccessible clamber down spiny-ridged limestone. Luckily, she'd rented a car, and after adapting to the harrowingly narrow roads filled with traffic hurtling straight at them, they'd found the beach not far from where they were staying.

The main thing had been to get away. Everything else had been secondary. Life for Grace Descanso had changed in an instant on a sunny October day in San Diego when a monster had reached into her world and grabbed her daughter, and by the time Grace had gotten her back, nothing was ordinary ever again.

Mac was back, for starters.

She'd contacted him in the middle of the kidnapping, when she was desperate and cornered. He'd represented the best hope of getting Katie back. The only hope. And now Grace couldn't say, *Gee thanks, for saving my life and helping find our daughter, but you can leave now.*

Katie Marie had no memory of the kidnapping, but Grace relived it beat by beat, startling at sudden noises, tensing at the sound of alarms, always looking for the shadow with the long arm that could snag into the shot and blur out of frame, loping away with Katie in its jaws.

The price of getting her back was constant vigilance. Even worse was the guilt, and Grace feared that would never go away. She had lied to Katie growing up, telling her daughter that her father was dead, and now here he sat, sucking down a canned mai tai and criticizing her parenting skills.

'You know this isn't healthy.' His voice was mild. 'You need to take a breath. Relax. The bad guy's gone.'

She snapped her eyes back to his shoulders. She'd been watching Katie with the intensity reserved for photos on a post office wall. Mac had the kind of skin that never burned, turning golden and ripe as a peach and then browning. Katie had that skin, and his hair color too, but she'd inherited Grace's dark Portuguese eyes and a dimple that appeared whenever she smiled, and Grace had to admit she'd been seeing a lot more of it lately, ever since Katie had learned her father was still alive.

'And you know the bad guy's gone because?'

'I have the money and resources to figure things like this out, that's the *because*. He's not getting back into the States, don't worry.'

'We're not in the States.' She glanced around the quiet beach and saw a sand crab busily

10

dragging the corpse of a small sea anemone across the sand.

'Still.'

'Daddy, Daddy, Daddy,' Katie crooned. She clasped her small hands together as if she were holding a Mr Microphone in a karaoke bar. 'I just want my daddy.'

'I'm coming, princess.'

Pet names. He'd met Katie face-to-face for the first time exactly twenty-four hours before, and already he had a raft of them. Little dimple toes. Miss periwinkle flippy hair. Sunshine happy girl.

He clambered to his feet and reached for a towel.

'Do you remember that old movie, *A Man and a Woman?*' Grace twisted the cap back on and tossed the suntan lotion aside.

'I wonder if I should take off my sunglasses.'

'Remember, Anouk Aimée, and she loses her husband, and then she meets this race car driver, and they both have adorable kids and then they all go out to dinner? Or maybe she lost her race car driver husband, and met somebody else, I can't remember.'

'She'll probably splash all over them, right?'

'Well, it's not like that here.'

'What are you talking about?' Without the sunglasses, his eyes were a brilliant green against his skin. He dropped the sunglasses onto the blanket.

'The kids. In that movie. They were there. But somehow in the background. They were present, but didn't take over the whole thing. The grownups still had a nice, normal dinner and

11

they were flirting to beat the band and — '

'So.' Mac shot Grace a swift, evaluating look. 'Are you thinking about the dinner or the flirting part?'

'I am hungry.'

He smiled, his teeth very white, and she felt her body flush.

'Daddy.' Katie flung her arms wide.

'I'm coming, sweetie girl,' he called, his eyes still on Grace. 'Ten minutes. Then I take you and your mom back to your place so you can get changed for dinner.'

They'd already agreed to that; it was just that he said it with such *authority*, and she thought about that as she gathered up the blanket and stowed it in the car. What she didn't want was Mac upsetting the balance she had with her daughter, and it was already too late for that.

He had come over in the morning in his rental — a classier, cleaner car than the cheap one she'd rented before he got there — and picked them up, and now he was driving them back, and it seemed, incrementally, that he was in the driver's seat a lot. She still wasn't certain how she felt about that.

From the moment yesterday when Mac had flown in and found them, the life she'd shared for five years with Katie had been over. She'd stepped over a threshold into another world, and it scared her.

What was worse, she had no idea what it was doing to Katie.

Katie had been subdued — shocked — when she'd met him, stealing quick looks up at his face

12

before moving out of reach. Mac had taken it slowly, never pressing, and that, too — his restraint — pressed a guilty place in her heart and made Grace want to run.

That first night, they'd eaten dinner in a small local café, the only outsiders. The wife of the cook served them steaming plates of rice and fish and when Katie yawned as the plates were cleared, the server said in a musical voice over her shoulder as she swayed back to the kitchen, 'Looks like it's time to get your little one home.'

Home.

They were so far from that, all of them. Far from the safety of home. From the idea of it. And Grace feared she'd never find her way back, and that even if she could, she might be returning empty-handed. Losing the one thing that mattered most.

She watched as Mac and Katie came up the beach toward the car, wrapped in damp sandy towels, Katie chattering. There was a warm gusty wind but suddenly Grace felt chilled, the growing tug of distance, separation.

She gripped the side of the window as Mac bumped the car down the narrow rutted road that led to her bed-and-breakfast. They turned a corner and a haphazardly built octagon painted a startling shade of Creamsicle purple appeared, set back in a tangle of undergrowth.

A truck idled in the drive. The back looked like a flimsy covered wagon held together with duct tape. A sunburned man with a nest of red dreadlocks sat hunched in the driver's seat, talking on an iPhone. He clicked it shut and sat up and eased out of the truck as Grace and Mac got out of the car. Mac was taller and bigger through the shoulders but the other guy was younger. He smiled.

Grace made a sound. 'He's back. That's my landlady's son. Clint. He likes to stop by unannounced.' She reached into the backseat to help Katie out.

'Swell,' Mac said. 'And he has the key, right?'

'Actually the door doesn't lock.' Grace unsnapped Katie's seat belt and she scrambled free.

'Ah.' Mac nodded.

Clint plodded over and pulled a crinkled envelope out of the pocket of his board shorts. The flap had been opened and resealed with a piece of cloudy Scotch tape.

'Here.'

She ripped the envelope open and pulled out the single sheet, scanning it.

'Is that who I think it is?' His voice had a lilt to it, as if he'd had a couple extra beers and couldn't quite shape the hard vowels anymore.

She glanced up.

Clint was staring at Mac.

'No, Clint, you're getting them mixed up.' She refolded the letter and put it in the pocket of her cover-up. 'The other guy's better-looking and works for Fox.'

Clint frowned and brightened. 'Oh, I get it. A joke. Very funny.'

Mac touched her arm. 'Okay?'

She knew he was talking about the letter. She shrugged. 'Why don't you ask him, he's already read it.'

Clint ignored her, hitched up his board shorts and padded over to a twisted tree that stood in the yard.

'It's from my uncle Pete,' she said to Mac. 'Wants me to call him. Said it's business. He works for the FBI in Palm Springs. Whatever it is, it can wait.'

'I didn't know you had an uncle in the FBI.'

'He's not even a blip on my radar, Mac. We haven't talked in years.'

'Forgot to tell you, Grace, about this tree.' Clint cleared his throat importantly. 'Katie, this is important for you, too.'

Katie started to trot forward and Mac shot out an easy hand and stopped her.

Black sap oozed from creases in the bark. Clint scooped a finger of sap and held it out. 'See this sap? Don't touch it. It's called a poisonwood tree, because that's what it is.'

'Poison?' Katie cried. Grace instinctively reached for her but Mac was there first. He rested his palm on Katie's curls.

'Yes, Katie, it can kill you.' Clint leaned on the word *kill* like it was a horn. 'Some people are immune, like me.' He wiped the sap onto his board shorts and left a trail. 'But no worries! It stands next to this tree.' He patted an ashy colored tree with flaking bark. 'It's the antidote. I haven't figured out how to use it yet, but it's here, if you need it.'

'Ah,' Mac said again.

A black snout poked through the slats of the truck, followed by a second, more massive head.

'Oh, and don't worry about those guys.' Clint

gestured grandly to the dogs. He walked down the path toward the front door of the B-and-B. 'They only attack if they smell fear.'

He pushed open the door. 'Got anything to drink?'

'Okay,' Mac said. 'We're done.'

★ ★ ★

Half an hour later, Mac moved them. He turned in both cars, took them by water taxi to Harbor Island five minutes away, and relocated them to the Pink Sands Hotel, owned by the man who started Island Records. Now they stood in the living room of a villa.

Katie dropped her backpack, her eyes wide. 'Wow. It's got flat-screen.'

'And movies, Katie. I can rent whatever you want.'

Katie flung her arms around Mac's legs and Grace looked away. The windows and French doors opened onto a patio that faced a three-mile pink-sand beach dotted with lavender beach umbrellas, sand as soft as corn silk, the water a turquoise that slid into mauve at the horizon.

'Come on, I'll show you where you'll sleep.'

Katie took his hand and skipped beside him and Grace trailed behind, the sherpa hauling suitcases. It occurred to Grace that Mac already knew where the bedrooms were.

'Here's where you and your mom can stay.' The room held two queen-sized beds with a view of the beach. 'My room's on the other side, and the bathrooms are in between. Want to see?'

Katie nodded, her eyes round.

'I'll wait,' Grace said. Mac shot her that look again and she flushed.

That night they ate in the hotel dining room at a small table covered in brocade, next to a plaster wall of vivid pinks and oranges, wooden mermaids hanging in the archway. Katie sat next to Mac and insisted he cut her chicken, and he bent over it as if it were a sacrament. Nobody bothered them.

Clemens, the manager, explained that their villa had housed kings and queens, heads of business and Hollywood royalty, and that one of the hallmarks of the place was the other guests' exquisite ability to leave those whose faces were familiar alone.

That, and the staff's attention to detail, anticipating every need and silently meeting it.

It was as if the ground were slipping, but it was *quality* ground, a finer silt than Grace was used to. Even the towels she used to dry Katie after her bath felt better. Fluffier. Softer. Whiter. Part of Grace loved being taken care of. And part of her feared it. But Katie seemed to be slipping into this life with Mac effortlessly — and that, too, scared her.

She'd been alone for so long, making every decision about Katie, and now here was a man — her man, he'd been, a long time ago — reverently embracing his role as dad. Daddy. The big guy. Mr Right who could do no wrong. At least not in Katie's eyes. Part of her wanted to yell, *Hold it! Wait! Who's the parent here,*

17

anyway? Not wanting to hear the answer.

Some uneasy thing tremored under the surface and Grace knew what it was.

Sometime soon, Katie would look her right in the eye and ask out loud why Grace had lied to her about her dad. Lied about the most important thing in Katie's life.

And Grace didn't have a good answer.

She doubted she ever would.

★ ★ ★

'How do you want to handle this?' They were sitting on lounge chairs on the patio. From the bedroom, Katie murmured in her sleep.

Mac reached across the dark expanse and took Grace's hand, his fingers warm, touch solid.

Past the railing and down the terraced walks, waves foamed whitely against the dark expanse of sand. Landscaping lights illuminated the palm trees and Grace saw a man and woman wading along the edge of the waves, holding hands in the growing dark.

The setting sun was turning the water a soft pink that glowed as if it were lit from within, and the air was heavy with the scent of hibiscus and the sea.

'We have to take it slow,' Grace said.

And then she got up and sat down next to him on his lounge chair, placed her hands on either side of his face and kissed him. He kissed her back, and pulled her on top of him. The rush was instantaneous, greedy, joyous, drugged with heat and desire. He rolled to his feet, picked her up, and carried her to his bed.

The clothes came off, and she wished again she'd packed better underwear, but who knew that instead of playing four rounds of Candyland she'd be sliding her hands over a man voted by *People* magazine as one of the top 100 sexiest men in America?

Last year's list, she reminded herself. Although he still looked pretty good. His chest gleamed with a fine sheen of sweat. He shifted and she felt him against her. Liquid fire.

'Oh, brother,' she said. 'Oh, oh, brother.'

She rolled away and wrapped a sheet around her. She took a long shaky breath. She rolled back toward him and put her hands on the flat of his chest. His skin burned the palms of her hands and that close, his eyes were heavy-lidded, his gaze intense.

'Grace.' He kissed her shoulder blade, the hollow in her throat where her heart was beating. 'Talk to me.'

'It means too much.' Her voice was quiet. 'If we made love and it didn't work — and it would be making love, Mac, not just the physical part, what it means.'

He slid his hand under the sheet and cupped a breast and she sucked in a breath, almost in a panic, her body flooded with warmth.

He removed his hand with effort. He was breathing through his mouth. He had a nick on an incisor. He'd chipped it as a kid using his teeth to cut a fishing line. She was doomed. She already knew how he'd gotten all his childhood injuries. His knees touched her

19

shins and shifted away.

He regarded her, loss and desire on his face. 'What do you want, Grace?'

Her eyes filled. She felt his breath, soft, on her face. He searched her eyes. All the bones in her body seemed to soften; she was warm wax in his hands.

'For the last five years to go away. Not the part with Katie. The part without you.'

He rolled onto his back and stared at the ceiling. In the moonlight, his eyes glowed bright. 'But see,' his voice was low. 'That's just it, Grace. That was the part without Katie. For me. That was the part.'

She couldn't breathe. Her throat closed. The night air felt heavy against her face. She had done this, she had done this. And there was no fixing it.

She rolled away from him with effort and slid free of the sheets. She stood. Her legs trembled. Their clothes lay in a jumbled trail across the Saltillo tile floor and she took a shambling step.

'You bolt at the first sign of trouble.' There was no accusation in his voice; it was as if he were tracking the beats of a song, figuring out its rhythm. She realized her heart hurt.

'I bolt.' The floor was cold. She found her T-shirt and put it on. She needed underpants. She needed distance. She needed to remember to take her birth control pills.

'It's as if you're there one moment, and then you flip a switch and you're gone. I don't want you to go.'

Mac flung off the covers and stood. The heat

between them was old, and raw and real. She looked away, but not before she'd seen that he'd seen it, too, in her eyes, on her face.

He pulled her to him and kissed her and she wrapped her arms around him and stood trembling, feeling the shock of his presence, the immediacy of his reaction. His arms seemed harder, somehow, than they'd been five years before, his muscles knotted.

'Hunger does that.' His voice had an edge.

She could feel her heart start to race. 'That's a little scary. Reading my mind.'

'I've had five years' practice. You were squeezing it,' he added.

'I beg your pardon?'

'My arm. The muscle. You were squeezing it as if you were testing its strength against your memory. My arm won.'

'Yeah, memory's a tricky thing.'

'Been my experience.' His body shifted and tensed and she felt the familiar fit of his body, both of them wanting more.

She dropped her hand to his back. She could still feel the sun in his skin. 'Have you had a lot of that? Experience?'

'Do my best.' He slid a hand down her back, and she could see him tracking its impact, evaluating mentally the way her back tensed, the short intake of her breath when his bare hand slid from her T-shirt to her skin, the hooded light in her eyes.

And then it rounded a corner again, what she was feeling, and her eyes filled.

He stopped his hands and moved his naked

strong body a fraction away.

'I did this to us, okay? I made it be *not simple*.'

'So now you're beating yourself up.' His hands found her hips. He pulled her gently toward him and she felt again the blurring sweetness of desire, the melting heat. His palm grazed her buttocks, his eyes still on hers.

She was going to have to push him away. If not now, then soon. Her breath came in short gusts. 'What are you offering, Mac?'

'I think that's pretty clear.'

'No, I mean it.' She rocked back away from him, but all that did was position her closer. If he moved, even slightly, toward her. Into her.

'Okay, what am I offering. The truth. Ask me anything.'

'Risky business.'

'Riskier not to.'

He touched her breast, her belly, the soft part of her that melted under his touch. They stood together in the dim light, their bodies naked except for her T-shirt. He swallowed. Sighed as if it took everything he had. He pushed her gently away.

'Truth then. I get the feeling you're a whole lot of work. Maybe I'm not up to that. Maybe I'd give it my best shot, and still come up short.'

Her heart was beating very fast.

'You kept Katie away for five years. When I think about that too much, it makes me crazy.'

She couldn't breathe.

'Maybe it is too late. Not for Katie. But for us.'

His room held a king-sized bed, a mahogany

side-board, a bar, a flat-screen TV. Through the French doors she could see the ocean. She looked everywhere except his face.

'So that whole 'sticking around when you're not sure' — that stuff you said after you got out of the hospital and flew here to surprise us and meet Katie — that's bullshit?'

'I don't want to do this anymore. Not here. Not this way.'

He was a big man, his movements economical. He found his shorts and pulled them on. It was abrupt, final, and changed everything. The small window he'd offered — the one through which she could have slipped without penalty or disguise — had closed.

It would take much more now to open it.

Yet as Grace returned to her solitary bed next to Katie's, listening to the commingled sounds of the surf and Mac gargling into his sink, it seemed as if they'd been doing this forever, or a version of it, and maybe when things evened out, they'd add back in the sex part and get married.

A fantasy she'd construct brick by fragile brick.

3

Friday

They spent the morning in a golf cart touring the candy-colored clapboard Harbor Island village, stopping at Angela's Starfish for fresh conch, searching for Jimmy Buffett's Cheeseburger in Paradise. Mac had been polite and remote with her, lavishing attention on Katie and right before Grace's eyes, their daughter bloomed.

There had been one reoccurring speed bump, an awkward one, when she noted it: she seemed incapable of letting Katie and Mac hold a conversation without interjecting herself into it, trying to change the focus, not to her, but so that Mac was closed out.

He'd point at a modest wooden house set back from a road and tell Katie it was a library. Grace would turn her in the other direction and point out the sea.

As the morning wore on, the tendency became more pronounced until Katie and Mac's defense was to close Grace out entirely, and it was then that she finally lost her footing on the emotional cliff face she was climbing — this strange new territory with no toeholds — and slid a good distance backward, scraping parts of her psyche she didn't know existed.

Battered, she thought jauntily. But still there.

On the heels of that thought, she felt it start in

24

her throat, and then behind her eyes. She'd found herself close to tears.

Now she and Mac lay on lounge chairs at the pool, watching Katie paddle in the shallow end, her water wings bright glints of inflatable pink plastic against the turquoise. A brilliantly colored wall of bougainvillea shielded the pool from the walkway. There were other people sunbathing on towels, but Grace didn't get the sense that anybody was actively listening. It was only the two of them side by side, and the quiet sounds of Katie paddling and singing a small, tuneless song.

'I talked to my folks.'

'And?' She reached for her lemonade and drank.

'They were wondering if I could take Katie back to Atlanta for Thanksgiving. They live about an hour away. They could drive in.'

'You mean, by herself?' Grace kept her voice steady, but the panic was rising.

'Well, me.'

'That's in less than two weeks.'

He was silent.

It hadn't occurred to her until just that moment that maybe rehabilitating herself with Mac would be the least of her worries. The image of grandparents, bewildered and furious at having had a grandchild withheld, suddenly rose in her mind. It was another prick threatening the bubbly bliss of Grace's imagined life.

'She's barely five years old. I thought we were going to try trips, the three of us.'

'This is sort of one.'

'You flew out. I wasn't expecting you.'

'I wasn't going to meet Katie while I was in the hospital, Grace. We agreed. I didn't want to scare her. You'd told me any time I was ready was fine with you.'

'Yeah, well, people usually call first, but maybe that's me.'

He started to speak and stopped. This wasn't going the way she'd envisioned.

'She's got a whole other side of the family, Grace, she's never met.'

'She's got plenty of relatives she hasn't met on my side either, she can start with those; I barely know them myself, we can start together.'

She stopped. It was exactly what she'd done all day; promised herself she wouldn't do again.

'I found us a therapist. Elise Lithgow.'

She sucked in a breath.

Mac scribbled a phone number on a napkin next to his Coke and passed it to her. Grace glanced at it. It was a Mission Hills prefix.

'She wants to meet both of us separately first, to see if we're each comfortable with her, so if it's not a good match, I'm open to something else, Grace, if you've got another idea.'

Grace shook her head. Katie grabbed the side of the pool and kicked. She was wearing pink nail polish on her toenails and every so often the color winked in the water.

'Grace, when you stopped me last night — slowed me down so I could think through what I was doing — I realized something. You were right.'

'No, no, I wasn't. Do over. Let's do a do-over.'

'Let's just do it *right*.' He looked at Katie and hesitated. 'When I was in the hospital I worked with a Realtor. I bought a place near your house; with the market sliding, everything's available. It's a condo in the Rondolet. Right around the corner.'

'I know where it is.'

It stood on Shelter Island, an enormous round building with views on one side of the San Diego Yacht Club.

'It's far from perfect right now; it's packed with an old person's furniture — I bought the place from an elderly woman moving into a nursing facility — but it's a place, and it means Katie will have her own bedroom when she visits.'

It sunk in. He had planned this. The whole time he was in the hospital, while she sat by the edge of his bed. While they talked about how the light fell on San Diego harbor and the exact timbre of their daughter's laugh. He'd been working with a Realtor.

'Lots of kids wind up going between two houses. It's not ideal, but it's not the worst thing, either.'

Dissolving into sparkly bits! The big candy-colored house with the granite counters and the security gate. *Evaporating into air!* The three of them climbing, skipping the stairs to some phantom life where Mommy and Daddy lived in the same bedroom and Katie was down the hall and everybody ran in slomo in fields of daisies like some personal hygiene commercial. *Fragmenting into pieces!* The dream of laughing

27

around the kitchen table *ha ha ha* and having the only silences be good ones, not the lethal kind that took years of explaining and apologies and therapy to sort out.

Gone, gone, gone, not ever having to work at it, and never, *ever* having to say she was sorry.

She started to say, *Right!* Say it with conviction and nonchalance and stopped, straightening in her lawn chair.

A Royal Bahamas policeman was bicycling to a stop outside the gate leading to the pool, and even before he scanned the sunbathers and locked eyes with her, she knew he'd come for her.

4

They walked the beach. Pink sand foamed into a burst of white, the waves a dark green flattening into a purple so deep it looked inked. On the horizon a sailboat stood motionless.

Grace cut him a look. He was slightly built, very black, his gray shirt and shorts still crisp despite the humidity. He was wearing sandals. His name on the tag read EPSTEN and when he spoke his voice was a deep baritone. 'Thaddeus Bartholomew. Does the name mean anything to you?'

Grace shook her head.

He glanced around. No one was close enough to hear. A man in a leg cast and crutches limped away from them down the beach, his wife walking ahead, holding a cooler and a blanket. The wife never turned to check on him, striding briskly away from her husband as if he was paying for something not quite current in the marriage account. She seemed to be picking the least steady ground, the softest sand. He followed, a resigned slant to his shoulders, his wedding ring a dull flash against sunburned fingers.

'You received the message from FBI Special Agent Peter Descanso.' Epsten peered at Grace, his eyes bright.

'I'm on vacation.'

'Yes. With your daughter and her father.'

Grace shot him a look of surprise.

He said mildly, 'Not all white people look the same, but those two do.'

'She has my color eyes,' Grace said. A rogue wave washed toward them and Grace took a step back. 'And a dimple. You can't really see that from where you stood, but it's there.'

He started to speak and stopped.

'Some people think that Mac's the one with the dimple, but he really isn't. His is more of an indentation.'

He looked at her a long moment. 'Thaddeus Bartholomew,' he repeated gently.

'Name's vaguely familiar but that's as close as I can get.'

She was still smarting that a stranger had immediately seen the connection between Mac and Katie. What if it wasn't just physical? What if it transcended any bond she'd built with her daughter? And wow, the wrongness of that. Already putting Katie between them in a game of cosmic tug-of-war.

'He died in Palm Springs two nights ago. He was a history professor at Riverside University. Somebody shot him with an arrow. A bolt, they call it, in the States.'

'Special Agent Descanso — my uncle Pete — has been trying for years to get me to spend more time with him and his family. If you knew him — '

Officer Epsten shook his head.

' — but if you did, you'd understand this is so. Like. Him.' She was working up an aggrieved tone of voice. Soon she'd be able to thank

30

Officer Epsten nicely and he'd leave, reassured that she'd done all she could, had nothing to offer. 'Tracking me down on a family vacation so I could get pulled into something I know nothing about. Have no relationship to.'

Epsten stopped walking. 'Special Agent Descanso, he didn't explain in the letter?'

She shook her head.

'Mr Bartholomew left a clue, one investigators think *does* involve you. He was dying, but resourceful.'

Epsten's voice was measured and Grace realized in that instant she'd underestimated him. He wasn't going away.

She was.

That's what he'd come to tell her. She stared at the water. A teenage girl stood in the waves, her hair a springy golden mane against perfect skin.

'He sent a message to his home phone right before he died. At first, they thought it was just clicks, a child perhaps, playing. He had an old-style cell phone, no text messaging.' He turned. 'It was Morse code.'

She snapped a look at him. He stared at the water. From the side, his profile was strong. A slight graying near his glasses betrayed his age.

'He spelled out your name, Grace.'

She licked a lip. 'My first name? Because spelling out the word *grace* when you're about to get killed by a maniac with a crossbow is probably standard stuff.'

'Both names. Actually the exact message was *Find Grace Descans*. He was cut off before he

31

could add the o. He picked you, and they'd like to know why.'

He stooped and picked up a shell. It was small, fan-shaped, a soft purple and cream. He wiped off the sand and tucked it in the pocket of his shirt. 'My granddaughter collects these.'

'I don't have any choice, do I?'

'Not really.'

The teen in the ocean turned. It was a woman in her forties who'd had very good work done. A little too tucked around the eyes for Grace's taste, but still.

'It's bigger than somebody dying randomly in a field. Isn't it?'

Three horses picked their way carefully down a path toward the water, riders gripping saddle horns, and Grace turned back toward the Pink Sands cabana on the beach where a Bahamian attendant named Bolo smiled, waiting to offer a towel and a mauve-colored lawn chair. Grace smiled and shook her head and kept walking, taking the soft sand trail cut into the side of the hill that led back to the villa. Officer Epsten kept pace.

'Are you going to answer my question?'

'There's an international agricultural convention hosted by the United States government that starts in Palm Springs tomorrow and runs through Monday night.'

'Heard about it. Its official name is the International Ministerial Conference and Expo on Agricultural Science and Technology.'

He stared.

She shrugged. 'A friend has a friend who's involved in it.'

'Apparently Mr Bartholomew was involved in it, too.' He scuffed the sand with the heel of his sandal. 'He was not who he appeared.'

'How so?'

Epsten stared at her soberly. 'You'll have to ask Special Agent Descanso that.'

The villa was coming into view and she could see Katie on the balcony. She waved, and Katie bounced up and down and waved back. Mac appeared on the patio and he put his arm easily around Katie's shoulders and Grace felt hollowed out, light.

'If you know about Katie's father, then you probably know we haven't had much time together.'

'And I am sincerely sorry for that, madam.'

Katie was laughing, Mac bending over her saying something only she could hear. Katie impulsively reached up her arms and hugged Mac hard.

Whatever Grace's uncle needed her to do in Palm Springs was far less important than the likelihood of Mac forging a bond with Katie that forever altered the relationship she had with her daughter.

'I'll be back to drive you to the water taxi, which will take you to Eleuthera. On Eleuthera, there's transport waiting to drop you directly at the plane. They're holding it for you.'

'Am I supposed to go right to Palm Springs?'

He handed her a sealed letter with an FBI insignia on it. 'That, I do not know, madam.'

'How much time do I have?'

He glanced silently at the villa. Mac and Katie had disappeared inside, the balcony empty. He looked at her neutrally.

'Enough to say good-bye.'

★ ★ ★

'Mommy! Mommy mommy mommy mommy mommy!'

Katie threw herself at Grace. She was still in her swimsuit; her skin smelled of chlorine.

'Daddy's going to take me out in the golf cart later, just the two of us. We're going to find a store where they sell kitties. We're not going to buy one, just look. I want to hold a fluffy one.'

Grace met Mac's eyes over their daughter's head. He shrugged and Grace felt a territorial tug.

'You need to take a bath, sweetie.'

'There was a bird that flew onto the balcony. It had orange on its head and a very, very big beak. This big.' She held out her hands in front of her nose.

'Sweetie, that's great. I need to talk to Daddy a minute, okay? Let's get you out of this wet swimming suit.' Her tone held just the faintest hint of criticism, and out of the corner of her eye, she could see Mac tense.

It eased something in her. She rested an open palm on her daughter's shoulder.

'Come on, kiddo, I'll start the water for you.' She moved toward the bathroom, Katie skipping next to her. 'I'm going to show Daddy how hot

34

to make the water, so he knows.'

She glanced back at Mac just in time to see his jaw tighten. After a beat, he followed.

*   *   *

'What's going on?'

Mac followed her into the bedroom and closed the door partway. From the bathtub came the sounds of quiet splashing, Katie singing an off-key version of 'Itsy Bitsy Spider.' Grace could feel his eyes on her as she moved to the closet and pulled down her suitcase from the shelf.

'I have to go to Palm Springs and help Uncle Pete with something. Today's Friday. Katie's got Monday off — it's a teacher planning day — she has to be back in San Diego for school Tuesday.'

'Katie stays here. You're not taking her.' It wasn't a question. It was a statement. A bold squaring off.

Her intestines felt spongy. 'No. I know you need time with her.'

He crossed his arms loosely. He'd scuffed up his right hand somehow and the knuckles looked chapped. 'I still want her Thanksgiving.'

'Can we talk about this later?'

'Now.'

The splashing stopped. 'What?' Katie called.

Anger surged and spread through her body. Love was better, but this still had a warm glow to it. She shot Mac a look as she moved past him to the door.

'Everything's fine, honey,' she called through the open door.

35

'I heard my name.'

'Daddy and I were just talking.'

'About what?' There was alarm in her voice and Grace went into the bathroom. A flotilla of rubber duckies bobbed in the water. A soap bubble bloomed on Katie's shoulder, like a glittering corsage.

Grace sat on the edge of the tub and reached for the shampoo.

'About what a cool daughter we have.'

'You sounded mad.' Her eyes were dark and wide.

Grace massaged the shampoo into her scalp. 'We're fine.' She heard Mac come in behind her. 'Aren't we?'

'Absolutely.' His voice was a little too hearty.

'Lean back, honey, I'm going to rinse this off.'

Katie took a breath and held on to her nose and sank back into Grace's hand. Katie's hair floated in the water like a sea nymph's, her lashes dark against her cheeks. Her head felt fragile in Grace's hand, easily injured.

'You want me to — '

'Everything's fine.'

He tried again. 'But I could — '

'I'll be right in, Mac, okay?' She lifted Katie up and squeezed out the water. She felt him moving away from the door, felt the absence of him.

'I held my breath.'

'I saw. When you're done playing, I'll rinse your hair again.'

Katie nodded, peering up at her uncertainly as if there was something that needed asking. That

36

needed clearing up. That threatened world peace as she knew it.

'Okay,' she said finally.

Mac was leaning up against the door jamb, waiting for Grace when she got into the bedroom.

'She hears everything,' Grace said pleasantly, her voice low.

'I got that.' He smiled back pleasantly. 'But let's talk about *you*. What I especially liked was the bit about how hot to make the water. I think I can figure stuff like that out.'

Grace picked up a straw hat and a pair of espadrilles and carried them to the suitcase. She and Mac hadn't danced this one before, but she remembered it from the times her parents did the steps.

'Go on, say the rest. The even-though-I've-never-had-the-chance-to part.'

He smiled. 'Even-though-I've-never-had-the-chance-to.'

'Thanks to me,' she prompted. She lifted a clump of underpants and dumped them into the suitcase.

'Thanks to you. Here. Let me help you.'

'Gladly.' She was keeping her voice down, but it rang with hurt and her need to be right.

His eyes were bright with calculated interest. As if he'd waited a long time to play this game. As if he'd spent years studying the rule book. As if all bets were off.

He went to the set of drawers, yanked open the top one, and carried it over to the suitcase, upending the bras and tank tops into the suitcase, shaking the drawer hard.

'There. All set.' He tucked the drawer under his arm and carried it back to the dresser, shoving it back into the slot. 'Anything else?'

'I'm good.' She unhooked a row of hangers and flung the shirts and pants in a clattering heap into the suitcase. 'Ready to leave.'

'Works for me.'

The air left her body. A bullet of pain lodged in her belly. Not exactly a direct hit. He just needed more practice.

She was certain he'd been aiming for the heart.

She straightened. 'I'll be back in San Diego Monday night. Tuesday morning at the latest.' It sounded like a warning.

'Take your time.'

'You're not keeping her.' It slipped out and the ferocity of it took her by surprise and made real the possibility of Katie leaving for good.

He looked at her as if he were seeing her for the first time and not quite liking it.

'Why are you doing this?' His voice was even. 'She's my daughter, too. Mine. And frankly, that's all I've been thinking about. What you did. What it cost.'

She slipped the shirts and pants out of their hangers, one by one, not looking at him. The hangers were wooden, well made. She carried them back to the closet and hung them up. They clicked together. The only clothes that hung now were the dresses that belonged to Katie, a small bright row of pink and lime green, splashes of yellow and orange.

'Grace?'

'Don't think I won't be checking with the school, to make sure she gets there safely.'

'Nice.' He shoved past her into the hall.

★ ★ ★

'Okay, so it's going to be really fun.' Grace cradled Katie in her lap as she dried her hair with a towel.

'Why are you going?' Katie sounded worried.

Grace kissed her. 'Oh, honey, I have a couple of days of work to do, that's all.'

'But I want you to stay.'

'I do, too, sweetie.'

'But Daddy's going to be here, right?'

'Right here.'

'With me.'

'Every second.' Grace lifted Katie down from her lap. The towel had left a damp splotch on her shorts. 'Okay, what do you want to wear? A sundress, shorts?'

'Do you like Daddy?'

The question caught her by surprise. She turned away from the closet. 'Very much. Why?'

'I think shorts. Those pink ones.' Katie dropped the towel and scampered to the set of drawers. 'And the pink underpants. Everything pink.'

From the back, she was golden except for the pale band where her bathing suit had been. 'Does Daddy like you?' Her voice was muffled as she dug through her underpants and pulled out a pair.

39

'I hope so. Sure. Maybe. Probably. The main thing is, Daddy likes *you*. Lots. I'm going to get the lotion we use on your hair, so we see the curls.'

Grace went into the bathroom she shared with her daughter and stared at herself in the mirror. A woman she barely recognized stared back. Her eyes were dark, intense, her face looked hunted. She slicked on gloss, smacked her lips together, recurled her eyelashes and fringed on mascara, her mind blank, back on Katie's question.

Does Daddy like you?

She found the hair conditioner and went back into the bedroom.

Katie lay sprawled on her stomach, next to the open suitcase, shorts and a ruffled top a pale pink against her glowing skin. 'How am I getting home?'

Grace sat next to her and worked a dollop of conditioner into her hair. 'I'm glad you got dressed. That's good. You'll fly with Daddy and then stay in his house.'

Katie yanked up her head in surprise and Grace gently tipped it forward again. 'He has a house?'

'Daddy bought a place almost right next to ours, so you'll spend Monday night there, and then I'll pick you up after school Tuesday.'

'He lives in San Diego in Point Loma?' Her voice was astonished.

'Not too far away. He bought it when he found out about you. He wants very much to get to know you and be a real daddy.'

Katie sucked in a breath, her head still bent.

Her curls were damp ringlets against her scalp. 'He *is* a real daddy,' she said, her voice almost inaudible. 'He's mine.'

Grace nodded. 'Yes, honey. He is.' The bullet now was burrowing, worming its way up toward her heart. It was one of those time-release ones, guaranteed to keep chewing up her insides for some time to come. She wondered what it would take to get rid of it.

'All done.' She carried the conditioner into the bathroom, found what she was looking for and returned.

Katie sat with her knees up, her face down, protecting herself.

'Sunscreen.' Grace put it on the dresser. 'Even if Daddy forgets. Don't *you* forget.' The bottle was bright orange and had a cartoon of a fish on it.

'Mommy.' Katie's voice was muffled, forced. 'Did *you* just forget?'

'Forget.' Grace looked around the room, her eyes settling on the open suitcase, mentally reviewing the contents. It was a jumbled mess.

'I think I packed everything.' She closed the lid and zipped it. 'If I forgot something, bring it back with you, okay?'

'No, silly, that I had a *daddy*.'

Katie raised her eyes and looked at her. Her eyes were wide, dark brown, fathomless.

Katie's aim was much surer than Mac's. It was a direct hit.

Grace felt the aftershock first, the trembling as her body braced for a blow that had already come, and then she felt the pain coursing

41

through her. It was hot, electric, a wire that stung with recriminations and truth.

Grace had tried to leave Mac behind for good. What she hadn't factored in was how much that decision would cost Katie.

'Am I interrupting something?' Mac stood in the doorway, a hopeful look on his face, the parent at the fence, the one on the outside.

There was a split second when Grace could have said something, fixed whatever it was between her and Katie, a single word and everything would have been okay, but in that blinding moment of time, Katie turned toward the sound of his voice. Grace had always reached out to Katie, instinctively, joyously, but now she stalled, free-falling, unable to move. She stared at Katie and for the first time felt the awkwardness of not reaching out, embracing her, and in that instant she lost her standing as a mother. Not with Katie, perhaps, but with herself.

'He's here. That's what I came to tell you.'

Katie turned to take a look out the window. Officer Epsten sat in an idling golf cart. Katie trotted for the door.

Grace made a small sound.

'Wait,' Mac said. 'Give your mom a hug.'

Katie came limply into her arms, her body angled away. Grace felt an elbow. Katie squirmed free, leaving behind the familiar scents of new-mown grass and lemon.

Grace swallowed. She felt faint and afraid. 'My cell doesn't have an international connection. I'll call you from a landline when I get in.'

'Sure,' Mac said, his hand touching Katie's curls.

Grace walked the two of them out the wide door and to the golf cart. Mac stowed the suitcase in the back.

Epsten eased the cart forward along the bumpy path and Grace grabbed hold of the frame to steady herself, and by the time she angled her body around to take a look behind her, they were gone.

5

Grace drove past the shop, circled the block, and found a place to park on Newport Avenue. It was two blocks from the boardwalk in Ocean Beach in San Diego, not far from the YMCA youth hostel. She walked past a row of antique shops.

The sky was a paler blue than the one she'd left behind in the Bahamas. Mixed in with the sharp smell of the sea was the odor of dirt and sweat and grimy cement.

A group of glossy-haired teens stood panhandling in front of the grilled door. They looked at her and scattered, starting a game of bocci ball farther down the street as she opened the door and went inside.

Helix yipped and clattered over on his fake leg, tail wagging joyously, and Jeanne looked up from her work. A fan shot a current of cold air across Grace's body.

The shop was empty except for a fragile-looking woman in the chair wearing shorts, a tank top, and headphones the size of Egg McMuffins. Her eyes were closed and her mouth had dropped slightly open. She was sleeping.

'You're back early. I wasn't expecting you until Monday. Where's your sidekick?' Jeanne put down her needle and reached for a new color.

44

The beginning of a unicorn glistened on the client's left calf.

'Hey, buddy.' Grace bent to Helix and scratched him behind his ears and he licked her face and woofed. 'You sent Mac down there. To find us.'

Jeanne sorted colors, held up one to the light, put it down. 'The light in here is for shit. Turn on the lamp, okay?'

Grace clicked on a standing lamp and positioned the light. Jeanne's hair was a startling shade of red. Age had wrinkled the rose tattoo on her arm so that it looked wilted, the petals convoluted.

'You gave me directions to the beach you said you went to.'

'As a precautionary measure, Jeanne. Not so Mac could fly down there.'

Jeanne looked at her sharply. 'You are talking about Mac McGuire, the hero in this deal, right?' She picked up a bottle of eggshell blue ink and squirted it into a cup.

'Is Jeanne feeding you?' Grace rubbed Helix's belly.

He groaned and wriggled. He was a mongrel mix, black and white, with a fake leg that spasmed in the air like a Rockette executing a tricky high kick.

Jeanne rolled the calf gently and held it steady as she positioned the needle, delicately stippling the skin. The woman flinched slightly and Jeanne swabbed the calf with an antiseptic pad. 'What's going on?'

Grace swallowed, suddenly close to tears.

'Why does something have to be going on?'

Jeanne stared at her over her glasses and went back to work.

'Can she hear us?'

'She's listening to the Dead full blast. I'd be surprised if she could hear anything after this.' She shrugged in the direction of a chair. 'Sit.'

Grace pulled a chair over from another workstation and positioned it so that she was facing Jeanne over the legs of the client. They were skinny legs — a kid's — and Grace wondered if Jeanne had carded her before starting. The girl didn't look old enough to be making a choice that lasted a lifetime, but then again, Grace knew age hadn't protected her from doing things that cost. Were still costing.

She clasped her hands between her knees. 'Can you keep Helix until Tuesday?'

Jeanne shot her a measured look, bent over the calf and inked in a shadow along the unicorn's legs, so that the animal looked as if it were springing off the skin in a three-dimensional leap.

'Did you hear me?'

'I heard you.'

Jeanne put down the needle and swabbed the skin. It was pink around the fresh needle marks. She tossed the pad into the trash.

Grace blinked. 'I'll put him in a kennel.' She started to get up.

'Sit. *Sit*.'

Helix wagged his tail and sat.

'Not you, *you*.'

Grace sat.

46

'Of course I'll take him. What's this about?'

Grace felt tears leak onto her hands. Jeanne yanked a Kleenex from a box and Grace reached for it blindly and dabbed her eyes.

'He wants to take her for Thanksgiving.'

'He's her father, Grace.'

'Without me.'

Jeanne looked at her steadily. 'How close are you?'

Grace licked a lip. Her mouth felt dry. She reached into her purse and took out a miniature bottle of bourbon and put it down on the worktable next to the bottles of ink and a glass container of doggie treats.

'Honestly, on the plane? When the stewardess made the announcement that she'd appreciate correct change, I told myself I was helping her out, buying this.'

Jeanne smiled briefly and reached for a new bottle of ink. 'You didn't drink it.'

Grace inhaled, blew the breath out.

'Take a meeting.'

'Can't.' She felt rubbed raw. She stole a glance at the small bottle of bourbon and wondered if she could get it back in her purse.

Jeanne shot her a look and went back to work. Grace stared at the far wall. A crumbled set of terracotta pots lined a high shelf. Somehow Jeanne had managed to get tulips to bloom, and the bright yellow and orange and pink waxy petals bobbed on some invisible current as if they were watching a tennis match from the bleachers. Leaning against the wall under them was Jeanne's cane, its thready topknot wearing a pink Barbie-sized baseball cap.

'I need to drive to Riverside County. Examine a body in a morgue.'

Jeanne looked at her a long moment. 'It's not Guatemala, Grace.'

'I don't know if I can remember that, when I see it.'

'I could say it's time you got over it, and you don't want the bad guys to win by giving up a piece of who you are, but the truth is, we all give up pieces, every day, just to get by.'

Jeanne reached for a new color, a soft red the shade of old blood.

'I thought you couldn't go back to work until they health-checked you.'

'It's not the crime lab. I have an uncle who works in Palm Springs for the FBI.'

'Your uncle's dead?'

Grace made a small sound. 'You're busy. I shouldn't even be talking to you. You'll ink in an extra leg.'

'I did that once. Told the client it was an Asian fertility symbol. I didn't know you had an uncle in the FBI.'

Grace lined up bottles of ink. The bottle of black was bigger than the rest and she lined the cap up neatly so that the caps were straight across. A tear splashed onto a bottle called pink ochre and she wiped it off.

'He did something to my family that was pretty unforgivable.'

'That changed the course of family history?'

Grace dropped her hands. 'I'm not joking, Jeanne. It was when my dad died, and things

48

were bad. I haven't talked to him in years, and the idea that I'm getting dragged into something that's *his*, having to fix something that belongs to *him* — '

'Honey, if you want me to give you hell, you're going to have to give me more to go on.'

Grace fished a treat out of the jar and fed it to Helix. 'You're lucky, you know that. I get you home, we're working on that belly. Doggy aerobics.'

Helix smacked the treat down, snuffled the floor, picked up crumbs, and looked up at Grace expectantly.

'Don't even think about it.' He thumped his tail and Grace scratched his white chin. He had a narrow jaw, little teeth. He slopped out his tongue and kissed her. Grace bent down and scratched the place right in front of his tail and he raised his rump and wagged his tail.

'I get called into this by some guy. Asks for me by name when he's dying. So in the airport in Florida, between flights, I go to a business center and Google him. Turns out he stormed a lecture I was giving last month to forensic biologists on DNA and profiling. Storming a roomful of police nonsworns, can you believe it? Probably set some record for speedy arrest. Thaddeus Bartholomew.'

A clatter of bottles. Grace looked up.

'You okay?'

Jeanne had knocked over the bottle of red ink and it spilled across her fingers. Grace caught a swift smell of vomit and wood sap, a sharp image of bloody hands bent over a prone body, chest open.

Grace closed her eyes and waited it out.

When she opened her eyes, she was back in the tattoo shop. Jeanne groped for a Kleenex to mop it up. She missed the box and tried again.

'He's a bad actor, Grace. Ted Bartholomew.'

'I wondered if Frank knew him.'

'We ran right into him, the day he died. Palm Springs isn't that big.'

The skin around Jeanne's eyes was getting crepey, and the eye shadow she used clumped in tiny balls of violet that made her eyes look very blue.

The teen in the chair stirred and Jeanne patted her calf heavily and stared out the front window. Grace had helped Jeanne paint the words ROSE TATTOO in ornate red letters on that window years ago. Last year, Jeanne had added the words AND REMOVAL, and Grace wondered how long it would take for the girl in the chair to come back for that part.

'Frank's been putting this ag convention together now for over a year. That creep Bartholomew — sorry to be disrespectful of the dead — has been on his ass for most of it. Calling him a killer for GM-ing crops. *Frank*,' Jeanne said wonderingly.

Grace remembered Jeanne's boyfriend as tall, with long, expressive fingers, smelling faintly of mulch, wearing brown boots and a laminated California state ag tag on a plaid shirt. Two geeks in a pod, Jeanne called herself with Frank.

Jeanne had met him at a conference for

50

genetically modified crops, an interest that had morphed naturally out of her retirement as a scientist, and dovetailed with her lavish gardening efforts. A recent blue rose crossbreed had earned her a blue ribbon at the Del Mar Fair.

'I heard Bartholomew was killed in some field.'

Jeanne's mouth tightened. 'Well, he was alive when we saw him in Gerry Maloof's. Frank hasn't bought a single new thing for himself in years, and I made him go with me to get some pants. He has to introduce the secretary of interior, for crying out loud. He's so hard to fit, with his long inseam.'

Grace didn't want to hear about Frank's long inseam, or any other part of Frank's body, either. The small, homely beats of a relationship reminded her too much of Mac and what she might never have.

'And that's where you ran into Bartholomew.'

Jeanne stippled in the red and the unicorn glowed. 'It's a fine, fine store. They were having a sale on these lovely linen pants.'

'What was Bartholomew like?'

'I'm not exactly an impartial witness here, Grace.'

'Your impression.'

Jeanne moved the needle, drew another line on the pale skin. 'Fiery. Passionate. Threatening to sue.'

'On what grounds?'

'You need grounds?' The needle made a small metallic whirring sound. 'No government oversight. Accidental gene transfer to new crops.

Disastrous, life-threatening killer bad stuff we don't even know about yet, and somewhere, a monarch butterfly is keeling over dead in the food chain. The usual. And if that doesn't work, he vows to shut down the conference by force, if necessary.'

'By force. He used those words.'

Jeanne nodded. She swabbed the skin with a fresh pad and the sharp odor of astringent cut the air. She dropped the pad into the trash.

'What was Frank's reaction?'

'Subdued. He's maxed out, Grace. Has meetings from early in the morning until late at night. Probably knows your uncle better than you do.'

'Then he needs to be careful.'

Jeanne tightened her arms against her body, as if trying to warm herself. 'Frank can only tell me a fraction of what's going on, but everything he says, Grace, scares the hell out of me. You have no idea how many times a day bad guys threaten to maim or blow up or poison somebody.'

'Uh. Yeah, actually, Jeanne, I do.'

'I'm talking about Palm Springs, Grace. Crumbly, aging, jaunty-faced Palm Springs. Every time they slap a face-lift on that old girl, the plaster crumbles. She's still got the moves, but it's motor memory. She's harmless. And an ag convention dealing with world hunger. That sounds safe, doesn't it? Except lots of countries ban GM crops. Frank says he thinks the protests have tapped some big nerve.'

'Mad as hell and I'm not going to take it anymore.'

'Exactly. I loved that movie, too. Liked it less when I saw it in the middle of men's sportswear waving its fist at my Frank. Oh, and get this. Then Bartholomew whips out this throwaway camera and takes a picture of me.'

Grace shifted in her chair. The fan feathered cold air along her arms.

'He did the same thing the day he crashed my lecture. Got right up in my face and snapped a shot.'

Jeanne looked at her. The cracks along her mouth seemed to have deepened in the weeks since Katie's kidnapping. 'Why?'

'I have no idea.'

'What are you supposed to do there?'

'You mean, today? It's one thing to go to Palm Springs and tell a bunch of FBI agents the gist of my lecture. That's my only intersect with the vic and maybe they can find something in there. It's another getting dragged into the middle of a murder investigation, and that's exactly what Uncle Pete's doing. He booked a room for me. I'm there for the count.'

'Except that's not your only intersect with the vic.'

Grace looked her.

Jeanne glanced at Grace over her glasses and hunted through bottles, picked one up, held it to the light.

'Bartholomew didn't call out Frank's name. Or mine, either. He asked for *you*.'

A dark green liquid sloshed inside, as if it were a vial of alien blood. She twisted the cap off and inserted the needle.

'Look. I didn't like that guy any more than you do, Grace. And my reasons were a lot better.'

'Yeah, but he had the nerve to send for *me* when he was dying.'

'There you go. Good reason to stay away. Why get involved if it's not about you?'

'I guess what I'd like to know,' Grace tried to keep her voice light and failed, 'is whether it's okay not to go. Not to do some things. Even if we're asked. Even though we're called.'

'What's the cost?'

Outside, someone went by on Rollerblades, the cracks in the sidewalk making the rollers clack. It sounded like steel balls in a garbage disposal.

'Maybe nothing.'

Jeanne shook her head as if Grace were a very slow pupil. Grace held her gaze defiantly.

'Go in peace, my girl. Live.'

Grace looked away. 'I've worked hard to hang on to this anger, Jeanne.'

'Be a shame to give that up.'

'Uncle Pete hurt my family.'

'And you're trying to come to terms with the guilt you feel about lying to Katie and Mac by doing what again, exactly?'

Grace checked her watch and slipped her bag over her shoulder. 'I have to go.'

Helix cocked his head, looked from Grace to Jeanne, whined, his tone urgent, mournful.

'Shit.' Grace sat down. 'A recipe for living, please. In English. Make it snappy.'

'All I'm suggesting is that maybe by pushing into whatever snarled-up mess is waiting for you in Palm Springs, you'll find a way through the stuff that matters.'

'Let me guess, it involves sacrifice, right?' She held out her hands, palms up. 'Slit my wrists right now and be done with it.'

'Actually, the real question, Grace, is what are you *not* willing to sacrifice.'

On the wall were posters of body art. Grace's gaze settled on a skull filled with flowers.

'I'm going to lose her, Jeanne. I'm going to lose my daughter.'

'I think you're underestimating the power of forgiveness.'

'Hers? Or Mac's?'

'Try yours.'

It was a strong, sweet sucker punch and it took a moment to recover.

'Can't see myself trying that, Jeanne. Not anytime soon.' She got up. Helix thumped his tail once and put his head between his paws. 'I'll be in Palm Springs.'

Grace was almost at the door when Jeanne spoke. 'I need you to do something.'

Grace turned. Jeanne pulled on her lip. She wasn't looking at Grace, and then she did, and her eyes were filled with anxiety and defiance. 'It wasn't just any field.'

Grace waited.

'Where Bartholomew was killed. He picked Frank's field to die in. My Frank. He got my Frank involved.'

'As a suspect?' Grace felt as if she had slipped down a rabbit hole.

Jeanne shook her head. 'I don't think so. I

don't know. Frank didn't tell me, Grace. I had to find it out on TV. It's all over the TV. He's not telling me squat. And another field went up in smoke last night. He's trying to protect me, and all I want is the truth. Help me get the truth.'

Grace tightened her grip on her bag and nodded.

'Two fields burned, Grace, and a man dead. Be careful. Come home to us safely.'

'Sure. Will do. Easy. As soon as I find where that is.'

Jeanne put down her needle and held open her arms. 'Come here, sweet girl.'

Grace went to her and knelt, the embrace clumsy. Jeanne's skin smelled leathery and rich.

She stayed that way, her head cradled in Jeanne's arms, a long time.

6

Grace got caught in truck traffic heading north on the 15. She had a low-grade headache that carried her past the brown and yellow scrub of Camp Pendleton, the blackened burn area from the Indio fire through the checkpoint as officers glanced into cars looking for illegals, and on past the auto dealerships and neat rows of identical condos stitched together with soft red roofs.

She passed a nursery with palm trees on a brown stony hillside, trunks cut so that they looked like rows of crosses. She stopped at a roadside stand in the heat and bought organic cherries and then found she couldn't eat them. The heat bled the juice onto the paper bag like spatter at a crime scene. She put the bag in the trunk, changed her mind, and tossed it in the trash.

She reminded herself that Guatemala had happened a long time ago. Before Katie was born and she was five now. What had happened there had been serious enough that she'd quit medicine and taken a job in the San Diego Police crime lab, working with fluids and not people. She'd stopped the drinking and reached the point where she could work crime scenes, handle spatters, dead bodies, compartmentalize. But since the kidnapping, the fragile boundary between reality and nightmare was porous again, and it took all her energy staying in the moment.

Not going back. She wasn't ready to see a dead body.

She pulled in to a rest stop when she got to Highway 215. She had a fresh shirt in her suitcase and she put it on over her tank top. A row of hang gliders floated high inland as she took the Perris exit. They hovered against the sky like a band of delicate, mutant butterflies.

She pulled into the parking lot next to the sand-colored coroner's office and parked. She turned off the ignition and immediately the air in the car grew suffocating.

Her nostrils felt pinched. She took little sips of air, as if she were rationing it, delaying going in, and finally burst out the door in a damp gulping rush, hurrying down the white bleached path to the sliding front door.

Deputy Coroner Jeff Salzer met her at the front desk and led her through a work space of laminated counters and computer stations. His hair was starting to thin. He carried himself like a retired military man, shoulders back, as if tensing for a bullet that hadn't been fired yet.

Air-conditioning blasted. A chunky deputy in rolled-up sleeves glanced up from her notepad as they went by in silence.

Salzer closed the door and motioned for her to sit. Through the window, her car already looked glossy with heat, as if the chrome were melting. She took the seat across from his desk.

'Special Agent Descanso said to give you whatever you need on this one.'

His desk was swept clean except for his computer. It was on, the screen blank.

'I thought the body would have gone to the Indio morgue; that's closest to Palm Springs.'

'Would have, but the air-conditioning in Indio blew out in this heat. We've gotten all of them for a week now. They come in refrigerated trucks. Full house. Let me get the file.'

Salzer pushed away from his desk and his pecs bunched under his shirt. He riffled through a file drawer. Grace tried not to visualize what *full house* looked like in a morgue.

He pulled out a thick file and handed it to her. 'You can use the conference room. You can't make copies, but you can take whatever notes you'd like.'

She nodded and followed him into the corridor. She caught the faint whiff of formaldehyde. Her stomach churned and she tasted acid.

'Palm Springs is a real dog's breakfast right now with that ag convention. Where's your hotel?'

'Right off Palm Canyon.'

'You're going to get a dose of it then. They start at the Convention Center and spill out onto the main drag.'

'I heard a second field was torched. Anybody else killed?'

A deputy rolled a rack of files down the hall and squeezed past them. Salzer shook his head and resumed walking.

'No, but a couple of delegates were hospitalized for smoke inhalation. It's going to get nastier. Protest organizers took out a march permit for eight thousand people. They've blown right through that number. We expect ten times that amount. The last time the U.S. hosted this conference was in Sacramento. Major protests. That came on the heels of riots in Seattle during the World Trade Organization, which led to looting and the declaration of martial law. You know how many rioters showed up for that one?'

Grace shook her head.

'Close to a hundred thousand, Grace. We have two hundred cops, security guards, and a handful of National Guardsmen piled in, from as far away as L.A. The FBI's running the show. Not bad, but it's not good, either. Makes everybody nervous. Plus, we got people drinking, raising hell, so we've had a rash of unrelated accidents, car crashes, partygoers using loaded weapons. A mess here. We've got three autopsies backed up. I can rustle up coffee, water, maybe some soda.'

'Water's good.'

He nodded and closed the door. She took a seat at the long table in the quiet room. Empty bulletin boards with tacks adorned the walls. A detailed map of the Coachella Valley hung over a coffeemaker. The coffee smelled burned.

She opened the file. Stapled to the cover page was Bartholomew's DMV photo. A heavyset man in his sixties stared back, with beetling eyebrows and shrewd blue eyes, looking into the camera with a mixture of intelligence and amusement, as if he was party to some small secret.

He was wearing a blue oxford button-down shirt, open at the neck, and a tweed jacket. His silvery hair was long, parted in the middle, his face a series of pouches: fleshy jowls, pink balloons of cheeks, and smaller, bluish bulges under his eyes. He looked impatient and tired, a combination Grace remembered from the day he'd burst into the lecture hall in Indio, not far from where she was sitting right now.

That day he was yelling, waving a sign and pointing a camera like a weapon:

DOWN WITH RACIAL PROFILING. POLICE PIGS ARE WHITE SUPREMACISTS.

He'd been cuffed and hustled out, and as they'd closed the door and she'd resumed her lecture, she'd heard him screaming, 'Sow it, you'll reap it!'

From Martin Luther King's 1967 speech, taken from the Bible. Grace was just Catholic enough to have felt immediately guilty.

She'd never seen him again. Palm Springs police had taken her statement, but they hadn't needed her to testify: He'd pled guilty and spent three days in jail for disturbing the peace. A month ago. And now he was dead.

She turned back to the file and studied the crime scene photos. Bartholomew had been reduced to looking like a charred piece of meat, the arrow still embedded in his chest.

She'd seen plenty of crime scene photos. She could get through these.

She looked up as the door opened and Salzer came in with a bottle of water.

'Thanks.'

He nodded and sat. Grace turned the page and read the report.

'Tracking?' She twisted the top and took a gulp of water.

Salzer nodded. 'The way they think it went down, Bartholomew was driving, and he was either surprised by the perp there, or they rode out together. My guess? The UNSUB was in the car, directing him. Bartholomew parked badly and left his door open when he got out. By the time he entered the field, he was in a major hurry to escape whoever was after him. The police found a scrap of his tweed jacket on the barbwire, where he tore it. He stumbled, at some point, and when he got up, his stride was uneven, shorter. He'd injured himself, apparently, when he fell.'

She took another drink. 'How about footprints, did they get anything they can use?'

Salzer shrugged. 'It's not in the coroner's file if they did. The official cause of death was massive blood loss due to a direct arrow hit to the heart, and thermal injuries.'

'Thermal injuries?' She took a long swallow of water and wiped her lip.

'Yeah, Grace, he was still alive when his body was set on fire.' He got up. 'Ready to take a look?'

7

The short answer to that would be no, she thought.

A wave of nausea washed over her and she felt her skin grow clammy. Salzer stared at her sharply.

'You okay?'

'I think it's the heat.'

'It's cooler in there.'

She nodded and followed him in. The autopsy viewing suite was a windowless room, filled with two empty tables, stainless steel sinks, metal filing cabinets equipped with scales for weighing and measuring the cost of death.

The body lay under a thick white plastic sheet on a metal table that was raised on the edges to catch fluids. Salzer hesitated briefly, as if to issue a warning, but Grace knew no warning from him could soften the images she was about to see. There had been fire in Guatemala. And death.

She nodded and Salzer slipped the sheet free. The odor of burned flesh permeated the room. 'I'll be right back.'

She went into the hall and leaned against the wall. Gradually the walls stopped moving. She went back inside and closed the door behind her.

He offered a box of gloves and she took a set and put them on, as if stepping into the hall was the most natural thing in the world. Maybe in that room it was.

The body lay on its back, claws pointed toward the ceiling, blackened arms frozen over its head as if trying to protect the face from the accelerant that was about to be dumped onto its dying body, but the face was curiously intact. The hair had been burned off, along with the eyebrows and ears, but in the shape of the brow and the slope of what was left of the nose, the face was still recognizably human.

Especially in the shape of the mouth, open in a frozen scream. The scalp had been cut open in a coronal incision from ear to ear and closed with white stitches. White thick stitches also closed the Y chest incision. The torso was severely charred, the tissue blackened and peeled back in some places to expose red flesh and bone underneath. The chest cavity was collapsed and sunken around a blackened hole.

The underside of the body was still intact. Shreds of what looked like khaki pants, a tweed jacket, and a beige shirt still were visible.

'The clothing remnants weren't removed?'

'I took samples. They're fused to the body.'

His feet were unharmed, and seeing two pale feet rising above the blackened carnage of his torso made the damage even more real. This had been a man not long ago, and the doer was still out there somewhere.

'Any genetic material found on the body?'

'Not human. A dog hair. The lab's got it. As you can see from the severe charring of the midsection, the perp dumped the accelerant directly onto the body in the chest area and then lit a match.'

The smell was an overpowering mix of chemicals, residue from the fire and the decomposing body. Her mouth tasted of death and she blinked and stared across the room, her vision blurred. Salzer glanced at her and dropped his gaze to the clipboard. Grace appreciated that. She stared at the linoleum until the pattern came into focus.

'Bartholomew had first been hit by a bolt from a crossbow, and from the distinctive cracking pattern in the ribs, the killer tried to extricate the bolt and failed.' Salzer pointed at a section of tissue. 'Normally, a wound of this kind would have been tight. He used an expandable broadhead, a tip that explodes a barb on impact. The bolt would have plugged the wound and there wouldn't have been profuse bleeding.'

He lifted a clipboard off the wall and scanned it.

'In this case, fifteen hundred ccs of blood were recovered from his chest cavity. Where you see the raw pink and red tissue and white rib bone, under the blackened, charred skin in the concave of this chest, is the area where the bolt had been. I removed it in the course of my examination.'

'Who has it now?'

'The Palm Springs police were first on scene, followed by the Riverside sheriff's deputies. The area's just close enough to the outskirts of town that sometimes they both show up, especially now with the convention. As for who has the bolt now . . .'

He skimmed the clipboard, found it.

'Police. The bolt had lacerated a lung and

65

punctured the heart in the upper right quadrant of the left ventricle. Death would have been certain, and imminent, but this guy didn't want to wait around. In essence, Bartholomew was bleeding out as he burned to death.'

Salzer hung the clipboard back on the wall next to a grease board where four current autopsies were listed, amounts and weights itemized in neat columns.

'What was the carbon monoxide saturation level?'

'You mean in his airway?'

She nodded. She was still thinking about what Bartholomew's last moments must have been like, pinned to the ground by the bolt, in shock, still alive enough to know what was happening, yet incapable of preventing it.

'Toxic saturation levels, but not lethal. His lungs were heavier by a couple hundred grams from fluid produced when the lungs were seared and his airway had narrowed to protect the lungs.'

He covered the body again with the sheet and waited as she went through the door. He turned off the lights and locked up and they walked down the hall.

'I worked the Esperanza fire,' he said quietly. 'The burn-over on this one would have been just a few minutes.'

'Burn-over.'

'Fire literally can burn over the top of things. Here, there was a limited amount of fuel and the body was only partially cremated. Bodies cremate at between fifteen hundred and three thousand degrees.'

They were back at the deputy bullpen. He pushed open the front door and the heat smacked her like a living thing.

'Get this guy, Grace. He's a nasty piece of work.'

She nodded and stepped into the parking lot.

After the door closed on him, Grace trotted behind her car and threw up.

8

She took 10 to the 111, navigating switchbacks of purple hills cut with dark brown trenches and expanses of sand. Miles of desert stretched ahead. Wind turbines stood close to the road, marching in regiments up the brown hillside, protecting what looked, at a distance, like a compound of windmills — a family — the big ones towering over the little ones. She passed shopping outlets and a billboard advertising dinosaurs. Next to the road, the Union Pacific carried freight in a steady stream of double boxcars.

It was just after four and the dry desert sun turned the asphalt a shiny black. Just after seven in Harbor Island. She'd tried reaching Katie that morning when she'd flown in to Lindbergh Field and taken a taxi home to pick up her car and pack a few things for Palm Springs.

No answer. She'd tried again, compulsively, right away, and this time, the hotel desk clerk had apologetically said he'd thought they were already out.

Maybe they'd be back by now, Katie brimming with news.

Or not.

Maybe Katie wouldn't want to share a piece of the day she'd had with her dad.

Grace hit the gas and passed a slow truck. The wind punched against her car and lifted it sideways in a scalding wash of blowing sand. It was a bump, a hiccup, a swat of a giant invisible hand, but its power sent a flush of heat up her body. She gripped the steering wheel and steadied the car. A row of giant windmills gyrated in a frenzied dance and the boxcars rolled on in a yellow swirl of dust.

Traffic was stalled on Indian Canyon Drive and Grace cracked her head out the window, straining to get a better look. Up ahead a police siren wailed, the sound undercut by the murmuring roar of protesters. The cars crawled forward.

Through her passenger window, Grace caught a glimpse of a brown valley sweeping down to her right. Wind turbines churned on the ridges. Dust spumed across a dirt road leading to a small train depot.

She put up the windows, adjusted the air conditioner, and spread MapQuest on the seat, wishing she had a map to navigate what came next.

★ ★ ★

It was an older neighborhood off Ramon Avenue, fading apartments and duplexes and cottages with cracked sidewalks. Grace missed it the first time and circled back. Bartholomew's house was set back from the street, a cement pebbly structure with an iron gate. Barrel cactus lined the sidewalk.

Yellow police tape stretched over the paint-blistered front door. There was a padlock below the door handle. She pulled to a stop at the curb behind a police unmarked and locked up. A big guy fighting flab got out of the unmarked. He came over and they shook hands. Homicide Detective Mike Zsloski. Older, face permanently flushed, right on the edge of having a stroke.

She followed Zsloski up the walk, trying to recall which case they'd worked together. She went back in her mind through the cases in the last year and found it. A black gang member working out of north Palm Springs in the Gateway Posse Crips, who'd ended up stuffed into a sealed drum in San Diego harbor.

Zsloski offered a pair of gloves and she put them on as he took off the police tape and unlocked the padlock. 'They finished up an hour ago.'

Grace nodded. It had taken from Wednesday night until midday Saturday to process Bartholomew's house. She wondered why. He hadn't died there.

The living room was an explosion of books, papers, folders, stacked against the wall, burying the carpet, spilling out of the bookshelves, piled high on the coffee table. Crime lab print powder crusted the books and walls and light switches.

'Not that Bartholomew read much,' she said.

Zsloski smiled briefly. 'We're due there in fifteen. What you want to see's in here.'

He took her down a short hall, opened a door and stood aside, letting her walk in first. Letting her see it.

Her stomach flipped.

It was a small room. In a normal house, it

could have been a child's bedroom, or held a TV and favorite books and some comfortable chairs.

But there was nothing normal about this room.

Small school head shots covered the walls. A dizzying blur of faces smiled back, eyes friendly, direct, frozen in time, photos placed so thickly together Grace wasn't sure what color the walls had once been.

Under each photo Bartholomew had carefully block-printed out the name of the student. His handwriting was neat, precise. The hairstyles in some of the photos went back thirty years — lacquered helmets and mullets and bubble cuts, and the tape holding the photos and names to the walls was yellowed and cracked.

At some point, Bartholomew had run out of room and had started using the floor and ceiling. It looked like a fungus encroaching, a swirling mass of color and imagery so intense and dislocating Grace had to stop herself from walking out.

It was stuffy in the room but Grace felt cold. She walked around a desk he'd constructed out of a wooden door propped up on cinder blocks, stacked with foot-high columns of books and papers. A brown plastic kitchen container held pens and pencils instead of knives and forks. Buried in the middle of the papers was a Remington typewriter with a piece of paper wound into its platen.

Grace twisted the cartridge. The paper in the typewriter was blank. She looked around the room, trying to absorb it. Trying to slow her heart. Trying not to run.

'What do you think?'

'Reminds me of John Nash.'

Zsloski was silent.

'That schizophrenic mathematician at Princeton who created game theory and later went on to win a Nobel prize. He had a room like this. Only not photos. Equations and —

'Oh my God.' She rocked back on her heels as if she'd been hit in the face. Her stomach clenched and for the first time, she felt a jolt of fear.

Zsloski followed her gaze.

Grace went over to the corner, where two walls connected.

Amid the swirling cacophony of images, taped onto the crowded wall was a blurry snapshot of Grace, her name block-printed under it. Next to the photo, also taped to the wall, was an article from the *Desert Sun* about the lecture and Bartholomew's arrest.

Zsloski nodded. That was what he'd brought her here to look at, she knew that now.

'He took that picture that day he crashed my lecture. A month ago.'

'Any idea why?'

She shook her head.

He nodded as if he expected that. 'They'll be asking you about that. And the lecture. You've got the address, right?'

She nodded, her eyes still on the photo. She'd seen evil before, more times than she cared to remember. But never such a clear manifestation of insanity. It was a darkness at the end of the road. A troubling message from the grave, every bit as potent as Bartholomew's Morse code summoning her.

She wondered if somewhere in the room, hidden in plain sight, Bartholomew had taped the face of his killer to the wall.

If even now it was staring at her, smiling.

9

The FBI substation was tucked in a group of brown office buildings trimmed in succulents. Perry Como was singing through speakers as she crossed the covered parking lot. There was no identifying sign on the building, nothing in the lobby.

Upstairs, the door was made of steel. To the right was a keypad, to the left, a buzzer. She scanned the ceiling and found it, what looked like a gray convex ceiling light.

Behind the locked steel door were video screens, and on one of those screens she stood in the hallway, leather satchel in hand, a woman of uncommon beauty.

She'd added that last part to make herself smile. Always good to be smiling when caught on a camera in front of an FBI door. It didn't work. The room in Bartholomew's house had knocked the smile out of her.

She pressed the button and was buzzed into a small anteroom where an agent stood behind Plexiglas. He was wearing a sports shirt and slacks with no ID tag. He didn't introduce himself.

There was a metal slot in the glass, like a tollbooth, and she slid her ID in so he could check it. He looked up briefly, making sure the picture matched. She resisted the urge to tell him she was much better-looking at night after he'd had a few drinks.

He slid her ID back and buzzed her through an adjoining door that opened into a small conference room. A beeper went off: the all-clear signal that she wasn't carrying.

'They'll be in soon.' His hair was brown, without a trace of gray. He could be any age from thirty to sixty. He was wearing a wedding ring and blue veins roped the backs of his hands, old hands, which had the curious effect, Grace thought, of making his face look even younger.

He glanced at the bag she was carrying. It was leather and brown with straps. She'd bought it at a Coach discount store in Cabazon when she first started working in the lab.

'There's a wall outlet here if you need it.'

She nodded and pulled out her computer.

He closed the door and left her.

★ ★ ★

Grace looked up from her flash drive and for an instant, it felt as if she were flattened in another dimension, looking into her life from a distant place. There was no air in this other place. She couldn't breathe. Her head felt squeezed, elongated.

Her dead father stood in front of her, bulkier, with drooping lids and fierce brown eyes. A welter of lines cracked his face as his lips moved.

He smiled with no tenderness.

'Uncle Pete.'

'SA Descanso in here.'

His voice was lower than her dad's had been,

75

and she could almost guarantee this man had never hit the high notes singing 'Louie Louie' as a good-night song. She actually couldn't imagine him singing much of anything to his five kids, now that she considered it, and for a moment, she wondered what her cousins' lives had been like in some airless, cheerless dimension with a man who didn't smile easily.

'Ready? They're on their way in.'

She noticed he didn't wait for an answer.

* * *

'What do you know about racial profiling using DNA?'

She looked down the table. Zsloski slouched next to her uncle. Across the table sat an investigator named Thantos from the Riverside sheriff's department who was part of the joint terrorism task force, and another Palm Springs FBI agent named Beth Loganis.

The sounds of a busy office carried through the closed door into the room; somewhere a fax machine churned and phones rang. A small window had been cut into the door of the conference room; Grace caught a glimpse of two agents rushing past in the hall, voices urgent and muted.

She waited for it. Usually it took a beat before they got it.

Zsloski was frowning and doodling on a pad. He raised his shaggy head. 'Wait a minute. Race is in the DNA?'

All the heads came up.

76

'We've been able to do it for a while; we just don't call it that in press releases. We can figure out a suspect's race from collected DNA found at a crime scene. We say *race*, and people think *target*, when what we're actually talking about is the narrowing down of a suspect pool, catching a bad guy before he does it again.

'If you knew from collected DNA that a suspect was a white male whose skin easily sunburned, wouldn't you want to know that chances are the perp has red hair and freckles? Figuring that out is a little complicated, but — '

Zsloski threw down his pen. '*Un*complicate it.'

She was trying not to stare at her uncle. In the way he held his pen she saw her dad; in the slope of his shoulders, her grandfather.

'It came out of an innocuous pastime, people wanting to trace family trees, get a handle on their ancestry. Now police use it to flag suspects. Somebody kill the lights.'

She started her flash drive as the room went semidark, illuminated by the ghost stamp of light still coming from the hall.

'First off, what the tests do is break down *percentages*, not actual race.'

She tapped the keypad and her first graphic came up. It was a map of the world with three small silhouettes standing along the bottom. She was using the wall as a screen; it worked fine.

'Basically a lot of our DNA is junk. It's a matter of geography. Let's say — a long time ago — we've got an Asian who lives someplace in the Pacific Rim. Let's put him, for our purposes, in China.'

She transferred a small figure to China and filled in the figure with slanting lines.

'His family stays there for generations and over time, there are a few minute variations, some hiccups in his DNA that naturally occur randomly, and once they occur, they get passed down through generations. Those are called polymorphisms in the DNA, or SNPS, pronounced *snips*.'

She waited as the scribbling subsided and the group was ready for her to go on.

'Now let's move a different guy to Cape Horn. He started out there and his family lives there for generations, long before recorded time. He's called a sub-Saharan African.'

She placed a second figure in the south of Africa and filled in the outline with gray pixels.

'Same deal. Lives there eons and *he* has random snips that are passed down through his line and everybody in his part of the world has some of these same snips, but and here's the key thing: the guy in Cape Horn probably never went to China, not to move there, not even on vacation — we're talking thousands of years ago, not now, jumping on a plane. So, the guys in Asia are going to have different snips than the sub-Saharan Africans living at Cape Horn.'

She danced the third figure into what looked like the middle of France.

'Here's our third guy. He started out in what is now Europe. He has his own snips that go way back in time and that we still see coming up in his relatives alive today. He's called Indo-European.'

She filled the third figure in with dots and turned to the audience. 'These snips insert themselves randomly and are then copied and passed down through generations. Different continents fostered different snips. We fast-forward to today.'

She tapped the keypad again and figures appeared across the world, each a mix of slanting lines, gray pixels, dots; each figure different.

'Nobody's stayed in a neat little box, but we can pretty accurately trace percentages, how much percentage of a person comes from each of these subgroups. The most sophisticated tests involve one hundred and seventy-six of those snips, narrowing the ancestral pool pretty conclusively. Lights, please.'

Zsloski blinked in the sudden light, looking confused, and Grace amended it.

'It means that after testing a sample, the most sophisticated tests can accurately say that a person is maybe — say — ninety-two percent Indo-European and eight percent sub-Saharan African.'

'So we'd be looking for a white guy.'

'In that example, Mike, yes; if you had this DNA sample at a crime scene, you'd be focusing on white suspects, because it would be genetically impossible for the perp to have come from a predominantly different subgroup. It stands to reason that it would serve to narrow the suspect pool in a reasonable way and save valuable time on the street.'

'I got it.'

'It's not an exact science but I can tell you this, there's a DNA printing outfit in Florida that's a leader in this type of thing; they routinely do blind tests and nail it, every single time, just based on DNA. That means that if they analyze a sample that's predominantly Indo-European, the features of the actual person will express in Caucasian features and skin tones, ditto if it's Asian or African.'

She clicked off the graphic.

'Any questions?'

FBI Special Agent Beth Loganis raised her hand; not really a hand, the merest flag of a manicured finger elevated for the briefest of seconds. She was about Grace's age, early thirties, with the burnished look that always spoke of enriched preschool and normal childhoods with mothers who remembered to lay out lunch money and buy laundry soap. It was a look that, despite years of faking, Grace knew she'd never get right. Knew that all a woman like Beth had to do was take one look at her to know that, too.

'This is the lecture Bartholomew crashed?' A faint tinge of condescension colored Beth's question.

Grace swallowed her irritation. 'Pretty much. Little simpler this time, but yeah.'

Zsloski harrumphed into his hand.

'What do you think Bartholomew was trying to tell you?' Beth clicked her sterling silver pen and readied it.

'The only time I met Professor Bartholomew,

he was lunging at me with a protest sign and spouting sound bites from the Bill Ayers playbook.'

Pete nodded. 'At the time of his death, he was a full-tenured professor at Riverside University, teaching a popular undergraduate-level course called 'Silent Voices.' It was about the ones history forgets — the ones on the bottom. He was arrested at Grace's lecture by a Palm Desert cop in a roomful of forensic biologists.'

The sheriff investigator patted the pocket of his tan shirt. He had penetrating mahogany-colored eyes the same color as his skin and wore his hair close to the scalp. His brass ID bar read T. THANTOS. 'So he wanted to get arrested.'

'Looks that way,' Pete said. 'He got press, if that was the plan.'

In her mind, Grace saw the Desert Sun article taped to Bartholomew's wall.

Thantos pulled a Mars bar out of his pocket and unwrapped it. 'DNA testing for race would definitely have pushed Bartholomew's buttons. From what we've got so far, he was all about how human dignity was compromised by putting racial groups in boxes.'

'Bartholomew could have been trying to tell us we're looking for a racist,' Grace offered. 'But if the doer was using racial percentages somehow, the question is why? What's the point? Why would those be flagged?'

Zsloski shifted his bulk in his chair. 'It doesn't have to be a racist. Could be somebody in law enforcement. Based on what you said. I mean,

81

we're the guys who use this stuff, right?'

'Or some genealogist with a grudge,' Beth suggested.

'Or it's possible the suspect had a genetic anomaly shared by only a small subgroup.'

Grace shut down her computer.

'Any idea yet what kind of crazy Bartholomew was?'

Her uncle shook his head. 'We're doing cross-checks with every face on that wall. Dividing the photos into subgroups — class, gender, race. Whatever it is, it's not mentioned in either his university file or medical chart, so right now we're shooting in the dark.'

The group was already starting to gather notepads and pens and tuck them away. Grace looked down the table. 'Any more questions?'

Agent Beth Loganis flipped open her cell phone and checked for messages. Grace felt a slow burn.

'Good, because I've got some. What in the hell is going on here?'

Faces looked up. The noise stilled.

'Two fields torched and somebody's died. What is this?'

She stared at her uncle. He stared back, dark eyes inscrutable in a face creased and grooved and furrowed, as if everything he'd seen in his job had chiseled out a piece of him. Another couple years and he'd be left with nothing but a skull.

'I've flown over three thousand miles through the night and driven in from San Diego. I think I deserve to know.'

Her uncle grew still. She could feel him weighing what to say.

'You understand this is information that you are not to share outside this room.'

She couldn't believe he'd actually said that. 'Or you'll have to kill me, right?'

'We've had lots of experience. There won't be seepage.'

He waited.

'Fine. All right. I get it. I'm not going to say anything.'

'We've gotten word from FIG, Field Intelligence Group, out of Norwalk. They did a threat assessment on the convention. My SSA and the OCC's involved, and when FIG passed along — '

Acronyms made her testy. 'Okay, so your boss in Riverside and the operational control center out of L.A. — '

'Right. OCC is set up to manage big situations. We've been lining up assets and manpower for months, pulling in bodies from all over Southern California. Field Intelligence monitors Internet chatter, blog sites, confidential sources. We have reason to believe a group calling itself Radical Damage has plans to disrupt the agricultural convention during closing ceremonies.'

'What is it?'

'A violent offshoot of ELF out of Northern California.'

He shifted in his seat.

'These guys aren't worried about collateral damage. They've taken credit for explosions in three labs that have led to the deaths of four scientists and crippling injuries to five others. One guy was left blind and without hands. The victims all worked with genetically modified plants. Here's what's at stake. There are delegates from every state and almost sixty countries at this ag convention. Frank Waggaman's had death threats. He heads up the teams that created ten fields of GM crops here, six soy, a couple of sugar beets, and two corns.'

'I didn't think any of that stuff grew here.'

'That's why they picked Palm Springs for the convention. The genetic modifications — each field tweaked differently — had to do with making crops drought-, pest-, and weed-resistant. Ag convention director Frank Waggaman believed that one field in particular, USDA Experimental Crop Project 3627, held the key to helping solve world hunger.'

Grace stared. 'And that's where Bartholomew was killed? In USDA Experimental Crop 3627.'

Pete nodded. 'This whole thing could explode in our faces. The GM fields are off-limits now to delegates, but all we need is a foreign delegate killed and an international incident on our watch.'

'Monday night.'

'Monday night.' He glared at Grace, his eyes small balls of bright fury under drooping lids. 'Two days from now. We need to figure out what Radical Damage has planned and stop it. The clock, as they say, is ticking. And *damn*, I hate that expression.'

'Same old Uncle Pete. You still haven't told me how I fit into this.'

He glared. 'Same old Grace. Always pushing it.' He stepped away from the table. 'We're done here. Not you, Grace. You're coming with me.'

10

She followed her uncle past a gray fabric wall with notices tacked to it. On the other side of the wall was a row of workstations with access to a balcony that ran the length of the agency. Her uncle's silence made her review every wrong thing she'd ever done. He kept walking and that gave her a chance to flip it, and think about every wrong thing *he'd* ever done, and by the time he opened his office door and motioned her in, she was herself again.

He stood uncertainly, as if wondering whether to hug her, and Grace pretended to dig through her bag. She dropped into the chair across the desk from him, and when she looked up, he was seated.

He looked smaller, somehow, diminished. His shirt had a button loose and he needed a shave. 'Thanks for coming.'

'Did I have a choice?' She folded her arms.

He studied her a long moment. 'I don't think there's anything I could have done that would have changed it.'

Grace looked away. The walls were devoid of personal touches except for a framed photo of a much younger Pete in a SWAT group shot, but family photos jammed the top of the filing cabinets behind him. Her eyes settled on a black-and-white of three dark-eyed skinny boys shivering in wet swimming trunks, arms around each other. Her body knew it before it registered in her mind; heat coursed through her and pressed against her eyes. Her dad smiled back, the one in the middle, a tooth missing, squinting at the camera.

'He always looked up to you.' Her voice caught.

'When your dad ran off with Lottie — '

'We were cut out of almost every family gathering, and why? Because he'd married outside the faith? Outside the Portuguese community? Give me a break.'

'Look, you don't know how it was.'

'I know exactly how it was. I lived it. It's the first story I ever learned.'

Her dad, Marcos, the middle son and two years younger than her uncle Pete, had impulsively stopped by a bar one night on his way home after cleaning his boat, *The Far Horizon*. He was twenty-three.

He'd been at sea for three months chasing tuna, sunburned and exhausted and dry mouthed, and it was his dry mouth that night that had gotten him into trouble he never quite got out of. At least not easily.

Not until the night he disappeared for good.

But that night in the beginning, Marcos, the shy, methodical man not given to bouts of spontaneity, blinked in the sudden blaze of the spotlight as Lottie pranced onto the dusty beer-washed stage, shimmying and sparkly, with platinum hair and fishnet stockings, and inexplicably, hours later, he'd decided to drive to Las Vegas with her and get married.

In the faded photo Grace had of her parents shot in the Temple of Love, Marcos stood up in his reeking, fish-slimed jeans, a glazed and thunder-struck look on his face, mouth gaping open, as Lottie leaned next to him, her spandex top somewhat obscured by the yellow rain slicker he'd given her as a cover-up. Her head was cocked and she had a triumphant smile on her face, but the lines around her eyes and mouth were those of an exhausted woman, as if she'd just landed the biggest fish imaginable after a long and harrowing battle at sea.

'He was engaged to a Portuguese beauty from a good family,' Uncle Pete said feebly.

'Well, your wife seems to have gotten over him.'

'I was comforting her.'

Grace threw up her hands. 'All I'm saying is, this cord was severed long before I ever came into the picture, and you — you were the favorite son, the favored son, the oldest. One word from you and things would have been different. You did nothing.'

'That's not true.' He looked pained.

'I was eleven when Dad died. I spent the rest of my childhood living out of suitcases while Lottie worked the West Coast, playing in country-western bands. She dragged Andy and me all over the place.'

'She never told you? Aunt Chel and I tried to get you. Both of you. Fold you into our bunch. What's a few more? Your mother wouldn't hear of it.'

The blood drained from Grace's face and her skin felt damp.

Her uncle stared at her wonderingly. 'Jesus. She didn't tell you.'

Her heart pulsed in her throat; she could taste the anger. She wondered if he'd told himself that lie so long that he believed it.

Grace scraped a hand through her hair. 'We both know you're lying.' Her voice was raw.

She shoved her chair back.

'I can't do this. I absolutely can't do this, so if this is what it is, I'm out of here.'

'You will sit.' His voice was low.

As a child he'd scared her. He scared her still. In her father's eyes, she'd hung the moon, a bouncy, luminous pumpkin moon. In her uncle's, that same moon withered and dried and blew away in a gust of stony fragments.

The silence stretched. Her uncle cleared his throat. She averted her eyes, hating him. She sat heavily back down in her chair and stared out the window. The field office wasn't far from the Agua Caliente Indian reservation, and her uncle's office overlooked a row of date palms and government buildings. The San Jacinto Mountains rose in a cliff of jagged granite.

'In your mind, this wasn't my coming in to brief you about my lecture.'

'What?'

'This was you, bringing me in for questioning.'

He looked away. She followed his gaze to a set of Callaway golf clubs leaning against the wall. Dusty.

'I talked to your supervisor.'

'Sid? That guy's a joke.'

'That's odd. Because he speaks so highly of you And — '

'I can't believe this — '

'And, Grace,' he continued calmly, 'he's gotten permission from San Diego Police brass that if you do this job, providing you work with your own shrink, and as long as you don't screw up and go Waco — '

'*Waco?*' she interrupted, outraged.

'You're going to be able to go back to work, no harm, no foul. I assume you have your own shrink.'

'Waco's not a good example to use, Uncle Pete, since as I recall, it was the FBI who shot up the place like a video game.'

'Are you in, or not?'

A silence.

He smoothed the front of his shirt with his hand.

You bolt at the first sign of trouble. That's what Mac had said to her in the Bahamas. The fury she felt washed over her like an acid wave and with it the dull realization that Jeanne was right. In some way she couldn't quite articulate, finding her way through this tangled maze of old anger she'd trapped herself in with Uncle Pete had everything to do with setting things straight between her and Katie and Mac. It was as if she'd spent five years in a holding pattern, waiting for the letter that had come for her in the Bahamas.

Waiting for a dead man to call her name.

Waiting to find her way home.

Did Grace believe in holy deaths? She wasn't sure.

But Bartholomew's was about as unholy as they came.

An image of his body, lying still in the morgue, flashed into her mind and receded. An outline lingered, as if burned into her retinas. Bartholomew had been a man not long ago, opinionated, angry. Alive. Suddenly it became even more important to her to find his killer.

'Monday night. When the convention closes, I get a free pass back to work at the San Diego Police crime lab. To my job.'

'You left out talking to your shrink, but yeah.' He opened a drawer, the movement random. He closed it.

'What do you see me doing here?'

He toyed with his pen. 'Do you know what a coat-holder is, Grace?'

She waited.

'A guy who gets two other guys riled up enough to fight each other and then says, 'Here, I'll hold your coats.' We think that's what Bartholomew did. Stir up fights and stand on the sidelines, coat-holding.'

'But not this time.'

'Not this time. He was killed Wednesday night and the GM soy field burned.'

'Where is it?'

'Not too far from the Union Pacific railroad sidings as you leave town, if you're taking the 10 toward Indio. You can't miss it. It's the blackened earth that looks like it's been hit by a meteorite.

91

Surrounded by cops now, so flash this from here on in.'

He opened the desk drawer again, and this time pulled out a laminated tag identifying her as an FBI consultant. Her driver's license photo stared back, big dark eyes, black hair, pale skin. Next time she'd put eyeliner on and more mascara. Her eyelashes disappeared completely against the blue background. And blush. Always blush. Something nice and pink. She clipped the tag to her shirt collar.

'This, too, if you need to show it around.' He pulled out a copy of the DMV photo of Bartholomew that Grace had seen stapled to the cover sheet of the coroner's report.

She folded it and put it in the back of a notebook she'd bought at a Qwik Stop in Escondido on the way there.

'I heard Bartholomew had a running conflict with Frank Waggaman over genetically modified crops. And that he attacked Frank in a clothing store the day he died.'

'You mean, could Frank be good for it? Think about it, Grace. If Waggaman shot Bartholomew he would have let us know. He would have spelled out Waggaman's name in Morse code, or enough for us to get it. God knows, the man knew how to spell.'

'You've got a list.'

'Suspects? Yeah. We're working some.'

Annoyance flared. His inability to open up mirrored his lack of generosity when she was a child. Everything had a cost. He seemed to sense her thoughts.

92

'Last night, a second field was torched, also a GM crop — sugar beets this time. Twelve arrests, misdemeanor vandalism and destruction of property. The thing we don't know is if the murder and fire in the soy field is more than superficially connected to the second torching.'

'Same accelerant?'

'Different. Car gasoline, unleaded, burning Bartholomew's body in the soy crop. Diesel fuel in the sugar beets.'

'Anybody taking credit?'

'You mean for the second one? It started as an opportunistic student call to arms against Bartholomew's murder, organized on Facebook. It morphed into something else.'

'Opportunistic?'

'Finals start next week at Riverside U.' His voice was dry. 'What better reason for not studying than honoring a dead professor by taking over a genetically modified crop in his name. There were about a thousand kids. It was a candlelight vigil that turned into a swarm. The ag convention head, Frank Waggaman, was giving a tour to delegates in the sugar beets field when it happened.'

She digested that. Jeanne's boyfriend, Frank Waggaman, in the mix again.

'A lot of it's caught on tape.'

'They must love that over at Channel Two.'

'It's Three, here in the Valley, but yes.'

He leaned on an elbow, pressed a finger to his temple, massaged his forehead.

'I love this place, Grace. The Palm Springs Film Fest and the White Party and the Coachella

Stagecoach and the tennis matches at the Grand Champions and the Bob Hope Golf Tournament. I love the little stuff, too. I love the statue of Sonny Bono and the horses carrying tourists and lovers. How people can walk down the street here safely holding hands, no matter if they're green, purple, or polka-dotted, and trust me, I've seen them in all those combinations. This is a place with a huge heart, Grace, and it's my job to protect it.'

He lapsed into silence.

'So you want me to do what, again?' Grace asked.

'Oh, yeah. Lost my train of thought; too busy listening to the 'Marine's Hymn' in my head.'

She half smiled. She didn't want to like him.

'Grace, you didn't know Vonda very well.'

She remembered a tea party she'd orchestrated; her younger cousin's shy delight at the way Grace had placed teddy bears and dollies in a circle, a toy plate holding a crumb of doughnut in front of each. Downstairs, the voices of the adults had been soft, relaxed, mingled with the cries of the boys playing a raucous game of tag in the backyard.

One of her few, undiluted golden memories of a time when things were easy.

Interrupted by other memories — Vonda teetering blindfolded on the edge of the pier, screaming on the handlebars of an older brother's bike, running into traffic for the sheer rush of seeing terrified drivers slam on their brakes.

Grace remembered Vonda well enough to be

afraid of her. For her.

Her uncle rubbed a finger into his eye, exhaled. 'She's our youngest, our only girl. I guess we always babied her. She's — how old are you again?'

'Thirty-two.'

He nodded. 'She's twenty-six.'

He glanced behind him and Grace saw a frame of Popsicle sticks painted in blue poster paint and decorated with sparkly buttons. In the photo, a young Vonda stood smiling in a party hat, eyes shiny as black buttons.

'Married. We thought that would settle her down. She lives here now. That was one of the reasons I requested a transfer to this field office. I've been here six months.'

'Just? Explains the holes in the wall.'

His gaze went to the wall.

'The guy before you had pictures.'

Pete picked up a crystal paperweight embedded with a gold FBI seal and put it down gently. 'Vonda might be involved in Bartholomew's murder.'

Outside, the silence was cut by the faint drone of a jet.

'What do you mean?'

'That's what I need you to find out. Report to me. You won't attend briefings. I want an outsider's perspective. See if there's anything I missed. I'll make everything available. Whatever you need, ask. Here are contact numbers and directions to the murder site.'

He scribbled on a pad, tore it off as if it were a prescription, and passed it over to her.

'Should have been a doctor, Uncle Pete.'

'What?' His face was shot with worry and blank love.

'Got the handwriting down.' She stuck the paper in her bag. 'I take it her alibi's checked out for Wednesday night.'

'Her husband's. Hers, not so much.' He opened his mouth as if there was more, closed it, and rocked back on his chair.

'You're not telling me what those alibis are?' She kept her voice pleasant, but inside, she was fuming. It felt like a clumsy version of 'I'm not telling until you guess,' a game Katie was brutally good at.

'It would be more helpful if you did your own investigation, came back with what you find.'

'If you think Vonda's involved, how can you work this case?'

'Conflict of interest, you mean. Columbine settled that one for the agency.'

'Columbine.'

'One of the lead agents, Dwayne Fuselier, had a son who went to Columbine, graduated a few years before the massacre. While he was there, he'd helped edit a video. Of a massacre. Taking place in Columbine. With kids in trench coats.'

'Wow.'

'Exactly. But Fuselier's son had nothing to do with Klebold and Harris gunning down defenseless students and teachers.'

'You're hoping I'll find the same thing with Vonda.'

He was silent. His eyebrows had started turning gray and his hair was combed straight back. He dug his finger into his temple again, as if trying to extricate a piece of shrapnel without anesthetic.

'I can't lie. If I find something — '

'I don't want you to.'

'Find something, or lie?'

He pushed his chair back, stood and walked to the window. Across the balcony, the San Gorgonio Mountains glowed in the distance. Snow feathered the peaks.

'Either one. I'm counting on you to do the right thing, the professional thing, Grace. Hell, you probably have authority issues that would keep a trainload of shrinks busy. Your dad left — '

Heat flushed her face. 'He fell overboard.'

'He was my brother, I knew him better than you did, but yeah, okay, have it your way, *overboard*; you did an end-run around the cops when Katie was snatched, speaking of which, why in the hell didn't you call me? Never mind. It's going to be some bullshit reason anyway and the point about Vonda is — '

'I had just over twenty-four hours.' A wave of heat shot up her face. She scooped up her bag as he went to the door. 'I called somebody I trusted in my lab to help me. He'd tapped the line; he *knew*. Told me he'd send me Katie's finger in a box, I tried it again. Or worse. He was going to kill her. Right there on the spot, kill her.'

Uncle Pete frowned. He had two sets of grooves in his forehead and they moved in unison, like synchronized swimmers. 'Oh, hell, Grace, they all say that. That's right out of the bad guy handbook.'

He walked to the door and she followed him out. He moved fast. She trotted to catch up. She raised her voice.

'And you're right, the biggest bullshit reason I never called is because we've been so *estranged*, I forgot I even *had* an uncle Pete, let alone *an uncle Pete in the fucking FBI*.'

In unison the two terrorism task force reps raised their heads over their cubicle walls. She recognized one from the briefing, the sheriff's investigator. The other guy was balding and wore brown-rimmed glasses that matched his eyes.

'We're fine,' Uncle Pete said. 'Just a friendly family squabble, nothing to worry about. Go back to checking for lead in underpants or whatever the hell you're doing.'

A distracted wave and the heads disappeared.

'Lead?'

'You'd be amazed and appalled at what's smuggled into this country on a daily basis, Grace, the point being, maybe Vonda will tell you things — things she doesn't even know are important — that can help us stop whatever bad thing's coming.'

An assistant went past in the other direction and handed Pete a stack of messages. He sorted them moving. In front of them was the bank of video screens and the Plexiglas barrier.

'Where is she?'

'Jail.' His jaw bunched. 'She won't let Stu — that's her husband — spring her out.'

'Making her own point. The daughter of an FBI agent won't be treated differently.'

'Embarrass me is more her style.' He talked quietly without moving his lips, like a scarred, lumpy ventriloquist. 'And it's not differently. It's more severely. The tapes we have don't give any indication she was responsible for the GM sugar beet crop burning. But she stood there, wrists out, waiting to be cuffed, *daring* them to arrest her. Most everybody's out by now. This is vintage Vonda, digging in her heels. Aunt Chel's a wreck over this.'

On a bulletin board hung a crowded wall of wanted posters. Her uncle scanned the faces, as if looking for someone in particular.

'One other thing. She's pregnant.'

Grace felt her scalp prickle, right along the hairline.

He opened the gray door leading to the anteroom. 'This is her fourth try.'

Grace put her hand on her face, as if to anchor it. The skin felt hot.

He let the door shut behind them. 'She's lost three others early on. She's due in two weeks.'

He held the door to the hall open, and for a moment, his gruff mask dropped and she saw a flash of despair.

'I know you're not a doctor anymore, Grace. But maybe you can talk some sense into her. If she loses this one, I think she's gone for good.'

'I'm not a doctor. I can't pretend I am.'

'I'm counting on you.'

'Don't.'

11

Grace drove down Civic Drive, past a gate with a silhouette of a German shepherd and the words *K-9* on the arch, and parked in front of the memorial to two fallen policemen framed by a piece of sculpted, mangled car.

She was still angry. Her uncle was good at creating his own universe. Boxing people in. Making them cry uncle.

Only it wasn't going to happen this time. Not with her.

Under the anger was fear. He couldn't expect her to respond as a doctor. If she did, she'd go under.

The outside of the Palm Springs Jail looked like a brown brick junior high school in Northern California that Grace had attended for a few months as a thirteen-year-old — no visible windows and a sense of lost hope.

There was nobody behind the Plexiglass wall. Grace pressed the buzzer and a disembodied voice told her to speak. In the small waiting area, a man in his late thirties paced back and forth, anger rolling off him in palpable waves.

His face looked oily and pale, as if he'd been working hard in the bowels of a submarine boiler room and had only recently climbed into the light. Grace placed his age a few years older than Mac, late thirties. He was wearing a sky blue uniform with a decal of a windmill and a tag that said SODERBERG.

A correctional officer in gray short sleeves and pants came to the other side of the Plexiglas window. She had curly hair she wore skinned back into a ponytail, and strands had come loose, creating a fuzzy halo around her face. She looked scrubbed, Mormon. She glanced nervously at the man and licked her lip.

Grace smacked the FBI ID against the Plexiglas wall a little too hard and the CO jumped.

'Drop it in the slot, please.'

The CO's fingers clicked as she entered Grace's information off the ID tag and slid it back. 'You're here to see . . . ' She waited, fingers poised.

Grace realized she hadn't asked her uncle Vonda's married name. She reclipped the ID badge to her collar. 'Vonda,' she said with authority.

The jailer frowned, looking at the screen. 'Last name?'

'Soderberg.' The man in the jumpsuit was at her elbow.

His eyes were a dark gray and he had thin sideburns the color of yellow ash. He stuck out his hand. His fingers were hot.

'Stu. I'm Vonda's husband.'

'Grace Descanso. Vonda's cousin.' She tried not to stare. He was older than she expected, and now that he was standing in front of her, better-looking. His hair reminded her of Mac's — styled, not something from a barber — and

101

his eyes crackled with intelligence and smoldering rage.

His eyes slid to the ID. 'FBI.' His tone changed, became guarded.

'It's going to be a few minutes before we can take you back. Have a seat.' The corrections officer was talking to Grace, but her eyes were on Stuart.

His fist shot out and hit the glass. 'Damn you. I thought she was getting out.'

The CO jumped backward. 'Mr Soderberg, I explained to you — '

'No, this is wrong. You've seen how pregnant she — '

'Outside.' Grace clamped a hand on his arm.

Stuart Soderberg jerked his arm free and banged through the door.

'Back in five.'

She did the little pirouette and dip that people do when they're embarrassed and backing out of a room, stopping just short of fanning her pants out in a curtsey.

Stuart Soderberg stood on the sidewalk facing the granite wall of Mount San Jacinto, visible past the busy traffic on Tahquitz Canyon Way. The sun was setting, turning a row of barrel cactus bright orange.

He shook a cigarette out of a pack, stuck it in his mouth, and scraped a match along a decorative boulder in a sandy garden, cupping his hands around the flame until the match caught. He still hadn't looked at her. In profile, his shoulders looked big.

'Whose side are you on?' His voice was rough.

102

He took a long drag of his cigarette and held it.

'Nobody's, I guess,' Grace answered honestly.

Stuart blew the smoke out in a gust, inhaled again, and dropped the cigarette. He ground it under his boot and picked it up carefully, blowing off the dirt before he put it back in his shirt pocket.

'She *promised* me. She had no business getting involved in this stuff. None. Not with her history.' His voice was pained.

He was talking as if he knew her. Grace wondered why. 'Have we met?'

'You're the one who got away. Actually your dad. He broke the purity of the line when he ran off with Lottie.'

A mocking smile curled at the edges of his mouth, so she'd know he was kidding. 'Your father opened the door to indiscriminate mating.'

She smiled back. 'That explains it.'

He snapped a look at her, his eyes suddenly wary.

'I expected somebody Portuguese, that's all.'

'And maybe a decade younger.'

She was silent.

'On my first date with Vonda, she told me how Nana only wanted her to date Portuguese boys. She thought it was funny.' He grinned wistfully at the memory, and the angles in his face softened.

'Nana's a pistol.' Grace had a sudden flash of her grandmother, sitting on a stuffed pillow at the embroidered dining room table, folded in, like an ancient predatory bird.

'The best,' he said loyally.

Grace wondered how hard it had been for him, facing Nana's sharp tongue. Nana had made it clear to her as she was growing up that there was safety in being Portuguese; outside the fold was danger, and Grace had straddled both worlds, feeling safe in neither.

Stuart tilted his wrist and checked the time. He had an army watch with a cracked face and Grace wondered if he'd bought it at a secondhand store, or earned the damage in some desolate spot.

'When you see her, tell her I love her.' He dipped his head and studied the toe of his boot. 'And that I'm sorry I yelled.'

He glanced sideways at her, eyes bright with pain and humiliation.

'You're worried about her.'

'I have to go to work.' He walked away, toward the parking lot, his long legs churning.

'I could meet you.'

He stopped walking, considered it. 'I've got a break at midnight. We could talk then.'

There was lonely pride in his voice, a man struggling with himself, and she wanted to tell him it wasn't charity that was driving her, but selfishness. She wasn't trying to help him, only get through the long night that lay ahead without Katie and Mac in it.

She rummaged through her bag, walking, and gave him a pen and the notebook, open to a blank page.

He scribbled out an address. 'I'll see you at midnight. We'll talk. I'll tell you everything I know. And a lot I only suspect.'

12

Grace didn't know how it was in other families, but in hers, Vonda had been prepping to wear the crown since she was a baby, and Grace had been trained to pull the wagon where the queen sat.

It had been one of her earliest memories, Vonda sitting in a sundress, rolls of baby fat cascading down her sturdy toddler body, teetering in a sitting position, waving at her brothers lined up to fling things at her, the harder the better. Grace had wanted to do the sitting and waving and have one of the boys pull the wagon, but Aunt Chel had insisted Vonda get in some early training.

And then Grace's brother, Andy, had tripped her and she'd tilted the wagon and Vonda had gone flying. The only person who screamed was Aunt Chel.

'Again!' Vonda had cried.

She'd seemed impervious to danger. Grace wondered if that had changed. And if it hadn't, what it meant.

All she knew was that Bartholomew was dead, he had Grace's photo on his wall, and Grace's uncle feared his own daughter might have helped kill him.

Grace followed the corrections officer through the dark corridors that would lead her to answers.

Vonda was wearing a wilted orange pumpkin costume that stretched over her pregnant belly. Wadded tissues littered the gray floor. On her head tilted a green beanie with a felt stalk that curved up. She sat on a mattress in a holding cell with two women dressed as a banana and an apple. They looked like leftovers at a farmers' market at the end of the day after prices had been slashed.

'Hey.' Grace smiled. Behind her, the corrections officer relocked the doors leading to the holding cell. They'd had to bend protocol, putting Grace in the cell with all three women, but Grace had wanted to meet the women in Vonda's life who were important enough that Vonda was willing to lie to her husband to spend time with them.

The apple shifted on the mattress. Her eyes were a bright green, her hair a frizzy red that made her look strangely festive, like a Christmas ornament.

'Are you the lawyer?' Her voice was hopeful.

'That's no lawyer. That's my cousin Grace.'

Wide smile. Vonda flung open her arms. A woman's face had been delicately inlaid over the teenager Grace remembered: hair a glossy black to the jawline, eyes a familiar dark brown, but the thing Grace remembered most, that still exuded from every pore, was her intense unpredictability.

It was as if a motor hummed deep inside that had somehow kicked a notch off center, everything vibrating, threatening to explode into hard, disintegrating shards.

When Grace was a kid, it had made her feel helpless and alarmed and protective. After all these years, the same feeling welled up.

She sensed that Vonda's friends felt the same way. They pressed in on her, soldiers closing ranks, flinching when Grace leaned in to kiss her.

All three had colds, their noses chapped and raw, and Grace kissed the air next to Vonda's cheek before stepping back. Vonda dabbed her nose with a tissue.

'What, no snacks?'

'The linguiça's out in the car right next to the crown I stole.'

Vonda laughed. It had a hard edge to it. The banana looked confused.

'Last time I saw Vonda, she was queen of Festa do Espirito Santo. Major Portuguese festival in Point Loma — in San Diego — that's where we were raised,' Grace said. 'The same crown's been used in Festa since 1910. Wearing the crown's a very big deal.'

'Grace brought linguiça — this sausage — and forgot about it and left it out in the car.'

'I didn't forget. Your mom put me to work in the kitchen. For six hours.'

Everybody pulled shifts at Festa, but Aunt Chel had seen to it that Grace's lasted until the party was over. And then Aunt Chel had asked her to leave.

She had. She wondered now why she had let her aunt have such power, but at the time all

107

she'd wanted was to run. She was the product of the union between her aunt's first love, Grace's dad, and the bleached-blond floozy warbler who had stolen his heart away. Being humiliated and banished had seemed a small price to pay for the sins of her parents.

Vonda's gaze slid to the FBI badge clipped to Grace's shirt. Her eyes dilated.

'Wow. A baby in there.'

'Sam.' Vonda was still looking at the badge.

There was no one in their family named Sam. 'After Stu's dad?'

'Mom. Samantha. I never met her. She died before Stu moved to Palm Springs. Grace, what are you doing here?'

'I could ask you the same question.'

'There were twelve of us crammed in here this morning. Two butterflies, three apples, the banana — Andrea — me — how many's that?'

'Too many,' Andrea snapped. The heat had wilted her hair so that the curls were pasted against her scalp making her look like a blond Kewpie doll.

Vonda frowned. 'Did my dad send you?'

'Of course he sent her. Look at the badge, Vee.'

Grace shifted. 'And you are?'

'Pissed,' Andrea spat. 'I told you, Vee, your dad's trying to pin Bartholomew's murder on us — on me, I swear to God.'

'What makes you say that?' Grace kept her voice neutral.

'Besides sending *you*?' Andrea smiled. Her teeth were small and white. 'Well, Mr Bozo head was here for a long time — '

'I told you, Andrea, don't call my husband that.'

'Well, he is. You're a grown woman, Vee. Entitled to make your own choices. He has no right blasting in here forbidding you to protest. It's not a good match.'

'Andrea, shut up.' Vonda's voice was tired.

Grace saw an opening and took it. 'I'd love to meet the latest member of the family.' She smiled at Vonda. 'How about tomorrow I bring breakfast over.'

'You can't, Vee!' Panic washed over Andrea's face.

'I can't?' Vonda stiffened.

'You need to rest.' Andrea's eyes flicked to Grace, back to Vonda. 'That's all I meant. You don't need visitors.'

'Seven?' Grace kept smiling. She could be a Miss America contender, that smile of hers.

Vonda shot Andrea a small defiant look. 'Nine's better. Stu comes home for a couple of hours then before he goes back to work.'

'Directions.' Grace pulled out a pen and notepad and watched as Vonda scribbled the phone number and directions.

The apple reached out and touched Vonda, her eyes shifting. 'Andrea didn't mean any harm. She just means nobody understands like we do, Vee. That's all.'

'And you are?'

'You don't have to talk to her,' Andrea said.

'Who's your other friend, Vonda?' Grace's voice was easy.

'Sarah. Conroy,' Vonda said.

'Fuck you,' Sarah said.

'With an *h?*'

'She's my cousin,' Vonda said. 'She can come and have breakfast with me, for chrissake. It's not like I'm under house arrest.'

'Why are you here?' Grace repeated.

'Rat testicles,' Sarah said. 'Mice and rats. Fed GM soybeans, they had dark blue testicles.'

'Instead of what?'

'Scientists at the Russian National Academy.' Vonda leaned forward over her belly. 'They fed female rats genetically modified soy two weeks before they mated, and over half the group died.'

'Yeah, and a bunch of GM offspring couldn't even get pregnant,' Andrea said. 'Not at all.'

'We're not goofballs, Grace, dressing up, protesting to get attention.' Vonda's eyes clouded. 'We belong to a special, horrible club. All of us have lost babies the first three months in utero. And not just us, either. Everybody in our group.'

The blood rushed from Grace's head. Her body felt heavy, stolid, as if the two parts of her were connected by the thinnest cord that could snap at any instant.

She let the words in one at a time. *Everybody in our group*. 'How many people?'

The women looked at each other. Vonda shrugged. 'Comes and goes. Two women moved away. After. There's been — what, seven? Does that sound right?'

'Becky, too,' Sarah said. 'She adopted.'

'Right. Okay, so eight.'

Grace thought of empty rooms in silent houses, bassinets waiting for babies that never came.

'I'm sorry.' She meant it.

Grace had gotten pregnant immediately with Katie, as if her body had only been waiting for Mac so they could get busy on a long-term science project that required teamwork.

'What do your doctors say?' That was a dangerous question, and the instant she asked it, she wished she could call it back. Something wild thrummed in her chest, as if it were trapped, trying to find a way out, explode into the sky, to freedom.

'The usual.' Sarah shrugged, her voice brittle. 'Imperfect fertilization. Damage to the placenta or umbilical cord. Fibroids. Endometreosis. These guys don't know.'

'We've had chromosome workups,' Andrea said. 'They look inside our uteruses like they were peering up there with flashlights. You don't want to hear this.'

They were right; Grace didn't. Not as a doctor.

She realized in that instant she was reacting as a crime lab investigator. She wasn't interested in solving their medical problems as much as in how they'd used their grief to justify anarchy.

She understood something else in that moment. She wasn't going back to medicine. The light in the cell looked refracted, altered, and she felt a curious sense of lightness.

She would use her past, who she was. Shape

her future. Whatever it turned out to be. She wasn't faking it anymore, pretending to be a crime lab investigator but feeling like a fraud, always resisting the urge to explain her choice, make excuses. She belonged in this world. Or not. But that was enough for now.

Andrea was talking. 'Chickens fed GM corn died twice as fast as the others.'

'And mice eating GM potatoes,' Vonda said. 'Their pancreases were messed up. We have to warn them. These people from poor countries, coming here getting a load of crap about how GM crops are going to save their people from hunger. Nobody has a fucking idea what's really going to happen, or when. They're getting lied to and it has to stop.'

'And you're the ones to do it.'

Andrea looked at her. 'You have to be willing to die for your beliefs.'

Traveling from bar to bar with Lottie had taught Grace a few basics: always get a room on the ground floor, much easier to leave through a window in the middle of the night that way; stand by the door if given the choice; and never discount that shiver that started at the base of the spine, a shiver that when pronounced enough, raised hairs along the nape of the neck.

Grace rubbed her neck. 'Is that what happened to Bartholomew? He died for his beliefs?'

The outside cell door opened and two jailers came in, the new one swinging a set of keys like nunchucks. They crossed the dining area and he unlocked the holding cell door.

'Okay, you three, out.'

'What if we don't — '

'Enough, Vonda. Don't want to keep your fans waiting.'

13

Grace sat in her car in the parking lot. They were shooting the TV interview in front of the monument to the downed officers, using the twisted metal as a stage backdrop. It was dark now, and in the spot, Vonda's skin looked gray and damp. What had Vonda gotten herself into?

You have to be willing to die for your beliefs. That's what Andrea had said.

And killing. Was that part of it? Had someone in Bartholomew's group killed him to get things started?

The spot went out and Grace sat up straighter. A cab glided through the parking lot and stopped at the curb, motor running. The cameraman eased Vonda into the backseat. Andrea and Sarah climbed in after her.

Bobbing above the television van like a flying saucer was a white satellite dish, and the cab followed it out of the parking lot and onto Tahquitz. Grace kept a car between her and the taxi. Protestors in costume marched on both sides of Tahquitz, holding signs. A woman dressed as a grim reaper darted into traffic and Grace slammed on the brakes, cursing as the light changed and the satellite dish sailed down the street, the cab right behind it.

Grace sat in her car, fuming. She pressed her window down and stuck her head out, straining to see up the street. It was getting more

114

crowded. She spotted a yellow wink of the cab as it rounded the corner onto Palm Canyon Drive.

She pressed the bumper of the car in front of her and ran a yellow. Two yellows. She made Palm Canyon Drive just in time to see a blur of yellow banana spilling onto the sidewalk and darting up tiled steps to a Mexican restaurant. Andrea. The taxi slid into traffic and kept going.

Grace parked in a no-parking zone in a bank lot and jogged back to the restaurant.

A harried hostess in a layered skirt checked her chart. 'Sorry. It's going to be twenty minutes at least, place is jammed.'

Grace was still panting. 'Late. My group's inside. No worries. I'll find them.'

A three-piece band belted out 'Let the Good Times Roll.' The area in front of the band pulsed with people in costume. Grace slid into a booth with a sight line of the sunken dance floor.

She scanned the dancers, looking for Andrea. She saw three other bananas, but not her. An elderly couple jounced through the crowd on the floor, dancing with elbows akimbo and pivoting knees swiveling like Elvis, the man's shirt a bright turquoise in a sea of red and green and yellow. No Andrea. Grace shifted and stole a look at the diners behind her.

'Looking for me?'

A burst of heat shot up her body.

Andrea slid into the booth across from her, followed by a man in his early thirties dressed in black, a pack of Marlboros protruding from his shirt pocket.

'What do you want?' His voice was drowsy, as

if he wasn't quite awake.

A drink. A nice margarita blended, with salt and a frosty lime wedged on the rim, but she wasn't going to tell him that. 'Information.'

He barked a laugh. 'Don't fuck with Andrea anymore. Got that?'

He played a riff on the table with his hands, and Grace wondered what imaginary band he was part of. He reached for a chip, doused it in sauce. It left a red dribble across the wooden table. He crunched down hard on it and the dark stamp of hair on his chin moved. He had a fleshy nose and a gap between his two front teeth and he parted his brown hair on the wrong side so that a cowlick stood up, making him look like the *What, me worry?* icon on *Mad* magazine, if the image had been age-progressed by two decades.

'That's Vonda's cousin,' Andrea said, her eyes on Grace.

'Just in time for the blessed event,' Grace said. She smiled.

Andrea blinked. 'It's all arranged. I'm going to be there. So is Sarah.' Her voice rose.

'Good. We'll have a girl party. I'll bring the nail polish and the weepy movies.'

'She doesn't need you. She doesn't want you. She's got us.'

Grace stared. She'd followed Andrea purely on instinct, trying to get a handle on how she fit into Vonda's life. Into Bartholomew's death. So far, Andrea's biggest reaction was territorial, and it was over a defenseless, unborn child.

Grace reached for a chip and ate it. Fabulous chips. Salty, slightly greasy, cracking and

116

melting, the sweet taste of corn in her mouth. She chewed.

'I don't know how much you know about babies, and if you've lost a bunch, maybe not too much.'

It wasn't nice, but it worked. The hardness fell away from Andrea's face and left the wound exposed underneath. Her nostrils pinched and her mouth trembled.

'Vonda's about to deliver any minute and if you're any kind of friend — '

'She's my best friend.'

'There you go. She can't be doing this protest stuff, Andrea.' She caught a waitress's eye and smiled. 'Just have her lick envelopes or something. No, not that, Internet terrorist stuff; that's nice and clean. She can't be making bombs, got it?'

'What did you tell her, Andrea?' His voice was just short of a scream. He swiveled in his seat his face darkening.

Grace grew still. Bombs. Were they building bombs? Was that what Radical Damage had planned for the Convention Center Monday night?

'Protesting is not against the law. Protesting is our right. Our duty.'

'Shut up, Andrea.'

'Here's a news flash, Nate. I'm going to say the fuck what I want.' Andrea shoved her finger at Grace. 'If you think burning that field is the last of it — '

'That's it. We're out of here.' Nate pushed Andrea out of the booth.

'No, Nate, she needs to understand.' Her voice was shrill. 'This isn't some kiss-off thing that people dip into like they're testing the water to go swimming. Everybody in this struggle now needs to get a gun. That's where it's going.'

An elderly woman wearing golf shorts in the next booth looked up, alarmed.

'Get a gun, people,' Andrea shouted.

Nate glanced toward the street and Grace followed his gaze. A solitary car idled at the red light and shot through the empty intersection, tires squealing. She caught a side-angle view of the driver, eyes wide. Scared.

Grace riffled through her wallet, found a ten, and left it under the chips. When she looked up, Nate and Andrea were gone. A tremor rippled through the shifting crowd, as if in the same instant, everyone became aware that something was happening outside.

Grace made her way through the tables and trailed outside after four people dressed as green zucchinis with spongy heads. They sang off-key, voices raised and chins high. New lyrics to 'Old McDonald.' Something about chemicals and waste.

A police car glided down the street. A man stood immobile on a bench holding a sign: FEED THE NEEDY. NOT THE GREEDY.

Grace jogged around the corner and opened her car. A woman dressed as a bee darted out of an alley, smiling radiantly, yellow tennis balls wobbling like antennae.

Ghostly soldiers in a strange war trotted through the intersection, armed with garden

118

hoes. Adrenaline surged through her body and she slammed her car into drive and pulled into traffic. The light turned red and the car ahead of her took a chance and shot through the intersection.

A second police car squealed past, going the opposite direction. The air seemed to shift, grow electric, and she caught the sound of chanting. Up ahead, a puff of smoke clouded a roiling mass of bodies. A tinny voice on a megaphone urged them to disband before it was too late. The light was still red.

Grace kept an eye on the store windows. Dark reflections spilled across the glass fronts. Three. Five. A group shifting in the glint of her headlights.

They stepped out of the alley.

More than five. Much more. Somehow, they'd gotten around the police line. They were here now, on her block, twenty at least, brandishing low-grade weapons. They trotted closer, a merry band of travelers, spilling up the street, eager and hungry.

She wasn't going to wait anymore for the light. Maybe the light was broken. She swung wide, to the right. A man in a burlap sack scampered after her. He was fast. He held a bat in his hands. He smashed downward, aiming for the car, and she saw the swift blur of heavy wood winking past her windshield as she punched the gas and her car shot forward. The bat smashed the asphalt as if it were a wrecking ball.

For an instant, the shops she was passing seemed to shiver and melt into huts boiling with fire and smoke. The humming sang in her ears, the signal that things could get bad. She slid down the window and took deep gulping breaths.

She wiped her mouth. They were shops again, shuttered and silent, and the man with the bat was running slower, stopping. He waved the bat over his head. In the burlap sack, in the glowing light of whatever protests lit the rest of the street, he looked atavistic, primeval. She was the kill that got away.

14

A lizard sat immobile on the sidewalk in front of her room at the Comfort Inn. It scuttled out of sight down the walkway as she unlocked the door. Her room was on the first floor not far from the swimming pool, protected by a fence from the parking lot. She could hear the murmuring shuffle of protesters and the shrill of sirens a block away.

The desk clerk told her that the protesters had been going down Baristo Avenue since Wednesday, a trail of ants headed for Palm Canyon Drive, every night growing in number. Grace dead-bolted the door and threw the latch. She'd bought some sodas in a machine by the pool and she put them away in the small refrigerator next to the sink.

It was a fine room; it just didn't have Katie in it. Mac, either. Two framed etchings of palm trees hung over the king-sized bed. There was a coffeemaker and she made a pot, channel-clicking until she found what she was looking for.

She caught a glimpse of a National Guardsman in a flak jacket wrestling to the pavement a man dressed in commando gear. A shivering wall of bodies crashed through police lines in a blur of jumbled footage.

Someone smashed a car windshield with a bat. In the brief instant before the camera changed

121

focus, it looked exactly like the enraged man in the burlap bag who had raised the bat over the hood of her car before she'd gotten away.

The door to an appliance store burst open; looters poured out with HDTVs, price tags dangling, and scattered into the street. Grace thought again of the miniature bourbon she'd left on Jeanne's ink table.

She switched the channel.

Vonda stood in front of the jail, supported under each elbow by her friends. In their fruit and vegetable costumes, they looked like a Fruit of the Loom chorus line.

The reporter had big hair and a tiny body that made her look like a lacquered bobble-head doll. She lobbed three questions at Vonda, pointed ones about her father as an FBI special agent. Each time Vonda stole a quick look at Andrea. Waiting for a nod, eye blink, a glance back before answering. Andrea was the leader. Vonda followed.

The reporter beamed at Vonda as if they were old friends, her lips so glossy they looked sticky. Behind her glided a cameraman.

'Channel Three received a letter today from Radical Damage, saying that it's planned something special for the last night of the convention, and the question on all of our minds is, what are they going to do?'

Andrea slid a look at Vonda and Sarah. 'What makes you think we should know?'

'Are you part of Radical Damage?'

Andrea's lip curled. 'You think I'd tell you?'

A knock on the door interrupted Grace's

concentration and she sprang to her feet, heart hammering. The door handle jiggled. She crept closer.

'Grace?'

'Goddamn it. Uncle Pete, you scared the hell out of me.' She undid the bolt and held open the door.

Her uncle stood in a pair of jeans and a rumpled sweatshirt, holding a pizza carton.

He looked past her toward the television. 'Oh, good. I see you already got the movie on.' He squeezed past her and sat on the edge of the bed, adjusting the sound.

Grace relocked the door.

'I have ten minutes, tops,' he said. 'Eat fast.'

There was a small love seat next to the bed and Grace sat there. She reached for a piece of pizza. On television was an expanded version of what Grace had already heard: abnormal cells in the small intestines of rats, stomach lesions from genetically modified tomatoes, pigs that had given birth to stillborn piglets, sheep with black spots on their livers.

Pete ate neatly through three pieces of pepperoni pizza, eyes on the screen. Grace stalled out after half a piece. He turned off the television and stood up.

'Boy, I'm going to have some heartburn tonight.' He refolded the cardboard lid into the box. 'What did Vonda tell you?'

'Let's start with this.' Grace threw away the crust and wiped her hands. She didn't look at him. 'What did you tell Child Protective Services about my mother?'

She heard a swift intake of breath. She turned. A muscle in his right eyelid twitched. He smoothed the grease away from the carton lid, wiped his hand on a crumpled napkin.

'Aunt Chel was worried. We both were. We'd get calls from collection agencies, school truancy officers, up and down the coast.'

Her heart was starting to trip. She felt the way she did the first day at every new school, angry, hyper-alert, ready. The way prisoners felt transferred to a new facility, knowing it was going to get ugly, that it would always be ugly.

'You haven't answered my question.'

'It was a long time ago.'

'Not for me.'

She was twelve years old, it was her third school that year. She was standing in seventh-grade science class, making a model of a cell. She'd just double-bagged the Ziploc baggies and poured Karo syrup into the baggie to represent the cell membrane and the cytoplasm.

Ricky Mellen was her lab partner and she could smell a faint whiff of boy sweat and something she later identified as aftershave. Ricky reeked of the stuff. He held the baggies open wide as she carefully poured.

His hair stood up in a stiff gel cut that looked like freshly mown grass. At the last second, he cracked her up by sneak-eating Gummi Worms and three chocolate-covered peanuts, part of the stash that had been set aside to represent the various organelles inside a cell. He was telling her overcrowding of organelles was a serious problem, especially among the amino acids and mitochondria.

He had no idea what he was talking about and mispronounced everything; Grace had read the book cover to cover at the motel they were staying at; but he was cute and she realized in a tentative, heart-stopping way that he was flirting. With her.

Grace, the new kid with no prospects who had to lie about where she spent the night. He offered her a Gummi bear and she took it.

And then the door opened and Mrs Caltriter from the office, who always wore pink, poked her head in, with the saddest smile on her face. Behind her stood a woman Grace didn't recognize. And her brother, Andy. He was crying.

Grace dropped the baggie and ran. 'Is it Mom? Is it my mom?' Her voice was high and choked. Heads craned, the class turned, grew silent.

'This is Mrs Altheria, Grace.' Mrs Caltriter's voice was clear and it carried across the smeary lab counters, across the playground, probably up to Mars and back, and certainly carried into the deepest reaches of Grace's heart.

'She's from Child Protective Services. She's here to help.'

If Grace had to rank an order of badness, she'd be hard-pressed.

There was getting separated from Andy for a while. The foster home where the kid in the bed above hers wet the bed every night. Being yanked out of school. Being returned to the same school. Having Ricky look right through her, embarrassed. Missing her birthday. Sitting alone at lunch. Sitting alone on the bus. Sitting alone at recess. In class. After class. The corrosive shame of being different, having no one.

Being a tribe of one.

And then her mother at the window of the home one night. The whispered hurried conference through the screen. Grace going to school and melting into the shadows, waiting in the blistering heat as her mother's rickety car screamed to a stop and the door flew open.

Good times.

Mac thought she was good at leaving. She came by it honestly. It was one of the genuine gifts of her childhood.

Her uncle seemed inordinately interested in the pizza carton lid. 'We didn't make that call.'

Grace felt light-headed, looking at him carefully for any sign that he was lying. The skin on her face felt rubbed raw, as if she'd been crying a long time. 'You didn't call Child Protective about my mom.'

She needed to hear clearly what he was saying. There was too much noise in her head. He looked at the carpet. Nodded.

'But you did talk to them when they called you.'

He was silent.

Her voice was on the edge of shaking. 'You think you can walk on this one? Skate? This twisted me in ways I don't even know yet.'

Her uncle sighed.

'Who got them involved?'

126

He shook his head.

'Who called CPS, Uncle Pete?'

He flicked his eyes at her and she could see in them a darkness, and something else, a truth. 'This is going to sound nuts, Grace, but I think it was your dad.'

The blood rushed from her head and she sat. 'Grace?'

'My father washed overboard.' Her voice was careful. There was a thread loose in the bedspread. She reached over and tugged on it.

Pete nodded. 'You asked. I answered. My turn.'

'Not so fast.'

'Grace.' His voice was gentle. 'I have theories about what happened to him and sometime we can talk about that, but right now, I need your help.'

She smoothed the thread out, careful not to rip it. Never knew what you'd tear loose, if you ripped it.

She looked into midspace. *Daddy Daddy Daddy*.

'What did you learn?'

She allowed herself one bright memory of her dad, his face, the merry dark eyes and wide smile, a memory of sitting on his lap and how he smelled of the sea. She put that memory carefully away, so that all the corners were crisp.

She could compartmentalize as good as any guy. There was no girl her equal when it came to closing doors, moving on. She'd take that out later. She'd spend a long time on that later. But for now, she'd rather have her arm twisted behind her back and her knees buckled and her mouth packed with sand — the way it had happened once — before she let on how much she needed to know what her uncle knew about her dad. About what happened to him.

'Andrea thinks you're targeting her for Bartholomew's murder.'

'Good. That's good, she's on the defensive. She's talking to you.'

'Screaming, mostly.' Grace told him about following Andrea to the restaurant and the fight between her and Nate. Andrea telling everybody to get a gun.

'Nate flipped out when I brought up bomb making. I'd just thrown it out there to bait her, but he jumped all over it.'

Pete processed that. He looked exhausted and in need of a shave.

'Who's this Nate guy?'

'Nate Malosky. Andrea's husband. For all their radicalism, they got married a couple years back in a Unitarian church. Nate is Bartholomew's teaching assistant. Or was.'

'Might be interesting to see if he benefits at school from this sad, sad death.' She cut a look at him. 'Vonda's too pregnant to be involved in any of this.'

'Think I haven't said that? So has her husband.'

'About Stu. He's not Portuguese.'

'You noticed.'

'Hard not to. I would have thought after the shit you gave my dad — '

'Life's funny that way. It whaps you up the

128

side of the face with whatever prejudice you thought you were entitled to.'

'Karma's alive and living under the Portuguese flag. How's Nana with it?'

'She pretends she doesn't see him.'

'Going to be harder not to see him when they've got a kid. Plus he's what? Thirteen years older than she is?'

Her uncle looked tired. 'Nana called him shopworn when she saw him. That sealed the deal. Two weeks later, Vonda ran off with him. He doesn't have a sheet.'

'You checked.'

'She's my only daughter, Grace. Of course I checked.'

His eyes scanned the room and settled on the small refrigerator. He walked over and returned with two Diet Pepsis. She felt immediate irritation.

'Need a Pepsi, Uncle Pete? Because if you do, there's a diet one in the fridge. Help yourself.'

He ignored her. 'When Andrea told everybody to get a gun, then what?'

'She said torching the field was just the beginning.'

He cracked open a Diet Pepsi and drained half the can. 'The field. She didn't slip up and say fields.'

Grace thought about it and shook her head.

'Oh, and in jail, it was creepy. She made it sound like Bartholomew was a martyr. Made me think, maybe he was killed by one of his own, to jumpstart things.'

Pete looked at her approvingly. Warmth

129

flushed up her chest, the heady glow that came when a piece clicked into place. Uncle Pete might be parsimonious when it came to doling out information, but if she dogged it hard enough, he'd fill in the blanks.

'Aren't you supposed to call me Cricket?'

'It's Grasshopper, and we don't have time. In the last two hours, it's escalated. Pathologists have found soybean rust in some of the GM fields.'

He said it evenly, with no emotion.

'It kills things, Grace, big-time. It's been making its way north and west since it was discovered in the States in 2004, but before now, the farthest west it's been was Nebraska.'

'And now it's here.'

He nodded. 'Its pattern is weird. It's only hit the genetically modified soy fields grown for this convention, the fields along Highway Ten.'

'So chances are, somebody stepped out of a car, did whatever they do with soybean . . . '

'Rust,' her uncle supplied. 'They'd dab spores on leaves.'

'And then got back into their car for an easy getaway.'

'The USDA's climbing all over it. Trying to figure out the boundaries — stop it from spreading.'

'How does it spread?'

'Wind, mostly.'

Grace thought of the windmills churning as she rode the gusts down a hill and started the slow descent into Palm Springs. 'Lovely.'

'Oh, that's just the beginning, Grace. Our

major trade countries are threatening an embargo to prevent infected soy from coming into their countries. We're going to have to spray every soy field west of here, clearly an impossibility, so you get the magnitude of this problem. If we can't get a handle on this we're going to have bigger trouble here than even the subprime crashing.'

'It's just a couple of fields, Uncle Pete.'

'For now. When you're talking about messing with the food supply, you're talking about things going south fast.'

He shifted the pizza carton to his hip and scratched the stubble on his cheek with his other hand.

'There was this wheat fungus on seeds, about ten years back, not too many seeds, not too bad a fungus, and a bunch of countries turned our wheat back at their ports, wouldn't let the wheat in. Cost the U.S. about — oh, roughly, five hundred *million* dollars before people felt safe eating sandwiches again. It's huge. Everything's connected. Take a guess what the export value of shipping our soy to China is.'

He cracked open the carton and lifted out another piece of pizza. The cheese had congealed to the box and he scraped it up and folded it onto the slice.

'Close to a billion dollars, Grace. Just China.'

He tore a chunk off and chewed, his jaws grinding.

'E. coli. Salmonella. Remember what happened with spinach? And tomatoes? Nobody would eat them for months. Way past the time when they got a clean bill of health. And rice. Remember how there was a run on it? Shortages, panic, prices doubling per bag. Well, I got a news flash for you. Soy's in everything. Sauces, cake mixes, chicken coating, motor oil — probably the cardboard box this pizza came in.'

He took another bite and swallowed it almost whole.

'So how does Bartholomew's death factor into all this? He was a history professor, not a biologist.'

'Yeah, he taught history from the point of view of the ones on the bottom. It was an angry class, taught to a bunch of entitled kids with too much time on their hands. We're teaching a whole nation to feel bad about the things that made us strong, made us who we are.'

She opened her mouth and her uncle cut her off.

'I don't need a lecture here, Grace, about women and blacks and Indians and how it's time somebody stood up for them. All I'm saying is, Radical Damage could be trying to shatter public trust in government.'

'If you can't trust the government to keep food safe.'

'Exactly. If you can affect the food supply, and it's a big enough hit, it's gold.'

'Do you think Bartholomew was involved in Radical Damage?'

'I'd bank money on it. The question is whether Vonda is.'

He took a savage bite, put the crust back into the carton and reclosed it.

'As of tonight, across the rest of California, plant pathologists are busy with spore traps. We can't let this thing spread. And we still don't have a handle on what's planned for Monday night at the Convention Center.'

He tried to burp and failed. It came out a croak.

'Damn. The skills that fade as you grow old. It's rock-and-roll time, Grace. If you're planning on sleeping much, I'd give it up. This thing's on the move. It's getting worse. And we're running out of time.'

He balled up the napkin and made a one-handed shot. It dropped with a soft thud.

15

Every meeting was different, depending on the group and time of day, but the coffee was reliably weak and bad and the folding chairs hard. This group met downstairs in a rec room of a Methodist church off Alejo.

There were seven of them, Grace the only one from out of town. She didn't feel like sharing and nobody pressed but it got her through an hour where the anger and tumult she was feeling surged under the surface and made her want to try reckless things.

She could handle the anger; what scared her was what was under it. Waiting in a bubbling stew of raw emotion was pain. Always pain. She sat and let it wash through her, head down, knees quaking, shuddering.

She held the Styrofoam cup in her hands and thought of Mac in Guatemala, his hands on her body, the way he'd worked next to her in the makeshift clinic. She flashed on women in China years ago who'd had their feet bound to keep them small, and how in a movie she'd seen once on late-night TV, a woman had died from the pain when the wrapping had been suddenly ripped off. The scream had seemed very real; a compelling life lesson about not unwrapping things, even if the binding left you crippled.

Forgiveness. How could she get that? She wasn't ready to offer it to her uncle, she knew

134

that. What she didn't know was if those two things were inextricably linked.

Her uncle wanted her to say it was okay; his talking to Child Protective Services and not defending Lottie's parenting, his attempt to break up her family, the years of snipping them out of family events. As if she could wave a wand over the past and have everything not hurt.

The idea that her father might still be alive, and that her uncle might have a piece that could lead her to him, stunned her and made her light-headed.

'Are you okay?'

Grace opened her eyes and realized the woman was speaking to her. She had gray eyes and yellow teeth. She wore her sandy-colored hair short and parted to the side, a gold band on her finger.

'I'm fine.' Grace drank coffee and pretended to listen. They were past the part where somebody talked about how bad things got before they got better and on to particulars of the week. Apparently the woman with the gray eyes had been speaking. She turned back to the group.

'Anyway, it's creepy. I called and called. I was so afraid. Just stood there, screaming her name in the dark. We live close to the cliffs. It's this wall of black rising up, this *presence*. Like it's breathing, listening. And then the next morning, I go out for the paper, here she is, huddling on the step, shivering, this little ball of fur, bloody.'

The group shifted in the chairs and made appropriate noises.

'I scooped her up and took her right in and the vet said, and this is the weird thing, it looked almost like Peaches' midsection had been nicked, and I said, nicked? And he said, yeah, by maybe an arrow.'

Grace shifted her cup, alert.

'You mean, somebody might have tried to hurt her?' It was a tanned elderly woman, wrinkled knuckles studded with rings.

The woman nodded. 'Her paws were all messed up. He thought . . . ' She shifted in her chair. 'This is the truly awful part. He thought maybe somebody had tried using her for target practice.'

The room grew very still.

'Isn't that a stretch?' It was a man with a rumbly voice and a gray ponytail, wearing board shorts and a tank top that revealed a mat of curly hair.

The woman wet her lip. 'That's what I said to him, Lou, and then he told me he thought it was a lot bigger than that. He said it was the third one he's seen this week.'

★ ★ ★

The lines to get into the Convention Center stretched almost to the street. It was dark and cool outside. Under the swooping cement archway, recessed lighting cast a bronze glow over the delegates and volunteers waiting to clear security.

Grace inched her way past a cascade of boulders, palms punctuated by gravel and a

136

bronze sculpture of a cougar on high alert.

The cougar made her think of her mother. Midfifties, Lottie had never met a vinyl miniskirt that wasn't calling her name.

The Oasis ballroom swarmed with conventioneers wearing name tags, some in burkas, and salesmen in booths shilling everything from crop dusters to fertilizer and irrigation systems. The energy level was high and manic; everyone aware of the ramped-up security, jumping at sounds of farm machinery roaring to life in showcase booths, jerking away from contact as shoulders accidentally bumped. A roiling stew of smells greeted her: perfume and sweat and popping corn and motor oil.

Grace pressed through a crush of people and found an information booth. A bright-faced young woman wearing a red-white-and-blue name tag with HELLO! MY NAME IS MINDY! directed Grace toward a door on the far side of the room.

Mindy looked familiar. They all looked familiar. Shiny straight hair, glowing eyes, skinny. Grace showed her FBI ID to an armed guard who rapped on Waggaman's door and stood aside as Frank motioned her in.

Frank Waggaman's office had been set up in a small, cramped space sectioned off the ballroom. The cacophony of noise wasn't blocked when he closed the door behind them. He looked more drawn than she remembered, but the geek factor was still high.

He wore sturdy shoes over work pants and a wrinkled shirt. He had egg yolk on his lapel, and his hair along his jawline was coming in a bristly gray. He looked as if he hadn't slept since Bartholomew's body had been discovered Wednesday in his burned crop of soy.

He gave her a rough hug. He smelled of the woods and fresh soap.

'This place is jammed.'

'We've got thirteen thousand industry execs and sixty agriculture and environment delegates here from all over the world. Sorry for the mess.'

He raised his voice to be heard as he led her around a column of bubble-wrapped boxes stacked against a wall.

'I need to warn you, we're going to be interrupted. Secretary of agriculture's due to show up and I'll have to break away.'

Bags of seed lined the wall, along with a half-empty bag of dirt, fertilizer, and a coiled rubber hose and sprinkler. On the makeshift wall was a taped poster of what looked like a hairy pod of peas. The caption read: GOT SOY?

The room smelled like mulch and old tires, as if moldering tennis shoes had been left out in the rain. 'Where are your linen pants?'

'What? Oh. Over here.' He made his way to a metal locker. He had a comb-over in the back, his bald spot pink.

'And a shirt. I bet you've got a shirt in there too, right?'

He cracked open the locker as if he were seeing the shirt and pants hanging inside for the first time. 'Forgot all about these.'

He motioned distractedly to a platter perched on his desk amid a stack of bulletins.

138

Butter-crusted potato wedges.

'Hungry? These are really good. They've been GM'd with cholera and hepatitis B vaccines.'

'No, thanks,' Grace said hastily. 'Hand me your clothes.'

He looked alarmed and clutched at his shirt.

'Not the ones you're wearing, Frank, the ones in the closet. I'll clip tags. Where are the scissors?'

He patted the desk and moved on to the bookshelf behind him, searching under a stack of binders.

'Monday night. Closing. Do you have anything special planned?'

'Of course; nobody throws a party like they do in Palm Springs. Skits, kids drumming, party favors like you wouldn't believe. Seven sharp.'

'Party favors.'

'A free windmill, Grace, to each delegate and to the delegates from each of the states.'

He found the scissors under a piece of garden hose and gave them to her.

'What's freaking everybody out is that letter to Channel Three from Radical Damage, threatening something bad happening. Do you think it's going to happen, Grace?'

He looked at her anxiously. Grace clipped the tags from his pants. She hung them on a hanger on the doorknob, a visual reminder to him that he needed to change. She reached for the shirt.

'I'm going to ask you some stuff that's off the wall. You know my uncle, Special Agent Pete Descanso.'

'He's your uncle?'

'Yeah. The thing I need to know is if you've ever met my cousin Vonda.'

'Sure. I see her every couple of months or so. Her and Stu both.'

She looked up. It wasn't what she expected. 'How's that?'

'I have a side business. Selling organic soy seed. Takes me all over California.'

'They have a greenhouse?'

'Good Farms. Vonda makes bread from the organic seed and sells the bread at the farmers' market on Thursdays. For being her cousin, you don't know much about her.'

That rankled. She snapped the shirt to get out the store wrinkles and put it on a hanger.

'Isn't that some kind of major conflict of interest?'

'You mean my selling this organic seed when my job for the state of California is promoting genetically modified crops? It's okay with my boss. Nobody's complained. I started growing organic seed back in 4-H. I'm not against organic. Far from it.'

He was pacing, exhausted, speaking rapidly, jumping topics, as if preparing for the speech of his life. Maybe he was.

'Here's the thing. Cheese. You eat it, right? That's genetically modified food. They've even found pottery stained with fermented beer — pottery so old it dates back to the cavemen. Beer, that's a GM product, right there. Do you know what the average temperature is in Africa near Mauritania?'

Grace shook her head.

'They have five months of temperatures over ninety degrees. Everybody's seen those pictures of cracked dirt where nothing grows. That picture's haunted me since I was a kid. It's one of the reasons I got into GM-ing in the first place, trying to figure out a way to bring what we have — this *abundance* — to people who need it most.'

He stopped at the potato platter and scooped one up, tossing it down and chewing. His hands were crusted with orange. Grace pulled a Kleenex from her bag and stuffed it into his hand. He looked at it blankly, nodded his thanks, and rubbed it into his palm.

'You grow soy, you live. It's that simple. Soy likes heat. But it needs water, and that's one thing it doesn't always get in Third World countries. We spent *three years* working this problem. And now it's literally gone up in smoke.'

'Sounds like a compelling reason to kill somebody, in my opinion.'

She'd needed to surprise him and she had. He locked eyes with her, confusion followed by a click of understanding. He balled up the Kleenex and dropped it on top of the tags in the trash.

'You mean *me*. You mean, I might have killed him.'

She shrugged.

Something furious crackled under the surface. Something close to hatred.

'You done? Because I've got work to do.'

'Where'd you GM the seeds for the fields,

Frank?' She stood in front of the door, her voice quiet.

He blinked rapidly as if he were about to tell an elaborate lie. He wouldn't meet her eyes. 'Mostly out of high-tech labs at UC-Davis.' He hesitated. 'And Riverside U.'

'Ever run into Bartholomew there?'

He didn't answer, just dropped into his chair. 'Frank?'

He tried smiling. It looked forced. 'I can't remember every single person I've ever met.'

She didn't respond.

'Grace, I was training a bunch of convention volunteers the night he was killed. Don't believe me, ask your uncle.'

'Doesn't it fry you that a field you worked hard to create — the GM sugar beets crop — Vonda worked hard to burn up?'

His face convulsed. 'They can't even identify most of those kids, they were wearing costumes with masks, but Vonda. Yeah, it pisses me off. I'm not selling to them anymore. I don't care where the hell they get their organic seed from now on.' His voice was hard and angry.

'These GM fields that you created. You could plant again. You're talking about solving world hunger.' She was the good cop, bad cop, hoping he'd keep playing.

Frank smiled with bitterness. 'It's not just the planting part. We've got serious perception problems here, and with good reason. How many people believe the American government's the good guy? All you have to do is look at Hollywood movies to get the answer to that one.

We've had over forty countries unilaterally ban the import of U.S. genetically modified crops, and more are joining in every day, and meanwhile, a third of the world's kids go to bed hungry every night.'

Her gaze drifted to the potato wedges. 'I've got to be honest with you, Frank, and I'm a scientist. I understand why European countries are holding the line, trying to stop the influx of GM products. I don't want to eat that stuff, either. It — feels weird. All we need is one thing to go wrong. We don't know the long-term effects of any of it. And all this mixing. I think we've got a powder keg on our hands and — '

He looked horrified; close to tears. Under that she could feel a growing swell of rage.

'It's just that they have a good point. And once it's out there, there's no way of calling it back, and I don't believe our government is leveling with us completely, telling us everything that's — '

A sharp knock broke her thought.

'Come in.' His face had darkened.

The door opened and revealed a brunette in a plaid skirt wearing an intern tag identifying her as Rachel. She blinked when she saw Grace and ducked her head.

'Mr Waggaman, oh! Sorry. Didn't know you were busy. She's here, sir.' She stood poised to run.

'Thanks, Rachel. Good job. I'll meet you at the podium.'

She nodded and fled.

Grace picked up her leather satchel, looped it

over her shoulder, and headed for the door. 'This soybean rust. If a field's infected, how long before that shows up?'

'You mean in the field? Two or three days.' He hesitated, as if chewing something in his mind. 'Here's the truth. I probably would have killed him, if I could have gotten away with it. He was an evil man and he was targeting me, and I was relieved when I heard he'd died. And pissed that he picked my field to do it in.'

He scraped his chair back and stood. 'You need to leave now.'

It was a side of him she'd never seen. On the surface, his bony shoulders, the soft, malleable face, the eyebrows ruffing in a semicircle around his eyes, he seemed harmless. Now she wasn't so sure.

'I'll be back.' She smiled.

'I'll be ready.'

She threaded her way out through the sales booths and into the lobby. In the next room over, a man in a powder blue Homeland Security jacket stood at the podium, his voice amplified by a microphone.

'American farms are under attack, or could be, and soon. And frankly, we're almost powerless to stop that. This country has about two million farms. Farms that cover one billion acres of land. Hard to patrol. Easy to sabotage. Mad cow, hoof-and-mouth, wheat smut fungi dropped from crop dusters, whiteflies engineered to carry a virus genetically modified to make botulinum toxin in maize . . . '

Grace walked outside. The air was cold. She

counted back three days. Wednesday. The day Bartholomew was murdered.

The same day somebody dabbed soybean rust spores on healthy plants.

Were those linked? Was Bartholomew involved in sabotaging the fields with soybean rust? Was that why he was killed?

One thing was clear as she headed across the parking lot and unlocked her car. Frank Waggaman was more complex than he wanted her to believe. A man genetically modifying crops as part of his job with the state, who ran a business selling organic soy seed to the same people who helped burn his GM fields to the ground.

She wondered what Frank was hiding. And why. She wanted for him to be the good guy. Jeanne deserved that.

But more than that, Jeanne deserved the truth. They all did.

All I want is the truth. Help me get the truth.

Grace checked her watch. After nine-thirty. Too late to go to Riverside U and get anything useful. Too late to do anything unless she pressed.

She shrugged and flipped open her cell phone.

16

The Palm Springs Police property evidence room was downstairs off the break room, empty except for a patrol officer hunched over a paper cup of coffee. She passed a tan row of evidence lockers. They had the same system for storing evidence where Grace worked: sealed evidence was placed in a locker, the handle twisted, a button secured; at that point the contents of the locker could only be removed inside the property room.

The property room was the last defense against the darkness. The evidence there spoke for the dead. Grace wondered what she'd find.

A sign on the tan door said SAM'S CLUBHOUSE. Grace pushed the intercom and a woman's voice answered.

'Sam?'

'On vacation.'

'Homicide Detective Mike Zsloski called ahead. I'm Grace Descanso.'

The door opened. 'Evidence Tech Knudtson. Madge. This better be important.' Madge was brisk, gum chewing, the kind of woman who looked like she once may have taught gym to incorrigible girls. She motioned Grace into the warehouse crammed with numbered evidence boxes and relocked the door. Grace caught the familiar mix of dust and chemicals. To her left was a small office and directly past that, a section

146

of the warehouse enclosed by blue mesh wire and secured by a lock.

Madge caught her looking. 'That's the blue cage, off-limits except to evidence techs.' In there lay homicide report murder books, closed cases, DNA refrigerators, and homicide evidence, in rows of 187 numbered cardboard boxes.

'I'm missing *Law and Order*. Speed it up.' Madge unlocked the office and waved Grace in.

Tan file cabinets stood along the back wall next to a safe. The evidence lockers, secured by keys, opened into this room; the evidence rechecked and entered into a computer and stored.

An island table extended out from a pair of workstations. Grace recognized Bartholomew's homicide case number on two evidence boxes Madge had already placed on the table, next to a box of nitrile throwaways.

'I'll get the stuff out of the safe.'

Grace slipped on gloves, signed and dated the chain of custody log on top of the first box.

There was always a moment where her stomach fluttered. Viewing the physical links between a victim's last breath and whatever evil took him always did that to her.

But this time, layered on top of that, was the sharp memory of Bartholomew's madness, the blinding specificity of photo after photo, teeth and eyes and cheeks.

She braced herself and opened the first box. It was long and narrow. Inside lay a bolt, smaller in circumference than a man's finger and over a foot long, ruffed on one end with molded plastic feathers, bright orange and yellow. The other end was stained the color of rust, but of course it wasn't rust. Grace felt a squeezing pressure in her chest that tightened and receded. The tip was sharp metal that flared out so that it resembled a fighter plane, its wings wide. She thought of the hole in Bartholomew's chest, and how it had gotten there.

She put the lid back on and gave the box to Madge, who signed the evidence in and restowed it as Grace moved on to the second box. Inside were his shoes, socks, wallet, and briefcase. The briefcase was brown, old leather, with buckles. She undid the buckles. She hadn't realized she was holding her breath until the moment she let it out.

Pencils and highlighters. Tums, Blistex, a linen hankerchief and a black comb. She unzipped the back panel and pulled out three books: *A People's History of the United States* by Howard Zinn, the United States Constitution, and a well-marked slim volume of Sun Tzu's *Art of War*. The book fell open to a yellow highlighted sentence: *In conflict, straight-forward actions generally lead to engagement, surprising actions generally lead to victory.*

What had Bartholomew planned? What war was he in, and who would win?

There was no DayTimer, papers to grade, flash-drive, disc, CD, or computer. Either the killer had left with those things, or Bartholomew traveled light. She thought of his home and typewriter. Maybe he didn't use a computer; it would make his assistant Nate Malosky even more valuable to him and Nate's rage, a possibility.

Madge put down a baggie holding a gold wedding band and what looked like an expensive watch. Grace knew that anything that came in contact with a dead body was labeled Hazardous Waste, but it was unsettling to see a wedding ring tagged that way. The inside of the band was etched in script: TED AND LIZZIE LOVE ALWAYS.

'I'm good,' Grace said. 'I don't need to open this.'

Madge nodded and restowed the jewelry in the safe.

Grace emptied Bartholomew's wallet and sifted through the scraps of paper. She pulled out her notebook, and copied down the homely beats of a frugal man living alone: coupons for free coffee with any Grand Slam breakfast at Denny's, 10 percent off at IHOP for pancakes, an extra drink with a meal at Arby's.

A solitary man; places he frequented. Or maybe the killer worked there.

Or maybe a very large dirigible was going to float down from heaven and bump her on the head and bestow the smart gene.

She sorted the receipts and found one from an ATM for two hundred dollars, dated the day he died, and one for a belt purchased at the store where he'd bumped into Jeanne and Frank Waggaman.

'You don't need to see the money or credit cards, do you?' Madge stole a look at her watch.

It was right on the edge of sarcasm and Grace let it go. The evidence log said there was close to

149

two hundred dollars in the wallet when it was found, money now in the safe, along with five credit cards, his driver's license, parking validation, and university ID.

Grace shook her head.

There were three photos and she spread them out, photos of a woman growing older. The last photo revealed a still-beautiful woman, her hair a white cloud around a face that looked ravaged by illness. She was staring steadily into the camera, a look of intense love and quiet certitude on her face. She was seated in a rocking chair that Grace recognized from Bartholomew's living room.

The light had caught her face in deep angled shadows, as if the eyes were glowing in a darkness that, bit by bit, was extinguishing them. Grace wondered if she'd have that, at the end. Somebody who cared enough to be there. To record. She thought of the photos on the walls. Lizzie must have known about Bartholomew's secret obsession with faces and names. Grace didn't see any fear or tension on Lizzie's face, only love.

'I'll start reboxing.' Madge reached for the empty wallet.

'Wait a sec. Let me see that again.'

Madge put down the wallet on the counter and went back to refiling evidence.

A prick of white — the barest scrap of a corner of a photo — curled in the crease of the wallet where it folded. Grace flipped it open again, wormed in a finger, and worked free a photo, wedged deep.

From somewhere far above at street level, a siren screamed and died away.

It was a picture of Frank Waggaman, Jeanne's boyfriend and director of the ag convention. He was standing in a crop field, and his Adam's apple caught the light like a small tulip bulb. His fuzzy eyebrows rounded over deep eye sockets, like small tilted exclamation points.

There was a red slash through his chest, made by red ink. It was a thin line, but delivered with great pressure, so that part of Frank's chest appeared to have opened.

'Have you seen this?' Grace put it on the counter.

Madge frowned and checked the sheet. 'It's not listed. Where'd you find it?'

'This pocket in here.' Grace showed her.

She gave the wallet and photos to Madge, and picked up a sock and inspected it and set it aside, repeating the inspection with the second sock. The shoes were tan loafers with ridged soles. She checked the inside of the shoes; nothing caught under the pad or in the seams between the soles and the leather body of the shoes. She turned them over.

Pale plant material winked in the grooves of one of the soles. She pointed to the sole. 'What do you think? Soy?'

'Not my area,' Madge said. 'Have to ask the lab and they're not in until tomorrow.'

'Mind if I take it?'

'Have to check with Detective Zsloski.' Madge flipped open her cell. She blinked in time to her gum chewing, a diminutive female Jabba the

151

Hut, muttering into the phone. She thrust the cell phone at Grace. 'Wants to talk to you.'

'You do know that Bartholomew died in a field of soy, right?' Zsloski's voice rumbled.

'I do.'

'We left the soy in his shoe because it has nothing to do with the way he died.'

'Makes sense.'

A pause. 'You know this is pissing off Madge. She's going to have to redocument since you're splitting up evidence.'

Grace was silent.

'Whatever the hell you find, you give it to me first. Agreed?'

'Agreed.'

Longer pause. 'Why exactly are you doing this?'

'I work with DNA where I come from, so I gravitate toward doing any kind of test I can think of. Maybe I can find something that will point us toward where he was earlier in the night. Who he was with.' She paused. 'It's a long shot.'

'No kidding. Let me talk to Madge.'

'Wait, now that I got you on my side, you know of a lab in the Coachella Valley that handles plant DNA?'

'Jeez, I got to do everything, don't I? Meet me at Bartholomew's murder site tomorrow morning, nine a.m. sharp.'

Grace handed the phone back. Madge chewed vigorously, grunted twice, eyes on Grace. She closed the phone and tucked it back into her pocket. 'He says take it.'

Grace bent over the shoe, studying the plant material. It looked thready; fibrous. She heard Madge rooting in a cupboard and sensed her presence and, without thinking, held out her palm. Madge placed a pair of tweezers into her hand.

For a dislocating moment, it felt exactly like a surgical OR and nausea rushed up her body in a trembling gust. She tasted the sour flood of acid heaving from her stomach and fought to steady herself.

'You okay?'

Grace didn't answer.

'Want water or something?'

'I'm good.'

She tweezed out the material, dropping it into the envelope and sealing in the larger EDP envelope. Her mouth was beginning to taste a little less like the inside of a rancid tire.

She was just clearing the office and heading to the double-locked exit door when her cell rang.

'Zsloski here. Fuck it, Grace. There's something you need to see.'

17

Grace parked at the hiking area pull-off in Andreas Canyon and waited. The city wasn't far but it was already out of sight and the sky glittered with stars. She thought of other nights. Other stars. A light bobbed down the canyon path and a stocky man came into view. In his flashlight beam, his Palm Springs police shoulder tags glowed like epaulets. A set of goggles dangled in his hand and as he got closer, she saw he was wearing a pair, his face blank.

'I'm Officer Stanger, and you can tell how glad I am to have to walk down here and pick you up.'

She thought of an old Mae West line about heavy breathing and thought better of it.

He handed her the goggles. 'Put these on. It'll save you from stepping in a shitload of cactus.'

'Don't you mean cacti?'

'It's the shitload part you have to worry about. It's up this way.' He turned and headed up the hill.

She slipped the goggles over her face and adjusted the strap. Stanger's back glowed in a nimbus of yellow and green light; climbing up the hill, he looked exactly like one of those dead guys walking toward the light.

He pointed at a clump of beavertail cacti rising at the edge of the trail, spiny pads yellow-green in her goggles. She moved carefully around it.

The sand and stony arroyos sparkled like pale

crystals. A barrel cactus burst into view, sharp and spiny as a fish. A giant hairy scorpion five inches long skittered out from under a rock, clicking delicately across the path in front of her, ghostly green in the goggles.

An owl cruised overhead, its eye a coin winking in its body, circling lazily. A vole poked cautiously out of its hole and tracked a beetle, unaware that it, in turn, was being tracked.

It didn't take long.

The owl dropped silently, claws wide, and snagged the vole in one clean movement. The vole squeaked and writhed as the owl carried it straight through the night sky, heading for the cliffs.

They hiked single file for five minutes. The night sounds took over, silky whisper of wind, owl hoots, the scrape of shoes on the ground. The creosote smelled like tar. A lizard scrambled over the trail and slithered away.

She saw in a thick creosote bush the trembling green outline of almost translucent ears. They twitched. Suddenly a jackrabbit thrashed out of the creosote and sprang away.

At the top of the incline, the hill fell away in a series of gullies.

It was easy to see: lights, crime scene tape, techs, detectives crouching around a still form.

Stanger kept his rover tucked in his shirt pocket, the lapel mike coiled and clipped to his shirt pocket, so he could access it if he were running. He tucked his head to the side, pressed the button, spoke into it, and before long, a familiar bulky form detached from the group. By the time they'd slid the last few yards down the gully, Zsloski was holding up the crime scene tape as she followed Stanger in.

Stanger seemed relieved to turn her over. He rejoined the group. Grace saw her uncle in the mix and Deputy Coroner Jeff Salzer and Thantos — whatever his first name was — the sheriff's deputy with a work station in the FBI office.

'So the terrorism task force is involved.'

'Thantos? Yeah.' Zsloski pointed. 'Before I take you in, what does that look like to you?'

She followed where he was pointing, and found tracks in the dirt glowing through the goggles, the distinctive marks leading through bent stems of sand grass.

It made her tired, looking at them.

'Footsteps. Somebody small. Moving fast. The distance growing bigger between sets, more erratic. Somebody scared. Running.' She hesitated. 'Followed by somebody big.'

Zsloski nodded. 'He hunted her, Grace. Like game. And left her there for the coyotes.'

He turned toward the body and they went in. She could feel the anger and outrage in the tender way he squatted next to the body.

In the circle of light lay a girl, not more than a child, really. She'd been shot through the back and the force of the bolt had thrown her forward into the sand, her hands splayed wide, her legs bent. She was wearing a halter top and jean shorts. One sandal was missing. The blood pooled darkly in the white center of her back, under the shoulder blades, where the bolt had lodged.

156

There wasn't as much of the haft exposed as she'd imagined. Most of the bolt was wedged into the girl. A tech squatted next to the body and rolled it gently and one of her legs came into view.

Grace's ears hummed and she felt as if she were falling. Shock waves radiated into her hands and feet, and for a moment she couldn't breathe.

'Grace?' Zsloski swiveled his massive head.

'Oh my God.' Her voice was thick.

He stared at her.

'I know her. I know that tattoo.'

The leg was thin and very white.

On the left calf bounded a unicorn.

18

Another murder, and this one of a girl who looked barely out of high school.

Grace wondered who she was, and what her life had been like, if she'd had somebody who loved her and even now was expecting in a few hours to see her come through the door.

Grace took the 10 out of Palm Springs, driving toward Indio. The day had been long and it wasn't over. She drank coffee. Through the passenger window, the Union Pacific train rolled on into the night, a dark wall of metal.

Indio wasn't far from Palm Springs, about twenty minutes in the car, but it was another country when it came to personality.

Working in the police crime lab in San Diego, Grace had a view of Indio at odds with the image that came out of the glossy PR pamphlets — date farm capital of the world, center of a burgeoning country-western community, an agricultural mecca of opportunity and promise. The Indio Grace knew had youth gangs made up of homeless, abandoned, throwaway kids. Transient farm workers. Hispanic gangs at war with black gangs at war with Asian gangs at war with skinheads. Broken glass and graffiti.

She wondered which Indio she'd be seeing this night.

She took the off-ramp past a row of gas stations onto the frontage road. The area had built up since the last time she'd been there at night and it was bright with motels, a Denny's, and a row of Mexican restaurants.

After the commercial area came houses, their lights softer and smaller. A crossing light stuttered in red and she heard the wail of an approaching train. She put up her window and locked her doors. The train roared past her.

She found Jackson Street and the bridge over the railroad tracks and made a right turn into the dirt driveway that led to the Union Pacific switching yard.

Her pulse was starting to trip. She'd seen the switching yard in daylight and it had unsettled her then. This was worse.

It had once been an active freight switching yard, but that was years ago. Ahead of her rose the tattered hulk of a roundhouse, a former diesel machine shop.

Concrete pillars rose like jagged stalagmites, and in the wash of her headlights she caught a glimpse of glinting broken beer bottles, violent graffiti, drug paraphernalia, a half-fallen ceiling of broken tile and asbestos.

Surrounding the roundhouse were smaller buildings, all abandoned: old crew shanties and field offices, moldy with ancient mattresses and broken doors. Shadows darted. A mangy dog slid out of a doorway, its eyes yellow in the sudden light, a blink of dog in the headlights, swallowed up by darkness.

Grace bumped her car over a set of tracks and kept going. A freight engine with three boxcars stood on a siding and workmen trotted in a tight group nearby, waving their arms and shouting instructions, and Grace felt immediately better. There was life here. Workers with jobs and responsibilities and flashlights. The train slowly eased backward onto an alternate siding that held four new boxcars.

A short set of tracks ran from the main yard a couple hundred feet into a building, and this building blazed in light. The name had been painted in bright blue letters above the door: WINDLIFT.

The tracks ended inside a hangar-sized garage, the space dominated by a boxcar and a man on a forklift swinging a crate into its interior. Grace drove around to the side of the building and found the parking area. In her rearview mirror, she caught a glimpse of a policeman dressed in black, and she locked up the car and waited.

A cold wind spatted gravel across the parking lot and dug into the back of her scalp. His ID badge read JOHNSTONE and the shoulder patches on his arms identified him as a Union Pacific policeman. His bulky Sam Browne belt was loaded with a Sig Sauer, radio, magazine pouch, and two handcuff cases.

'Cold night to be out.' He was all business, but there was warmth there, too. Sweat creased his face — cold sweat — from the wind, she thought, and she wondered how long he'd been working.

She nodded. 'I'm here to see Stuart Soderberg. He expects me.'

She gave him her FBI ID and he took a flashlight from his SAP pocket, on the back side of his thigh, and studied the ID a moment before handing it back.

'He should be inside. You can go anywhere except down by the tracks. Stay away from the loading area inside the factory. We've got a lot of freight we're moving out tonight.'

She nodded and took a step backward and her ankle turned on a rock, just enough to let her know she had to be more careful.

'I've got an extra penlight on my key chain, you need it.' His voice was dry.

'I'm good.'

He nodded and stepped away, the light plowing a path toward the tracks. She made herself walk into the building without limping.

It was hot inside and the air rang with metal on metal, the scrape of machinery, the clang of steel. Under the lights, workmen glistened with sweat.

The ceiling was high and metal-beamed, with a row of small windows near the flat roof. A row of gleaming white egg pods stood on the floor. The center of each opened in the midsection, revealing high-tech gears inside. A man in a blue uniform climbed out of one, a wrench in hand, and when he straightened and stood, Grace realized the egg was bigger than he was.

Wind turbine towers lay in pieces like a giant Erector set, their size clear only in comparison to the men crawling over the parts. Lilliputians. Young and solidly built, climbing over the metal scaffolding.

Through a wide door, she saw in an adjoining room windmill blades stacked in neat piles,

161

tagged and wrapped in steel bands for shipment. A compact interior crane hoisted a heavy gearbox into a crate as workmen steadied it and lowered it into the straw-filled crate.

Metal ladders led to a second level of work-stations along a narrow platform. A man in a protective mask bent over a piece of steel tubing, sparks of fire scattering from the end of a welding torch.

She walked the length of the room, through canyons where windmill blades hummed on vibrating machines, glancing at the men pushing pallets on wheeled wagons over to the garage bay, their muscles tanned and glistening and ropey.

She felt someone's eyes on her and looked up. A man with biceps the size of hockey pucks stared down at her. A tool kit poked from his belt.

She motioned to him, mimed asking him a question. He climbed down, his boots grating on the rungs, and swung a massive studded boot within inches of her face. She flinched and took an instinctive step back and caught him smiling.

'Need something?' His eyes slid to her ID.

'Stuart Soderberg. You see him?'

He scanned the room, the spitting fire torches, the glistening men. His eyes shifted as if he were considering the best way to answer that.

'Try down at the tracks.'

He reached a hand up and grabbed the lattice and lifted himself one-armed up to the first rung.

★ ★ ★

The temperature was dropping when she stepped outside. Over by the tracks, workmen were standing clear as the main line was switched.

Maybe that's where Stuart was. It was worth a shot. Johnstone had told her to stay clear; she'd stay clear of *him*, that was all. She wished she'd said yes to the penlight.

She hiked past the spur track and the boxcars. That close, they rose like blank-faced buildings.

'Grace,' Stuart shouted. He ran after her, out of the warehouse. His studded boots crunched the gravel and a tool kit banged at his waist.

'I was inside, up on level two. It took a while to come down.'

'How much time do you have?'

'It's my dinner break but I'm not hungry. We could walk if you're up for it.'

She nodded. He carried himself with a relaxed watchful energy that reminded her of her younger brother, Andy. She wondered when she'd called Andy last. She couldn't remember.

'There's a crack of moon out tonight. You have walking shoes on?'

'You've been married a long time.'

'How's that?'

'To immediately think about what kind of shoes a woman is wearing.'

He half smiled. 'We won't go far. Enough away so they can't hear us.'

He followed an invisible path that cut into a low rise of hill. They walked in silence. Loose

163

gravel skittered and slid as they dislodged it.

Something small and wild thrashed ahead of them and Grace caught a glimpse of white before it burrowed out of sight. About fifty yards up the path Stuart stopped. Grace turned and looked down at Windlift and the abandoned buildings. From that perspective, the building and activity in the freight switching yard was a small stamp of light in a vast, unsettling wilderness of decay.

'Come here a lot?'

'Every chance I get. It helps put the crap into perspective.' He pointed at the sky. It was jet black pricked with a canopy of glittering lights. The lights didn't seem to go up far enough to affect the great stillness above them.

'Look. You can see the Milky Way.'

Grace looked up. Standing in the darkness next to Stuart, looking up at the sky, was an utterly different experience than the darkness she had just inhabited looking down at the girl's broken body in the desert. She didn't trust it.

'There it is. That band.' He showed her.

It looked like a glittering bracelet.

'I invited myself to your place tomorrow for breakfast.'

'You didn't tell her you were here, did you?'

She shook her head.

'Don't. I don't want her thinking I'm going behind her back.'

'You didn't bring me up here to look at the stars.'

Stuart tamped a cigarette out of a pack, cupped a lighter in his palm, dipped his head and when he came back up he was inhaling. He choked and coughed and inhaled.

'I see stuff when people don't know I'm up here. I pull double shifts right now, lot of them nights.'

He pointed with his free hand at the switching yard. 'What's happening right now is a yard locomotive is pushing that load of boxcars up the hump — hill,' he translated. 'And as the freight cars go down the hill they're disconnected and roll to a stop in the switching yard. They throw retarders — brakes — so they don't smash into anything and then they're reconnected to the line they need to go out on.'

He took another drag on his smoke.

'And there, that open boxcar Johnstone's coming out of, with that woman — that's the boss, by the way, Judith Woodruff — they're checking contents against a bill of lading before the boxcar's sealed and locked.'

Grace saw Johnstone clambering out of a boxcar and climbing down the rungs to the ground followed by a tall woman in jeans. Even from that distance, she looked tense. Johnstone nodded at something she said, turned and slammed shut the boxcar door. It sounded like a piece of gum popping. Grace could only imagine how loud it actually was, over the creaking, grinding noise of the boxcars backing up to join the existing train, and the grinding metallic roar coming from the factory.

'Okay, so follow that track down past Johnstone's car at the perimeter by the rusted boxcars.'

Grace studied the edge of the yard where the darkness overtook it and made out the shadow of a car parked near a set of abandoned oil drums.

Stuart touched her arm and pointed.

'There. Where it disappears in the dark. If the moon were fuller, you'd be able to see it.'

'And?'

Stuart inhaled again. She let him take his time.

'The train's gathering speed as it pulls out. About three months ago, I saw a guy run alongside one of those boxcars with a pair of bolt cutters. Half a second later, he climbs on and I see this box bouncing down off the boxcar, followed by seven others. I just stood there, counting boxes. I couldn't believe it. Sure enough, pretty soon, coming in the dark bumping over the ridge I see this truck. Pulls up against the track and picks up the boxes and the guy. Whole thing took maybe twenty seconds.'

'I don't get it. This place has security. I just met Johnstone and he carries.'

'He's got a rifle in his car, too, locked in a rack inside on the ceiling. But the Union Pacific police aren't here all the time. Right now we're moving inventory onto boxcars. It's intense, it lasts a couple of days and then it's over, and when it's over, he'll be gone. He has an insane area to police — Pomona to Gila Bend to Utah.'

'Wait, you're talking three states.'

'It's not just him covering that area, but what I'm saying is, the railroad police guys are spread out. Anyway, three months or so back, like I said, I see this guy stealing stuff off a moving train. And I've seen it twice more since then.'

166

'You tell Johnstone that?'

'I'm telling you.'

'The anonymous tip?'

He shrugged.

The wind shifted and brought the metal clang of the switching yard with it.

'I gave notice. I don't want to leave my boss stranded, though, so that's why I'm pulling extra shifts. I'm the QA guy for the project.'

'Just to get it out of the way, where were you Wednesday night?'

He shot her a look. 'So it's like that.'

She was silent.

'Here.' His voice was toneless.

'You have witnesses?'

'I've been checked out. They've done everything but look up my ass, I'm clean. You see those pods in the warehouse? That's my area. The gearshift boxes, the levels, magnets — everything has to be calibrated and checked. By me. I sign off on one and it's time-stamped, the exact second I did it. I time-stamped all Wednesday night. I'm the only one with access, to protect the integrity of the project.'

'There has to be somebody else. What if you get sick?'

He smiled bitterly. 'Like I said, I'm quitting. God, I'm going to be glad when this convention's over.'

'It's not always this busy?'

'Hell no. You see those big windmills as you come into Palm Springs? That's not us. Our windmills are about half that big. Which makes them perfect for farms, or homes, or even

167

dirt-poor villages. Everybody's going green now. Look at what that oil guy Pickens is doing. My boss got this brilliant idea to send a windmill home with every delegate. Put that windmill someplace where it can do some good, a small pocket of good in the world. That's fifty states and about sixty foreign countries. Took over a year to put funding together. Grants from big chemical companies and state and federal money.'

Grace thought back to what Frank Waggaman had told her about the world's most expensive party favors.

'We started sending them out this morning. The last one goes out — '

He rolled his wrist and peered at the luminescent numbers. 'Hell, I'm too tired to know.'

'Going behind her back.'

'Say what?'

'Sounds like you and Vonda are going through a rough patch.'

'We buy organic soy seed from Frank Waggaman and then she's part of the group that torches his GM sugar beets field. Yeah, I'd say we're going through a bad patch.'

'What made her do it?'

'You mean who. Here's the irony, Grace. In Washington state, I taught a bunch of classes to kids just like Andrea and Nate, classes on how to survive in the wilderness. Grow your own food, purify water. That's one of the things I love about Vonda. Her connection to the land.'

Grace looked out over the buildings. 'You ever

teach kids how to use a crossbow?'

He shot her a swift look. 'Come on, Grace. You can't think I killed him. Sure, I taught kids that, a long time ago, not now.' He shoved his right hand up so that it stood illuminated in moonlight. The joints on the two middle fingers were thick, the fingers tilting.

'Pretty, huh. It's the beginning of rheumatoid arthritis. Another reason I'm quitting. Quitting the job, quitting smoking. I'm getting all my smokes in now. The baby comes, I'm done, that's what I told Vonda, but the truth is, it's getting harder to do certain things. And it hurts like hell to climb around in that building there and do my job. So if you think I killed Bartholomew, think again.'

He inhaled, let it out. The smoke drifted in a lazy curl toward the warehouse below them.

'Any way you cut it, Grace, everything that's going on today — gasoline prices out of sight, the ice pack breaking up, the subprime fiasco — the scariest to me is what's happening with food. My area's microbiology. I know what's possible. There could be things that have been put into our food supply that we're eating right now we don't even know about, because nobody's telling us. So I *get* what all the protests are about.'

'But you don't want your wife on the front line.'

'I think the protests are lame. These guys are going about it the wrong way. Dressing up as vegetables? Give me a break. They get themselves arrested, get their fifteen minutes,

169

and then what? Nothing's changed. That's one of the reasons why I came to Riverside U to work on my doctorate. I want to be a watchdog, Grace. For the little guy, for all of us. And it's bigger than our country. It's the world.'

His energy was all male, a coiled exhaustion. In his Windlift uniform, standing in the dark, his shoulders looked strong. She wondered what Mac was doing. Thought about his shoulders. The rest of him.

'I came to Palm Springs four years ago. Vonda worked the houseplants aisle at a nursery where I went to buy some yarrow and then I ran into her on campus.'

'And ran off with her.'

'Chel — your aunt Chel — was pissed. What she never got was that I was following Vonda's lead. There's something crazy wild in Vonda. She wants what she wants, that's it. And she didn't want her folks throwing a wrench in it.'

'Coming up with a nice Portuguese boy as a consolation prize.'

'They'd have found one, believe me. Especially when she dropped out of school right away, senior year. I was against it, but have you ever tried reasoning with her?'

Grace was silent.

'She wanted to be a mother, that's all. And right away, she gets pregnant.'

'And loses the baby,' Grace finished quietly.

Stuart ducked his head, blinked.

'Her doctor said she was priming the pump, as if she were a piece of machinery. We changed doctors. We were thrilled and scared when she got pregnant a second time. Andrea got pregnant around then, too, and I was relieved Vonda had a friend to go through it with. She cut back her hours. She was lifting fertilizer bags at work. There were things she couldn't do anymore. I ramped up my program, tried to wrap things up faster, but with research and lab work — some things you can't push.'

The cigarette was almost to the nub now and he pinched it carefully and inhaled. He exhaled for a long time, as if breathing out the story he was about to tell; its sadness.

'She loses number two. Andrea does, too.'

'Don't you think that's a little weird?'

'You mean that both of them miscarried? Not as weird as you'd think. The doctor said some women miscarry without even realizing they're pregnant.'

'When did you start working here?'

'That was when. After my wife lost number two. They're trying to bring industry back to the switching yard. I've been here since the beginning. I dropped out of school.'

'Penance?'

He shot her a swift, evaluating look. 'Yeah,' he said simply. 'And good medical. I hadn't been taking care of her.'

'You're saying losing the babies was your fault.'

Stuart grew silent. She could see his throat move. 'You have no idea how helpless it made me feel. It was this nightmare we couldn't climb out of. Vonda was spiraling into a depression. We both decided to eat organic. Organic everything.

Doctors couldn't tell us shit. She was losing her mind. We'd saved money to put down on a house, and I took all of it and used it as a lease on a greenhouse for her. We were already growing joy and making organic bread for friends, but now I figured she'd have a chance to build a business. And eating fresh. That was a main thing.'

'You're a lucky man. Organic bread.'

'Actually, it tastes terrible.' It slipped out and it made him laugh. 'Lord, never tell her I said that.'

Grace grinned. Her shoe had come untied and she bent and retied it and by the time she stood up, she wasn't grinning anymore. 'Did you know Bartholomew?'

'We all did.'

'Friend, foe?' She stared out across the warehouse.

'Vonda took classes from him a few years back. That's where she met Andrea. You met Andrea in jail, right?'

'Creamy skin, blond hair, wearing a banana suit.'

'A banana suit. Great. Yeah, that's her. The pit bull. Bartholomew was Andrea's advisor in school and now he's a silent partner in her business.'

Grace's antennae tweaked. 'What business?'

'A nonprofit that's supposed to help women in Third World countries sell their products in the U.S. Square Pegs. She's the one who got Vonda all riled up about GM crops. Vonda was always green, but her pal Andrea carries it to a whole new level. Her company's a cover for something. I'd bet money on it.'

'What kind of stuff?'

'I knew that, you could canonize me. Everything she's done, Vonda's followed her like a lemming. I'd come home, working sixteen-hour days, Vonda's off protesting for gnatcatcher habitats or fairy shrimp. What in the hell's a fairy shrimp anyway?'

He exhaled, patted his pocket absently, pulled his hand away.

'And now we've finally got a child with a shot at making it into this world. She promised me she wouldn't do this anymore — step back, that was the deal, step back. Instead, I come home, find a message on the machine that she's gone off with Andrea and chances are, she's in jail. Vonda's not capable of doing harm, that's the one thing I need to stress. I believe that with everything in me.'

'But Andrea is.'

'Absolutely.'

A bright red car rolled into the parking lot and stopped next to the factory door, its motor running. Stuart squared his shoulders.

'The irony is, I'm the one who suggested Vonda form a grief group. I thought talking through it might help. If not her, at least me. Sounds cold, but it's the truth. I'm a guy. I don't want to hear that shit. I want to fix it and there was no fixing miscarriages and it was making me nuts.'

The driver's door opened. A woman climbed out with a paper bag and jounced into the

173

building. Under the light, her auburn hair spilled in a ratty mass over a comb. She'd changed out of her apple costume into jeans and a shirt. Still an apple shape.

In the incremental seconds it took to register, Grace went from staring at the woman, recognizing her shape, sketching in details, to filling in the beats of when she'd seen her last and then the shock of realizing she was here, at Windlift, in the middle of the night. Sarah Conroy, the third person in the cell with Andrea and Vonda.

'What's Sarah doing here?'

Stuart scowled. 'She's married to one of the welders, Tony. Brings him dinner.'

'You don't like Tony?'

He tossed the butt down and ground it into the gravel. 'We don't share the same political agenda.'

'Oh, what's that?'

'People I disagree with, I like to leave alive.'

The wind snapped against Grace's neck, cold and grainy. 'He kills people?'

'The owner likes to hire people with records, that's all I know.'

'Sarah's husband has a record.'

'Murder two. Served twelve in San Quentin. Killed his first wife. Threw her out of a moving car and then ran her over.'

In the crime lab, Grace was used to dealing with the aftermath of blind rage or blind drunkenness or blind stupidity. When she rolled semen, swabbed saliva, studied spatter patterns, spun DNA into pellets, always the word *blind*

174

seemed to be in there somewhere. Six degrees over from the word *evil*.

'Show him to me.'

Stuart shook his head. 'Can't tonight. I'm backed up. I think you met him.'

'Guy in the red tank top, bandanna, black boots, pocket ripped.'

'Man, you're good. Yeah, that's him. Okay. Well.'

'Think he might be involved in the cargo theft or Bartholomew's murder?'

Stuart shrugged.

'Anything else you want to say?'

'Vonda's folks. Pete and Chel have made a career of holding on to Vonda. And now that we have a baby coming . . . ' He stopped.

'Say it.'

'Pete did a background check on me, we first got married.' Stu's voice rang with contempt. 'One early arrest for possession of grass. Not for sale, even. A joint in my pocket. That was it. It was like Pete was pissed he couldn't find more.'

He crossed his arms over his chest. Moonlight angled across his face.

'And Grace, I don't know how you fit into it, but I can tell you this. Be careful. Truth is, Pete's looking for some reason to hold on to her. Still have her be their little girl. They'd love it if I was out of the picture.'

'One more question. Where was Vonda Wednesday night?'

It was dark outside, but she could still see him stiffen. 'I have no idea.'

19

Sunday

French tourists swarmed over the breakfast room in the Comfort Inn, chattering happily, as Grace carried an orange and a cup of coffee back to her room. It was seven-thirty, three hours later in the Bahamas.

For November it was hot in Palm Springs, close to eighty. The air smelled of desert heat and sage. The cliff wall of the San Jacinto Mountains crackled like crumpled tinfoil against the flat blue of the sky.

She dialed the Pink Sands Hotel, picturing the front desk with its scalloped, pink and orange plaster arch limed in shells, the polite and efficient clerks. It rang into space. She was on the edge of hanging up when a musical lilting voice answered and asked which suite.

She remembered their villa — and all the suites — had names. She remembered nothing. She had no idea.

'Mac McGuire. Please.'

Grace inspected her toes. It was hot enough for the sandals she was wearing, but a bad idea if she ended up tracking a bad guy into the desert. Rattlesnakes, scorpions, and cacti. Oh my. She'd change after the call.

'I'm sorry, madam, but he and the little one appear to be out.'

The air really was sucked out of the room then.

'Ma'am?'

Grace tightened her grip on the phone.

'Would you care to leave a message? Oh wait, wait just a moment.'

A voice in the background, laughter, and then remarkably, his voice coming across the distance.

'Hey.' He sounded tired and relaxed. She could hear Katie chattering happily in the background.

'Hey.' Tears spilled.

'Honey, are you okay?' It slipped out, and the concern and warmth derailed her.

'Is it Mommy?' Katie squealed in the background. The happy sounds of exuberant chaos. Mac raised his voice.

'Yeah, buttercup. Want to say hi?'

A scream of joy and the phone was transferred. Katie sounded breathless.

'Mommy! We had breakfast at this place all blue, and they fix whatever you want, and yesterday, Daddy took me to a pool with a rock that spouts into a slide and he got me a pencil thing so I can use it when I swim.'

Grace pressed the phone to her ear. She could almost smell the chlorine in her daughter's soft tangle of curls.

'That's great, sweetheart. Having fun?'

'Yes, double-yes, triple, all of the numbers.'

Grace could hear gales of laughter and Mac joining in. It went on a long time. She crimped the bedspread and smoothed it flat.

'Sorry, Mommy. Daddy's being his silly self.

There's fishies here in the main place.'

'The lobby.' Grace closed her eyes. 'They're koi.'

'Daddy let me have two scoops of ice cream and a cola and bye! Love you!'

'I love you, too, honey, so much.'

'And here's kisses.' The sound of wild kissing and silence.

Mac's voice. 'I'm back.'

He sounded happy, and for some reason, that made her angry.

'Two scoops of ice cream and cola?'

He was silent.

'I'm sorry. I'm sure you're doing fine, it's just — '

'Just what?' His voice turned cool. 'Grace, she's fine. I have to go. We've got a busy day planned, swimming and then taking the golf cart to drive to lunch.'

'She needs milk.'

'I think I can handle that.' His voice had a definite edge now.

She couldn't seem to stop herself. 'When you tucked her in?'

The air between them grew heavy and she could picture, like one of those CSI shows, her energy spiraling down the coiled wire, sparking like a synapse across a continent, burrowing under an ocean, roiling up intact into Mac's ear, her immaculate, angry, pitch-perfect timbre of neediness: 'Did you find the *Anne of Green Gables*? I left it on the dresser. I'd marked it where I left off, I just forgot to tell you, but Katie probably did. She's been really

178

excited about that book and — '

'She wanted *Green Eggs and Ham*. Over and over. That is all I've read to her the last two nights.'

'Good choice.' Katie hadn't wanted *Green Eggs and Ham* in at least two years.

'I bought it as a gift.'

The silence grew heavy. 'Have fun.'

'We will. We are.'

Too fast, she said, 'Did you have fun today?' She'd already asked that. She already knew the answer.

'Look, Grace, I need to wrap this up. We were walking by the front desk when you happened to be on the phone. I hate to tie up their business line.'

'I'll call later.' She was falling. Spinning into space. 'When's a good time?'

'Let's play it by ear.' He hesitated. 'She really is okay, Grace.'

★ ★ ★

Twentieth Avenue to Karen. Second mailbox to the right.

Grace drove slowly down Twentieth, a frontage road of I-10, looking for Karen Street. Wind turbines towered in gleaming white columns, and the wind, as it went through them, whined like a living thing.

She passed a sign advertising windmill tours, and a row of metal mailboxes. On the seat next to her, three orange juices and three coffees sloshed in a cardboard container.

179

Karen turned out to be an avenue, optimistically named, in Grace's opinion. The road dipped and she slowed, one hand holding the cups so they wouldn't spill. The smell of freshly baked cinnamon rolls filled the car and her mouth watered.

On the side of a post a faded For Sale sign had been tacked, with a newer sign slapped on top: SOLD! TINE REALTY!

Her car bounced down the path and then the road opened out again and she saw a building shaped like a bubble. An oasis suspended in blowing dirt. Nothing stirred.

The greenhouse. The building looked deserted, but through the blowing sand, Grace could see a stucco house up ahead. She was passing the greenhouse now. A small, hand-painted sign stood on a wooden post, the words already nicked by the constant blowing sand. She slowed her car to get a better look: GOOD FARMS.

She'd slept little. She'd found herself thinking about Vonda. Hearing Stuart's pain made it real. As a doctor, she'd worked with parents of sick children, but she'd tried hard not to cross a line. Practice compassion, but maintain a boundary. Doctors who forgot that important lesson and let patients get close enough to grab hold always got dragged under.

She could feel the currents in her cousin's story threatening to pull her under. She was too tired to defend against it. She couldn't afford to drown so far from shore.

Grace drove up a gravel driveway leading to the carport and parked behind a battered, mustard-colored van. In the carport, a U-Haul stood with its back hatch open. Inside, a mattress lay folded over a kitchen table.

They were leaving, from the looks of it. And soon.

20

The door opened and Vonda stepped outside, smiling. She was wearing her hair in a braid and she flipped it and it settled at the nape of her neck. She shuffled down the steps in a pair of fuzzy blue slippers. Her ankles looked like they'd swollen since Grace had seen her in jail the night before.

'Hey. You made it.' She grinned and patted her swelling stomach. She was wearing a blue T-shirt that said BABY ON BOARD, an arrow pointing at the bulge. A bulge that to Grace looked lower.

Grace reached into the car and took out the carton of juice and coffees and the grocery bag. 'I didn't know what you liked, so I brought a little of everything.'

'I can carry something.'

'You already are.'

Vonda laughed and wiped her nose with the back of her hand.

'This damn cold.' She shuffled ahead of Grace and held open the door. 'Stu's taking a shower. He'll be done soon.'

'Who's moving?'

Vonda cracked a look at her, and for an instant, Grace saw the kid she'd been, darting into traffic, the same smile.

'Stu's job is winding down, and the greenhouse sold out from under us. Time to move on what the hell.'

'Are you nuts? Crazy? You're days away from giving birth.'

'Stu's been accepted to Stanford. We'll live in student housing. We'll drive up, take our time.'

She held the screen door open. 'Come on, Grace, ease up.'

The living room was small and spare, separated from the kitchen by a pony wall. Moving boxes lay in high stacks against the wall next to the door. The only furniture left was a half-emptied bookcase, a sofa and coffee table. Shower noise gargled from down the hall.

Grace set the bags down on the kitchen table. Stacks of homemade bread lay on the counter, in piles. Cranberry seemed the most popular; there were only three left in that stack.

'Coffee, yay. I can have one cup a day.'

'There's a little thing of milk, too, if you need it.' Grace unpacked the cinnamon buns and Vonda's face fell.

'Oh, I was going to serve homemade banana bread.'

Which was why Grace had brought buns. 'I'll bring a loaf home.'

Vonda brightened and cracked open her coffee lid.

'I hear you sell it in front of the Hyatt on Thursday nights.'

'Farmers' market.'

Grace busied herself with the yogurts. 'I was just wondering.'

'What?' Vonda took a sip, relaxed, oblivious.

'Where you were Wednesday night.'

Vonda put down the cup and went down the

hall, her back rigid. She entered a room across from the bathroom and closed the door. Grace followed her down the hall and knocked.

'Vonda?'

Silence.

'Vonda, let me in. I'm coming in.'

It was a baby room with a decorated crib and a chest of drawers with a changing table. Boxes of Pampers stood against one wall next to a baby carseat.

Vonda was standing in the baby room, digging her hands into the quilt, trying not to cry.

'Vonda.'

'Don't.'

'I have to ask everybody that.'

'Why? Because my dad tells you to? He's not going to believe me anyway.'

'Try me.'

Vonda grimaced. She smoothed her fingers over the crib. The wood was oak.

'Stuart didn't want to put the crib up this time. Not until we were closer. Now I can't stay out of this room. I made him promise it would be the last stuff to go.'

'Try me.'

She exhaled. 'I was walking. I was walking around outside. I knew we'd be leaving soon. I was walking.'

'Alone?'

'Yes.'

'That's it.'

Vonda raised her dark eyes, her face so like Grace's. 'I told you, you wouldn't believe me.'

There was nothing to say and Vonda knew it.

She turned and went past Grace down the hall. There was something lonely and deliberate about the way she walked, as if she'd been walking alone for a very long time and still had trouble getting used to it.

By the time the bathroom door opened, they were sitting at the table, drinking coffee, or pretending to.

Stuart padded down the hall, toweling dry his hair. He was wearing worn jeans and a pullover. In the daylight, his sideburns were salted with gray and his abs looked taut. He glanced at Grace, went into the kitchen and kissed his wife.

'You okay?'

'Grace, my husband, Stuart. Stu, this is Grace, the cousin I was telling you about who knows a lot about microbiology.' Her voice was toneless. The joy had gone out of it. 'That's what he's doing at Stanford, going back to finish up his doctorate.'

He blinked as if he'd forgotten the script. He was still staring at his wife, and Grace could see the confusion in his eyes, and tenderness. They might have bumpy spots, but this was a man who loved his wife.

Grace said, 'Actually, we met briefly last night at jail. He was just leaving.'

'Hey. That's right. Good to see you again. Starbucks. Wonderful.' He put the towel around his neck and reached for the last coffee, cracked open the lid and took a small sip.

The room grew silent. Vonda blinked, close to tears. Stuart moved behind her and rubbed her neck with one hand.

'What kind?' Grace and Stuart were going to have to lug this conversational ball up the hill together, and it was a heavy one.

'What?'

'Microbiology. It's a big field.'

'Oh. *Agrobacterium tumefaciens*. Are you asleep yet?'

Grace smiled. She waited. A fly buzzed. 'You're starting Stanford winter quarter then.'

Vonda stared stiffly at her cup, refusing to make eye contact.

'Right after Christmas. If we leave now we'll be settled in for a couple of months before I have to go to school. We've been saving some money, I've got student loans, and I'll be working part-time. We'll be okay.' Stuart dropped his hand. 'Honey, do you know where the spoons went to?'

Vonda shrugged.

'I brought plastic ones,' Grace said.

He found spoons and put one next to each place along with a napkin. He smiled at his wife again but Vonda shook her head. A silent, pained communication snapped from her eyes to his. He sat down.

They ate in silence, fishing out melon wedges from the container as if they were ripe pickles.

'How's your mom taking the move?'

Vonda exchanged a quick glance with Stuart. Her lower lip trembled.

'You haven't told your folks yet.'

Vonda wet her lip. 'Mom's at Curtis and Sandy's, baby-sitting. They live on the coast — Carlsbad, not far from you, Grace. Curt won

186

this big sales award and he and Sandy are on this cruise.'

Grace vaguely remembered a row of Vonda's older brothers, dark and mischievous, Curt second from the oldest.

'So your mom's going to come back to an empty house here, is that it?'

'It's not like that, Grace.' Stu's voice was sharp, his tone preemptive.

'He thinks I've fallen in with a bad crowd.' Vonda tried to make it a joke and Grace could tell by the grim set of Stuart's mouth that this was an old battle, wounds raw.

'Andrea's a good friend. I could stay with her. I'm not due for a couple of weeks. You could go ahead and be back in time. That way, I wouldn't have to be at Mom and Dad's but they could still — '

'You're not staying with your folks. They have zero respect for us. Go on, tell her.'

'About the . . . '

'Yeah.'

Vonda raised her chin, angry and resigned, and when she spoke, it was as if the words were a set piece she'd committed to memory.

'I was repotting a bunch of stuff in the greenhouse and came home for some lemonade, and here's my mom and dad, going through drawers in the kitchen. Mom said she was just going to make some iced tea and surprise me with it, but it freaked me out.'

She turned to Stuart. 'Happy?'

'Not particularly.'

'I think it's a good idea, staying with Andrea.'

187

Vonda darted a glance at Stu and this, too, was the Vonda that Grace remembered. Goading to get a response. 'I don't see what the big deal is.'

'Andrea's got an entire room set up in her house for our baby, that's the big deal.' His voice was low and thick with emotion. 'She's got more gear than we do. What do you think that means, Vonda?'

Vonda blinked rapidly. 'She just wants me and Sam to be comfortable when we visit, that's all. Why are you going off on her?'

'You mean, why in particular? Because I don't trust those girls to give him back.'

Vonda sucked in a breath. 'What are you talking about?'

'Think about it, Vonda. Your pals Andrea and Sarah have worked hard to drive a wedge between us. And it's working. I kept trying to figure out why, and then it came to me. They want that baby.'

Vonda's hands instinctively flew to her belly. 'No.'

Grace busied herself with the melons, putting the lid under the container as if she were an extra on *Martha Stewart*.

'They like our baby too much, Vonda. I think everything Andrea's talked you into doing — all of it — and God, I don't want to know what it is, only that you've stopped — is so that Andrea will have a shot at raising this kid.'

'What? You think I'm going to get arrested?'

'Are you?'

'For what? You mean, for his *death*? Bartholomew's death?'

188

'Okay, there's more yogurt, more melon, nobody's touched the cinnamon rolls yet . . . ' Grace surveyed the table.

Stuart's eyes darkened. A look of fear crossed his face. 'Tell me you haven't done anything.'

'For God's sake, Stu, that man was a hero.'

It was bad timing, but what the hell. 'Were you ever in his house?'

'What?' Vonda snapped her head around and stared at Grace; her face was blank.

'His house,' Grace repeated. 'Were you ever in Bartholomew's house?'

Vonda frowned, her eyes back to Stuart. 'No, he was a private guy, never wanted company. Stu, I can't believe you're saying all this stuff.'

'Well, somebody killed him,' Stuart snapped. 'I'm sick of coming home, not knowing if I'll find you here, not knowing if you're all right. Not knowing squat. I want you safe. I want you mine. I want to start over with a baby and our life.'

Grace looked at them brightly. 'Anybody have a knife? I'll cut these rolls.'

Vonda frowned and turned to look at her, as if seeing her for the first time. Stuart bent over a box. 'There's one in here somewhere.'

Three things happened at once. Vonda accidentally knocked over her coffee. Stuart came up with a carving knife.

And the kitchen door burst open and an armed federal agent crouched into position, weapon drawn, and screamed, 'FBI. Freeze!'

21

A Jack in the Box butted up against a welding shop called Hole in the Wall where a monster metal spider crouched in the dirt-packed yard. Crooked pieces of black pipe bunched like legs, welded onto a black VW body that hung as a fat midsection, so that the spider appeared to be poised to leap. Grace glanced at the scribbled directions from her uncle and took the frontage road at the 10.

The fields were on Bureau of Land Management land, on the outskirts of a neighborhood called Garnet. A forest of windmills stood near the road, the columns white and sculpted as pieces of art. The blades churned as wind gusted through them. Snarls of creosote bushes leaned sharply into the sun, a dark slash marking an ancient fault line.

Advancing up the ridges past the column of hightech windmills stood regiments of heavy windmills — the old kind — with blades as big as the propellers on rusty ships. A wind popped through the canyons, banged into the blades, and they turned.

The sun beat down on the San Jacinto cliff faces that rose thirteen thousand feet straight up from the desert floor, the gray and chalky stones, purple crevices, orange scrub etched in brutal clarity. Cables looped across the sides of the mountain, suspended and fragile as webs. Grace saw a small ball of cable car slide across the face of a cliff and shoot out of view.

She turned onto a dirt road and drove past sharp spurs of acacia and three irrigated patches of crops — nonsoy — bright green stamps against the alkaline sand, the only fields not at risk of infection of soybean rust or burned to the ground. She passed the GM sugar beets field that had been torched by protesters, and fields tinged in orange — the distinctive color of soybean rust. An army of workers moved through the fields, spraying.

The closer she drove to the field where Bartholomew had died, the heavier her chest felt, as if the heel of a hand pressed, just enough to be noticed. She took a dirt road that dead-ended in a parking lot.

Three cars were parked under the feathered shade of a tamarisk tree. Grace parked and walked across the sun-bleached dirt to the edge of the crime scene field, marked off with police tape.

An empty folding chair guarded the crime scene. Under the chair was an open box of water bottles and a trash bag, crumpled in a gelatinous ball, melting.

Grace immediately saw the gaping hole in the fence through which Bartholomew must have fled in his desperate attempt to escape his attacker. A sign identified the plot as USDA Experimental Soy Project 3627. She moved closer and peered into the field, careful not to touch anything.

'This is a crime scene investigation. No one's allowed back here.'

She jerked her head around, startled. Instinctively her hands shot up, palms raised. She hadn't heard anybody. He was dressed in a tan Riverside County sheriff's uniform and wasn't smiling. He had cropped brown hair and cold blue eyes, a Glock in the holster under his arm. There was a bulge toward his ankle, too. Hopefully he wouldn't shoot something off. Like his mouth. Or a foot.

'Grace Descanso.' She put her hands down. 'FBI.'

He came a step closer, studied the ID tag, adjusted an ear pod, and stuck out his hand. 'Rogener, deputy sheriff of Riverside County.'

They shook.

The sun bounced down his face and his cheeks shone. Sweat ringed his armpits and streaked the front of his shirt. 'What do you need?'

'Meeting Homicide Detective Mike Zsloski here.'

'Wait a sec, I have to find my partner and then I'll take you in.'

He pulled his handie talkie from his shirt pocket. A hot gust of air blasted over the parking lot; pebbles sifted and raked the dirt. The deputy's hair riffled and his collar shot up and he turned away from the wind, speaking into his hand.

'He'll be here soon. He's walking the perimeter.'

'I got her.'

It was a familiar rumbly voice, and Grace turned back to the field. Palm Springs Police

Homicide Detective Mike Zsloski ducked under the crime scene tape and lumbered over. His face was flushed a deep shade of red. His stomach tilted over his belt, shorts a size too small, his knees scraped.

He was wearing navy silk stockings and Nikes, which made him look like an aging Swiss yodeler, the kind in a *Prairie Home Companion* skit advertising a fake brand of hot chocolate. He clamped his mouth shut, jerking his shaggy head from side to side, as if shaking off a bad smell.

'Nice knees.'

'Don't give me hell. My wife's visiting her sister in Milwaukee. I ran out of clean clothes two days ago. You're late.'

'I got a little tied up.' She thought back to the last hour at Vonda and Stuart's house. 'Did you know my uncle was going to send the FBI to raid his own kid's place?'

Zsloski shoved his hands into his pockets. 'Everybody's on the list, Grace. It would have been weird if she wasn't. Think about it. She's part of the protest group that torched the sugar beets. She gets herself arrested. She has the resources to grow this soybean-rust crap. We're trying to figure out where it comes from, that's all. The plant pathologist I was going to have you meet, give the evidence to, he's wandered off again. I swear to God that man's driving me crazy.'

A fine sheen of sweat greased Zsloski's face and the gray hair in his ears looked damp, but it was his color that concerned her. His face was the shade of old cheese.

193

'You're taking water in with you, right?'

'What are you, my mother?'

'Yes.'

Zsloski hefted his bulk, reached under Rogener's chair, and came back with two bottles. Grace cracked open the cap and drank. The water was warm.

Mike lifted the crime scene tape and she ducked under. The faint smell of gasoline still hung in the air, along with a sharp odor of soy.

'Did you sleep at all?'

He shook his head. 'You?'

'Some. Not really. Do you know who she is yet?'

'Her name's Tammy, at least that's what was on the fake ID she showed your pal, Jeanne Bigelow. She paid cash for the tattoo, made the appointment the day before by phone. Everything on the waiver she signed was shit, so the name could be bogus, too. Jeanne had never seen her before. The San Diego Police are flashing her picture around Ocean Beach but so far haven't come up with any hits. We're going through the Missing Persons CLETs right now, see what we can find, but it's a crapshoot.'

'Another crossbow. Is it related to Bartholomew's death?'

'Too soon to say. The markings that get made when a bolt starts to fly are slightly different. A cargo shipment of crossbows and goggles was stolen off a Union Pacific train car a couple months back.'

'Which means a killer with access to a lot of crossbows.'

194

'Or a group.'

'So they could use crossbows at the Convention Center.'

'They could.'

They took a breath, almost in unison, inhaling the deep mulchy flavor of soy. And then the gasoline aftertaste came into Grace's mouth and she took a long drink of water. A group of killers. Hunting.

'They were practicing with animals.'

He turned. His energy grew still. 'And you know this because?'

She had a hard time feeling good about herself, but she'd learned that the less she betrayed others, the easier it was to salvage something decent at the end of the day. Telling Zsloski she'd heard it in AA fell into that category. 'I can't tell you.'

'Of course not.'

'Check the vet hospitals, Mike. Dogs. They've been hunting family pets. How much are you telling the media?'

'We're keeping a lid on the method of death, but we'll see how long that lasts.'

'Bartholomew carried a photo of Frank Waggaman in his wallet with a red line through it.'

Zsloski frowned. 'You find that last night in the evidence room?'

She nodded. 'If there's a group, he could be targeted.'

Grace glanced back to the parking lot, where the deputy was sitting on the chair, eyes closed, legs stretched out, face to the sun.

'Nice to see all I had to do was flash the FBI tag.'

'It's not like TV, Grace. We all play pretty well in this sandbox. Any ego clashes come farther up the food chain. Not us in Palm Springs. We rely on each other too much. Anyway, we asked the FBI in. That's the way it works here.'

She nodded. 'That's how it works where I come from, too. Bartholomew's phone. I take it, it hasn't been used since he sent the Morse code.'

Zsloski shook his head. 'He had an old cell phone, apparently prided himself on not upgrading it. Didn't have a GPS embedded.'

Zsloski wiped his forehead and smoothed his hand on his shorts. Light sifted over the stalks of soy, and a fine mist of dust swirled in the air, creating a soft nimbus of light around the face of the aging dectective.

'The UNSUB took the phone with him when he left.'

'On foot.'

'Only way he could have gone.'

'No footprints?'

He shook his head. 'High-wind area, and looks like he went to the trouble of scraping the prints with a branch. No tracks except the girl's up on the ridge, either.'

'You think he was picked up on the highway?'

'So far, we haven't found evidence of either a hitchhiker in the vicinity or a car parked along the side of the road waiting. It's possible he cut through the desert.'

The sharp cry of a train whistle bit through

the wind. 'I saw a depot off on Indian Canyon.'

Zsloski rubbed the back of his sunburned neck and the thumbprint left a white mark on skin that flooded immediately to pink. 'He could have caught the Sunset Limited, heavy on the limited; it slows at the crossing by the depot and nobody's on duty unless there's a scheduled passenger.'

Grace nodded.

Zsloski tilted back his head and swigged water; somehow, he'd managed to sunburn the underside of his chin; it was an angry orange-red. 'It's a mile and a half of boulders and sand wash and barrel cactus across to the depot. We fanned out in a ninety-degree radius from the kill site for a mile into the wash, and didn't find anything human.'

Grace swiveled and studied the cut barbwire. 'Here's where he caught his tweed jacket?'

Zsloski nodded. 'What do you think?'

'Couple of things,' she said finally. 'The perp probably cut the wire in advance. It would have been tricky cutting wire and holding a weapon on the vic at the same time.'

'That makes sense.'

'It means he picked this site on purpose. The area was familiar. If he cut the wire, he probably pretested going under the wire himself. You don't want to get your own shirt caught as you go in. The barbwire's been tested for fibers, right?'

Mike nodded. 'Our lab handled the CSI. Besides the chunk torn from Bartholomew's jacket, it came up clean for stray fibers. Nothing, either, on the kill route and the soy.'

'They've been interviewed, everybody who worked this site?'

'So far, their alibis hold. Nobody remembers seeing Bartholomew or anybody strange. But there weren't guards here until after the homicide. 'Course, with last night, there's a whole other angle we're exploring, since it's up on Indian land.'

Zsloski pointed at a path through the soy that ran adjacent to the crime scene. 'CSI wants us to use this corridor.'

Grace turned and studied the path that Bartholomew had taken into the soy. The soy fronds were hairy and green, rising to midchest, the crushed route of Bartholomew's flight made obvious by the damaged stalks flattened in a narrow swath. It looked as if a large, frightened animal had plowed headlong into the field, trying to get away.

Zsloski turned and headed into the soy. She followed him in, slipping on the uneven soy, which caught in her shoes and dug into her ankles. She grappled for purchase at some point, trying to right herself, and had an uneasy sense that Bartholomew must have done the same thing, under far more desperate circumstances.

They kept walking. The soy pressed in, the air hot, claustrophobic. She ducked under a soy frond. Zsloski stopped at the end of the path. The ground was stained by gasoline residue and darkened blood. The plants closest to the fire were blackened scarecrows, the leaves curled, fronds crackling in the wind. She wiped her forehead. She should have brought a hat. At least sunscreen. She hoped Mac was remembering to use sunscreen on Katie.

'I had a sit-down with Andrea,' Grace said. 'She talked about Radical Damage. Nate kept trying to shut her up. She runs a small business, importing from Third World countries. She partnered with Bartholomew.'

'We did a background check on Professor Bartholomew and that came up.'

She nodded. She expected it. 'That crossbow theft might be part of something bigger.'

'Also know. Working with Union Pacific. They have their own police to monitor trains.'

'Might want to check out a guy named Tony, works at Windlift as a welder.'

Zsloski stared at her.

'He's a convicted felon. Murder two. Killed his first wife.'

'We got that already.'

She felt a slow burn. It had to be clear she'd gotten an FBI consulting ID but no deep briefing. 'Then you got everything I know. Don't need my help.'

'You're doing good, though. You've been here, what, forty-five minutes?'

He was trying to make her feel better and she appreciated it.

'Maybe a bolt cutter — like the kind used in the cargo thefts — cut the wire on that fence there.' She took another gulp of water. Of course he knew that; she was trying to save face.

'Might be worth finding out what they've imported lately at Square Pegs, and where the stuff has ended up. Anything useful yet from his house?'

'He had a housekeeper he paid in cash. Her prints haven't come up in the system. Only reason we know about her was that he spilled that he had a maid during the part of his class dealing with sexual oppression. It chewed on him: paying a woman to clean for him every two weeks so that he could lecture about how women were held down in the marketplace by low pay and traditional jobs.'

'Interesting that he let anybody in there. Must have been somebody he trusted.'

'Like I said, no match on the prints yet.'

So it wasn't Andrea.

'We're finding nasty shit, Grace,' he said quietly. 'He had a complete set of Jolly Roger cookbooks inside a John Muir biography.'

At the Mexican restaurant, Nate had reacted when Grace spitballed the idea of explosives. 'I met Nate last night. I brought up bombs in the conversation.'

'That sounds nice and light.'

'He turned on Andrea, wanted to know what she'd told me.'

'So you think it could be a bomb Monday night.'

'Sure. A bomb and then pick off any survivors with crossbows. Bartholomew flag anything in that cookbook?'

'We're checking the pages that are most thumbed to see what we get.'

Out of the corner of her eye she saw something on the periphery of the field.

Zsloski straightened. He was a lot taller than Grace and whatever he saw enraged him. He turned and plowed past her, back the way they'd come, bellowing and sliding over the soy. 'Hey, hey, hey, what did I tell you about stepping into the crime scene?'

He disappeared ahead of her and she was left enveloped in a green dusty wall of soy higher than her head. *Tell her, Vee. Tell her about the GM soy turning the rat testicles blue.*

She shifted uneasily, slapped a hand over her nose, and tried not to breathe.

Not that she had testicles to worry about. But still. She put her head down and followed Detective Zsloski out.

22

Deputy Sheriff Rogener stood outside the tape in a heated argument with a man Grace didn't recognize, Zsloski bearing down, waving his fists and bellowing, everybody talking at once.

'It was only a little.'

'He sneaked, Detective. He went right by me and sneaked in.'

'And how did he do that *exactly*?' Zsloski growled.

'I have permission, that's what I'm trying to tell you. From the FBI.'

The speaker had white hair tufting far back on a receding hairline, a bulbous veined nose, and a too-wide smile that made him look alarmingly like a clown named Bobo who had terrified Grace as a child.

She'd forgotten all about Bobo until that very minute. She was a person doomed to go through life remembering, reconnecting the perilous parts of her past in a painful voyage of rediscovery.

He was wearing what appeared to be a safari outfit, the kind Grace had seen on sale in the gift shop at the San Diego Zoo. Strapped to a wide cotton belt jangled a set of plastic sample containers filled with dark orange bits of leaves. He'd slung a canvas bag over a narrow shoulder. It appeared to have everything he'd need for a long journey except a porta-potty.

'Grace. Dr Gordie Turngood. Turngood, Grace Descanso. He's a plant pathologist I was telling you about, checking the soy for soybean rust.'

Dr Turngood nodded, gripped two sample bottles convulsively and pulled, as if he were milking them. He looked ready to confess. To whatever it was.

A police radio crackled to life and Zsloski cupped it in a massive palm and spoke into it, his voice a mumble.

The plant pathologist's gaze wandered and Grace saw him look with longing at a soy frond, just out of reach. He leaned his body toward it, feet on the ground, eyes down as if he really wasn't ready to whip his hand up past the crime scene tape, snap off the frond, stuff it into a fresh bottle and cap it. Grace had seen Helix do exactly the same thing, creeping toward a stray cookie.

'This is a crime scene. Nothing is removed from here and *you* — ' Zsloski pointed a square finger at Gordie Turngood and the scientist flinched and bobbed to an upright position, a bouncy toy. 'Stay with *her*. Deputy, I suggest you sit in your chair, stop listening to the pregame chatter.'

Sheriff Deputy Rogener's hand clapped over the ear bud in his left ear.

'I'd hate to have to confiscate that before kickoff.'

Zsloski cracked up the crime scene tape for Grace and she scrambled under it. Up close, Gordie Turngood smelled of cinnamon and

203

musk, liberally applied.

'I've got work to do.' Zsloski headed back to his unmarked. 'The perimeter, Grace. Don't let Gordie Turngood under that tape.'

* * *

'It's sporulating like crazy. Not this field, but the others.'

'And that's a bad thing?'

They were walking back to the cars. A fine cloud of dust sifted over the parking lot where Zsloski's unmarked had been. Deputy Sheriff Rogener was on the folding chair, back listening to the game, a finger wedged in his ear to hide the ear pod.

Dr Turngood fished out his car keys from his pocket. 'Oh, that's a very bad thing, Grace. There were six different strains of GM soy planted in fields here. All of them have been hit.'

'But not this field.'

He looked longingly back at the field and tried again. 'I wanted a sample of the gasoline residue, that's all.'

'For what, so you could sell it on eBay? Are you married?'

'Not anymore. Why?'

Grace thought of her mother, Lottie, who never met a boundary she couldn't do an end run around, usually in hot pants and stilettos.

'No reason. What makes soybean rust so bad?'

'You want the stomach-turning version, or the regular one?'

'I've got a great imagination. Stick with the facts.'

'Pustules,' Gordie Turngood said matter-of-factly. 'Brown, squishy ones shaped like sci-fi miniature pinecones that, if left untreated, erupt with a volcanic surge of spores that — '

'Okay, I get it,' she said irritably.

'Actually, it's worse than that. It's a parasite. It needs green, living tissue to survive.' He unlocked his car door and grappled his pack into the backseat.

Grace had never thought of soy as 'green, living tissue' before. It gave her pause.

'It's host specific. Affects only soy.'

'Well, there you go,' Grace said. 'There's no other soy around for miles and miles. This is date palm country.'

'You don't get it. It's already gone by now, on the wind.

'Like snowbirds, soybean rust likes to hunker down, winter in warm climes. We found it on Florida beggarweed.'

'In Florida?'

'Georgia. Misnamed. It can wipe out eighty percent of a soy crop. And it can respore, so it comes back. And some strains appear to be resistant to every known antidote, so we have to GM the soy to stave it off, and that takes time.'

A sudden wind snapped through the parking lot.

'This stuff was deliberately placed. It's jumped about six states to get here; on this wind, it's halfway to Monterey by now.' Gordie Turngood undid his belt and carefully put the samples in the front seat next to him.

205

'I've got a sample of something I need you to process.'

He shook his head and the curls bounced. 'Can't get to it for at least two weeks, with the backup from this.'

'It might have something to do with this case.' Grace pulled the evidence envelope out of her bag. 'These came out of the vic's shoes.'

'The *vic*?' He blanched. 'You mean the victim? Professor Bartholomew.'

She nodded. 'I need you to tell me where these came from.'

Dr Gordie Turngood's lab was in a medical and technical building off Date Palm Drive, gray glass windows and beige cement. Palm trees and yucca studded the lawn. She parked and followed him up the exterior staircase to the second floor. He unlocked a door across from a clinical psychologist's office.

Files buried the desk. A putting green poked out from a debris of papers on the floor, the hole for the ball filled with paper clips. A half-finished charcoal sketch of a nude woman stood positioned on an easel. A Gibson guitar leaned against the wall, its strings sprung and curling in hard wiry strands. If there was a phone and computer, filing cabinets, Grace didn't see them. Silently, she cursed Zsloski.

'Looks like you're too busy to do this. I'll just take it — '

'You're put off by the mess.' Turngood managed to sound affronted. 'Understandable. It's adult ADD. Diagnosed when my kid was evaluated. Your choice, but I'm the only game in town here, if you're in a hurry. And clearly Homicide Detective Mike Zsloski must believe in my abilities or he wouldn't have sent you my way.'

Reluctantly, Grace held out the evidence packet and he signed for it.

'I go all over the world finger printing vegetables, not just the Coachella Valley.'

'I'm with the San Diego crime lab. We analyze DNA all the time.' She was trying to make nice. It made her face itch.

He rooted through a stack of papers, found something, and passed it to her. It looked remarkably similar to human DNA: a series of sharp, well-defined peaks compressed tightly together, resembling a supermarket bar code.

'This is a date palm bar code from a farm in Indio. A strain that's been cultivated to yield richer-tasting, plumper dates. They patented their procedure, but these guys have to protect their project, and this is a way of doing it. I profile the DNA, and that way, if it turns up in some other farm's product, there's a way of collecting. It's big business and that means theft is right behind it.'

'So you could tell me what this is and where it came from.'

'If it's plant, sure, I could tell you where it *didn't*, at least. There's a library of bar codes I'll compare it to, but not every grower goes to the trouble of registering his strain. The USDA and a lot of universities have overlapping programs, and some of that's on the Net, but there's a long way to go. They haven't even completely decoded the soybean genome. Humans have about three billion bases — building blocks — in just a single cell. The humble soybean only has a third of that, but that's still a lot of bases to cover.'

He smiled at his little joke.

A bell went off in the lab and he turned toward the sound, remembered the packet and came back for it.

'Got a timer on. Got to go. I'll call. Make sure you lock that door when you leave.'

He darted into the lab and closed the door behind him. Grace ripped off a piece of notepaper from her pad and block-printed her name and cell phone number. She stepped over the debris and slid it under the lab door.

'Got it,' Gordie Turngood said, his voice muffled and distracted.

Grace hesitated, staring at the door, wondering if she needed to write a reminder and slip it under the door again.

She locked the outer door behind her as she left.

23

Grace took Bartholomew's photo to IHOP and flashed it around. None of the servers recognized him; the same with the Denny's on East Palm Canyon Drive. But at the Denny's on North Palm Canyon Drive, she hit pay dirt.

The place was jammed with college-age students and families with restless kids drawing on place mats, enjoying a late breakfast or early lunch.

Grace walked once through the restaurant and spotted a table toward the back with three old guys in shirtsleeves and bifocals, all finishing Senior Grand Slams. They were drinking coffee, the *Desert Sun* spread out next to their plates.

'Yeah, it's Ted. Helluva thing.' The man speaking had a voice box he had to touch to get sound, and when the sound came out, it was mechanical and tinny. 'Who are you again?'

'Manners, Arnie,' a sunburned man in the chair across from him chided gently. He was wearing a hot pink shirt and a pair of lime yellow shorts with athletic socks and loafers. His legs were white and knobby. 'I'm Wes. Arnie's our version of Mr Inquisitor, and the guy over there buried in the sports page is Raymond.'

Raymond looked up and grunted a greeting, his blunt finger on the line he was reading about high school girls' tennis.

'Grace Descanso. I'm from the crime lab in

San Diego, here giving a hand to the FBI, trying to get a bead on what happened.'

They shook hands all around. Wes smiled benignly up at her and blinked and his lenses caught the light.

'Is it okay if I sit, have a cup of coffee?'

'Oh. Sorry.' Wes pulled out the empty seat and she sat. 'It's been a long time since we've had a pretty girl join us for breakfast. I forgot how to do it.'

'You pull the chair out,' Arnie squawked through his box.

'Even longer since a pretty girl joined one of us for breakfast after joining one of us for dinner,' Raymond said under his breath.

'You'll have to excuse Raymond, he's never had a pretty girl join him for *anything*. Arnie and me are widowers. Raymond's like that Lonesome George tortoise in the Galápagos they keep trying to find a mate for. He's way past confirmed bachelorhood.'

'At least I'm not crazy about interior decorating.' Raymond turned the page and kept reading.

Wes shifted in his chair. 'So I like to freshen up my place, is that a crime?'

'How did you find us?' It was Arnie, the voice box man again. Through his glasses, his eyes were shrewd and penentrating.

Grace thought about the coupons in Bartholomew's wallet in the police property room.

'I got to thinking,' Grace said. 'Mr Bartholomew was a widower. And breakfast is a pretty intense meal to make, especially when you're on your way to work. I remembered my own grandfather used to gather with a bunch of guys once a week in a coffee shop. Every week for years.'

'Your grandmother was dead?' Raymond took a bite of bacon and a swallow of coffee.

'No, she just made lousy pancakes.'

Raymond smiled. He had wavy silver hair he wore parted and age spots freckled his broad expanse of forehead. 'So you went from restaurant to restaurant until somebody recognized that photo?'

'Something like that.'

A waitress stopped momentarily in her path across the floor, holding steaming plates of food, caught Grace's eye, and nodded. Grace nodded back.

'It was like that for us,' Raymond said. 'How many years now?'

'Two,' Arnie said.

'And a couple of months,' Wes added. 'Remember, Lizzie, Ted's wife, died of cancer that summer and then we saw Ted there at the counter all by himself, looking like a lost little kid. We folded him in. First thing he did, he got us all together and took our picture.'

Grace blinked.

'Didn't even have a moment to prepare.' Wes shook his head. 'I use this cucumber scrub if I know I'm going to be photographed, gives my skin a nice, peachy glow. The rest of us have been coming here for what? A decade?'

'A decade,' Raymond agreed.

'When did you last see him?'

'Tuesday morning,' Arnie said. His finger on the voice box trembled. 'We always get together Tuesdays, Thursdays, and Sundays.'

Raymond nodded and shook his head. 'Terrible thing.'

'Tuesday,' Wes repeated. 'He didn't show up Thursday, and didn't call.'

'He always calls if he has to cancel,' Arnie said.

'And then he didn't.' Raymond poured himself another cup of coffee.

'I get the special on Thursdays.' Wes smoothed a wrinkled hand over his shorts. 'We'd just ordered from Janey. Raymond here had gone outside to buy the papers. We take turns getting them. At our age, it's a long walk outside to that machine.'

'They ordered for me, they always know what I want.' Raymond nodded and the ropey skin cording his neck swayed. 'I brought the papers back in, sat down, and then I opened mine up so I could see the whole front page at a glance. That's the way I like to do it. That way I can tell if there's something I want to avoid.'

'Janey was the first one to see it,' Arnie said. 'Ted's face was right there.' He took his finger off his voice box and punched a place on the current paper, right under the fold.

'Exactly,' Wes said. 'The order book fell from her hands.' His hand on his knee spasmed.

'And then she collapsed,' Raymond said. 'Slipped to the ground like she'd been clubbed. I used to be a farmer. We used to club hogs.'

'We don't need to hear about the hogs again.' Wes cleared his throat loudly.

212

'Just like a hog,' Raymond said. 'You enjoy your bacon, Wes. Well, it comes from somewhere.'

Arnie sighed heavily and soundlessly, his finger off the speaker button.

'Did he seem upset, when you last saw him?'

The three men looked at each other and away. Nobody spoke.

'You must be Wes's daughter, Amy. I'm Janey.' The waitress smiled down at Grace. She was tall, almost six feet, with dishwater hair turning to gray and her posture was hunched, as if she'd spent her lifetime apologizing for some wrong that had never quite been explained to her.

'Oh,' Grace and Wes said simultaneously.

'I'm Grace Descanso,' Grace said.

'Grace is a hotshot investigator,' Arnie said, his voice squawking at the last syllable. He adjusted his finger on the box.

'Who needs a cup of coffee, Janey. If it's not too much trouble,' Raymond said. 'Anything else?'

'Small salad and a cheeseburger sounds good,' Grace said.

'And a small salad and a cheeseburger,' Raymond warbled.

'No dressing, no french fries, cheddar for the cheese, and a to-go box just in case.'

'No dressing, no french fries,' Arnie chimed in, 'Cheddar for the — '

'I'm not hard of hearing.' Janey reached over to a nearby empty table and filched a cup. She poured from a pot on the table. 'You investigating Ted's murder?' Her voice had a

213

quaver in it. Her eyes were deep wells of suffering.

Some antennae tweaked in Grace's brain. 'Sounds like he was a good man.'

Janey's eyes filled and she nodded a little too hard as she put the coffee down in front of Grace. She took her time refilling the other cups.

'Mine's unleaded, Janey, you know that,' Wes said, putting his hand over the top of his cup.

He was avoiding looking at Janey, they all were, as if by ignoring her emotions long enough, the threatened tears would go back to whatever hormonally charged netherworld they'd originated in, instead of hovering behind her eyes, threatening to spill.

'You knew him pretty well, didn't you?' Grace said softly.

Janey reared her head back, and Grace caught a glimpse of the whites of her eyes. She expelled a breath and half laughed. 'Yeah, you could say that.'

'Excuse me, miss? Miss.' It was a well-fed man in a booth with a busy family, eating. He raised his voice. 'Could we have some more butter here?'

Janey straightened, and the terrible softness hardened into a mechanical smile. 'Be right there.' She turned back to Grace, all business. 'Cheeseburger and small salad coming right up.'

'And a little more decaf,' Raymond reminded her.

She lifted their breakfast plates into a stack on her arm and escaped.

'So now you know,' Wes said.

214

'We would have told you,' Raymond said.

'Were planning to,' Arnie squawked.

'But you're a hotshot investigator, didn't need our help.'

'Must be why they pay you the big bucks.' Raymond leaned back and smiled.

'Not that big,' Grace said. 'I'm not springing for breakfast.'

'She's good,' Wes said.

Grace pulled out her notebook and put a pen down beside it. 'I need your names and phone numbers.'

'Yippee.' Raymond reached for the pen.

'Why you? Why do you get to be first?' Wes grumped. 'He's not the most important one, I want you to know that.'

A young male Hispanic server came over with a pot of decaf and refilled Wes's mug. Interesting that Janey had sent somebody else over. Grace waited as they finished writing. She took back the notebook and positioned the pen.

'Okay, so what's the story here.'

They leaned in, exchanged a look. 'It's all confidential, right?' Raymond said.

She narrowed her eyes. 'Guys, if you know anything, cough it up. He was your *friend*.'

Another look. An imperceptible nod and Raymond said, 'Well, we first noticed it a couple weeks ago. He and Janey had been an item for — what, maybe six months?'

'Seven,' Wes said. 'This is November. Remember, I'd just given all of you flowers for Easter that I'd arranged — '

'Except I'm Jewish,' Arnie squawked.

215

'What, Jews don't like flowers?' Wes folded his speckled arms.

'It's not about the flowers, it's about the *event*,' Arnie said.

'April,' Grace said. 'They'd been an item since April. Ted Bartholomew and Janey here.'

Wes nodded, miffed, still not looking at Arnie. 'Ted was getting all red-faced around Janey, and she was always standing next to him when she took our orders.'

'And Wes would notice something like that,' Raymond said. 'Besides flower arranging and interior decorating over there at that night school, he was taking a class in body language.'

'Had just finished it. I wasn't taking them all at the same time.' Wes tossed his head defensively. 'So what if I'm exploring my feminine side. There's nothing wrong with that. You guys could use a little of that yourself.'

'And so you noticed that Janey was attentive to him,' Grace prompted.

'Exactly. She's here for the breakfast-lunch shift and, well, being us . . . ' Wes squared his bony shoulders. 'We started ribbing him about it.'

'We didn't know there was anything to it,' Raymond said.

Arnie nodded. 'Or we never would have.'

'I think our exact words were, 'Teddy's got a girlfriend, Teddy's got a girlfriend.'' Wes rocked in his seat. 'Only being guys, it was kinda high and singsong.'

'Like on the playground,' Grace said. She was poker-faced.

216

'Exactly,' Wes repeated. 'Well, anyway, that's when we realized, I saw it first, of course, and once you knew the signs, it was hard to miss, his face turning bright red, and this little grin.'

'So that's when you realized — '

'There was more to it,' Arnie finished.

'Turns out they were dating, and had been for some time,' Raymond said. 'He'd taken her on a tram ride.'

'And over to the Agua Caliente museum,' Wes said.

'And the Follies,' Arnie said.

Wes shook his head. 'The Follies.' He fanned himself with his napkin.

'It's all these retired blue-haired women in their twilight years, kicking it up in fishnets and flimsy little costumes,' Raymond explained.

'Not just the women, either,' Wes said.

His friends looked at him.

'Well, you need to be fair. The men in the Follies have had long and illustrious careers, too, and it's no cakewalk wearing tights and an athletic cup so — '

'What happened at the Follies?' Grace asked.

Raymond sat back and folded his arms. Age spots covered the wrinkled skin of his forearms. He waited as Janey placed a cheeseburger and small salad in front of Grace and immediately retreated.

Grace doused her bun with catsup, closed the burger and took a big bite. She looked up. All three men were staring at her cheeseburger, mesmerized.

'Oh, what I wouldn't give to be fifty again,'

Wes said mournfully.

'The Follies,' Grace reminded. She lifted her cheeseburger to her lips and their eyes followed it as she bit into it.

'Oh, right, he took Janey opening night. Starts in November. Two weeks ago.'

'Only, well — '

Arnie leaned in and pressed the button on his voice box. In his eagerness, his finger slid off the *down* arrow and hit the arrow adjusting the volume up.

His voice pealed, 'It was *over*. He had met somebody new. That's what he told us on Tuesday.'

Diners looked at them. It was one of those slomo moments, where the forks froze halfway to mouths, people pouring syrup seemed to pause, the syrup itself seemed to freeze in its path to the plate.

Janey was bending over a nearby table, putting down plates. At the sound of Arnie's voice, at what he said, she reared up, a look of pure panic on her face. She put down the last plate and fled through the double doors into the kitchen.

They watched her go. 'That's one way to find out,' Wes said.

'Any idea who it was?' Grace had finished half her burger by then and she took a long drink of water.

'We've got our theories,' Arnie squawked, 'especially since — well, since he turned up *dead*. We're pretty sure Janey didn't do it. She doesn't look like an ax murderer.'

There was a reverb problem developing in

218

Arnie's voice box, and the man with the family in the nearby booth turned around and glared at the words *ax murderer*. 'I've got kids here, do you mind?'

'You shouldn't use so much butter,' Arnie squawked. 'It's bad for your health, to say nothing of your kids. You want to make them huskier than they already are? Don't you read the AP stories in the *Desert Sun*? We're raising a nation of fatties and it starts with *Y-O-U* and those supersized waffles.'

The voice box was making him sound like some large, mechanical parrot. Grace half expected him to sing out: *Is that a tanker in the next booth, or is that just your wife?*

'Arnie,' Wes admonished.

The man turned purple and started to rise and his wife put a restraining hand on his arm.

Arnie turned his back on him. 'Well, he *engaged*,' he harrumphed. 'He didn't have to horn in on our conversation.'

A high piercing whine emanated from the vicinity of Raymond's right cheekbone and his hand stabbed at his ear. 'My damn hearing aid,' Raymond muttered. 'Don't say anything important until I get it calibrated.'

He twisted a few invisible wires that only served to make the sound more piercing. Raymond closed his eyes and opened his mouth wide and for an instant, Grace saw his uvula vibrating in a good imitation of the haunted figure in Munch's *The Scream*. He twisted harder and the sound stopped.

'Fine,' Raymond said, 'I killed it. It's dead

now. I didn't need it anyway. I was just wearing it to humor you.'

'You need it,' Wes said. 'You can't read lips.'

'I heard that,' Raymond said.

'What exactly did he say,' Grace tried again, her voice a little louder and slower.

'About what?' Arnie squawked.

'What do you mean, about what? Aren't you paying attention?' Wes glared across his coffee cup. 'She's trying to figure out how Janey fits into this whole deal.'

Janey picked that moment to reappear through the swinging doors, carrying plates of food. Her face was pink and splotchy from crying and her lips glowed with fresh crimson lipstick. There was something valiant and sad about the way she walked.

'She might not factor in,' Grace said. 'Probably doesn't. But I'm not going to know that for sure until you tell me everything. Even the parts you think don't matter.'

'Well,' Wes leaned in, casting a quick look behind him to make sure Janey was a distance away. 'She cooked him dinner Sunday night. That was the big turning point.'

Raymond nodded. 'Ted had all these dietary restrictions from his diverticulitus.'

'No popcorn on that menu,' Arnie said.

'Not even the seeds of tomatoes. It was discussed in detail. See, what happens is, things like that get stuck in his — '

'Grace doesn't need the details, Wes, for crying out loud. Janey served pork,' Raymond said. 'That's the long and short of it. It was nice and succulent from the sounds of it, because she went to the butcher and asked him to — '

Arnie held up his fork in a threatening manner.

'All I said was *pork*.'

Arnie made a growling sound low in his throat.

'Fine, fine, I'm done, but, Grace, if you ever need my help on where to position the knife to flense the shoulder — '

Arnie arranged the fork tines over Raymond's forearm and made a stabbing downward motion.

'Fine,' Raymond said mildly. 'I'm done.'

Grace picked up a chunk of iceberg lettuce and ate it. Talking to them was like standing on top of two stagecoaches, galloping teams veering in opposite directions.

'Janey made him dinner last Sunday night,' Grace repeated, getting things back on track.

'That's what we just said.' Arnie tapped the button on his voice box.

'And by Tuesday morning, he was making noises about breaking things off. But he never said why.'

The three old men exchanged looks.

'Oh, he said why,' Wes said finally.

'Do you mind telling me?' She was trying hard not to lose her patience. She opened her bag and found her wallet.

'He had met somebody who fascinated him,' Arnie said, a little too loudly.

'And that was . . . ?' Grace counted out cash and an extravagant tip, and left it under her cup.

'And that was what?' Wes frowned, confused.

She forced herself to speak slowly, clearly, distinctly. 'Who was the person who fascinated him?'

'Oh, for goodness sake.' Raymond snapped the newspaper closed and refolded it. 'Why in the world would you think he'd want to tell us that?'

'A man's got to have his secrets,' Arnie agreed.

Grace threw up her hands. 'Okay. Interesting. Thank you all.'

She dumped the salad into the take-out container, pulled a card from her wallet, and stood. It was the business card from the Comfort Inn. She block-printed her name on the back and handed it to Raymond, who was closest. Raymond shot her a coy look and smiled. He tucked the card into his shirt pocket and patted it with a liver-spotted hand.

'If any of you think of anything else, don't hesitate to give me a call. I'll be at the Comfort Inn until checkout time tomorrow.'

'Wait a minute,' Wes said. 'Why does Raymond get the card? I want a card.'

'Yeah, me, too,' Arnie said. 'I don't want to be the only guy without a card.'

She inhaled through her nose, rummaged in her bag until she found two more cards. The block printing this time was not as neat. 'Anything else?'

'You sure are a cutie-pie,' Arnie said. 'If I was forty years younger.'

'If you were forty years younger,' Wes said, 'Grace wouldn't even be born yet. Isn't that right, honey?'

'There is one other thing,' Raymond said

suddenly. 'At breakfast one morning, when he was pulling out his cash, he also pulled out this stack of . . . ' He paused.

Grace sat back down.

Raymond picked up his water glass and sloshed the ice around slowly, stretching the moment until Wes blurted out, 'Oh, for crying out loud, Raymond, you take the cake, pulling out a stack of stubs — '

'From the Follies,' Arnie squawked.

'He'd been going by himself, over and over again,' Wes finished.

'It's my story,' Raymond said. 'A man should be allowed to tell a story at his own pace.'

'Raymond, we're old. We don't have that kind of time. At your pace, we'll be dead before you get to the good part.'

Grace got up. 'Thank you. All of you. It's been very interesting.'

Wes twinkled, 'Oh, no, honey, *you're* the interesting one.'

'Where are these Follies?'

'Downtown at the Plaza Theater. Starts in half an hour.' Raymond leaned up, his hair a fragile tuft of delicate white cornsilk. 'And, Grace, I think her name is Jewel.'

24

Grace joined a long line of white-haired men and women in high spirits shuffling past a tiled kiosk and under three stuccoed archways into the theater.

She peeled away — these were people with tickets — and waited in the much shorter ticket line.

'Very lucky, are you,' the ticket seller said when it was her turn. Grace wondered if he'd been watching *Star Wars* a little too long.

She smiled.

'We are completely sold out, as usual — people buy seats months in advance — but we had a comp seat promised — well, to a wildly famous person, and she's been delayed and will attend another performance. That means you have a seat in row two, center stage. Ninety dollars, please.'

Grace swallowed. 'Alrighty then. Do you take American Express?'

★　★　★

It was like nothing she'd ever seen. On each side of the stage, the names of long-gone entertainers had been lit in orange neon, written in the crabbed flourishes of their own handwriting. Elvis, Jack Benny, Frank Sinatra, Dinah Shore.

The conductor, wearing a white tux with a red

silk hankie and black pants with a sequined red stripe, stuck his head up, grinned at the audience, ducked his head down, and waved a baton with a sparkling tip at what Grace was certain was empty air. Skillful empty air, though; the sound quality of a live band reverberated through the theater.

The women of the Follies came out in a clattering blaze of tapping and twinkly lights, wearing black-and-white tails with short skirts that resembled piano keys, accompanied by men in red-sequined suspenders. None of the women had cellulite. All of the men were able — in unison — to kick up their heels and click them together and find the floor again without losing their balance. It was remarkable.

Especially since the youngest cast member was fifty-nine and the oldest over eighty.

Grace looked at the faces of the women carefully, trying to spot a tell, a face blotched from crying, eyes red, feet stuttering. They were flawless, black false eyelashes curled over smooth cheeks, lips red and glossy. They looked like the senior set of Stepford Wives, choreographed by Fred Astaire.

She straightened in her seat when master of ceremonies and co-creator of the show, Riff Markowitz, hand in the pocket of his tux pants, introduced the men one by one, each dancer blurting into the mike a staggering laundry list of Broadway shows in which he'd participated.

The women had to be next.

Perhaps she'd been expecting giggles, modesty, a slightly apologetic *we're just kidding*

225

shrug to the shoulders.

Each came down a sweeping staircase alone, wearing little except high heels, a jaunty smile, and thirty-five thousand dollars' worth of boas and glitter.

Jewel was a tall blonde with perfect posture, dressed like an exotic bird. Scallops of red and silver sequins took the place of a fig leaf; a fringe of silver and red beads jounced wildly over her breasts. Attached to her rump and head fanned ten feet of green and blue feathers, red boas, crystal beading, and shimmering opalescent jewels, as if a costume designer had upended a box of sparkly junk he'd been saving.

Jewel was sixty-seven, she informed the audience, and had danced on Broadway in a blurring array of hits that spanned thirty years, and then dinner theater and touring in Europe. It made Grace want to seriously hit the gym.

Good eye contact. No sagging under the weight of the feathers, or catching a heel on a stair as she swiveled down the steps.

Grace's phone vibrated and she checked the text in the dark.

A volley of heat slammed up her body.

She scooped up her purse and climbed out over knees, apologizing, racing up the aisle to the lobby.

She burst through the lobby door and an usher in a pink shirt and a black fringed hat pointed toward an arrow. 'Ladies' room that way,' he said in a stage whisper.

She shook her head and kept running.

226

25

It took ten minutes to get from downtown Palm Springs to Karen Avenue, another five to reach the greenhouse, and in that time, Grace found a quiet place inside, impervious to stress or panic. She needed to distance herself from her own history. She needed to give her cousin a gift she didn't think she had.

Up close, the building was constructed of hightech polyethylene. The splintered door looked damaged by wind, but there were fresh gouges, too. She thought of the FBI raid that morning, the intensity of it.

Grace pulled in behind a car she recognized. Bright red. Sarah's car. If Sarah was there, it meant Andrea was, too.

The door wouldn't move and Grace pushed into it hard and it gave way. She tumbled into the building and regained her footing. Dim grow lights illuminated high frothy plants. The air was hot and cloying. Tall plants bristled in the gloom.

She could hear grunting and she stiffened involuntarily, her heart racing. She moved cautiously down a row of mulch-smelling plants and rounded a corner. Vonda was bent over, sitting on a wooden crate, panting. A green grow light cast a shadow up her face, illuminating the stalks behind her, as if she were an exotic bloom flowering in some lethal greenhouse.

Sarah and Andrea knelt in front of her,

murmuring encouragement. As if they were midwives and expected her to deliver there, among the plants.

Andrea sensed her presence and turned. In the green glow of lights, her eyes looked catlike, unblinking. 'What are you doing here?'

'Grace. You came,' Vonda cried.

'How are you feeling?' Grace shoved in between Andrea and Sarah, and Sarah lost her balance and tipped off the planting pot she was using as a seat.

'Jesus! Watch where you're going!' Sarah grappled for the planting pot.

'Give it to me. Now.'

Sarah bared her teeth and shoved the pot toward Grace, and Grace settled on it and pressed her fingers against Vonda's wrist, counting. Vonda's pulse was strong, so there was that, but her skin was moist and her expression interior, watchful. She shifted and clamped her hands around her belly.

'Vonda?'

Vonda made a small sound and scrabbled for the edge of the crate, her face popping with sweat. At her feet lay a denim bag that Grace would have recognized anywhere: the baby bag a pregnant woman packed getting ready to go to the hospital.

Grace shoved her seat closer. Her shoe struck metal. A second bag lay in shadows. This one velvet, half open. Inside, hidden in its soft, secret folds, the edge of a blade winked. Grace swiveled on her seat.

'Is that a siren? Do you hear the EMTs?'

Andrea and Sarah jerked to their feet and trotted in the direction of the door as Grace yanked up the velvet bag and shoved it into Vonda's hospital bag, looping the strap over her shoulder.

'Okay, sweetie, here we go. I'm taking you in.' Grace slipped Vonda's arm around her neck.

Vonda grimaced. 'Hurts.'

'I know honey, I know.'

Vonda made a small sound as she staggered to her feet. The weight of her body shot a pain through Grace's shoulder blade and they half shuffled down the aisle in a thicket of soy. An automatic sprinkler misted the plants and the air felt humid and wet.

They rounded a corner. A bright stamp of light fell across the floor. Andrea stood illuminated in the doorway, blocking the exit. She reached out her hands.

'We agreed, right, Vee? You're riding with us. We get to go in with you. Cut the cord.'

Grace braced Vonda's back with a hand. Through the cotton T-shirt, her back was wet with sweat. *Surprise actions generally lead to victory.* Sun Tzu. 'Andrea, you forgot something.'

'Vee, we'll put you right in the front seat. Sarah's getting it ready.' Andrea's voice was soothing.

'I'd rethink that one, Vonda.'

Grace kept her voice light and Vonda moving. They were almost within touching distance of Andrea and Grace got ready. She kept talking as if Vonda was having an actual conversation with her instead of caught in a seizing pain.

'See, Andrea packs a knife.'

That broke through and Vonda jerked up her head and locked eyes with Andrea, her gaze wild.

'She has a knife?'

'Not anymore,' Grace said. 'Andrea, we're going to need a little room here.'

'I don't have a knife.' Andrea took a surprised step sideways.

'Careful around that bag of potting soil, Vonda. What's the knife for, Andrea?'

'There's no knife.'

Grace could see her confusion, her mind racing. Grace kept steady pressure on Vonda's elbow. They were within feet of the door and Grace heard the sound of a car engine idling.

'She's lying, Vee.'

'I saw it. It's in a bag back there.'

Comprehension flooded Andrea's face and she raced down the aisle, searching under the ledges of pots. 'I was getting soy clippings. To start my own garden.'

'And maybe a knife to cut the cord. Here in the greenhouse. There's the doorsill, Vonda. Be careful.'

Vonda lifted her foot. It looked as heavy as an elephant's. Grace steadied her as she cleared the doorsill and Andrea looped back, rushing through the door after them.

'It's not there. What did you do with it?'

Grace squinted in the sunlight. Vonda shuffled her feet and flecks of sand spat into Grace's shoes. Sarah sat in the driver's seat of her car, waiting. Grace had her blocked; she couldn't leave without Grace moving her car. Vonda sighed unsteadily, focused on the grinding pain in her body.

'Doing good, sweetie.'

They were almost up to Sarah's car. They passed a scattering of cactus poking out of white bleached sand. Except for the sound of the motor, it was quiet.

Andrea raced ahead and opened Sarah's passenger-side door. 'Vee,' her voice was pleading, 'the important thing is getting you into the car, doing everything we've talked about.'

'And what's that, Andrea?' Grace turned to Vonda. 'I think Stu's right. I think she expects to share this kid.'

Through the windshield, Sarah frowned, realizing suddenly that things were not going according to plan. Grace slammed shut the passenger door with her hip.

'Don't you, Andrea?'

Andrea ran ahead so she could walk backwards in front of Vonda, her soft yellow curls almost white in the sun. 'Whoever was first.'

Sarah got out of the car. 'What's happening?'

'But it's my kid.' Vonda frowned and gripped her belly as if it were a basketball somebody was trying to wrench out of her grasp.

Andrea wet her lip. 'Vee, we can do this later. She's trying to bait us. Let it go.'

'No, what did you mean, whoever was first?' Vee stopped walking. She straightened. 'It's *my baby*. Understand? My baby doesn't even *see* you, unless I want him to.'

The mask dropped. Glittering fury crackled

over Andrea's features; she wasn't pretty anymore, not soft, and certainly not harmless.

'You have no idea how it is watching you. Every minute getting more pregnant. Having the one thing all of us want.'

Vonda rocked back on her heels as if she'd been slapped. A hand flew to her face. 'I'm leaving with Stu.' Her hand shook.

'You can't.'

'What do you mean, I can't. I get in the van, we attach it to the U-Haul, we leave.'

'You promised,' Andrea wailed. 'It's my kid, too. Do you understand?'

'A couple more steps now, Vonda, and we're there.'

Grace shifted her grip on Vonda and dug into her bag. She came up with her keys. She'd been having trouble with them lately; the automatic opener unlocked doors sporadically and never the trunk anymore; but she didn't need the trunk opened, only the passenger side.

The lights blinked and she heard the crunch of the door locks opening.

'Vee, you're staying. At least until Sammy's a toddler, then we can decide what else to do.'

'A toddler? Are you kidding me?'

Grace opened the passenger door of her car and Vonda grunted and slid in.

'No,' Andrea cried, her voice fierce. 'We take her in. Vee, we take you. I get to be in there. Sarah and I both do. Hold the baby afterwards first. You promised. We get to cut the cord.'

'You heard her. I'm taking her.' Grace slammed the door.

26

'Okay, now, honey, it's going to be a little rough here, going in.'

Vonda leaned back in the seat, gripping her belly, moaning as Grace hit a bump.

'Sorry.'

Grace eased the car down a gully of eroded sand. She checked her rearview mirror. Sarah stayed right on her bumper. Dust billowed over the road, obscuring the car.

Vonda clutched her arm, fingers damp. 'Thanks.' She talked through her teeth, as if the sheer act of moving her mouth caused pain.

Grace nodded.

'Call the cops?'

'No.'

'Call Daddy.'

Grace glanced over at her. 'You mean, did I? No. But you need to tell your folks you're in labor, Vonda.'

'No! After this morning? No way. Don't want him near my baby.'

The road dipped and Grace tapped the brakes to soften the bump as they passed a row of rounded metal mailboxes. A rusty barbwire fence roped off a field of wind turbines, sprouting like malignant mushrooms, the kind whose caps had already disintegrated into chalky spikes.

'Vee, can you talk?'

'Hurts.'

'Yeah, I know, honey.' Grace wet her lip. 'How about this. How about you just move one of your fingers for *yes*, okay? If you hear me and it's okay to talk.'

A pause. Vonda clawed her belly in a spasm of pain. A moist finger came up.

A middle one.

Grace smiled. 'Good. That's good, honey. Good to see you haven't lost your sense of humor.'

'Thirsty.' The word came out cracked.

'I know, sweetie, and I wish I had something. I'll get you there soon.'

Not wanting to tell Vonda that chances were, they weren't going to let her drink or eat anything from that point forward, except maybe ice chips.

They were still on the dirt road.

'Which hospital?'

'Desert Regional.'

'Do you remember where that is?' She waited as another spasm seized Vonda. She checked her watch.

'Indian.'

'Indian Canyon Drive?'

Vonda groaned.

'I'll take that as a yes.'

The road leading to Vonda and Stuart's house connected to a frontage road and Grace picked up speed, Sarah tailing them as they came up behind a school bus stopped at a light. Grace took off her seat belt, reached into the backseat, and opened the velvet bag.

'What?'

'Checking something.'

She clambered back into the driver's seat and put on the seat belt as the light changed. She turned right onto Indian Canyon.

'Vee, what happened after I left this morning? You've got five minutes, honey, before the next one hits.'

'Scared. He's okay?'

'I know it,' Grace lied. 'He's a healthy, beautiful little boy.' She wet her lip. 'Can you tell me about this morning?'

Grace glanced at her, saw her mustering energy for one brave torrent of words. Vonda screwed up her face, concentrated, and in a rush they came.

'They didn't find anything. No soybean rust. I can't believe Daddy thought I had something. I'm organic. He knows that. At least I thought he did. That stuff's as nasty as it can be. Did Dad honestly think I'd grow something to harm people? He doesn't know me at all.'

She collapsed back against the seat, gasping for breath.

Grace smoothed a hand on Vonda's shoulder, careful not to press too hard. Pregnant women were sensitive to touch and smells. Vonda squeezed her eyes closed and rocked her neck so that her head was against the seat.

'Vee? About what Andrea said.' Grace kept her eyes on the road. 'Are you worried about that?'

Up ahead traffic was slowing to a standstill and Grace felt her stomach knot. This was not a good time to be stalled in traffic, caught in a protest.

235

'A knife?' Vonda panted, her mouth open. Her tongue looked gray.

'You mean, in the bag? No. Gardening shears. She probably wanted clippings like she said. But the other part. Sharing your baby. Does that make you rethink things?'

Vonda raised a finger briefly and for an instant, Grace thought it must be a reflexive movement from her belly quaking. If Vonda was rethinking her friendship, maybe she was ready to tell what she knew. The finger curled, straightened.

Sweat pooled in tiny beads on her fingers, as if in a commercial for a fancy emollient. She squeezed her belly again and moaned.

'Vee, this is important. I need to know if they've planned anything that could hurt somebody.'

Vee twisted her head. Her face looked clammy and pale. 'How much longer?'

Her voice raised in timbre, the panting more pronounced, and her body bucked in on itself and a leg spasmed. Grace had been around enough women giving birth to know the signs.

'No worries,' she sang out. 'You're ramping up. Perfectly normal.'

Grace rolled down her window and squeezed onto the bike path, inching her way forward. A traffic cop approached, a whistle clamped in his teeth, the sound shrill. He was lean, probably ran Iron Mans before breakfast. She made herself relax. It was all good; he could fling Vonda over his shoulder and carry her there if he had to.

'Okay, lady, what in the — ' He thrust his head

in the car and immediately reared back, holding up his palm, whistle shrilling. He stopped Sarah's car behind them.

'Go, go.' He waved Grace through and slammed up a hand on Sarah's car. 'You. Stop.'

*   *   *

Desert Regional Medical Center was a complex of buildings tucked off Indian Canyon Drive, surrounded by date palms and low-impact succulents. A tiled roof decorated in yellows and blues adorned one of the front buildings.

Grace drove to the emergency entrance and parked haphazardly, flinging open her door and racing into the building. The sliding glass doors opened onto a waiting room, green walls, wailing children, gray-faced people in pain, watching television.

'Emergency outside,' Grace shouted. 'I need doctors. She's giving birth.'

Vonda wasn't, not yet, and Grace knew it, but it certainly helped move things along, and by the time she'd yanked open the passenger door, two EMTs were already rolling a wheelchair down the ramp toward Vonda's writhing body.

Grace found the seat belt and unlooped it. It was like freeing a jumbo balloon from its mooring.

'Grace.' Vonda's voice was feeble.

'Here's your bag, honey.'

'Get Stu. His cell phone doesn't work at Windlift. It's a dead area. You'll have to go get him.'

'I can't go right away, Vonda.'

Vonda reached up and convulsively grabbed Grace's hand. 'Hurry.'

Grace hated this. 'I can't drive to Indio right now and get him. I've got someplace I have to be.' She hesitated. 'I could call your dad.'

'No!' Vonda's fingers clutched at her. Her face looked damp, gray. 'Promise me. Promise me you won't tell my dad.'

'That's a terrible promise, Vonda. Trade.'

'No!' Her voice was hoarse. 'No trade.'

Grace thought about the tangled trouble between Vonda and her dad. Uncle Pete's impulse to guard and protect wasn't surrounding his own daughter with peace; it was driving her away, running head down out of the gale of his wrath and the storms of his emotions, looking for sanctuary anywhere that did not bear his name.

Sending a team over to her greenhouse to check for soybean rust must have sealed the deal, from Vonda's perspective, and no matter what happened next between them, it was a country of arid ground and bad winds and Grace had no place there. It struck her as curious that Vonda would have given over her life to nurturing the soil, bestowing the very gifts she had never received in abundance from her father: light and air and healing rain.

'I won't tell your folks you're in labor. But you have to tell me what you know.'

Vonda searched her eyes. She sagged and licked her lip. 'They were playing some game. A hunting game.'

'Who, Vonda? Who are you talking about?'

'Friends.'

'Your friends are playing a hunting game. What kind?'

The EMTs counted to three and hoisted Vonda into the wheelchair and she cried out in pain. They made preoccupied shushing noises as they closed shoulder ranks and pressed Grace out of reach, pushing the wheelchair toward the doors that opened.

Grace ran ahead so she was facing Vonda for a split second. Her cousin's face was blind with pain.

'What were they hunting, Vonda?'

She clutched Grace's shirt and Grace leaned down, put her ear close. She whispered something.

'I can't. I don't . . . '

Vonda was racked by a pain in earnest and the medics pushed Grace aside and barreled through the door.

At the last second, Grace stopped them. 'Two women, Vonda will give you names. Keep them away from her. They're paparazzi, trying to get birth photos.'

27

Birth photos? It was the only thing that had come into her mind. The EMTs had nodded, as if they were always whacking paparazzi out of the way during deliveries in Palm Springs. Grace had climbed back into her car and waited for her heart to slow.

What Vonda had whispered in her ear had chilled her, but she had work to do and time was going fast.

There was no place to park on Palm Drive. She sprinted three blocks, certain she was too late. The lobby smelled like popcorn and butter cookies and the same usher smiled and pointed toward the women's room as she raced past him toward the auditorium.

In the audience, five frail seniors were standing and facing the stage, their posture stooped. They stood at attention, taking the salute, each a branch of military.

After that in a great heaving rush, everybody who'd served in any branch was invited to stand, and did. Lurching to their feet they trembled, blinking in the white light, as applause roared over them like a wave. Grace clapped and thought of her dad.

He'd served in Vietnam with the marines. Never talked about it, at least not to her, and it seemed like one more thing she had lost. She would have been the hoarder of the beats of his life; he would have lived forever through her. As it was, the memories she had of her father were separate and hard and distinct as glass beads on a bracelet. Beads for a small wrist, memories that were spaced apart, memories that could shatter if not treated carefully.

She joined in singing 'The Star-Spangled Banner.' Guns popped; fake snow fell; the show was over. She stepped into the lobby and waited.

The Follies women made walking look easy.

Patrons tottered up the aisles. The clang of walkers mixed with the scraping of wheelchairs. The aisles jammed.

A Follies man with thick yellow-white sideburns bounced into the lobby from a side door, took one look at Grace and grinned.

'So what do you think?'

'I think you're amazing,' she said honestly.

'Oh, you can come home with me.'

'Thanks. I'll remember that. Where does Jewel usually stand?'

He pointed to a door closest to the plaza and turned to greet the first woman out the door.

Grace positioned herself and waited. Jewel glided across the floor, six inches taller than the stooped audience members thronging around her. She shook hands with a row of elderly women and one older man whose wife finally nudged him along. Jewel turned to Grace. Her eyes were hazel brown and up this close, her cleavage was wrinkled and deep. She extended her hand.

Grace shook it. 'Stunning. A two-and-a-half-hour show, too, and eight times a week.'

'Thank you.' Jewel said it with warmth, already turning to the next person in line.

Grace tightened her grip. 'Actually, I'm with the FBI. I need to talk to you about Professor Bartholomew.'

Jewel's hand flexed convulsively but her smile was glossy, intact. 'You're holding up the line.'

'I'll be here as long as it takes.'

Jewel glanced at the next person in line, a stout short woman wearing good walking shoes and sparkly glasses. 'Be right there.'

She turned back to Grace.

'Give me five minutes.'

★ ★ ★

Grace followed Jewel down a lit staircase directly under the stage, past men in hard hats shifting a set of metal ladders against a tangle of pipes. A woman in sweats sailed by with a rack of sequined purple jackets. They squeezed by a teenager in black carrying a laundry basket piled with dirty leotards.

The door to the men's dressing room stood ajar and Grace stole a glance. A dancer had stripped out of his satin shirt, his chest hair a curly mat of white.

Jewel kept walking, shoes rapping smartly on the low-impact carpet. From the rear, her sequined blue skirt swished, revealing panels of red and white glitter, the skirt barely covering her rump.

She opened a door. A mirror stretched the length of the room. Opened vats of makeup and

242

foundation and tubes of lipstick spilled across the counter. Eyes stared vacantly down at Grace. She jumped back, startled, her heart banging.

They were Styrofoam heads, eerie silhouettes of smiling, invisible women wearing wigs: silvery bouffant, shoulder-length Cleopatra black, shiny pink. Jewel took off her blue military hat and put it on the shelf above her work space and peeled off the blue wig and put it on a wig frame.

Her natural hair was a soft brown, pressed into flat curls by the wig. Jewel sat in a chair and crossed her legs, facing Grace.

'Talk. You have three minutes, tops, before everybody comes piling in.' She bent her head and coughed into a hand. 'Sorry. My chest.'

'You were dating Bartholomew before he died.'

Jewel sighed. She turned the chair and faced the mirror. A vat of cold cream stood open next to a box of tissues and she scooped some cold cream onto a tissue and carefully took off her lipstick.

Grace watched her in the mirror. There was nothing calculated about her delay in answering, only weariness. She tossed the tissue in a trash can and turned again.

'You saw the end of the show, right?'

Grace nodded.

'That's a big deal. For all of us. We honor these incredibly — beautiful — old men — most of them men, sometimes a woman, who stand and accept our thanks for having served in the military, some back as far as World War Two.'

Her hazel eyes filled with tears.

'Let me take off my eyelashes before I screw them up.'

She bent and carefully peeled off the first one and put it in a box. It looked like a feathery spider. Something nice and big. A tarantula, maybe. She peeled off the second one. Her eyes were suddenly smaller.

'I first noticed him in the audience opening night, a couple of weeks ago. And then I realized, he was showing up at least three or four times a week. He always tried to sit close enough so we'd make eye contact. He never seemed to take his eyes off of me.'

'Creepy?'

'Not — particularly. I'm a performer. I wouldn't be onstage if I wasn't okay with that. But there was an intensity about it that at times was unsettling. Especially because, well, this is going to sound odd — but every time when he met me later, it was as if he was introducing himself for the first time.'

Heat shot up Grace's spine. Her face felt warm. 'He didn't recognize you.'

Jewel shook her head. 'Finally I asked Nate about him. Nate's always followed his own drummer. I never understood his fascination with — '

It came late. A delayed shock, a second one. Grace lived in San Diego; she was used to aftershocks. These were coming fast, rolling breakthroughs, small moments where the pieces fit.

'Wait a minute. Did you say Nate?'

Jewel nodded, puzzled.

'Nate who?'

A cautiousness crept into Jewel's eyes. 'Is he under investigation?'

'What's his last name?'

'He hasn't done anything, has he?' She gripped her fingers together so hard that Grace saw the knuckles turn white.

'You tell me.'

Jewel twisted her hands in her lap. 'Oh, God. His last name's Malosky. I went back to using my maiden name after the divorce.' She took deep breaths, wincing, as if inhaling ground glass.

A clatter of footsteps pounded down the metal staircase.

'I don't want to have to do this someplace else,' Grace said gently. 'Let's push through it and get it done. Am I the first person to talk to you about Bartholomew's murder?'

Jewel nodded. The door next to the women's dressing room opened and the booming voices of the men carried through the wall. Somebody guffawed. Jewel glanced in the direction of the voices. She shifted in her chair.

'Nate Malosky. Your son. Bartholomew's assistant. You were saying you never understood his fascination with . . . '

Jewel raked a hand through her hair and absently fluffed it.

'His fascination with alternate history — that whole 'everything that's ever gone wrong in history you can blame on old white guys.' To me, it seems just as racist a belief as the other kind, but not to Nate. Call me old-fashioned, but that's all they teach at university now. It would just be great if there was a balance.'

They heard female voices and a clatter of heels crossing the stage above them and Jewel talked faster. 'Then Nate fell in love with Andrea and she seemed to politicize him even more.'

'Did he help her with her business? Square Pegs?'

'Nate? Sure. *I* even help them with the business. It's like working at Nordies. I don't think I could work at that department store and ever bring a paycheck home. I saw something this last week at Square Pegs, loved it, would have bought two or three, but Nate jumped all over me and yelled, just for unwrapping it.'

'What was that?'

'*What* isn't important. Okay, they were drums. Goat-hide African drums. Very cool. He was trying to save me money.' Her voice was protective, the mother and her cub. 'I love this job, but I can't do it forever. I need to be saving for my old age.' She half smiled and then she took a shallow breath again and winced.

'You okay?'

Jewel glanced back at the door. People were in the hallway now, talking, coming closer.

'Getting back to his not recognizing you. He'd come, watch the show, meet you, and it always felt like he was meeting you for the first time.'

'When I realized who he was, I thought it was my chance at understanding my son, but Bartholomew's politics made me angry and sad. Everything about the military he hated — everything those guys did to serve, and all I could see in front of me were those men, standing at the end, small and frail and proud. I went for coffee a couple of times with him, that's about it. Some people give off this — odd energy — and Ted Bartholomew was one of them.'

'Odd. How so?'

Jewel glanced at the door again, leaned in, her voice almost a whisper. 'He thought of himself as this mild-mannered professor, intellectual, but not an activist. In his self-talk, I think that's what he was saying.'

'Self-talk.'

'Yeah, you know how we have this constant stream of stuff inside, this emotional ticker tape telling us who we are. Whether or not it's true. I think he saw himself as this thoughtful, articulate — I Googled him and all this stuff came up. Protests, arrests. And then there was that other part. Finally I asked Nate and he told me what the deal was.'

Laughter right outside the door now, and two women talking. Grace could picture a hand on the knob, a body turned, finishing up a sentence in the hallway and then twisting the knob, plowing in.

'The deal.'

'Professor Bartholomew had a face recognition problem. He was good with people he'd known a long time, but even with Nate, sometimes he'd forget. Nate said he had a cheat sheet in his desk. Green dots next to faces of friendly people; red slashes on people he had to be careful around; everybody named.'

'Did anybody else know?'

'I don't think so. He would have died if he'd thought I knew.'

She realized what she'd said and blinked.

'It's okay. I know what you meant.'

'Nate says Professor Bartholomew — Ted — was embarrassed about it. Nate found out by accident. The sheet was on his desk at work; little photos all in a row, like a high school yearbook or something, and Ted studying it like it was an exam.'

'What happened to it?'

'The cheat sheet? When Ted died, the first thing Nate did, when he heard about it, was go and find that piece of paper. He told me it was the last act of kindness he could do for his friend. Protecting him.'

'Where will Nate be?'

'Why?'

'Not now, in a couple of hours.'

Jewel looked at her steadily. 'You won't hurt him.'

'I might be the only chance your son has of getting out of this alive.'

28

Grace drove to Indio as fast as she dared, her anxiety translating into anger that could have easily spilled into road rage, except that nobody challenged her. The sky had started to turn. It was after four and a faint wash of color stained the San Gorgonio Mountains. It would be dark soon.

She felt diminished and small. She didn't like feeling responsibility for her cousin, and yet she did. Her cousin's happy ending — her husband by her side as she delivered her perfect little boy — seemed to rest on Grace's shoulders and it was a burden she didn't ask for and didn't want.

She wasn't good at happy endings. Not for herself, not for anybody else. That made her think about Jewel. Everybody was connected to somebody they loved. Even Grace. And loving somebody carried profound risk for damage.

Grace pulled into the parking lot at Windlift and darted through the building. It was emptier than it had been the night before, less noise, less activity, but it didn't make it any easier to find Stuart. Some counters on the second level had been swept clean. The egg pods were gone, as if overnight, they'd hatched into exotic creatures and flown away.

A grinding noise spilled out of the hangar and she followed it. A crate twisted on a crane next to a boxcar. Grace circled the room, staying clear as two crewmen wrestled the crate into the open side of the boxcar. Stuart wasn't in the hangar.

Grace walked out past the boxcar onto the siding and spotted the owner of Windlift gesturing to a group of three men, their heads down, hangdog and respectful. She looked as angry as she had the night Grace had stood on the hill with Stuart, watching her and Johnstone secure a boxcar.

Grace waited as a westbound train rolled through the yard, blocking her view. The front of the locomotive flared out in a metal scoop; above it the snout was painted with a Union Pacific blue and white bird, wings spread. The train gusted past, revealing the small haggard group and the furious woman.

One of the men was Stuart. The closer Grace walked, the more she saw it wasn't a hangdog expression on his face, but utter exhaustion. He stood the way she'd seen some livestock stand, dozing upright, jerking awake in a trembling instant.

'L.A. to Buckeye, that's an extra hundred seventy miles.' Judith Woodruff's voice was raspy and raw. 'You promised the uplink with the Kansas route at the Forty. I have a schedule to maintain. This is unacceptable.'

Stuart blinked his eyes and opened them wide, as if he could will himself to stay awake. Judith hadn't seen that, but she would soon. Right then she was busy tearing into a man sweating in a suit. He looked as if he'd spent his life indoors and wished he could get back to what he was most comfortable with, a good drink in the

250

afternoon, a secretary fielding interruptions, a schedule that worked.

'We had rail fatigue up by Windy Point,' the man said. 'The angle bar gave way. We're working on it.' He glanced up and locked eyes with Grace and she saw a spark of hope flare, as if he were praying for imminent rescue. Either that, or death.

Judith narrowed her eyes and shot Grace a look. 'What?' she barked.

Grace touched Stuart's arm and he flinched awake, focused on her face. 'Grace.'

'Great news, Stu. You're going to be a daddy.'

His eyes snapped wide. He was suddenly, buoyantly awake. 'She's in labor?'

'Sarah and Andrea know about it.' There was warning in her voice. 'They might try to get into the birthing room.'

'Not on my watch.'

'Indian Canyon's jammed. Overshoot it on Palm Canyon Drive and double back.'

He nodded. 'Oh, my God. I'm going to have a son.'

'Wait.' Judith spun out of the group and yanked on his arm.

'She's in labor, Jude. That was the deal.' Stuart shook her off and loped toward the Windlift parking lot. He called back over his shoulder, 'I'll write you, where to send the last check.'

Judith Woodruff whirled on Grace. 'Great. Thanks. Another thing gone to hell.'

'The QA's all done, what are you talking about?' It was the man in the suit again. Judith had pushed too far. 'The man's wife is in *labor*,

251

Jude. And his job is *done*. You know it, and I know it.'

Grace kept quiet. The truth was, Vonda was probably four hours away from delivery, but she figured Stuart deserved the chance to find that out the old-fashioned way, pacing the floor with his wife.

Judith cracked the brim of her cap down over her eyes, grabbed Grace's elbow, and guided her a few steps away. The light from the switching signal flashed across Judith's face. It was a strong, lean face. Grace thought it had probably been beautiful in makeup accenting the high cheekbones and sculpted jaw. Now there was the beginning of a good menopausal mustache bristling.

Judith's voice was low and angry.

'Look. I have a small company here. Top-rated. My aim is to create an eco-friendly environment. Sending these wind turbines out is the biggest contract I've put together, and I'm behind. Over a hundred windmills total. Get that? I'm a little guy trying to make it in a very competitive world. Do you have any idea what it's been like around here? With police roadblocks during protests, I can't get half my workers in to do their jobs.'

Perfect opening and she grabbed it. 'Tony Conroy.' Grace pictured Sarah's husband during the brief moment she'd met him, the way his boots came within inches of her face. The way he'd made her flinch. The way he'd smiled.

'What about him?'

'He here Wednesday night, around seven-thirty, eight?'

'You mean when the murder was happening in that soy field. I already gave the police a list. Who are you again?'

Grace held out the FBI ID tag, still attached to her shirt collar.

'Yeah, Tony was here. Had a bunch of guys call in sick. There's a nasty flu bug going around, as if I need anything else. Look, Tony's a good kid.'

'Just had that little rough patch when he threw his first wife out of a moving vehicle and ran her over.'

Judith cracked her knuckles. A train whistle sounded.

'We're done. I have to figure out a way to get Kansas where it needs to go.'

29

It took an hour driving to get to Riverside University. Traffic slowed on the 10 around Palm Springs, but she made up the time as she approached Beaumont and the 60 turnoff. The moon glowed, a dagger stabbing downward toward a hillside clicking with wind turbines. The sky was starless, silky, and black.

She passed a row of fast-food restaurants and realized it had been a long time since she'd eaten. She could wait. The idea of another fast-food meal turned her stomach.

She knew from the map that the school was near UC Riverside and she'd visited the UC school before on a case. But Riverside U was a private school; a professor had just been murdered; parents were spooked. She wondered what she'd find.

She got a map at the security kiosk and directions. Two stone lions, backlit so that their ruffs stood like ermine collars, guarded the entrance. A boulevard led into the school, both sides of the road landscaped with expensive, full-growth palms. Centered at the far end of the boulevard, a pointed clock tower constructed of pale rose marble stood erect between two low sculpted buildings. It looked like a Viagra commercial.

The campus was bright with lights, but the students walking kept their heads down and hurried along the paths, conferring worriedly with each other, darting quick looks at the road and traffic, startled and stepping back to avoid the occasional student on a bike or long board. Everybody looked weary and upset.

Grace turned at a side street that wound through the campus and drove past a row of brick buildings. A girl stood in a dorm window, brushing her hair. Grace wondered if she realized she could be seen from the road.

She found the band shack at the back of a glittering gym, parked illegally at the curb, and got out. She heard a brief burst of a trumpet, and as she got closer, laughter. The door to the shack was unlocked.

Inside was a kid's clubhouse. A silk-screen print covered most of a wall — Che Guevara: soulful eyes, wiry beard, wearing a beanie.

The room was crowded with toys: a foosball machine, a pool table, ping pong — the paddles worn. The net on the table sagged. She didn't see any balls. Beanbag chairs lay crumpled against the walls. A television set with the cord unplugged sat on its side.

The noise was coming from around the corner and she heard Nate's hypnotic voice over the trumpet.

'Me myself? I'm voting Republican next time.'

Laughter and a celebratory toot on the trumpet.

'I mean it. We teach this stuff, year after year, none of it changes, none of it means a damn, except a good man gets snuffed.'

A short burst of Taps on the trumpet; no laughter this time.

'Come on, Nate.' It was a soft female voice.

'T.A. Nate to you.'

Grace couldn't tell if Nate was serious about wanting to be called a teaching assistant, or just trying to bring the mood up after he had so successfully dampened it.

'Tits and Ass Nate?' A different female voice, slightly mocking.

A scatter of laughter; uneasy this time. The combination of death and sex had cast a pall.

'Wait, did you hear the door open?'

A patter of footsteps. Grace came face to face with a young woman wearing tights and a smock, her hair tufted in blue and white streaks. She looked at Grace doubtfully, and for a moment, Grace saw herself through the girl's smoky kohl-rimmed eyes.

'Are you lost?'

Grace didn't answer. She walked around the corner. Nate sat on a desk in a tiny room stacked with band equipment. He was wearing jeans and a soft striped shirt, swinging his feet, his hands clasped loosely between his legs. In front of him crouched a group of kids taking notes, mendicants at the feet of the oracle.

He'd managed to control his cowlick. He made sleepy eye contact with her and jumped off the desk. 'Okay, kids, find current examples of how the dominant culture reinforces *knowing one's place*, what steps you'd take to change things and — this is the most important part — *how those steps would change the culture from the bones up*. Everybody out, see you next week.'

Six students filed past, stealing quick glances at her and hurrying past. She didn't recognize anybody. Nate waited until they heard the door in the other room close and the last voices die away.

'You don't look surprised to see me.'

'Bad pennies, foot fungus, and Vonda's cousin, yeah, I thought you'd keep showing up. What can I do you for?'

He picked up a small spiral notebook and tucked it into his jeans pocket.

'I talked to your mom.'

He frowned. 'Leave my mom out of this.'

'She told me how much you wanted Bartholomew's job. How you would have done anything to get it.'

It stopped him cold and he half laughed, as if he couldn't believe what he'd heard. The stamp of hair under his lower lip jumped as he sneered. 'You are so full of shit.'

He walked out the door and flipped the light off behind him. Grace followed him into the bigger room.

'How long have you been carrying the load for him? A year? Longer? I bet in his office, he didn't even have a computer, did he? So who wrote up the lesson plans for the classes, who contacted kids if a schedule changed? And you're telling me you weren't sick of this guy?'

Nate darted his tongue between the gap in his front teeth and pressed, as if he were trying to pry his teeth apart. 'I didn't kill him.'

'Then who did?'

'How the fuck should I know?'

He yanked open the door. A cold wind gusted into the room.

'Security's going to be by if we're not out of here.'

'What's that class you were teaching?'

'A salon,' he spat. 'Not a class.'

She stepped outside and turned back to look at him.

Venom spewed from every pore.

'If you didn't kill him, who did?'

'Some fucking cop, that's who. Bartholomew's been on every hit list for years.'

He snapped off the light, stepped outside, and slammed the door shut behind them.

★ ★ ★

Grace was buzzed into the jail by the same corrections officer from the day before. The CO had gelled her hair and it lay flat against her scalp instead of drifting in a fuzzy nimbus around her face, but her cheeks were still pink, her face unpainted.

'SA Descanso and Detective Zsloski say to send you right back. Follow me.'

She led Grace to the booking area lined with a bank of video monitors, and an IN CUSTODY board with names in greasepaint. Past a blue wire locked door, two police officers flanked a prisoner duck-walking in chains down a corridor to another door. On the monitor, Grace saw that the door led to a parking garage where a police van idled, waiting to take the prisoner on the next leg of his little journey through life.

258

The not-so-pleasant part.

'That's where they go after they've been bound over for court,' the CO said, watching Grace watching the monitor.

And then three things happened almost simultaneously, information crowding in that changed everything.

A name she'd scanned on the IN CUSTODY board filtered into her consciousness. It was a name she knew well.

At first there was a jolt of surprise, followed by a surge of relief; it was a joke, had to be; then acid slammed up her throat as her gaze dropped from the monitors to the blue cage right outside the jailers' booking room.

It was Jeanne, hunched over her knees in the holding cell.

Grace must have cried out because Jeanne turned. It looked like she'd dressed in a hurry and Grace wondered if her uncle and his team had gotten her out of bed. A vein under her left eye bulged like a small purple worm. Her eyes were wide, dazed. She focused on Grace as if she were a drowning woman grabbing hold of the last floating thing in an ocean of dark. She was wearing a lacy brown bra under a yellow tank top, and a strap angled across her rose tattoo, as if it were crossing it out, a classic *no!* sign.

'What is she doing here?'

'She's wanted for questioning.'

'Are you nuts? Where's Mike? Where's Zsloski?'

She didn't wait for an answer. She yanked open the door leading to the hall that held the

259

cage. Jeanne limped over and dug her fingers into the wire that separated them.

Grace leaned in, her voice urgent. 'What in the hell is going on?'

'There was a dog hair on Bartholomew's body, Grace.'

'I heard. The coroner told me.'

'It's Helix's. It's your dog's.'

'What are you talking about?' The words didn't make sense.

Jeanne repeated them, more slowly, her eyes wide and desperate.

'Bartholomew's body. The coroner found a dog hair.'

'Right, he told me.'

'It's from Helix, Grace. A piece of his hair on Bartholomew's body. I didn't do it, Grace. You have to believe me.'

Her stomach roiled as if she were trying to stand on a tilting ship.

'Where is Helix?' Grace imagined her dog in the back of the cruiser car, tail thumping at the approach of any stranger.

'I called that vet place on Voltaire you use sometimes to board him. He's not here.' Jeanne looked at her. 'You're not getting any of this, are you?'

Grace shook her head. Her legs felt rubbery and she grabbed the cell wall that separated them and held on.

From the area next to the holding cell, she could see back into the jailers' nerve center. The door opened and her uncle walked in.

He saw her first in the monitor, dropped his gaze, and wordlessly opened the second door.

'Follow me.'

'I'm not going anywhere with you.'

'If you want to see her again, follow me.'

'I'll be back, okay? You hang on, Jeanne.'

Pete held the door open for her and they stepped into the corridor. She was close enough now to smell soap and aftershave and the pressed smell of a clean shirt.

He walked her past a bullpen that looked out on the main police lobby. He opened the door to a conference room. Grace followed. Jeanne had been picked up in San Diego. It didn't make sense.

Her uncle motioned to a chair and sat. 'This is a room that can record video and audio, but it's not recording now. Thought you'd want to know that.'

Grace stared at him in stony silence.

'She's wanted for questioning in a variety of terrorist activities.'

'Jeanne Bigelow. My AA sponsor. A terrorist. This is it. I was giving you this one little window — '

'Grace — '

'No, I don't even want to hear it. You set me up. Wanting me to investigate your daughter, my cousin, make sure she was clean. You just didn't want me anywhere near what you were doing to Jeanne.'

'How much do you know about your sponsor?'

Grace didn't respond.

Jeanne had been everything her real mother, Lottie, was not. Lottie was a drive-by parent, and the weapons — words lobbed like grenades, an unshakeable narcissism that put her at the center of every story, an unerring ability to go right for the pain and probe it — were perfected over a lifetime. It annoyed Grace no end that everybody overlooked Lottie's defects and was half in love with her, finding her flamboyancy by turns touching and hilarious, mesmerized by the swing of her tasseled boots and the twitch of her hot pants.

When Grace had gotten pregnant, the first thing she realized was how little she knew. She'd been lost, afraid, alone, a wandering young parent, terrified at making mistakes, without a guide. Later still, a drunk in shadows, with shadows. Holding a child of light. And Jeanne had stepped in and saved her life.

Grace knew all about saving her own life. But she'd made changes first for Katie, one small painful step at a time, long before she was able to muster what it took to do it for herself.

Jeanne was her safe place. The one person she could always count on to tell the truth.

If Jeanne were at the conference table instead of crouched in the holding cell next to the intake bay, she'd be busy telling Grace that Grace herself was the only one she could count on to be the truth teller.

That no truths were plain to see. That all truths were hard-won.

That forgiveness cost.

'Grace?'

Uncle Pete sighed, patted his shirt, and fished out a toothpick. 'She knew him. Did she tell you that?'

'Of course she knew him. She and Frank saw him the day he died. I told you that. Bartholomew attacked Frank at Gerry Maloof's. It's high-end. Great linen pants.'

'Jeanne knew Bartholomew years ago, Grace. They were lovers, and, we believe, co-conspirators in trying to blow up a dam in Northern California, a forest genetics lab, and two electric power stations.' He shoved the toothpick into his mouth and clamped down on it. 'Some other stuff, too.'

Grace closed her eyes. She patted for her face and missed.

'They had different names back then, Grace. She called herself Erica, Marie, Sonya. She didn't settle on Jeanne until she went on the run. We lost her for years, and then we got a lucky break on this one.'

It hurt to swallow. It was as if a metallic ball was lodged in the back of her throat.

'Jeanne saw Bartholomew the day he died at the men's clothing store. Easy transfer for genetic material. That's where Bartholomew picked up Helix's dog hair.'

'Except we found more of your dog's hair at Bartholomew's house.'

Grace blinked. 'Same deal. Bartholomew gets the dog-hair transfer in Gerry Maloof's over by the linen pants, and goes back to his house, sits down someplace, there it is.'

'Jeanne was there, herself, later that day. That's the way we think it went down. Knowing what they discussed would go a long way to clearing your friend, but so far, she's clammed up tight.'

'Wait a minute, you think she might have killed him?'

He was silent.

'That's not possible.'

Her uncle chewed the toothpick. He tipped the wastebasket next to a supply closet with his toe and spit the toothpick in.

'We monitor the line at the agency after hours, especially now, so even if nobody's available to pick up, we get to them pretty fast. We got a call in for you, last few minutes, from somebody named Jewel. She said you'd know where to find her. She sounded — how do I put this — angry and distraught.'

Grace grew silent. Jewel would be gone now, but tomorrow, same time, she'd be carefully navigating the glittering staircase at the Follies.

'I've got her home number, if you need it. The Follies are closed Mondays.'

He looked at her carefully. 'Jewel's not that common a name, Grace, especially Jewels who have sons named Nate who work as teaching assistants with dead professors. We ran a check on the cell phone number and the connection popped right up.'

'I visited Nate. His mother probably wasn't too happy.'

'What did you learn?'

A police detective stuck his head into the room. 'Agent Descanso. Sorry. Didn't realize you were here.'

'Need anything?'

'Cartridge and patience. Printer blew.' He came into the room, a big guy in navy with a

Glock at his side, his movements easy. The closet opened onto shelves of boxes: yellow tablets, pens, bottles of water.

'Can I have some water?'

She was asking her uncle, but the detective snagged one out of a box and passed it back to her.

'Thanks.'

She cracked the cap off and drank, using the familiar solidity of the plastic bottle to anchor her in the present moment. They waited as the detective pawed through a box, found what he needed, closed the supply door and left.

'Grace, two people have died badly and I promise you we'll find out who did it, and if it turns out Jeanne's involved, then God help you if you're withholding information.'

'Nate thinks Bartholomew was iced by an agent or a cop.'

Pete laughed at that. It was the first time she'd heard him laugh in years. It wasn't pleasant.

She put the bottle down and worked on a piece of the label, ripping it off. 'I called you, Uncle Pete — Detective Zsloski, too — because I do have something. Something big. Couple of things, actually.'

The door cracked open and Mike Zsloski came in. He'd changed out of his shorts into long brown pants. He pulled a chair next to Pete, squaring off, his movements tentative, as if under the pants, he'd sunburned his knees.

They waited, looking at her. She felt tired. She'd promised Vonda she wouldn't tell her father she was in labor. But Grace never promised not to talk about what Vonda had traded to extract that promise.

'I got something from Vonda.'

Her uncle's index finger on his left hand twitched; otherwise, he looked the same, his legs stretched under the table, his hands relaxed, folded on his stomach.

'She said friends of hers were getting together, doing some target practice. With crossbows. She's not sure, but she thinks it may be one of them killed a transient. She heard bits — but nothing concrete. Wouldn't give me names.'

Pete's face grew still. He kept his eyes down, as if he were tracking some interior quarry, going deeper into the recesses of his own heart, hunting something elusive and shadowy, going so deep, no one could follow.

'She part of that?'

Grace shrugged. 'I don't see how. Physically, she wouldn't be able to shoot a crossbow, at this stage of her pregnancy. I don't think Stuart's involved. He's got rheumatoid arthritis in his fingers. Pulling a crossbow would be excruciating. He's wildly upset at Vonda for putting their family at risk, protesting. He loathes her friends. It's mutual. They loathe him back.'

Pete was silent. He looked as if his face were collapsing inward.

'I met these three old guys — myself, I call them the Breakfast Boys — who had breakfast with Bartholomew three times a week for the last couple of years, ever since his wife died.'

She flipped through her notebook and found the sheet with their names and phone numbers.

266

Zsloski reached across the table and copied the information.

'He was dating a waitress named Janey and dumped her when he got fascinated with Nate's mother, Jewel. Came to the Follies two or three times a week, just to see her.'

Zsloski raised his shaggy eyebrows. 'Mutual?'

Grace shook her head. 'She only tolerated him because she thought it might be a way in to figuring out her son.' She leaned in.

'Jewel said that Bartholomew had a face recognition problem that he'd worked hard to keep hidden. That's why he had the room with the pictures and names. He studied the incoming class, every year, to try and get a handle on it. She said Nate ran in on him once at school, poring over a chart of faces and names.'

'Where's the chart now?' Zsloski shifted his bulk and rubbed the back of his knee.

'She said Nate got rid of it when Bartholomew was murdered. This face thing. I studied that some in med school. Prosopagnosia. One of the four hundred or so neurological conditions we had to identify on an exam one week.'

She looked up to see if they wanted her to go on. They didn't stop her.

'Like everything, it's on a scale of intensity. It can start with a brain injury, or be present from birth and something a person gradually becomes aware of. Usually there's a certain amount of shame attached. Nobody wants to talk to somebody at a party for an hour, and a week later, not recognize that person when they stop on the street.'

'That's what happens?' Mike Zsloski's face drooped, like it had been out in the sun too long and melted.

'It can. The point here is, it widens the suspect pool. Nate could even be good for it. When I saw him, he was acting like a prisoner who'd finally earned yard time. My guess is that Nate had carried Bartholomew for years, doing his scut work. The other thing is, if Bartholomew had a photo of Frank in his wallet, it could be that's because his face just kept getting 'unstuck' from Bartholomew's memory, and he had to carry a visual reminder to jog it. Also, if Frank showed up in odd places . . . '

Her uncle leaned in, suddenly animated. 'Like at Riverside U, for example.'

She nodded. 'He might remember that link if he saw him around campus a lot, especially if Frank ever audited any of his classes, but he'd be completely clueless about remembering Frank's connection to agriculture, outside of that. He'd disconnect those two parts. And as far as a name — forget about it.'

'Then why did he remember yours?' Not melted, Zsloski's face, more like the color of liver.

'That article in the *Desert Sun*. He had it on his wall. He'd remember names in writing. He wasn't trying to pick me out of a crowd or a lineup of a bunch of thirty-something Portuguese-looking women. Just the name.'

She took another drink.

'So that means he called me into the case because of the work I do. Something at the lecture is a tie-in to solving this case, if we can figure it out.'

Her uncle crossed his arms, tapped the table with his fingers. They were a builder's hands, broad, agile.

'Jeanne told me she didn't kill anybody,' Grace said. 'That's all I know.'

Her uncle slid an evidence baggie out of his shirt pocket and held it out.

She took it.

Inside the baggie was an old Kodak print, the kind with scalloped edges.

She stared at it a long moment.

'You understand what that is, right?' His voice was more gentle than before, as if he were talking kindly to a child.

She shook her head.

He took back the baggie and told her.

30

Grace found a seat in the back at a conference table, poured a glass of water, and scanned the delegates sitting at tables, taking notes. Onstage, an African delegate from Somalia passionately argued that the war on hunger wouldn't be won by genetically modifying crops, but only by addressing the poverty behind it, and for that reason, everything the United States was sending abroad was categorically tainted.

An American delegate from Iowa sat onstage, pressing his hands under his legs as if that was the only way to stop from leaping up and wresting away the microphone.

Grace made her way along the wall toward a side exit where Frank was sitting. She clamped a hand on his shoulder and he jumped.

'I need to talk to you.'

★ ★ ★

'You heard.' His skin looked pink along the scalp and around the eyes and nostrils, as if the pigmentation had been spread a little too thin at the edges.

'I saw.'

'How's she doing?'

'As well as she can. What do you know?'

He shook his head. He looked like he was wearing the same shirt as the day before. He reminded Grace of a hurricane or tornado victim, numb, eyes blank.

'When Bartholomew was killed, I didn't even tell Jeanne it had happened in my field. I didn't want her to worry. She worries all the time about me.'

Frank Waggaman had a stack of newspapers on his desk. Grace wondered if he'd opened any of them. The top one was dated the day the conference started and had a photo of policemen in helmets with visors and nightsticks, beanbag ammunition slung over their shoulders. In the background, a handcuffed naked man was being escorted away from a crowd of protesters dressed as ears of corn.

'I sent her home, after that thing happened with Ted in the store. I realized it was selfish, my wanting her here with me. She promised she wouldn't come back until it was over.'

Frank plucked at a newspaper corner. He smoothed the page down next to a headline: BIOTECH INSISTS ITS GENES ARE GREEN. His nails looked dirty but Grace knew it was the way fingers looked over time in soil, as if they belonged there.

'Yesterday she came back to Palm Springs.'

'They must have dragged her back.'

Grace was silent. She was hoping that's the way it had happened, but she wasn't going to tell Frank that.

'Police come to your house after Bartholomew's murder?'

He nodded. 'I expected it after how public everything's been. I thought they were looking

271

for prints. Then they asked me if I had a dog. Helix had been there with Jeanne for a while, when you were in the Bahamas.'

His jaw worked. His teeth were blunt. He chewed an imaginary mouthful of something that didn't agree with him. He swallowed, winced, knuckled his diaphragm as if he were being cored by heartburn.

'You think I liked not being able to tell Jeanne that the police had stopped by? I was under orders, Grace, to comply.'

'Nice. You know German, too?'

'Yeah, I do, actually, and that's uncalled for.'

'How did this start with Bartholomew?'

'He protested the use of migrant workers tending the GM crops we were producing for the convention. Then it got really nasty. Letters to the editor, threats.'

'Did Bartholomew ever come after you for anything you were doing genetically?'

Frank refolded the newspapers. 'I don't know what you're talking about.'

'You did work at Riverside U, modifying soy that eventually ended up in the experimental plots. Whose lab were you in?'

'I don't see what difference — '

'What lab?'

'Dr Denise Bustamonte. I did the work there. She gave me space last summer to finish it, but I've been there off and on for a couple of years.'

'Bartholomew ever attack you there? Threaten you?'

Frank inhaled and the ring around his nose

272

grew pinched and white. 'Nothing. Not any-thing, really.'

Grace put down her pen. 'Okay, Frank, here's my problem. I don't have a handle on what's happening here, but Jeanne's been tagged, and that means I'm not stopping until I know the truth, and so far, the only truth is, you're not leveling with me.'

Frank gripped his hands, rocked. 'He followed me to the parking garage and yelled at me. A security guard had to talk to him.'

'Name.'

'What?'

'The name of the security guard.'

'I never filed a complaint. It would have been early last summer. It was just after I started work in the lab again.'

'Time of day?'

'What? Oh. Afternoon, I guess. No, maybe morning. No, night, it was night.' He smiled apologetically. 'We don't get natural light in the lab, everything blurs together.'

'And then what?'

Frank turned away from her as if it was hard looking at her and thinking up a lie at the same time. Katie always did that when she was making up a big one.

'Then the nice parking lot guy gave him a talking to and — no, maybe he didn't. Maybe I just wanted him to. Maybe I didn't stop at all.'

Grace stared. Frank shifted. 'Are we almost done?'

'I meant threat. What was the next threat.'

'Oh. A dead canon wren on my patio. Thought

273

maybe it had crashed into the window. Happens sometimes. I found the note next to this potted cactus near the back door. '*If you know what's good for you, stop.*''

'You can buy that threat on the Generic Threat Web site.'

'There's a Web site called Generic Threat?'

'I've heard that one a couple of times before, that's all. You keep the note?' Already knowing the answer.

He shook his head.

'What else you got?'

'A note stuck under my windshield in the parking garage. It had a picture of a dead sheep.'

'Moving up the food chain. You keep that one?' She couldn't keep the sarcasm out of her voice.

'Couple weeks ago, he killed my dog, Grace.'

That one got her attention.

'Muffy.' He looked close to tears. 'This big, overgrown galumph of a rottweiler. Nobody messes with her. Or did.'

'What happened?' In the still place inside where things coalesce, she already suspected, she already knew.

'He *shot* her. At least, that's what the vet said.'

'How do you know it was him?'

'Some nights, I'd go out with Muffy into the desert hills. I'd bring along the littlest flashlight so I wouldn't kill myself by falling into a crevice or off a cliff or something, but you'd have thought she'd died and went to doggie heaven.'

He heard what he'd said and his face darkened.

'What happened?'

'I took her off the leash and she ran after something. She'd always come back, she's a good dog that way, only this time . . . '

He shifted and she waited.

'I heard this bloodcurdling cry, and then I realized it was Muffy, *screaming*. I ran toward the sound and I saw, illuminated on the hillside — '

'Wait, there was moonlight?' Grace readjusted the image in her mind to include a big dog hit by an arrow in the silvery cliffs somewhere in the back country near Palm Springs.

Frank nodded. 'I saw an illuminated figure. Wearing what looked like goggles. With a bow and arrow set on his back. He turned and melted away and then I saw Muffy, crawling toward me, with this bleeding *hole* . . . '

He blinked and looked away.

'How do you know the shooter was Bartholomew?'

'I don't. But it was, I know it. Or part of his group.'

'His group.'

Frank twisted his fingers in his lap. 'I was delivering soil and seeds — all organic — to Vonda's greenhouse. I was early. Nobody was in the house, so I thought I'd try the greenhouse and unload stuff to save myself a second trip.'

'What happened?'

He sighed and massaged his jaw with his hand as if his teeth hurt.

'There was a meeting, Grace. A bunch of them in back. This woman started speaking. It was a voice I didn't recognize.'

So it wasn't Vonda. 'What was she saying?'

'First of all, she called herself RD.'

'Like R2-D2.'

'That's what I thought. Later I thought maybe I'd misheard. Maybe it was 'Artie.''

'What did she say?' She tried to hide her impatience.

Frank exhaled heavily, as if trying to expunge a memory. 'She said everything was planned out, good to go. They were going to be moving the item in on time. And that one more shipment was coming in and she expected all of them to do their part. That's what she said. And she thanked them for *practicing*.'

Grace straightened. 'You told the police this?'

'And the FBI.'

'Any idea what the shipment is or when it's coming in?'

Frank shook his head. 'It's like everybody knew, she was just confirming.'

'Anything else?'

'When Ted thanked her, he called her miss.'

'Miss.'

Frank nodded. 'Like he wasn't sure of her name, maybe.'

'What else?'

'It sounds crazy.' Frank Waggaman nibbled his lip.

'Throw it out there anyway.'

'I don't know. I had the feeling she was telling them . . . ' He stopped.

She waited.

'Telling them something was going to be

'. . . released . . . at the convention.'

Grace straightened. It was the same thing her uncle had said yesterday. So it must have come from whatever Frank Waggaman had overheard.

'And you told the FBI this.'

He nodded. 'Have you heard of the Terminator gene?'

'Isn't that the one that if it's planted, it dies after one crop, and so the farmers have to rebuy seed every year?'

'It's one of the core reasons lots of countries are protesting the United States' stance on GM crops. It sounds too much like a diabolical marketing tool used against the poor.'

He glanced around the room as if he feared they'd be heard over the noise in the ballroom.

'Okay, I'll just come out with it. I think they're here somewhere, in the Convention Center, and they've smuggled something that could disrupt agriculture worldwide.'

'Why would they do that?'

'Grace, what better way to stop science in its tracks than to come out with the ultimate killer and then blame it on the GM scientists? Nobody would suspect do-good granola bar activists. Oh, one more thing. They called Bartholomew *Mars*.'

'Like the candy bar.'

He looked at her, his eyes glowing in hollow sockets. 'Like the god of war.'

Grace was silent. She was thinking about the girl in the field. How black the blood looked, draining in a pool down her thin chest. 'This voice. This RD voice. Did it sound young, old?'

'Young. Definitely. All of them did.'

'Frank, when you hire these young kids to man the volunteer booths, do you check them out?'

He picked at the paper. Shredded the corner. The corn protesters disappeared in a pile of newsprint.

'It's been so busy here.'

'I take that as a big maybe.'

'Maybe's about right.' He looked up and blinked. 'Kids'll know other kids. They do that Facebook thing if there's a job. We pay by the hour. Not that much.'

'And they get clearance.'

'Of course they get clearance. At least I think they do.' He gnawed on his lip. 'Of course they would. Why, do you think . . . ?'

'Monday. Tomorrow night, can you think of anything that could be a target? Any*body* that could be a target?'

He shook his head.

'Anything else?'

'I don't know. I just . . . I just get this feeling. Like there's something here already. Something I've missed.'

She stood up.

'Not much to go on in the threat department, Frank, but thanks. I'll share your concerns with the brass.'

She walked to the door and stopped.

'One more thing. It pisses me off, it saddens me, Frank, that Jeanne pinned her hopes for a future on some guy who hasn't said one word on her behalf in the last five minutes. *She* was taken away. You weren't.'

Frank linked his hands and bowed his head. 'She never told me she had a past.'

'You don't?'

He raised his eyes. 'You can't imagine the *shock*, Grace. Jeanne isn't who she said she was.'

'You are?'

He clapped a fluttery finger to his mouth, as if trying to contain a secret. After a moment he removed it and said reluctantly, 'Wednesday, when we were in Gerry Maloof's getting those fine linen pants — '

'I've heard about the pants,' Grace said irritably. 'Move on to the threat part.'

'Maybe it's not but — '

'Try it.'

'Well. I spotted him before Jeanne did. He was pulling something out of his wallet, staring at it hard, then looking at me, back and forth. He didn't even see Jeanne at first and then he did.'

'What happened?'

'They stopped stock-still, rooted, frozen, shock on both their faces. I was going to do the introductions but it seemed pointless. Except . . . ' His voice trailed. 'She looked at him and a word slipped out. John.'

'Maybe it's his middle name.'

Frank shrugged. 'I asked her if she knew him. She turned pale, which is hard to do when you're already a redhead.'

He said it with tenderness. Grace didn't think it was the right time to remind him that Jeanne's natural hair color was brown, now gray.

'She turns pale. And?'

'That's it. That's all. Except.' He ducked his

head and Grace saw a blush rise along his stubbled jawline. 'She makes me happy when I'm with her.'

'An inflatable doll can do that, if it's positioned right.'

'She likes me. It's not easy for people to like me, I don't know why.'

Grace walked to the door and opened it.

'I try and try with these kids. To be a hero. A leader. I can lead. And they picked Bartholomew. They always picked Bartholomew.'

She looked at him. He was shaking his head, rocking over his knees.

He stopped and looked up. 'Why did they do that, Grace? Why did they pick him?'

31

Homicide Detective Mike Zsloski met her at the jail door and took her back to the booking area. On screens, different shots of the brown jail exterior and tan interior were visible, including the inside of every cell that held prisoners. Grace counted four men lounging on beds, heads against walls, eyes closed, and Jeanne.

Jeanne stared up at the camera and it distorted her face so that her eyes looked unnaturally spaced apart.

'I'm taking her back.' Mike slipped his Glock out of the holster at his belt and locked it into one of the safe boxes, pocketing the key.

The corrections officer with the gelled hair glanced up from the bank of monitors. She nodded and handed him a ring of keys. 'This one. Lock her in and bring it right back.'

She turned back to the monitors. A man with a swastika shaved into his scalp jerked his hand up in spastic gang signs to the camera.

Mike padded ahead of Grace through the labyrinth of cells.

'I didn't see her walking stick.'

'You know she can't have that in there.'

'If she had a pacemaker, would you take that away, too, so she wouldn't use it to start an electrical fire?'

'You're welcome, Grace, for bending the rules so you can get in there tonight instead of waiting

281

until ten tomorrow.'

'You can't think she's good for either one of them.'

Mike looked at her, his gaze steady. His hair looked permanently fried, as if it had been flash frozen, the ends frosted. 'You've got ten minutes.'

He unlocked the door to the cell and stepped aside. She stuck her head in and pulled it out.

'Wait. That camera in the cell that looks like a motion detector. There's sound on that, too, right?'

He relocked the cell door.

'As long as you're bending rules, can you stick her in the VISITOR room?'

'Tell me you're going home soon.'

★ ★ ★

Grace waited on the visitor side. What she said in there wouldn't be taped and recorded. Before long, Jeanne limped through the prisoner door and sat on a cement stool anchored to the floor. She picked up a phone and pressed her other hand to the glass.

Grace did the same. 'I see I get the good chair.' It was brown fabric, nothing special except it was on the side where the door unlocked.

'Good to know. Next time I'll take that side.'

They smiled at each other and put their hands down.

'You eating okay?'

'Not so hungry at the moment; thanks for asking.'

282

She looked drained. The orange jumpsuit leached color from her eyes. Her hair was very red, except for a fine growth of gray right at the hairline.

'This is going to sound weird, but I need to ask you how you came in.'

'I'm not following.'

'Did a Palm Springs police officer burst into your shop, or go to your house? Did you ride back in a wire cage?'

Jeanne shook her head and Grace's heart sank.

'No. A nice man called Detective — I don't know, it's a Polish last name — '

'Zsloski.'

Jeanne nodded.

Son of a bitch. 'He called and said what exactly?'

'Just asked if I'd come in, that's all. They wanted my hit on the fight Bartholomew started with my Frank in Gerry Maloof's. And I was happy to, because, well, the thing is, Frank had made me *promise* to stay far away from Palm Springs during the convention, but if I was there to help the police . . . '

Grace stared. 'So you just got in the car and came.'

'Well, I took Helix in to the doggie kennel, like I told you. And then I gassed up. And then I came.' She studied Grace's face.

Grace could see her reflected in the glass; it was like looking at two Jeannes, each with a dawning comprehension, eyes snapping open, both leaning forward in alarm toward the Plexiglas, mouth open so that Grace could

283

clearly see two sets of crowns on her lower left back molars.

'What did I do?' The two Jeannes gulped air and their lips quivered.

Grace tried to soften her face.

'No, don't be pulling that face on me, Grace, just tell me what in the hell I did.'

'If a person comes in willingly to talk to the police, the police don't have to Mirandize that person until they have — oh, pretty much what they need to lock in an arrest.'

'They Mirandized me.'

Grace nodded. 'Sometime after the part where they asked you about your commitment to save the environment and where you went to school, right?'

Jeanne blinked and leaned back on the stool and Grace realized that the reason the stool was anchored in cement, other than so that it wouldn't be thrown through the window to launch an escape, was so that stunned prisoners wouldn't inadvertently tip themselves backward upon hearing news exactly like this.

'Oh,' Jeanne said. She grabbed hold of the counter on her side to steady herself.

'Want to tell me about it?'

Jeanne looked away. 'I've been waiting for it, for that shoe to drop, most of my life. It got to the point I thought it never would, you know?'

Grace nodded. She remembered hearing about the Rancho Santa Fe woman living a double life who had been arrested for leaving a jail in Michigan twenty-five years earlier. She'd said the same thing.

'We were in school in Humboldt County. Redwood country. That's how it started. Saving the redwoods. Tree sitting, in the beginning. I wasn't up in the tree, I was the support person. Easier for a guy to pee in a jar, or just over the side, so we sent up Ted. We called him John back then. Little play on words, for what he had to brace himself to do over the edge of that tree. He was a pretty private guy.'

Grace stared.

'You had to be there.'

'He sent down trash . . . and the john.'

'Right. I sent up granola bars and books.'

'You and Ted were — '

'Tight. We started with protesting the war, then added in the environment. We lived in this commune in the woods. We were arrested and convicted of vagrancy, creating a public nuisance — bunch of stuff. They tried to pin attempted assault with a deadly weapon on us, but it didn't stick.'

Grace shifted the phone.

'What was that about?'

'Tree spiking. We were monkey-wrenching the trees so that if they got serious, trying to saw them down, they'd get hurt. Nobody got hurt, Grace.'

'They just as easily could have.'

'I was stupid. It was a nature preserve they were tearing down, going to put up condominiums. It seemed wrong then, still wrong now, but the way we did it, that was wrong, too. The rest of it — car bombings. House explosions. Businesses burned to the ground — whatever other shit they want to pin on me, I didn't do.'

'Co-conspiring to bomb a forest genetics lab, a dam in Northern California, and two power stations.'

Her face turned pale. 'Oh my God. No. I left before any of that. If Ted were still alive, he could vouch for me, although I don't know if they'd believe him.'

'I take it when you knew him, he didn't have a face recognition problem.'

Emotions darted over her face: loss, love, and that click that comes when the piece falls into place. 'So that's why he took my picture that day. I sort of thought . . . '

She looked young for an instant, and very vulnerable.

'He did it with everybody,' Grace said gently.

'It's okay. It was a long time ago.'

Grace nodded. 'Uncle Pete showed me a photo of the two of you. It was sent anonymously to the *Desert Sun*. They're running with it tomorrow.'

'I hope I have my clothes on.'

'You were linking arms, rocking, and yes. It's ripped. Looks like somebody else was in it.'

A shadow passed over Jeanne's face. 'Probably Tasha. She broke us up. She was the reason I left the commune. She saved me, actually, from the worst of the bad stuff that came down, so I should be thanking her. Tough to come home, though, after a hard day of tree hugging, and find your man on an ergonomically, environmentally sensitive futon boinking his brains out with another woman.'

286

Grace absorbed that.

'So you left.'

'Walked off a work-release detail. We were sleeping in jail at night, cleaning roads by day. I only had two months to go on a six-month sentence. Dumb dumb dumb.'

'What happened to Tasha?'

'No idea. One thing I remember from that period. We all knew how to shoot bows and arrows.'

Grace nodded as if it were something she'd already heard. Inside, a train roared, exploding through her mind, blowing pieces of shrapnel and waves of debris.

'The guys were into hunting game, although most of the time that meant we were vegetarians. Nobody's aim was worth a damn and the idea of bringing down Bambi was a little too intense.'

'Bartholomew know how to shoot?'

'Even I did. Haven't done it in years. But I was thinking, since that's how he was murdered, I don't know, maybe it was somebody from back then.'

'You mean, somebody besides you.' The instant she said it, she regretted it.

Jeanne swallowed. 'They had me flagged as an escapee from a work-release program; I don't know if it's like having a late library book or owing something to the IRS, if they just keep piling on the penalty, but in any event, I'm here now, and it will be what it is.'

She shifted the phone.

'Grace, what am I looking at?'

'You mean sentence-wise? Hard to say, Jeanne.

287

After you left, you never saw Bartholomew, until last Wednesday.'

Jeanne nodded. 'Right.'

'So he recognized you.'

She nodded. 'Maybe the way it works is, he recognizes faces from before the injury. Probably one of those bombs took that away. I think I heard through the grapevine he was hit once. He definitely knew who I was; it scared the hell out of him. Frank told me where Bartholomew lived — of course he didn't know what I was planning — and on my way out of town, I stopped by. I threatened him, told him unless he left the convention and Frank alone I was going to turn him in. He flipped it, said all he'd have to do was pick up the phone and I'd go down, too.'

'So you kept silent.'

'Grace, I'm about as imperfect as a sponsor can be. I've worked the steps, but I haven't lived them, not as deep as I should. It all came down to turning myself in, but I had to tell Frank first. I owed him that much. And telling him when he was under such stress at the convention — well, that just seemed wrong.'

'So you cut a deal with Bartholomew.'

'I cut a deal. Bartholomew and the Radical Damage bunch he ran with would stay out of Frank's face, I'd stay out of his. That was my plan. Then I'd turn myself in Tuesday. Him, too, although I hadn't told him that.'

It was the core of everything Grace had been wrestling with. The substance of her despair, the dirt and dust of her potential rebirth. 'All that stuff about honesty. Did you ever think about telling me?'

Jeanne's eyes locked on to hers. 'All the time, Grace. All the time.'

The jailer came through the door on Jeanne's side. 'Time's up.'

Grace stood. 'What's your real name?'

Jeanne hesitated. 'Jeanne,' she said finally. 'Spelled differently, but Jeanne.' She put down the phone and went with the jailer back through the door.

* * *

Grace took a hot shower, put on her favorite nightgown and a fresh pair of socks, and went to bed.

But sleep did not come easily.

Jeanne had saved Grace with the simple words *Honesty, Grace. That's it. Getting clean. Staying sober. Speaking truth.*

Grace had counted on Jeanne to be her moral compass.

Broken. No true north for her. Not anymore.

And how was Jeanne's withholding truth from Grace worse than what Grace had done to Katie?

Grace had lied for no better reason than it was convenient. Through the years, she'd stolen moments alone watching Mac on television, hording a secret as guilty as any Jeanne had, and far more corroding, because Grace had used the clay of her daughter to mold it.

All the predators come out at night, the ones

289

in the desert, the ones in her mind. Tethered on a short cord were the ones with fangs, guarding a dark house of self-loathing and pain.

She shifted in bed, punched the pillow, made a small sound in the dark.

She had to make this work, get to the bottom of it.

Save her friend.

Save herself.

Find her way home.

32

Monday

It was two in the morning when the hotel phone rang. She was still awake, staring at the ceiling, but it took a moment in the unfamiliar room to find the receiver.

'Hey.'

It was Mac.

'Is she okay?' She came straight out of bed, her heart hammering.

'Oh God, of course she is. I'm sorry. Grace, it's okay, it's okay. I shouldn't have called. It was a bad idea.'

'No, no.'

She fumbled for the light switch and found it and then remembered she'd pulled the blackout curtains open and left only the sheers so the sun would wake her up in the morning. She reached up and turned off the light. There was a slight moon and it streamed through the gauze. Exactly the way it had the first night they were together in Guatemala. 'You okay?'

There was a pause on his end and she feared they'd been disconnected. He exhaled. 'I find myself thinking, Grace. You did this funny thing with your toes, when we were together. Sort of — curling them into mine. Did you even know that?'

She swallowed.

'Grace?'

'I'm here.'

'She had an accident today — not big, don't worry, please don't. She was running and she tripped on the sidewalk at the pool and got this scrape on her knee. And she started to cry.' His voice was low. 'And the first word she said was your name. *Mommy.*'

Grace closed her eyes. She felt herself unraveling, sitting in the dark in a strange room, her knees up. She opened her eyes and studied the pattern of light coming through the curtain.

'Do you miss medicine?'

Mac was the only one who could ask that question; the only one entitled to an answer.

'I miss how easy things were.'

'Before the end.'

'Yes. Before that.'

'Do you want other kids?'

She considered it. 'Yes. You?'

'Katie could use a sister or brother.'

A tear spilled and she touched it with her finger. She felt, through the phone line, him slipping away and wasn't sure why, as if he'd turned a corner in his mind, as if he was rooting through a variety of boxes, opening one and examining the contents, tossing it and reaching for the next, the tempo stepping up, shaking some of them to see if they rattled. She could picture him on his end, standing hip deep in boxes, contents scattered.

'So this visitation thing. Is that the way we do it?'

'I can't do this now.'

A silence. 'I shouldn't have called.'

'Mac — '

'No, no, I shouldn't have called. I'm sorry I woke you up.'

'Wait.'

But he was gone.

★ ★ ★

The air conditioner hummed and the sound mingled with an insistent rapping on the door. Grace rolled onto her back and frowned at the ceiling, trying to remember where she was.

The rapping again. She sat up. The clock radio glowed on the bed stand closest to the bathroom wall, and she crawled over the wide expanse of the king-sized bed and focused.

Three-thirty.

'Grace.'

She got up, groped back the other way, bumped into the love seat, hopped on one foot, and cracked open the door.

Her uncle stood in an FBI flak jacket. He straightened when he saw her and snapped his phone shut. 'Ever hear of leaving your cell on? I've been trying to reach you for the last half hour.'

'Why don't you just call the house line, everybody else does.' She yawned.

He rolled his wrist and stared at his watch. 'You've got thirty seconds to throw something on, if you want to be there when it comes down.'

33

'See, the thing is, they have the infrared goggles, like us, so it's like staring with binoculars off a balcony and seeing some other guy with binoculars staring back.'

Her uncle kept his voice quiet. They were on their bellies in the sand behind a stand of spiky agave, looking down at the railroad tracks. It was the same slope she'd hiked up with Stuart. Against the dark soil gleamed oblong patches of wood. She wondered what they'd been building, and what they'd left behind.

There was a single outdoor light on at Windlift, but no traffic. No boxcars on the industrial spur track connecting the building to the switching yard. No activity. Grace wondered if all the wind turbines had left the yard by now. It looked deserted.

In the abandoned buildings, she saw the unmistakable heat-sensor forms of animals: dogs, maybe a coyote. No people.

'Why no transients?' She kept her voice down.

'We did a sweep about a week back,' he whispered. 'Takes them a couple of weeks to slide back in, after we pull out.'

A signal light flickered and stopped, as if the wind had blown out the light. From a great distance came the shrill whistle of a train approaching. Almost immediately, coming from the highway, there was an outline of a truck bouncing over the road toward the switching yard.

Pete cocked his head and said something low and unintelligible into his handie talkie.

The sand was damp; it already had soaked through her sweatshirt. The desert clicked with skittering creatures and Grace had the uneasy desire to look behind her and recheck the status of her ankles.

'Stop squirming.'

A choking cloud of dust funneled down the hill and sprayed like yellow ocean spume over the desert floor. There were agents behind them on the hillside, too, Grace was sure, but she couldn't see them.

'If you've got something to say, say it.'

Grace thought of Jeanne, how she had to hang on to the wall to steady herself without her cane as she was turning to go back to her cell.

'If somebody does something stupid when they're a kid, and then goes on to lead a good life — an exemplary life — does the good life in some way help pay for the mistakes?'

'You're talking about an escapee from a work-release program who jumped a lawfully mandated sentence, went underground, and resurfaced only by accident.'

'She was going to come in.'

'Yeah, and there's enough water here that we can export it, ship it in barrels to some little pissant country that just happened to have run out.'

'I can see why Vonda's pissed at you.'

His jaw worked.

'I'm serious.'

'Grace, you're asking the wrong man about forgiveness. Mistakes are the one thing I plan on doing up until the day I die; in fact, the day I die I want to go out saying I was wrong; I want to take it back.'

He shifted on his elbows and slapped a sand fly away from his face. 'But the thing is, Zsloski and me and all the guys with us — we're the guardians at the gate. We take all that shit seriously about protecting and serving. We don't make the laws, we just take the scummy bad guys and trot their pornographic, skinny, smelly bad asses down into a holding cell where an irritable judge with a haircut that costs more than my golf clubs bangs down an arraignment gavel, and for a while, at least, we've got their shuffling, ankle-chained sorry selves in a place where they can't hurt anybody else. At the end of the day, that's all we care about.'

'Good, that's good, literary, even. But not very helpful.'

'Maybe not to you. But believe me, it is to the folks trying to get some sleep at night without getting raped, bludgeoned, maimed, or murdered. Let me tell you about this bunch. Those guys in the truck down there. The Palm Springs Police and the Union Pacific police have been working with the CAT team from L.A. — '

'CAT?'

'Cargo anti-theft team, FBI — don't slow my story down, Grace, it's too long as it is — they've been after this gang for almost a year. You take a regular-sized boxcar. Inside, it can pack twelve thousand dollars of merchandise easy, and that's the low end. You empty a boxcar carrying, say, computer chips or authentication certificates for a Microsoft Windows program, you're looking at millions. Pretty good for sixty seconds' work.'

He shifted on his elbows.

'This gang is so cocky, it actually wears monogrammed face masks with their initials. RD. They've even shown up on eBay. Not the gang. Face masks. One guy, sometimes two, runs along the tracks. The trains go slow, coming in and out of the yards, down to about twenty miles an hour, and they've timed it so they can get somebody up there with a pair of bolt cutters and — '

'RD.' It sunk in. The backs of her knees felt clammy. 'Radical Damage.'

Her uncle nodded. 'It's a sophisticated cartel, Grace. And we're busting its chops tonight. This is one of their drop spots. We've got teams set up to take them all at the same time. It's money laundering.'

'Through Andrea's company. Square Pegs.'

'They've been using the money to fund ecoterrorism. Paying for safe houses. Guns. Bombs.'

Her stomach felt hollowed out. 'Jeanne made an early mistake, that's all. She doesn't have anything to do with this.'

Her uncle looked at her. Through the night-vision goggles, his eyes looked dark, somber.

'We found the site of the soybean rust spores. Where it was being cultivated.'

297

Grace dug her fingers into her scalp, massaged her head right along the scalp line, where she could feel the muscles bunched.

'The desert's a lot more beautiful than I imagined, seeing it this way.' She pressed a knot in the back of her neck and felt a pain dart down her shoulder blade. 'Everything all glittery and alive.'

'You know that row of plants she had on that high shelf at her shop? Most of them tulips. But you look behind that row, it's agars of spore. It's right there on the shelf. She's been feeding it for months.'

She wasn't going to show him how much it hurt. 'Cultivating. That's what they call it.'

'What?'

'Cultivating. Not feeding.'

The rim of the San Jacinto Mountains glowed bright orange, the thinnest of lines, barely there, as if somebody had taken a fine-pointed pen and outlined the edge of the cliffs.

'I don't believe it.'

'Uh huh. And that's going to change it. Good luck with that. I was doing some work in St Paul, Minnesota, when Symbionese Liberation fugitive Kathleen Soliah was arrested driving a minivan on her way to school to watch her daughter get a sports award. Her doctor husband — who'd only known her as Sara Jane Olson in the almost twenty years they'd been married — claimed to be totally shocked — his words — at the arrest. Oh, and get this, besides being known for her cheese and noodle casseroles and hosting African orphans through her church, she had a reputation as a fine actress in Little Theater — specializing in those high-strung, difficult, and intense characters that are so hard to get right.'

Crossing lights flickered to life; a distance away a train whistle shrilled. Her uncle glanced at her, his mouth expressionless.

'At least I told you. It wasn't like me, finding out by accident my only daughter'd given birth.'

'She didn't want me to tell.'

'Works for me.' His voice was crisp. 'Cute little guy. Doesn't look a thing like me or anybody else in the family. Maybe that's a good thing. Start fresh.'

She was too tired for this; cold and tired and angry. 'You don't know your impact on the people you love, Uncle Pete.'

'I don't? Well, maybe it's an inheritable genetic flaw, Grace. Might want to think about that when you're so busy grading, which seems to be most of the time.'

He inched forward, his head still. Below them, the truck pulled in and parked behind a rusted-out boxcar. Exhaust curled into the sky.

'Stay put.'

She nodded.

'And stop nodding your goddamn head when you poke it around the bush. That's like a mirror flashing; you want to send up a flare?'

Through her goggles, a man carrying bolt cutters, his body lime green in the light, detached from the boulder where the truck was parked and trotted forward along the tracks. In the distance, she saw the bulky metallic girth of a Union Pacific freight train bearing down.

Everything happened at once. The man's legs pumped faster as the train slowed. The engine seemed to pass inches from his body, the floodlights illuminating the two dark lines of track. The man lunged for a metal rung on a third boxcar and swung himself up.

Within seconds a wide door slid open and he heaved a sturdy box over the side of the train. It bounced twice and cracked open, scattering what looked like, at that distance, Nintendo PlayStations. Before the second bounce, he'd tossed off three other boxes. The truck hidden behind the boulders rumbled down to the tracks and parked not far from the first box. New boxes continued to bounce off the train like boulders, cracking loose from a mountainside.

The truck idled and two figures burst out the cab doors, scampering to the first box and heaving it into the back of the truck. They ran to the second box and picked it up, their movements synchronized, effortless. The driver was already repositioning the truck at the third drop site.

A boxcar siding slammed open, revealing in Grace's goggles a crowd of bodies, all wearing guns.

Her uncle rolled to a crouch, slid his gun out, and danced down the hillside, sluicing gravel as he skidded down the hill, with what sounded like the cavalry right behind him. Grace covered her head and hoped they could see her through the dust they were raising.

The two crouching over the PlayStations looked up the hill. They were in face masks. One

300

of them raised a gun.

In that instant, the train came to a grinding stop, brakes screaming on metal tracks, boxcars lurching. Another door slammed open. Union Pacific policemen poured out of a boxcar. It looked like one of those telephone booth tricks; they kept coming.

They jumped down, flattened the pair by the box, ripped the driver from the truck, cuffed all three. Somebody's gun went off and Grace tucked herself into a ball. The small of her back felt clammy.

The man with the bolt cutters didn't have them anymore. Agents lifted him like cordwood off the train, ankles and wrists cuffed.

Grace sat up. Stretched her back. The sun washed the top of Mount Jacinto in golden light. She took off the goggles and rubbed her eyes.

Daylight was a mix of soft light and gray shadows. She clambered down the hill and found her uncle standing outside the circle of agents, talking on his cell. On the ground lay Tony, Sarah's husband. Grace resisted the urge to step close to his face with her boot.

He looked blankly up at her, through her. He smiled. It was still a chilling thing. He lay cuffed on the ground, hands behind his back, next to three prisoners still in face masks. An agent squatted and peeled one back. Sarah's curly red hair glinted in the morning light. She spat.

'Pig.'

Her uncle covered his phone with his hand. 'Yeah, Grace.' He was distant, his mind on the case.

Two more faces to go. Pete studied the prisoners and in a moment of tired understanding, Grace knew it was because he feared which face would emerge when the last mask was peeled back.

Andrea. Her face looked bruised from the ribbing of the mask. She smiled up at the agents, as if they were old friends.

'Call you right back,' her uncle said into his cell. He snapped it closed, waiting for the last mask to come off.

It was Nate. He grinned, the gap between his front teeth winking with saliva. Grace wondered if grinning was part of the terrorist playbook.

Her uncle exhaled.

'You were afraid it was Stuart.'

'Wait until it's your turn, Grace. Then we can talk about fears. What do you need?'

'Can we talk? Someplace private.'

He glanced at the busy swarm of agents and Union Pacific policemen. He turned toward the boxcars and motioned her to follow. His shoes crunched the gravel. They passed a dead-bolted boxcar with serial numbers dripping paint into the dirt. They kept walking. Up ahead they heard the whine of metal slicing metal.

Her uncle stopped at the boxcar that had recently held the crush of Union Pacific policemen and FBI agents. Above the boxcar on the roof, two yard workers squatted down and adjusted a heavy sheet of metal. It clanged down hard on the roof and a drill rattled, the whine of the drill changing as it pierced the metal.

'They're securing a roof plate. We modified the

boxcar for the raid.'

'Where does this boxcar go when it's not being used for the Ringling Brothers telephone booth trick?'

'No idea. Just know it has to be fixed; schedule to keep.' Pete grabbed hold of the first metal rung and climbed.

She hated heights. She was tired and cranky.

'Wait. It doesn't have to be that private, our meeting.'

Pete kept climbing. He swung his foot over to the boxcar floor and jumped free of the rungs, settling onto the floor and dangling his feet. Clouds of dirt misted the air. The air rang with the clang of feet on the roof, the drill slicing through metal and popping free, the sharp, swift clamp of a bolt piercing the roof.

'We won't be interrupted here,' Pete yelled down at her. He checked his watch. 'You have three minutes. I suggest you climb fast.'

The front of her jeans and shirt were already filthy from lying in wait on the hillside. She shrugged and started to climb.

The rungs dug into the arches of her shoes. It was like pulling herself up a cliff ladder at Mesa Verde, straight up. A narrow ledge lipped out from the open boxcar and she cautiously stepped onto the ledge, inched over, swung herself free and tumbled inside. Pete shot out a hand and broke her fall. She was facing the back of the interior and a metal ladder welded to the wall.

A bolt pierced the ceiling and Grace heard the sound of a lug nut being clamped down. Boots scraped along the roof and someone grunted. A new bolt was drilled into the ceiling.

The boxcar smelled of rancid grease and old sweat, the suffocating odor of an ancient, unwashed room. Grace settled next to her uncle and looked around. A plastic envelope the size of a file folder had been stapled to the wooden side.

'A bill of lading goes there when the boxcar's refilled.'

From that angle, the boxcar was bigger, the edges harder, the surfaces rougher. It gave her a new respect for the yard workers. The corrugated sliding door was jammed open by a metal bar and Grace took a welcome drink of air.

'Hate to be locked inside here.'

'Exactly why we cut a hole in the roof. Gave our agents another exit. That door slams shut, you could be locked in here for weeks before somebody finds you.'

'I'll add that to my must-miss list.'

'What do you need?' he repeated.

The sun beat down on the metal. From that perspective, the prisoners flat on the ground were surrounded by a swarm of blue and tan and black uniforms. Grace hadn't realized before that Homicide Detective Mike Zsloski was going bald.

A metal ridge dug into her thighs and she shifted her weight.

She lowered her voice. 'You think Radical Damage is still planning something for tomorrow night?'

'You mean tonight.'

She nodded. Time had melted.

'We got bomb-sniffing dogs in every room of

the Convention Center and at the exits, surveillance teams at key checkpoints, and five of the delegates are SWAT agents, plus a portable biodetection unit in place. We're sweeping for bacteria, spores, fungi, and ninety-five flavors of toxins. Nothing yet. I'll know more in a couple of hours, once the arrest count comes in, but I think we nipped this one.'

'You don't need me here anymore, right?'

'Checkout's noon. Stick around until then, just in case.'

He hesitated. 'I'm sorry about your friend. None of us are who we say we are, you know?'

'Except you. You told me you were an asshole, and you were right.'

He half smiled.

'Uncle Pete. What you said. About my dad. How you think he was the guy who called CPS on my mom.' Her heart pounded and she felt her face bead with sweat. 'Do you think he's still alive?'

Pete gazed down at the group of agents and policemen and when he turned back, his eyes were sad.

'I need to get back to my tribe, Grace. We're going to have to fix this one later. I can book a ride for you to your room, if you want.'

'Just answer me that one thing.' She tried to keep the desperation out of her voice and failed. 'You want forgiveness? Tell me. Where's my dad? Is he alive?'

'I wish I could say yes,' he said finally. 'The truth is, I don't know.'

* ★ *

The sky was turning pink when she returned to her motel. Her emotions careened like small, anxious children herded into a locked room. Her dad. Daddy. *Daddy Daddy I just want my Daddy*, Katie had cried, like a song, a key to a combination, a prayer.

Jeanne's eyes had been huge and haunted, facing down her past, staring into the cipher of an uncertain future, maybe charged soon with the murder of a teenage girl. Grace needed sleep, but more than that, she needed answers.

A man she didn't know had called her name on his last day alive.

find Grace Descans
As if that were easy.
find Grace Descans
Broken, bewildered, lost.
find Grace Descanso
She took a shower and got in the car.

34

'Can you think of any reason why Bartholomew would have asked for me? Anything in his past?'

Grace kept her voice down. They were both in the dim cell, sitting on the hard mattress on the floor, their backs to the camera. The corrections officers hadn't been happy to see her, but Zsloski had told them to give her whatever she needed.

'Anything about microbiology.' Grace was riffing. 'Forensics, maybe. Genealogy.'

Jeanne shook her head.

'Any reason he'd know Morse code.'

Down the corridor, a prisoner screamed curse words in Spanish. Jeanne's face looked haggard. She'd slept in the orange uniform and it was wrinkled.

'He taught himself that at Redwood State. He and Tasha used it for — they'd scribble out a Morse code — time and place — and leave it under a rock for their hookups.'

'What do you remember about Tasha?'

'Other than that she was a duplicitous, lying, avaricious, greedy little bitch?'

'Duplicitous means lying, Jeanne. Ditto avaricious and greedy.'

'So? Tasha McCollum was times-two everything. That's what I'm trying to tell you. As long as it got her what she wanted and didn't cost anything, she was in. And as far as how she looked — dark hair, I think. Can't even be sure

307

of that. You have to remember that was forty years ago, Grace. Janis Joplin looked fat to me then; now when I see her on those album covers? She just looks young. Ditto Mama Cass.'

'Jeanne, when you went over to Bartholomew's house, was anybody else there?'

'We were in his living room. I guess somebody else could have been in the house.'

'When you were arguing, were you doing it in the nice, polite way or the loud, messy way?'

'The just-short-of-throwing-things-at-each-other way. I'd taken Helix out of the car because it was hot. Helix heard me arguing and started howling on the front porch, as if he were a canine neighborhood watch. That's why Bartholomew let him in. To shush him up.'

'Did Helix try to go deeper into the house?'

Jeanne thought about it. 'I was focused on holding his collar and negotiating with Bartholomew.' She shifted her gaze midrange to the enamel wall. 'There was a sound in the house, now that I think about it.'

Grace shifted her legs. 'A sound.'

'A clothes dryer maybe. In the back of the house.'

So it was possible the housekeeper could have been there when Jeanne had surprised Bartholomew. 'The girl who got the tatt of the unicorn.'

'Tammy.'

'What do you remember about her?'

Jeanne rotated on her haunches and massaged her bad leg and Grace wondered again what they'd done with her walking stick.

'She seemed reluctant. I always give this

lecture to first-timers, tell them it's not too late to back out. No harm, no foul. She kept checking the window, as if she expected somebody. Finally she just said, do it, get it over with, put on the headphones and that was it. You banged open the door about twenty minutes later.'

'Did she come in a car or was she dropped off?'

'She was waiting for me when I got there, and afterwards, she walked off toward the beach. I had the feeling, frankly, she was one of these kids who just blew into town who have parents waiting somewhere, middle-class, middle-aged, and frantic.'

'Did she seem stressed about paying?'

'She counted her money out first, yeah, but that's because I always give them the stink-eye so they know I'm serious. Nobody's tried to walk on paying.'

Grace thought back to what the girl was wearing. She didn't remember pockets.

'Backpack, right?'

Jeanne nodded. Her red hair frizzed around her face in a haphazard nest, and Grace resisted the urge to tidy it up. From down the hall came the sound of a metal cart. Grace knew she was running out of time. When the cart came to pick up the breakfast trays, they'd be taking her out. That's the agreement she'd cut with the COs.

'Did you leave her alone for any reason while she was there?'

Jeanne pulled her legs up so that her chin rested on her knees and clasped her hands

309

together. Her soft orange nail polish was chipped.

'I went to the door once and shooed some girls away. They were playing bocci ball and smashing it against the window.'

Grace rolled cautiously to her knees. Her heart was starting to trip. 'I passed them on the way in.'

Grace was usually good at calling up details, but not this time. She'd been distracted when she'd seen them and now she eased into the quiet place in her mind and focused. She found her thoughts right away: roiling, preoccupied, exhausted from the flight, worried. She'd passed them with hardly a glance. Three teenage girls. Skinny. Averting their eyes when they saw her. Wearing cutoffs. Too clean. Hair too clean. Nails too clean. No smell of the street. Something light and floral.

They weren't panhandling. They were waiting.

Waiting for the right time to divert Jeanne's attention.

Grace swung an arm around Jeanne's shoulder and leaned her face close to Jeanne's ear. 'Did you go outside?'

Jeanne frowned, rocking quietly, rolling on her bad hip, and Grace wondered if the jailers would give Jeanne Tylenol if Grace insisted.

Comprehension flooded Jeanne's face. She shot a look at Grace, and then glanced at the camera. She swiveled her head down so that Grace had to lean forward to catch the words.

'Yeah, now that I think of it. They moved, but not off the window, just far enough away so I'd actually have to put down the needle and go after them. Tammy could have hidden the soybean rust spores then.'

'The kids who were outside. Are they regulars in Ocean Beach?'

Jeanne shook her head. 'I never saw them before.'

'Remember what they look like?'

Jeanne gnawed on her fist. She shook her head. 'They were clean canvases.' She glanced at Grace apologetically. 'I always look for canvases.'

Grace could feel the moist heat of her cheek, almost as if a spark of current shot through it. 'This is really important, Jeanne. I'm switching gears and we have to be fast. Did Frank ever give off weird vibes?'

Jeanne laughed. 'All the time. What do you mean?'

The cart stopped at the cell next to Jeanne's. Metal scraped. The food slot clanged. The inmate next to Jeanne was shoving his tray through the slot.

'Did you ever catch him in a lie, or did he ever pretend to be something he wasn't?'

'What are you getting at?'

'Just think about it.'

Jeanne exhaled, her cheek still close to Grace. She leaned her head into Grace's, her voice barely a whisper.

'He talked about the end of the world sometimes. Said it wasn't going to end in flames. Said we'd invite it into our homes. Serve it on a plate.'

'I can't arrest Frank Waggaman based on some half-assed remark by a woman who's spent the last forty-odd years lying about her identity, Grace. Of course she's going to throw him under the bus. She wants out of jail. Most cons do. Besides, he hasn't done anything.'

'At least check him out, Uncle Pete.' Grace shifted the phone. She could hear metallic screeching and the grinding of a train backing up.

'Go to sleep, Grace.'

'But — '

'Go to sleep.' He hung up.

Grace stared at the phone. She put her head down and curled into a ball. She couldn't think anymore. She'd hardly slept on the plane, when she'd taken the red-eye home. And the night before had been a constant stream of interruptions. Can interruptions stream? She wasn't sure anymore. Time was malleable, a Mr Bill clay body that could be re-formed into a lump of planets, a loopy grin, a springy bouncy ball. Re-formed and tossed off a building with a springy splat. Small fireflies of light exploded behind her lids.

A phone jangled her out of sleep and sent her rearing up in bed, disoriented.

'Grace?' It was a guarded male voice, one she didn't recognize.

'Yes.' Grace turned the clock radio around. Eight minutes to twelve. That couldn't be right. Checkout was noon. She looked around the room. At the explosion of clothes. She patted her way into a crouch, into standing up.

'This is Dr Gordie Turngood. You left the soybean fragments with me? You need to get in right away.'

She frowned, trying to pull herself together. 'It's going to be a while. I have to pack and check out.'

'Push it.'

Grace scraped back her curtains and blinked in the sudden glare. Light poured in. 'You found something?'

'Oh, yes.'

35

'I'll get right to it.'

Dr Gordie Turngood locked the door securely and led Grace back through the ruin of his office to the lab. He was wearing maroon bellbottoms and a hot pink turtleneck, with Teva sandals and white socks. His white curly hair stood straight up in springy curls, as if he'd touched an electric socket, and his blue eyes were red-rimmed and bleary. He smelled of Old Spice, her dad's cologne.

The lab was strikingly clean. None of the chaos of his paperwork and personal life spilled back into this pristine space, lit by two wide windows. Light touched a spectrophotometer, turning the gray edges gold. A centrifuge vibrated on the counter, drying down whatever sample it held locked inside.

He found a graph paper on his desk and handed it to her. Two bar codes banded across the page. They didn't match.

'I'm not . . . '

'Here.' He pointed at the first bar code. 'This is the bar code for Frank Waggaman's soybean crop, the one that burned. And this,' he pointed to the second one, 'is the one from the soybean fragments taken from the grooves in Bartholomew's shoes.'

Grace studied them. The bar code for Frank Waggaman's experimental crop marched across the page in a series of randomly spaced peaks. The other one seemed denser, messier, somehow.

'The second one's . . . *thicker.*' She couldn't think of a better word.

Gordie nodded, his white curls bouncing. 'Exactly. See that?' He stabbed a finger along the second bar code, tracing a jagged set of peaks. 'There are extra peaks that aren't supposed to be there.'

'You mean those lines.' It looked like a scribble under a taller set of peaks.

He nodded. 'They don't match,' Turngood said. 'That means the soy seeds in Professor Bartholomew's shoes could not have come from the soy field where he was killed. He was someplace earlier with soy.'

'And it doesn't match anything you've got.'

He shook his head. 'It's not from a registered sample, nothing I have on file.'

'What do the marks mean?'

He shook his head. 'Not sure. I've never seen peaks in this location on a soy code before, Grace. It may be that two soybean signatures are intermingled, but I can't find the mystery peaks in any registered signature. The dominant signature came from a strain in China, by the way. Deciphering this is completely out of my league, but I work with a colleague at Riverside University who retired early from Beltsville.'

'Beltsville?'

'Maryland. It's the crack USDA facility for soybean research. She just left there a couple years back. She also runs a state-of-the-art lab.'

'What's her name?'

'Nobody you know. A woman. Dr Denise Bustamonte. She's expecting you. I already called ahead.'

★ ★ ★

Grace parked in the garage closest to the liberal arts complex. It was almost two-thirty and the sky was a pale drift of blue and white. A bell shrilled. Doors burst open and students blinked in the sunlight, gripping binders and scuffing through fall leaves. Even in daylight, they stared timidly at her as they bolted down paths to their next classes. Even in daylight, they looked afraid.

Grace found the arts and sciences building, a brick and ivy edifice trimmed in fresh white paint, and took the stairs to the second floor past the steady murmur of voices coming from open classrooms. On Dr Denise Bustamonte's office door was a yellowed 'Far Side' cartoon, and a more recent one from 'Dilbert.' Both dealing with recombinant DNA.

Nobody answered her knock. Footsteps pattered up the staircase.

'Oh, sorry. I thought I could run over and make it back in time. I'm always trying to cram three bushels into a quart container. Professor Bustamonte. Denise. You must be Grace.'

Grace nodded: 'Thanks for meeting me.'

Denise Bustamonte was a black woman in her early sixties, wearing an orange silk caftan, sandals, and heavy gold hoop earrings. A brightly woven satchel hung from her shoulder. Her hair

316

was short and gray, tight curls accenting a beautifully shaped head and dark expressive eyes. Dimples on both cheeks. She wore orange polish on her toes that matched the skirt and she carried a cardboard carton with two carefully wrapped and cut sandwiches and two cartons of coffee.

The sharp odor of food made Grace feel faint. Denise handed her the carton as she rummaged in her bag for her keys.

'Didn't know if you were vegan.'

Grace checked out the sandwiches. 'I can do vegan. Cheese. Cheese is good.'

'Gordie thought you'd be hungry.'

'You have no idea.'

Denise found the key and unlocked the office. A hardwood Grace didn't recognize covered the floor, a rich golden red carefully crafted tongue-and-groove. French curtains on the windows, floor-to-ceiling bookshelves holding science books, hand-made baskets and early primitive art. A photo of Denise and a man with white skin and soft gray hair smiled out from its frame on her mahogany desk. A group photo sat next to it, taken at a picnic. Four relaxed-looking adult children in various hues of tan and copper and dark brown stood next to Denise and their dad and smiled.

'Our rainbow family.'

Denise sat, motioned toward the desk, and Grace put the carton down.

She waved a hand toward a brocade chair. 'Please. Sit. Eat. There's cream and sugar for the coffee, if you need it. I'm going to dig in.'

'Thanks. I will try not to make little noises while I inhale this.' Grace reached for the sandwich.

They both ate for a few minutes, Grace believing in her heart she'd never tasted a better combination: the nutty flavor of whole wheat, the cheddar biting against the sprouts, the avocado ripe but not mushy. She *was* making little sounds. She stopped and wiped her mouth, and cracked open the coffee.

'I always think a good meal helps calm the heart.'

Grace looked at her more closely and could see that she'd been crying.

'We just got the news. It raced through campus like it was — well, a virus. That's all anybody's been talking about.'

'What news?'

Denise looked at her soberly. 'There's been another killing. A sophomore girl. Tammy Hammond. The police aren't saying how. They're not saying much of anything. On top of Professor Bartholomew's death. It's scary here. Everybody wonders what's next. Parents are packing up their kids, taking them home before finals.'

The scientist's face grew soft with pain. 'I feel so sad for her folks. I can't imagine.'

The news must have come through when Grace had been asleep. It felt like a hard bad rain. Cold.

'Did you know her?'

Denise shook her head. 'Never had her in class. She was a liberal arts major from all reports.'

'What else have you heard?'

Denise sighed. 'Her folks reported her missing this morning. Some time over the weekend, she disappeared from Wenaka dorm and never came back.'

'Her roommate didn't report her gone?'

'Tammy was a free spirit, from what I hear. It wasn't unusual for her to disappear. But this was over her mother's birthday, and Tammy never would have *not* called. Her roommate didn't want to get her in trouble, but the parents kept pressing, and finally Sandra gave it up.'

'Sandra who?'

'The roommate? I don't know her last name.' She looked at Grace with a mixture of pain and hope. 'Gordie tells me you're bringing me something that might have relevance to what's been happening here.'

'Soy fragments to test. Did he tell you where they came from?'

Denise shook her head.

'These were in Ted Bartholomew's shoes when he died. If you test these fragments, are you prepared to be dragged into the middle of a murder investigation, perhaps be called to testify at some point?'

Denise wiped her mouth with a napkin and when she looked up, her gaze was steady. 'His death's affected all of us. Hell yes, I'm prepared.'

Grace took the evidence envelope out of her bag. 'Dr Turngood sequenced these soy pod fragments and apparently, there're some peaks that don't match anything he's seen. He thought you could run tests, figure out what's going on.'

319

Grace handed the small evidence envelope to the professor.

Denise handed it back. 'I have to sign for it, right?'

Grace nodded.

'We'll take this to the lab. You set?'

Grace nodded and helped Denise gather up the remnants of lunch. They were silent until they reached the stairs.

'Any ideas?' Denise's voice rang in the stairwell.

'You mean, about what's going on? Some.' She'd mulled it over during the drive. 'We got a sequence in the crime lab once that didn't make sense. Turns out it was a contaminated sample from a sloppy tech. They fired him before he could do any more damage.'

She kept her voice neutral, but she was thinking back to the explosion of debris in Gordie's office, and wondering if he'd slopped the sample in the lab without realizing it.

Denise shot her a look. 'Gord's the real deal, but we can recheck it anyway.' She opened the door. Outside, the sweet smell of fall grass washed over them. They walked toward a modern-looking gray building, three stories high.

'Isn't it possible,' Grace said slowly, thinking out loud, 'what Gordie tagged as a wild card could just be some type of processed food? Maybe somebody's doing work they haven't made public yet.'

'Or maybe they're doing work they don't *want* to make public,' Dr Bustamonte said. She opened the heavy doors to the building.

An atrium flooded the entryway with soft autumn light. The floor was gray marble, the walls a soft matching fabric that absorbed the sound of their footsteps.

'Lab's in the basement. Of course.'

When they were alone in the elevator, Denise said, 'We spent thirty years living in Baltimore, raising our kids. Henry — that's my husband — had some old football injuries kick into gear and translate into miserable tendonitis and deep socket problems. We needed a place where his bones weren't chilled in his twilight years. We handpicked this place, mostly for me and the opportunities this school afforded. Maybe I'd been working with adults too long. The Beltsville team was amazing. Like working with the space program. Fascinating projects, brilliant minds, good rapport. At least I've got a good lab. There's that.'

'You don't get stimulated by the kids?'

'Sure, some have crack minds. And some are just *on* crack. God, what a world.'

The elevator opened and they moved into the basement hall. Their voices echoed.

'Most of them don't know how to *work*. They don't have any *staying power*. And scholarship, truly original work, forget about it.'

Denise stopped at the door and unlocked it.

'Boy, I sound like a grumpy old woman. Another year of listening to myself, and I'll be ready to call it quits. Grab Henry and hang out in the south of France.'

She pushed open the door. It was a southern exposure, and watery light from high windows

321

slanted over the DNA thermocyclers, the autoclaves and incubators, the sparkling rows of pipettes and immaculate sinks. It was the kind of lab that Grace envisioned having in her garage. Some people had grunge bands or pottery wheels. Grace could see herself eighty years old and drying down DNA.

She missed the crime lab and what it offered; missed the way things had been the last day she'd awakened in her small bed in the Guatemalan highlands next to Mac, awakened to see him quietly packing, getting ready to leave. The moment right before the world changed.

Denise lifted a white lab coat off a hook and put it on, her hem an orange slash along the bottom. She signed for the baggie of soy, snapped on a pair of gloves, and dumped the contents out on a marble grinding pad.

'So what's the plan?' Grace leaned against the counter.

'I'll extract the DNA from the plant cells, do a PCR amplification, sequence some regions of the genome, and then feed what I find into BLAST.'

Grace had heard of it. 'Basic Alignment Search Tool. Soy's on the Web, even though it's not all sequenced?'

Denise nodded, intent on the soy. 'What they have is there for scientists to use.' She picked up tweezers and examined a small whiskery strand of plant material. 'BLAST has the map for everything that's been decoded so far. Hopefully, we'll find no surprises in this puppy.'

'Hopefully, we won't find a puppy.'

Denise shot her a swift look. 'Not out of the

question. Those squiggles on the bar code that looked weird? What I do here is going to tell us if anything's been added to the soy.'

'Added.' Grace shifted. 'What do you mean, added?'

'That's what I have to find out.'

36

Grace stood in the lab, watching Denise's familiar movements and feeling like the kid dying to get asked to the big dance.

Denise turned. 'Oh. That's right. You're on leave from the crime lab.' She added more gently, 'Sorry. Scientists gossip.'

'Police, too.'

She motioned a hand toward the back of the door. 'There's an extra jacket on the hook.'

'Thanks.' Grace slipped the lab coat on and snapped on a pair of gloves. 'What do you want me to do?'

'You can get this ready while I program the computer to synthesize the primer. I'm going to try some microsatellite marker screening.'

'What enzyme are we using?' Grace took over the pestle and ground the soy into a fine dust.

'TAQ. Thermus aquaticus, same as for humans. The recipe's over there.' Denise pointed to a lab notebook open on the counter.

They worked in silence, mixing the soy DNA with the material that would replicate it, and transferring it into the automated thermocyler.

Denise clamped the lid in place, ripped off her gloves, and hit a few keystrokes on her computer. She nodded.

'Good to go. This will give us a chance to call up what we know on BLAST, so we'll be set. Pull up a chair if you like; this shouldn't be long.'

Grace took off her gloves and positioned a chair next to Denise, silent as the scientist's fingers flew over the keyboard and the commands led to more intricate paths.

'Gordie said the soy strain — or at least the primary one — came from China.'

Denise nodded, not surprised. 'We actually use a strain from there in our work here in the labs. A couple more from Australia and nine from the States.'

'Where are you going?'

'Into the soybean genome that's been sequenced. Once we get our sample ready, I'll be looking for specific markers I know are on the Chinese strain we use here, to see if it's ours. Ah, here we go.'

A long, blurred set of letters — the soybean genetic code — scrolled past.

'How you doin', baby.' Denise breathed. She half laughed. 'I've been staring at this stuff for so long, fascinated with its mysteries, it feels like another kid to me.'

She pointed at the screen. 'The secrets to flowering, pod development, plant growth — all right there. You can do the paperwork while we wait, if you like.'

Grace nodded and busied herself for the next twenty minutes, meticulously recording in Denise's lab journal everything they'd done and intended to do.

The PCR dinged softly and Grace looked up and frowned. 'Do you have a warning bell on your PCR?'

Denise grinned and stood up. 'A year ago, this

325

company working on a faster prototype sent a flyer around. Somehow, it wound up in my in basket — I'm sure whoever dropped it there didn't understand its significance. I snapped it up. I've got one of the only working PCR and sequencing machines that pops this stuff out. I only have to write up reports every once in a while and rave about its beauty and versatility, easy to do under the circumstances.'

'It's half a day for PCR and sequencing, minimum, where I come from.' Grace's voice held admiration and a little wistfulness.

'And where you're going back *to*. Don't tell them. I'd hate to have it come up missing in the middle of the night.'

Denise used a pipette to extract a small amount of the DNA and inserted it into sterilized tubes for sequencing. Grace helped her load the rack into the sequencer.

It didn't take long before DNA was translated onto the computer screen in a long, steady stream of data. It was close to five and the light through the windows was a soft gray against the darkening sky.

'I've got Gordie's results on disc. I'm going to compare them.' Denise inserted the disc and the screen split.

Two bar codes, side by side. They matched.

Denise flicked a glance at Grace, consternation on her face. 'So much for the good news. Gordie didn't screw up. There was no contamination in his test.'

Grace studied the bar code. There were peaks on the page, the kind of scribble marks a toddler makes. And underneath, hugging the sequence, was a second set of peaks, jagged and irregular.

'I'm going to check first and make sure the dominant sequence,' Denise pointed to the heavier set of peaks on the screen, 'is our Chinese strain.'

She clicked a few keys and new letters spilled across the screen. She studied them. 'Well, the primary sequence did come from the strain we use here at Riverside.'

'How many schools use it?'

'Lots, so just knowing that isn't telling us much. It's a teaching tool in universities across America, but what it's telling me is that it's a mixed sample. Hard to understand.' Denise frowned. Her body language changed. She straightened in her chair, alert, serious.

'What is it?'

'We're getting into the area of the code that's been tweaked.'

'Is it bad?'

Denise studied the screen. She shook her head, then rolled her chair away from the screen and pointed. 'Just odd. Take a look.'

Grace saw a tumble of green letters spilling across the screen.

'It's not adding up. The codes aren't matching. Aren't even coming close in this section. I'm going to ask it how much of the soybean fragment we tested is the soybean genome.'

She rolled her chair closer and her fingers clicked over the keyboard, her face tense. The lines around her mouth deepened. She stared at

327

the screen. She pushed her chair away and rubbed her eyes.

'This is not good,' she said.

On the screen were the words: SOYBEAN GENETIC CODE 98.3%.

Grace studied the words. 'Wait a minute. So the underlying signature — that second squiggle on the page that's right under the bigger set of peaks — that's not soybean.'

Denise nodded.

'Maybe it's just part of the soybean genome that hasn't been decoded yet.'

'No.' Denise Bustamonte shook her head. Her gold hoop earrings moved heavily. 'The system accounts for that. That's factored in to this program. No, what this is telling us is that this soy fragment has been altered with something nonsoy. Something else.'

Grace felt a knot twist in her stomach. Where had Ted Bartholomew been, that he'd picked up a soy fragment that had been genetically altered so that it wasn't even completely soy? Had he stumbled into something he wasn't supposed to find? Had that discovery led to his death?

There had to be a reasonable explanation for the information on the screen.

SOYBEAN GENETIC CODE 98.3%.

'Nonsoy. You mean like wheat? Or corn?' A note of desperation had crept in, but she couldn't contain it. 'Maybe whoever tried this was working on a hybrid. It would make sense. There's the International Ag Convention going on right now. Wraps up tonight. Somebody easily

328

could have been working on something under the radar.'

'It's completely against the rules, messing with stuff that way.' Denise turned back to her computer and fed it new commands.

'But it's done all the time, isn't it?' Grace pressed. 'I mean, there's that new fruit, that cross between a plum and an apricot, right? And tangerines and oranges. Tangelos.'

Denise was silent, fingers clicking.

Grace inched her chair closer.

'Okay, boys and girls.' Denise stared at the screen. 'We got trouble. This is telling me it's not plant material. Whatever's been added to the soy was taken from someplace else.'

'Best guess?'

'Virus, from the looks of it.'

'You must see a lot of that, though, right?' Grace thought back to an article she'd read once in a doctor's waiting room when there was nothing left to read. 'Bean pod mottle, isn't that one of them? And there's that mosaic one.'

Denise shook her head and moved her fingers over the keys. New letters spilled across the screen. She turned and stared at Grace, anxiety in her eyes.

'It's not a soy virus that's in here, Grace. There's an overlap with some of the soybean genetic markers. BLAST is telling me the lower signature, that little squiggle on the bar code, is partly made out of a common-cold virus.'

'What does that mean?'

'The cold virus is one of the simplest delivery systems known to man. That *impacts* man. You

329

get a cold virus, it replicates its DNA in human cells.'

'And it's in there.'

'Along with something else I haven't identified yet.' Denise kept working.

Katie had a Magic 8-Ball at home she'd gotten with her own allowance once. It was heavy as a shot, hard gray plastic inset with green-colored windows. Katie would ask it a question, shake the ball, and the green answers inside the windows would dance, finally settling into one screen with a crawl of words: NOT LIKELY, or SURE THING, or NEXT TIME.

Grace waited as the words on the screen assembled: ANIMAL 1.7%.

Denise expelled a breath and shook her head. 'I'm going to compare this sequence against other life-forms, starting with the simplest and working up to the more complex, to figure out what's been incorporated. It could take a while, or we could get lucky right away.'

She took down a thick manual from a shelf over the sink and flipped it open. 'Read me this while I code it in.'

Grace studied the page. 'This is the genetic code for a simple bacteria?' It was short, less than a paragraph of numbers and letters.

Denise smiled briefly. 'That's the code to *access* the code. The genetic code for a prokaryotic cell is pages. We'd be here through Christmas trying to manually put that one in.'

'You're saying that the cold virus is riding inside something else, and that both of those are inside the soy?' Grace was trying to keep up.

'That's shorthand for it,' Denise said. She reached for the book and started clicking in the code herself. Absently, she added, 'Something's inside the soy, and until we figure out exactly what, we're not going to know what we're up against.'

'You're going to ask BLAST to start with bacteria, and work its way up?'

'That's too broad a focus. Its little brain would short out and then we'd have to stick it in rehab.' Denise finished and glanced at Grace. 'What? You're thinking of something.'

'I'm just trying to figure out if there's a way to word it, so we could narrow it down,' Grace said. 'That 'higher-lower' game on *The Price Is Right*.'

Denise cut her a look and turned back to the computer. Her fingers clicked. 'You've been home way too long, girl, if you're hooked on that stuff.'

'But you can do it, right?'

Denise kept clicking.

Grace sat silently, watching her work.

Denise straightened. 'Okay, here it is. It's starting.'

Rapid-fire shifts, with sparks of color. Occasionally the screen would slow and the letter would appear to crawl.

'It's hunting for a match now, then moving on. Kind of like one of the extreme-dating shows,' Denise said drily. 'And no, don't ask me how I got hooked on that one.'

She shoved her chair away from the computer and stood. 'Come on, I'll make coffee while we wait.'

331

She locked the lab door and unlocked a door across the hall. It was the professors' break room.

'Interesting times,' Grace said.

Denise poured water into the coffeemaker. 'What?'

'The Chinese curse. 'May you live in interesting times.' That's what we're living in.'

Denise dumped coffee into a paper filter and started the machine. 'Did you know scientists have found a soil bacterium that can actually jump kingdoms? It causes tumors in plants, and now it looks like it can do the same thing in humans. Reuters reported it.'

'You think that's what happened here? Some sort of bacterium that attaches itself to the plant, inserts its DNA and replicates?'

'We'll know soon.'

Ten minutes later, they were back in the lab, staring at the screen. A single word pulsed: *Higher.*

'Oh my God,' Denise said. She sat down. 'That was the parameter for apes.'

They looked at each other. Denise moved her fingers heavily across the keyboard and put in the parameters for a human.

It came back almost immediately: 1.7% MATCH.

Grace stared at the screen, disbelieving.

Denise took an unsteady breath. 'Okay. Here's what's happening. I'm not sure why. But this soy has been encoded with certain human snips. Little pieces of DNA.'

Grace stared at her, stunned. Someone had

encoded human DNA into a soybean plant, altering it in some way they couldn't imagine. Dark and violent images skittered through her mind.

'They used a simple cold virus as the transfer.' Denise's fingers clicked across the keys.

'I'm just wondering *why*. Why would a soy genome be modified so that a human cold virus could be used to transfer something to humans? What's been encoded?'

Denise shook her head. 'It's going to take time to pin it down. I'll have to feed the genes into a BLAST program and see where I find matching sites. Could take hours.'

'Call me when you get something.' Grace scribbled out her cell phone number and waited as Denise did the same thing. 'Did you work with Stuart Soderberg?'

'One of the brightest doc candidates I've worked with. Didn't surprise me when he left the program, though. He was passionate about his wife, and I guess she had personal troubles. One day he came in, said he had to quit. Just like that, he left.'

'Did you ever surprise him as he was doing something that — '

'You mean like this? Never. He was a law-and-order guy. Meticulous with his research. His area was soil bacteria that inserts itself into a wide variety of plants — all kinds of fruit trees, grapevines, almonds, even rhubarb — and kills it. He was trying to find the off-switch when he left.'

'Did you work with Frank Waggaman?'

'Yeah, I did.' Her voice held anger. 'He did most of his genetic modifications on crops in my lab.'

Grace pulled a chair close and took a notebook out of her bag. 'You're going to have to tell me everything you know about him.'

'I need to keep working this, Grace.'

'Short version, then. Did he strike you as angry?'

'Yes.'

'About what?'

'Everything. He'd go off on rants that had nothing to do with him. At first, I thought, what a lovely man. Say, raving about how despite generations of struggle, women are still only paid seventy-seven cents to the dollar, and how it's even worse for women of color. But it was a dark, uncontrollable rage, coupled with trying to get kids a third his age interested in vicious protests.'

'That's what Bartholomew was doing, the call-to-action part.'

Denise nodded. 'But Bartholomew had a following. Frank Waggaman was out there by himself. And jealous. Wildly jealous of Ted Bartholomew's gift. He'd actually audit classes from him, so he could disrupt the lectures. He started wearing those little chains around his neck, doing comb-overs on his bald spot. Standing up, yelling in the middle of lectures. Ted finally had to call security, have him removed. Even that didn't stop Frank. He'd pretend Bartholomew was out to get him. Nobody believed it. It was odd and weird and it never stopped.'

She turned and looked right at Grace.

'And then Ted died. And it stopped.'

334

37

It was dark outside, a cold November night, as she crossed the quad and got back in her car. The Wenaka dormitory was in the row of dorms Grace had driven past the night before, a three-sided, brick and ivy-covered building with small windows, set around an open space.

She tried the front door. Locked. She'd promised Zsloski he'd be first to know if she found anything in the soy. She dialed his cell number, remembering his frustration when she explained racial profiling, how the DNA worked, his plea to make it simple. But there was nothing simple yet about what was happening. Only the press of time.

'Zsloski.' His voice was abrupt. In the background a bullhorn blared, the words, unintelligible but the menace real, cut short by a swelling roar from the crowd.

'Yeah, it's Grace Descanso.'

'Where are you?'

'In Riverside. Over at the school. I'm working with a scientist named Denise Bustamonte. That soy in Bartholomew's shoes, it's been genetically modified.'

'What?'

'It didn't come from the soy field where he was killed.'

'Wait, I'm writing this down.' He cleared his throat and she could hear a siren whine, growing higher-pitched and closer. 'Just a sec, until it passes.'

The sound grew and on top of it, the sudden cacophony of voices, shouting, and the shocking crack of gunfire. 'Got to go.'

'But — '

'Call me later.'

'Mike?'

'Yeah.'

'Be careful.'

A cold wind slivered across the back of her neck. She stamped her feet, waiting.

The door burst open and two students spilled out, wearing short skirts, black tights and scarves, hands stuffed into the pockets of their fleece jackets.

Grace raced up the steps and grabbed the heavy door seconds before it closed. Inside, the hallway rang with the sounds of showers, stereos, and laughter. Somebody was playing a drum. She walked the length of the first floor and took the ornate stairs to the second. A girl toweling dry her hair stopped in the hall.

'Can I help you?'

Grace scanned the hall, looking for a spontaneous memorial. She didn't find one.

'Tammy's room is where, upstairs?'

The girl's eyes flooded. She nodded, glanced down at her flip-flops and fled. Grace climbed the stairs to the third floor. Five doors down from the unisex bathroom, she found it.

The door was closed. A message board hung on the door, covered in scribbled heartfelt messages. A papier-mâché wreath adorned the wall, with a photo of Tammy in the center. She had her head back, laughing, eyes crinkled shut. She looked nothing like the fragile girl in the earmuff headphones dozing in Jeanne's chair.

Grace knocked on the door. Nobody answered. She leaned her ear against the door. She didn't hear anything on the other side.

'She's gone.'

Grace jerked her head up.

It was an Asian student, thin to the point of anorexia, wearing a knit miniskirt with tights and ballet slippers. She clutched a set of textbooks to her chest. Her glasses looked smudged and her eyes swollen. At her neck she wore a thin gold chain.

She'd come out of the room across the hall. A message board hanging on her door was bare except for information about a memorial service for Tammy scheduled for the day before Thanksgiving break. The grease pencil handwriting was small, precise.

'Who's gone?'

The student chewed her lip. Her mouth worked. 'If you're looking for Tammy's roommate, she split a couple of hours ago. She couldn't take all the press. Her profs are letting her have compassionate leave. She'll do make-up exams after Thanksgiving.'

Grace nodded and waited.

'So if you're somebody from the press, none of us is talking.' She cleared her throat. She darted a look at Tammy's photo on the opposite wall, as if she still had trouble believing it.

Grace shook her head. 'No, no. I'm not from

337

the press. I'm from the FBI.'

The student hunched her narrow shoulders. 'I don't have anything to say.'

'You don't, or you're too sad or scared or stunned to say it.'

The woman's face convulsed and she ducked her head into her books and fled. 'I'm late. I can't. I won't.' The last was a cry.

Grace caught up to her halfway down the hall. 'Can I buy you a hot meal?'

'Who are you?' She was exhausted, but she still managed to make it sound withering.

Grace pulled out the ID badge. 'I'm Grace. And you're Elaine Choo.'

Elaine raised her eyes cautiously. She blinked. 'How did you know my name?'

38

'I guess I should have figured it out.' Elaine Choo wiped her fingers delicately on the paper napkin and left red blotches of catsup. 'We used to leave messages on each other's boards. So after she died, I kept doing it. I added a message to her board every time I left my room. It makes me feel less alone.'

Elaine blinked behind the glasses and shoved them up her nose. She detached a french fry and daubed it in catsup before nibbling the end.

'The handwriting on your message board about Tammy's service matched the messages Elaine Choo left on Tammy's door. It was pretty easy to guess that was you, when you came out of your room. How well did you know Tammy?'

'We were best friends since we met in Professor Bartholomew's class.' Elaine stopped eating the fry and put it down.

'When was that?'

'Last year, spring quarter. It was a two hundred-level lecture class called Silent Voices. We had the same class after it, a Russian lit class, and we started walking together between classes. Then we realized we were in the same dorm, a couple of floors apart. I was raised in a traditional Chinese family in San Francisco. My folks own a grocery store in Chinatown. My job was studying, no boyfriends ever, studying from early in the morning until late so I could get into med school.'

'I was a doctor.'

Elaine looked at her politely.

'You don't want to be a doctor, do you?' Grace said gently.

Elaine shook her head. 'I don't have any choice.' She examined the french fries studiously and picked a new one, repeating the ritual: a delicate daubing, a small bite, putting it down.

'And Tammy shared your work ethic in the beginning?'

Elaine smiled sadly. 'She was bouncy. My bouncy friend. Always encouraging me to take a study break. Go for a walk. Have an adventure. I felt like I was breaking out of prison, knowing her.'

'A friend like that, you probably'd want to room with.'

'My folks wouldn't let me. They thought she was a bad influence. They were furious when they realized I was living right across the hall from her. Felt like I'd sneaked one past them.' Elaine slid her necklace free and gripped the locket in a small hand. She tugged it back and forth until the necklace stretched taut.

' "Silent Voices". A mime class.'

Elaine took a small bite of cheeseburger. 'It was about legitimate rage, is the nearest I can describe it. A section on African-Americans and Asians, women and American Indians. Going through the beats of what the dominant culture here has done to hurt those groups and the duty we all had to stand up against it.'

340

'A class taken mostly by middle-class white kids. Bartholomew must have loved having you in class.'

'It was uncomfortable. He was asking me to relate to a discrimination I'd never experienced. After about the third week of prodding, he gave up on me.'

'And turned his attention to Tammy.'

'There were a pack of white kids who treated him like God. He folded Tammy in. The whole breaking-barriers theme ran parallel to his belief that ecologically, the world has been tipped into a crisis mode by the same white-dominance power groups and that it was our duty to strike a blow against them. He was counting down the days to the ag convention. And Tammy was gone almost all the time now. She'd be missing classes, living God knows where, and when I asked her about it, she told me not to worry. She was doing work that was going to change the world.'

Elaine moved the necklace again, back and forth, across her chin.

'Ever meet Nate, Professor Bartholomew's teaching assistant?'

Elaine rolled her eyes. 'He was always trying to get her to go to band practice, only she didn't play anything.'

'What's your necklace?'

'What?' Her hand clutched harder.

'Can I see it?'

She dropped the pendant inside her sweater. Elaine had a transparent face. Emotions roiled across her small features: alarm, panic, a

341

desperate need to come up with something. She licked her thin lower lip.

'It's from her, isn't it?'

Her eyes filled.

'About a week before she died, she knocked on my door one night. It was late. She looked nervous, scared. She wouldn't tell me what it was about, just that they'd been practicing. That's what she said. Practicing. And that soon they'd have to use what they'd learned. She talked about it as if — almost as if they were going to war.'

Elaine sighed. A tear rolled down her cheek and she took off her glasses and wiped her eyes.

'I told her I was scared, and for just an instant, she was the same old Tammy, a flash of laughter, and then her eyes dulled, as if a light had gone out. But in that instant, I could see that she was scared, too.'

'And that's when she gave you the pendant.'

'She told me to tell no one. That somebody might come by, asking if I have anything of hers. That it was important to lie.'

'But nobody came by.'

Elaine ducked her head. Tears welled. She shook her head.

'Elaine, we haven't found yet who killed your friend. Help us find who killed your friend.'

Grace reached across the table and held out her hand. Elaine reached behind her neck and undid the clasp. She lifted the necklace free.

It wasn't a pendant. It was a key.

39

'Elaine, you're going to have to come with me.' Grace slipped her cell phone out of her bag and punched in her uncle's number as she stood up and slipped the key off the chain. She put it into her wallet.

'I can't. I have to meet my lab partner for an engineering class. We're constructing a bridge out of ball bearings and toothpicks that has to sustain over thirty pounds of weight. They're graded at the end of the week.'

'People are going to die tonight, Elaine, unless you help.'

Her pale face flushed and she started talking more quickly. 'Then I have choir practice. And a meeting for next year's RAs. I've been picked to be an RA. I can't just blow off that meeting. And then I have to crank out a five-page paper from Odette's perspective on Swann in Proust's *In Search of Lost Time*. Wait. You said *die*?'

Grace nodded. The cell phone stopped ringing and her uncle picked up.

'Descanso.' In the background was a cacophony of noises. 'Got something?'

'Tammy's best friend from college. And a key.'

'A key. Any idea what it opens?' He went on without waiting for an answer. 'Where are you?'

'A Denny's right outside Riverside University. I'll drive her in.'

'No. Wait.' Elaine shot to her feet.

343

'The one on the twelve-hundred block of University Avenue?'

'That's it.'

'I'll have a Riverside police officer there in five.'

Grace looked at Elaine, gathering books together and quietly weeping. Her cheeseburger lay untouched.

'You're going to need somebody to talk to her professors. She's worried about assignments being due and missing deadlines.'

'I'm worried about the Convention Center going up in flames in an hour, unless we can figure out what's here.'

'Where are you taking me?' Elaine's voice was subdued.

'Somebody from the police is going to take you into Palm Springs, Elaine.'

'No, I mean *where*.'

'Tell her the Convention Center, Grace,' Pete barked in her ear.

'Everybody's at the Convention Center,' Grace said quietly. 'That's where they'll interrogate you.' She immediately wished she hadn't used that word.

Elaine paled. 'Grace, I just remembered something else. Tammy told me she was working there. She had a job at the Convention Center.'

Grace looked at her steadily. 'Uncle Pete, you still there? Tammy was going to work the Convention Center.' She lowered her voice and turned so that Elaine couldn't hear. 'Were the student volunteers at the ag convention all printed?'

344

'To work there, yeah. And we just came up with a match to prints for the housekeeper at Bartholomew's. A student named Mindy Coresu.'

'Mindy.' Grace searched her memory and found it: a dewy, glossy-haired student with a name tag: HELLO! MY NAME IS MINDY! Manning the information kiosk inside the Convention Center. If she was inside, and part of Bartholomew's group, then what they had planned for that night could have made it inside.

Time was running out. The dances, the celebrations, the speeches, started at seven. It was almost six. If Radical Damage kept to its original threat, something horrific would happen in less than an hour. She shifted the phone. It felt damp in her hands.

Outside the window, a black-and-white pulled to a stop at the curb and an officer Grace didn't recognize got out. Grace put cash down on the table.

'Ride's here. I'll send her on.'

'Where are you headed?'

Grace hesitated, looking at Elaine. She didn't want to say anything in front of her. 'I'll call you back, fill you in.'

Grace closed up her cell phone and escorted Elaine out past the booths and smiling hostess at the door. Elaine stiffened when she saw the police car and Grace laid a reassuring hand on her back.

'Anything else about Tammy that I should know? Anything strike you as odd?'

'When you said Mindy.' Elaine peered at Grace anxiously through her glasses. The red from the taillights on the unmarked washed Elaine's face like a watercolor.

'You know Mindy?'

'She was part of Professor B's group.'

'Wait just a sec, I'm going to give this key to the officer who's driving you in.'

Grace darted over to the black-and-white and put the key into the officer's hand. Elaine stood hunched in a tight ball of misery, waiting.

'This Mindy. Did she hang with Tammy?'

Elaine nodded. Her silky hair slanted across her face, obscuring her eyes. 'On campus, we have a clinic. Our folks want us to use it when we get sore throats and stuff, but nobody does. The guys there just blow off things — even when they're serious. You can be dying of pneumonia, and these guys won't catch it.'

'You were talking about Mindy and her relationship to Tammy.'

'Friday, Mindy stops by, picks up Tammy. They were going to catch a ride in on the Scoot, that's the free bus that takes you into town. Mindy said they were going to Target, but Tammy let it slip they were going to a clinic on Magnolia Avenue for shots.'

40

Grace hurried across campus to the parking garage, passing a deserted fountain. The cement fish that normally spouted water was dry now, the trough surrounding the fish a slimy green, littered with leaves.

Small stamps of light from the lampposts cast a glow across the flagstone, but the campus felt deserted. A cold wind shook the leaves of an oak tree, and a shivering cascade of dry leaves lifted off the ground and resettled.

There was a stone bench outside the parking garage and Grace sat in the light and called her uncle.

His voice vibrated across the line, crackling with focused energy. The noise behind him made it hard to distinguish his words. 'Give it to me.'

'Frank Waggaman used to audit Bartholomew's classes. He baited him in class until Bartholomew had him thrown out. He was wildly jealous of Bartholomew's hold on the kids.'

'What else?'

'How are things there?'

'Busy, Grace. What else?'

'The soy I took from Bartholomew's shoes. It's been contaminated — altered — with something.'

'Altered. What do you mean?'

'That's what I need to find out.'

347

'Bring me something solid, Grace. Otherwise, stay off the line.'

'Tammy, the murdered girl with the tattoo, was part of Bartholomew's gang. She went with Mindy into town last Friday. To get shots.'

'Shit. What kind of shots?'

'No idea. From a clinic on Magnolia Avenue in Riverside. That's from Elaine Choo, the student who's coming in with Tammy's key.'

His phone dropped out. 'Hang on. I've got a call coming in.'

Grace stared up at the parking garage. Light flooded the stairwells. A golf cart putted around parked cars on the first floor, carrying a security guard.

'Fuck.' Her uncle was back.

'What is it?'

'I have to go.'

'What?'

'Goddamn it.'

'Tell me what's going on.'

'Jewel Malosky, Nate's mother. Admitted this morning to Desert Regional. Tests just came back. She has anthrax inhalation. Those fuckers are going to release anthrax inside the Convention Center.'

★ ★ ★

Grace sat in her car with the windows up, doors locked. She had the motor running and the lights on so she could see better, but even with the heater on, she was cold. On her cell phone, she pulled up everything she could find on anthrax

348

inhalation. The way it worked was, information floated in sometimes and coalesced if she kept her mind still, but her mind was skittering, darting, and then a small piece of random information tapped into her mind, as if it were a chord in a song she'd heard before, or Morse code. Delicate, urgent.

Grace's eyes widened. She stared through the windshield at the cement wall. 'Oh, my God.'

Bring me something solid, Grace.

The car beams revealed ghostly pinwheels of turbines as she kept her foot on the gas, radio tuned to a local news station, her car rocketing toward Palm Springs in the wind tunnel created by a truck.

Otherwise, stay off the line.

★ ★ ★

A reporter was broadcasting live from the Convention Center. He interviewed Frank Waggaman, who kept trying to turn the interview away from the fields going up in smoke and Bartholomew's murder, back to the good that they were doing creating soy resistant to drought, but the reporter would not be deterred and Waggaman abruptly broke off the interview, screamed an epithet and strode off into the crowd.

Even better, from the reporter's perspective. Now he had something to talk about that was new: the rigid tilt of Waggaman's shoulders, the rage in his voice. The clip played twice in the time it took for Grace to get onto Palm Canyon

Drive. Stalled traffic again, with a patrolman on foot traffic.

Grace slid down her window and offered her FBI ID. 'Accident?'

He shook his head. 'All hell's broken loose at the Convention Center.' He waved her on.

Anxiety roiled through her. She pulled into the parking lot at Desert Regional Medical Center and darted through the lobby to the elevator. It stalled on the second floor. She punched the button again and heard the elevator settle on the ground floor with a crunch.

Intensive Care was on the third floor through a swinging door expressly forbidding any unauthorized entrance. She pushed through the door, shoved her badge toward a nurse, and kept running. 'Grace Descanso. FBI. Here to see him.' She pointed.

Sheriff's Deputy Rogener, the same deputy who had guarded the crime scene soy field where Bartholomew had been killed, shot out of his seat. He looked grim and jumpy.

'How's she doing?'

'No way of knowing.'

'Is she conscious?'

'I think she's in and out.'

'Can you get a note in there? It's important.' Grace scribbled a question in block letters.

He got a nurse to carry it in. She came back almost right away, eyes wide.

'I gave her the one blink for yes, two blinks for no. She blinked once. I tried a second time. Got the same thing.'

Grace trotted down the hall as she stabbed the

number. She felt a sense of lightness, a surreal quality. Her uncle picked up.

'This better be important.'

'Jewel. Nate's mother. The woman with anthrax.'

'Right.'

'Tonight, are there drummers, African drummers?'

'Grace, I don't have time to figure out the social calendar of — '

'She unwrapped an African drum, Uncle Pete. Nate and Andrea had them shipped into the country for their Square Pegs business. Probably the craftsmen didn't even know the skins carried anthrax. But Nate and Andrea did. Uncured goat hides, that's my guess.'

A nurse hurried by in the hallway, pushing a crash cart.

'The skins are hard-dried. That means they crack apart when they're hit. They only release the spores when they're banged.'

A silence. 'It's not an African tribe performing tonight for a bunch of chemists and GM scientists. It's a skit. The volunteers here. Mindy and — I gotta go.'

'Check out who's had an anthrax vaccination recently.'

He was gone.

41

Radical Damage had smuggled goat-hide drums contaminated with anthrax spores into the Convention Center, benign and harmless until the spores were dislodged by hitting the drums, and then the anthrax would become a lethal weapon.

Inhalation anthrax. A simple plan. By the time symptoms would manifest themselves, the members of Radical Damage would have picked up stakes, moved on. They had money from the cargo thefts, and even though Bartholomew had been murdered, and Andrea and Nate and a core group arrested during the cargo theft bust, there was still enough of a plan in place that the rest of the group would be able to move forward.

Grace thought about that. The seductive pull of terrorism. The winging-it thrill of living on the edge, breathing danger. Did Frank Waggaman kill Bartholomew so he could take over the group? The new king.

Bring me something I can use.

She took the elevator to the maternity ward. The waiting room was empty except for a father snuffling into his hand as he slept on a laminated chair. Above him, a TV was tuned to a woman with green hair swallowing a bug.

An admissions desk sat unoccupied between two closed doors under a sign: NEW VISITORS. SIGN IN. FOR ASSISTANCE AND/OR ADMISSION

PLEASE USE THE PHONE AT THE NICU ENTRANCE.

She pushed open a door. A nurse reading a chart glanced up.

'Vonda Soderberg.' Grace hesitated. 'I'm family.' The words held power. She said them again, more softly.

The nurse pointed and went back to the chart.

Grace found Vonda's door and knocked.

'Come in,' Vonda sang out.

She sat against pillows. Her face was pale, the nostrils pink and chapped, but her eyes burned with calm clarity. Grace remembered that feeling. When she'd delivered Katie, for a moment she'd felt invincible. That was how Vonda looked. She wore her hair loosely, glossy curves framing her strong dark eyes and soft mouth.

She cradled at her breast a small bundle, covered in the blue hospital flannel warming blanket. Dark silky hair fluffed over the blanket. A distinctive *thwup thwup* emanated from the blanket.

The blinds were tilted, letting in a crack of dark sky. A dog-eared paperback, *Making Organic Baby Food*, lay on the portable nightstand.

'Hey,' Vonda said softly.

Stacks of bread lay against the wall. *Handmade with love!* the tag said in a circular handwriting around the Good Farms label. *Wholesome soy in every bite!*

'I'm giving them out to the nurses here. They've all been great. You never got your loaf.'

'That's right.' Grace went to the stack and

353

squatted down. 'How about cranberry. That okay?'

'Whatever you want. Want to see him?'

'Love to. But let him nurse. Let's talk a while.'

At Vonda's breast, the tiny silky head moved rhythmically under the blanket.

'Vonda, the soy seeds that Frank Waggaman sold you. You ever have that stuff tested?'

Vonda frowned. 'It's organic.'

Grace nodded. She reached out and stroked Sam's hair.

'Why would we test it, Grace? What's wrong with it?'

'What needs to be tested?'

Grace looked up. Stuart lounged in the doorway. He looked tousled and sleepy and hard-bodied. He was wearing a dark gray T-shirt and a soft pair of jeans. He smiled at Vonda and she beamed and he came over to her and touched his son's cheek softly. 'Hey, guy. Hey, big guy.'

'You look good for having just been the coach.'

'I'm running on fumes, Grace. So what needs to be tested?'

'Maybe nothing,' Grace said. 'I'm just curious about the organic seeds that were used to grow your bread.'

'Frank Waggaman's.'

'Does he sell the seed to other growers?'

Stuart nodded, his eyes on his son. 'As far as I know. He had it enriched with a bunch of nutrients — it's all good.'

'I'd like to test it.'

His eyes shot up warily. 'Is there a problem?'

354

'I'd just like to get it tested, that's all. Do you still have a seed bag at the greenhouse? And am I going to need keys to get in there?'

'Wow. That sounds serious.' Stuart looked at her. His gaze was direct and penetrating. He had a fine nose, strong chin, good mouth. But his eyes knocked her sideways. They were gray and alert. He wasn't going to let her skate on this one. She could feel it. He was a father now. Every instinct in him was to protect his son.

'We got some in the van, remember?' Vonda shifted the baby to a spit cloth on her shoulder, smoothing his small back. 'Kind of like Johnny Appleseed. So we can get started at our new place with planting right away.'

'You're not leaving right away, are you? Not anymore.' A hard knot balled in her stomach, formed out of a raw welter of frayed relationships, angry words. Could people do that? Abandon their parents. Their family. Would Katie?

'Of course we are. A couple of days and we'll be set. The van's almost loaded.'

'What about your folks? Your mom. She's going to want to see the baby. You can't leave before she comes home.'

'She's flying up to see us. It's all arranged.'

'You can't leave your dad like this.'

Vonda grew still. 'Grace, stop trying to fix this. Some things, they get broken enough, they can't be fixed.'

Grace went to the window and stared out. 'I can't hear that one. Not now.'

'Grace, you don't have any idea what it's been

like.' Vonda's voice cracked and the baby stiffened under the blanket in a startle reflex and mewled.

Vonda stroked the top of his head and he rooted blindly for her nipple and latched on.

'This beautiful little baby. This healthy, beautiful little guy. Dad sees him and goes ballistic.'

'Ballistic. I don't understand.' The words made no sense. She only knew her head hurt. Her heart.

'I'll go with you, Grace,' Stu said. 'The van's crammed. You'll never find it.'

'Wait. She has to see him first.'

Grace came over next to the bed as Vonda carefully detached her infant. A bubble of milk beaded his lower lip on a small, rosebud mouth. A crater of shock rocked through her.

It was an Asian face. Dark blue irises stared back at Grace. Eyes set in epicanthic folds slanting down. A small nose against wide cheekbones.

'He's beautiful.'

Vonda was busy cooing at Sam, but Stuart looked at her carefully.

To see if she were lying? She wasn't sure. Sam *was* beautiful. But it was clear from the veil that had dropped over Stuart's eyes that he had seen her surprise.

She wanted to handle it properly, and that rocked her back a second time. She'd never thought of herself as being particularly conscious of race, and yet there she stood, choosing her words carefully, checking to see which ones were weighted, which ones held.

'They should tell people labor hurts.' Vonda grimaced. 'I had that Percodan or whatever it is that makes labor come like it's this fist grinding and then they finally took him C-section. It's hard to sleep; I want to hold him all the time.'

'You can stay with your folks.' Doing one more loop was risky. Grace wasn't ready yet to ask how two Caucasian parents came to have an Asian baby.

'I can't.' There was sadness and finality in Vonda's voice. 'I just can't. Dad's a hard-core law-and-order guy, with no room for mistakes, for *life*. When Sammy was born, it occurred to me. This was my shot at getting it right.'

Grace reached out and gently touched the infant's hair. It was soft as the inside of an egg. 'You did it. Both of you. You kept trying. And now you have Sam.'

'It was Stu's idea to use a sperm bank, try a genetic background different than ours. We'd tried for years. Then he got this idea, and I said why not?'

Vonda put Sam on her chest and patted gently.

Grace's cell phone rang. She checked the number. 'I have to go, Vonda.'

'I'll go with you. Be right back, hon.'

Vonda held up her arms to Grace. 'Wait. A hug.'

Grace wrapped her arms around her cousin and for a brief instant, Vonda held on convulsively.

'Family,' Vonda whispered.

'Family.' Her throat felt heavy. She disengaged.

'Wait. Don't forget the bread.'

'Right.' She picked it up and joined Stu.

In the elevator going down he said, 'Grace, what's going on?'

'You know I can't discuss — '

'Grace, if you've found something that could hurt my wife and baby, I deserve to know. We've waited too long for Sam to have anything happen now.'

'When are you leaving?'

'You haven't answered my question. Frank Waggaman promised us this seed was pure. Organic. I need to know if he lied.'

He stared at her tensely, his eyes searching. He must have seen something, followed some dark path. She felt the intensity of his probing. He reared back as if he'd been stung. 'Shit.'

The elevator doors slid wide.

'Shit,' he said again.

'I'm not sure what we're looking at yet, Stu. It could be nothing.'

'But that's not what you think, is it?'

She hesitated. He deserved the truth. 'No.'

She could see his energy coil. Something volcanic shot up his body. His hands curled into fists and she imagined for an instant what he would have done to Frank Waggaman if he'd been standing where she was.

Her cell phone rang. She checked the number and let it go to voicemail. 'I'm going to need to call this number when we get outside, Stu.'

'If Frank Waggaman did something to my

family . . . ' It was a low cry of despair and rage. He walked ahead of her through the lobby and when he turned, his face looked ashen. 'I'll bring the van around and off-load the seed bag while you make that call.'

She nodded. *You have to be willing to die for your beliefs.* That's what Andrea had said in jail.

Is that what Frank Waggaman believed, too? She mentally reviewed the contents of Frank's office. The fertilizer bags, the GOT SOY? poster, the high wall of bubble-wrapped boxes.

Boxes. Maybe they weren't boxes. Maybe they were drums. Goat-hide drums loaded with anthrax. What better way to guard them than to keep them close, in his office, sealed in bubble wrap and protected by an armed security guard at the door.

It meant he knew. It meant he was part of it.

Those drums had to have been brought in early, as part of his office. *Wheel in those three metal filing cabinets, stick them against the wall next to the wardrobe, and could you stack these bubble-wrapped drums laced with anthrax up against the door?*

She punched in her uncle's number as she crossed out of the lobby. A cold wind skittered across the parking lot. It was a damp cold, a cold that in the desert could cut to the bone in another month.

Frank Waggaman was competitive. That's what Denise Bustamonte had said in the lab. Maybe his competitiveness had driven him to snap, to murder.

And on the heels of killing Bartholomew must

have come the crashing realization that the soy field would be a murder site, off-limits to delegates. All Frank's work for nothing.

But his ego wouldn't let him leave it there. He still wanted to be part of the action. He set up the fire in the sugar beets crop as he was walking through it with delegates. Great footage. News at eleven.

And the soybean spores. Hiding them at Jeanne's.

Jeanne isn't who she said she was. That's what he'd protested to Grace.

You are?

He'd put his finger over his lips. As if to stop himself from giving up a secret.

'Yeah.' Her uncle barked into the phone. A shrieking sound in the distance, and a swell of voices and noise.

'Check the bubble-wrapped boxes against Frank's wall. I think that's where the drums are.'

He hung up without answering. Her cell phone rang again immediately.

'It's Denise Bustamonte,' the Riverside University scientist said without preamble. 'I've figured out what human DNA's been encoded in the soy. And Grace, it's gruesome.'

42

'I'm listening.'

Grace walked to a gravel island under a halogen light. She spotted her car a couple of rows over and unlocked the doors with the remote, and the lights winked in the dark. Stuart looked in the direction of the blinking lights, found it, and nodded. He peeled off in the direction of a mustard-colored van parked a distance away.

'You know about racial profiling using DNA?'

Grace frowned. 'Yeah, I gave a lecture on it in Indio a while back. Bartholomew was in the audience, actually.'

Denise sighed. She struck Grace as a solid, methodical, brilliant woman, unflappable. But something had disturbed her. She sighed again, and Grace realized she was trying to catch her breath.

Grace walked to her car, unlocked the trunk and lifted the lid, waiting. The keys dangled in the lock. Across the parking lot, she saw the lights of Stuart's van come on.

'Whoever doctored the soy — what he's done is insert a command that only affects a specific race.'

'What?'

The van coughed and sputtered to life and Stuart eased it out of its parking space.

The words made no sense. 'Wait, back up.

361

Something's embedded in the soy that affects a specific race. There's technology around to do that?'

'Oh, Grace.' Her voice was heavy. 'The USDA has given approval for the commercial production of rice that contains human genes to counteract diarrhea. An antigen for E. coli's been spliced into potatoes. There are edible vaccines now in tomatoes and bananas. Inserting a human gene that affects health is being done all the time. In this country alone there are close to two hundred million acres of GM crops, but GM crops are grown all over the world and a lot of those already have human genes in some form.'

Stuart's van bumped slowly across the parking lot, came to the row where she was parked, and turned in. Grace tossed her bag in the backseat of her car and slammed the door. She leaned against the car, waiting.

'Which race?' It was an easy question, only two words; her mind was already moving in short bursts of color, energy, making links, moving on, trying new paths.

Part of her already knew.

'The soy fragment found in Ted's shoes has been coded to target SNPS of Indo-Europeans. White people. The genes inserted stimulate an overproduction of interleukin-4.'

It wasn't what she was expecting and her mind took the disparate pieces and re-sorted. Her mind felt emptied, except for the busy work, moving, humming, building.

'Grace?'

She stared blankly at the van as Stuart pulled

362

up crosswise behind her. He left the motor running and slid open the side door. Mounds of clothing, books, and cardboard boxes crammed the back of the van. Stuart reached into the middle of the high jumble of debris and started hunting for the bag of organic soy.

'Grace? You still there?'

'Yeah.'

'You're familiar with it.'

'Interleukin-4, yeah. It's an essential ingredient in the human immune system.'

When she was training to be a doctor, her area of expertise had been pediatric transplant immunology, but she didn't have the energy to tell Dr Denise Bustamonte that.

'Why would somebody take the time to encode a human gene in a soybean plant? A gene that stimulates the production of interleukin-4. Any ideas?'

Stuart had disappeared into the interior of the van, sorting through clothes and setting aside books.

'There was a graduate study I remember at Cornell done on mice. Dealing with the overproduction of interleukin-4. The mice bred and the fertilized eggs were successfully implanted, but the overstimulation of the hormone created an angiogenesis inhibitor — interfering with the growth of new blood vessels in the fetus.'

'So the mice miscarried.' Denise sucked in a breath.

'Early in pregnancy.' Grace felt as if she'd been hit in the solar plexus.

Stuart turned in the van, half smiled, and

made a face, acknowledging the mess. He retreated again inside the van.

'So it's possible whoever did this with the soy was experimenting,' Denise said slowly. 'The 'go' switch that stimulates overproduction of this hormone is encoded in the soy, and the result is . . . what? If they eat the soy? Miscarriages in humans?'

'Miscarriages early in pregnancy.'

The mice miscarried. Early in pregnancy.

Just like Vonda Soderberg and the other women in her infertility group. Is that what Frank Waggaman had done? Reengineered the soy seed he'd sold to organic farmers?

'Whoever did this is targeting the reproductive systems of white people. But why? Oh. And whatever else they transferred, they encoded something so that when the soy's heated, the human genes aren't killed. They're intact.'

'So if something's baked, if the soy was baked and ingested, whatever was encoded in the soy wouldn't be neutralized.'

Grace's heart started to trip. 'Denise, the soy is encoded to stimulate the production of interleukin-4, right?'

'Yeah, it's shot full of the command to pump up production.'

'What's the cutoff?'

'You mean, to cause miscarriages?'

'How high a percentage of Indo-European snips has to be present before this stuff recognizes them as white and floods the system with the interleukin-4?'

'Fifty-one percent or higher.'

364

Grace shifted position. The jumble of pieces that had seemed so random suddenly sifted and clicked into place. She squeezed her eyes shut. A high wind screamed in her head and all the dark angels were unleashed. 'Denise — what if — somebody was tired of waiting around for the world to become less dominated by whites? What if that person had the technology and capability to ensure that this domination would no longer exist?'

'Go on.'

'The soy's been modified so that it only affects Caucasians, right?' Grace already knew the answer.

'Where are you going with this?'

'Miscarriages, Denise. The cold virus replicates the interleukin-4 and inhibits the creation of fetal blood vessels, but only in Indo-European snips. The people we think of as white. So if those white males mate with white females, the females miscarry. Those fetuses will never be carried to term. They destruct within the first three months in utero.'

'Other races, those wouldn't be affected,' Denise said slowly.

'Yeah, that's the beauty of it.'

'So you're saying if two white people try to have a kid — '

'They can't,' Grace finished. 'They just keep miscarrying.'

'But if a white woman matches up with somebody — say, with predominantly sub-Saharan snips, a black guy — '

'No problem. The cold virus hasn't been keyed

to recognize those snips, so the interleukin-4 doesn't kick into gear.'

'You're saying whites would have to choose partners from minority races if they wanted to have kids.' Denise sounded stunned.

Grace shifted her grip on the phone. 'Within twenty years, whites would effectively be stripped of their power. Their days at calling the shots would be over because *there wouldn't be any white race left*. They'd be history.'

Stuart eased out of the van, a bag of seed in his arms. He was smiling. The burlap bag looked heavy, awkward.

'But this is just how it looks on the computer.' Denise's voice held a faint tremor. 'It would have to be tested in real life.'

Stuart lost his balance and shoved the bag into her and she felt the cold snub nose of a gun. Fear coiled in her gut. A cold sweat washed over her. He put the bag down, the gun up. He pressed it against her head.

'Grace?' Denise's voice was tinny.

Stuart folded up the cell phone and tossed it into the parking lot and it skidded under a car. He grasped her arm and they half trotted around her car to the back.

'Now you're going to get into the trunk of your car, Grace. And we're going for a little drive.'

43

She curled into a ball, trying to still the sound of her heart. She heard scraping as he yanked the keys out of the trunk lock. Her keys. Hers. He relocked the doors, a quick grinding sound that delineated the walls of her prison.

A fine sheen of sweat creased her back. It wasn't daylight in the desert. Not yet. In daylight, the temperature inside the trunk could easily soar to over 160 degrees Fahrenheit. She knew that because there had been a smuggler in Calexico who'd been stuffed into a trunk as a payback. He'd literally cooked to death.

But that wasn't going to happen to her.

A little drive.

His shoes scraped across the gravel, receding. She heard the sound of a car door slamming. The rumble of his van retreating. He was driving away.

She replayed everything she'd learned about being trapped in a trunk, all of it easy, all of it things she'd never done, never had time to do.

Hide a second remote in the trunk. Keep a flashlight handy. A screwdriver, crowbar, tire iron. She rolled onto her side and started feeling along the carpet for the tab that would open it.

She found the tab and yanked it up. She put her hand down in it cautiously.

It was nasty, working at a crime lab.

Her memory was crammed with stories of six

hundred-pound boa constrictors named Baby Alice slithering loose in neighborhoods and winding up coiled inside spare tires.

The compartment was empty. She patted it again, harder this time, as if she could command it to appear. Nothing.

She remembered then she'd loaned the tire and the iron to Marcie, her crime lab friend. Helped change the flat in the police parking lot, both of them rushing out afterwards, her friend's grateful promises for dinners or cookies or a movie trailing in the air above her like a small galaxy of silvery lies.

She'd been late picking up Katie from soccer practice; that had been the only thing on her mind. How could she have forgotten to get the tire and iron back? She felt a flash of anger at Marcie, but it was old anger, not hot enough to use.

She rolled onto her back and stared at the ceiling. She wiped the sweat from her eyes and started patting down the cage. She'd believed his lie about rheumatoid arthritis. She'd never checked it. Never asked for confirmation. Believed him.

Believing the other lies had come easily from that one. A man with swollen fingers, fingers where the immune system was attacking cartilage, would live a life of compromise. A life that never could have included pulling back the inflexible swift cord, steadying the bucking fiberglass bow, taking delicate aim, letting the bolt fly.

Killing a man in a field of soy.

The alibi. Time-stamping egg pods for quality assurance. Sarah Conroy's husband, the ex-con arrested in the cargo theft bust, could have stepped in, taken Stuart's place for an hour or so, while Stu killed Bartholomew and slipped back to work. Grace wondered what Stu had traded for it.

She thought about Stuart, the way he looked at Vonda with love, how Vonda smiled back. Grace was a sap for the happy ending, the moment where the cowboys rode over the hill into the sweet, fragrant night.

It was harder when evil had a pretty face, a striking personality. Juice.

Solzhenitsyn had it right. Evil didn't separate countries, nations, ideologies. It ran through the middle of every human heart. Stuart had set it up perfectly. His grief over losing babies. His instinctive need to protect Vonda, protect Sam.

Only he'd orchestrated Vonda's heartbreaking miscarriages. He'd used her and her friends as research subjects. He must have been ecstatic when it worked.

He'd wanted to get next to Grace from the first time he'd seen her at the jail, find out why she'd been called in, what she knew.

When she'd asked for samples of the organic soy seed that Frank Waggaman had sold them. Stuart knew he'd have to act. The next step would have been comparing the organic soy that Frank Waggaman sold them to the soy seed he sold to other farmers. When the other soy seed came up untainted, Grace would have known Frank was innocent.

Known it was Stuart. Had always been Stuart.

Footsteps grated across the asphalt, coming closer, and for an instant, she thought maybe if she banged on the ceiling and yelled hard enough, whoever it was would stop walking to their own car and investigate. She pounded the ceiling and screamed.

A key turned, opening the driver's door and she stopped. She heard him slide in and slam the door shut. It amazed her how different things sounded, trapped in a trunk. Close. Sweat pooled off her face, or maybe tears.

In a normal tone of voice Stu said, 'I could fire this gun right through the backseat, use the cushion to muffle the sound. Have a pretty good shot at killing you.' His voice was pleasant.

He started driving. He wasn't leaving her there. He was taking her somewhere.

Stu tapped on the brakes and she rocked backward and pressed against the cage with her hands and feet, bracing herself. He drove faster than she was used to. The sound of other cars was close.

Grace's car was a Nissan she'd bought from a dealership. She'd gotten a good deal on it because it was that year that manufacturers were required to install trunk releases. Her car didn't have one. But it got good gas mileage and had some zip when she changed lanes.

The way Stuart was doing. The car tilted slightly and she splayed out her hands, trying to brace herself. She could feel the motion of the wheels under her.

A horn blasted right on the bumper, the sound

mechanical and angry at the same time, and Grace instinctively braced herself and covered her head.

The car made a sharp left turn and sped up. She took a breath. The air was hot. She needed to slow her thoughts, think. The traffic sounds were freeway noises: tires against pavement, occasional snatches of a song through a car window, metal grinding when gears shifted. They were on the 10, heading out of town.

Under the carpet, a cable ran from the driver's side to the trunk. If she could find that cable and pull on it, the trunk would open and she would be free. She did a cursory pat and found nothing.

Brake lights. If she could get to the brake lights, rip out the wires, a CHIP or patrolman would stop the car, write a ticket. Except everybody was at the Convention Center.

Time had lost meaning. Her feet were numb. She shifted position and pressed the soles of her feet against the far side of the trunk. Stinging pain shot up her legs.

The car was slowing. She heard the far-off sound of a train at a crossing light. The car bumped down a road, a dirt road, from the way the tires seized. He was taking her to the switching yard.

Her face was wet now and she wiped it. If they were at the yard, where was everybody? Where was the clang of machinery, the grinding gears of freight as a train was built?

The car picked up speed, bouncing over ruts, and Grace squeezed her eyes shut and gritted

371

her teeth. It was just the two of them. And whatever came next.

She felt a shifting in the underbelly of the car. He was slowing down. There was another sound coming closer, one that filled her with hope.

It was a car. Somebody was coming toward them. She scrambled to the driver's side of the trunk. The car would have to pass by. It was her one chance to make noise, to alert the driver, get help, end the nightmare.

She rolled to her knees, coiled her fists. She pounded on the wall in a flurry of blows, the sides of her fists stinging.

Stuart slammed on the brakes and she lost her balance and smashed into the opposite wall. Fresh pain shot up her shoulder.

'Grace. I know you can hear me. You make another sound, one move, and I'll put a bullet through the head of whoever it is that's coming my way. Can't see who it is in the headlights, but I guarantee I'll kill him. Tap once on the wall next to my seat, if you understand.'

She closed her eyes and curled her body into a small tight ball. Her heart tripped. She felt broken. She tapped.

For some irrational reason, she thought of banana pancakes and Mac, how they'd improvised in Guatemala, frying them over the campfire he'd built by the river, how they'd sat side by side on his hammock, the way the light filtered through the trees. How supremely happy she'd felt next to him. Safe.

She thought of Katie wearing a pair of clogs and a tutu, hanging upside down on monkey bars at Cabrillo Elementary, her brown eyes locked on Grace, screaming *Mommy Mommy Mommy look no hands!*

Grace needed to believe her life still would contain moments of such happiness again, but more than that, she needed to know that the life of the person approaching in the car, stopping the car, the motor idling, that person's life would also have the chance for small moments in the future of unexpected grace.

Stuart stopped the car, rolled down the window. 'Judith!'

Grace licked her lips. They felt cracked. Judith Woodruff. The owner of Windlift.

Stuart's voice was too hearty and Grace feared for her. She ducked her head into her arms. She couldn't breathe.

Judith said something unintelligible.

'Borrowed it.' Stuart's voice changed, tensed.

The car. Judith was asking about the car he was driving.

Another comment from Judith, something light. She half laughed at the end.

'She's Vonda's cousin. She's okay.'

More words from Judith.

'Yeah, the baby's great, Vonda's great. It's all good. Just swung by to check in, give you my keys. So everybody's gone, huh?'

Judith spoke again, the words lost in the rumble of the engines.

Grace heard keys jangling. Stuart must be separating out his keys to Windlift, passing them through the open window.

'I'm good. Thought I'd cruise down, take some night pictures from the hill. Don't know when I'll be back this way.'

More words, the noises someone makes saying good-bye, and Grace held her breath, wondering where Stuart's gun was, if he had it in his hand next to him on the seat, if he was getting ready to use it.

Judith's car pulled away and Grace sagged and let out a breath.

The car bumped forward for fifteen seconds and came to a jerky stop. The driver's door opened. He stepped out and slammed it shut. He walked away, his footsteps receding. Minutes went by. The sweat on her face turned cold.

Maybe he wasn't coming back. Maybe he had another identity already established. Maybe he'd never intended to stay with Vonda and Sam. He'd sell his doctored soy to the highest bidder. There had to be a market for it. Such a clean, elegant solution to what had proved, by the very shape-shifting fluidity of its nature, to be an intractable problem.

If everybody was gone at Windlift, that meant the Union Pacific trains would blast through; no reason to stop to pick up freight at an abandoned yard that only now was beginning to come back. She wondered how long it would be before she was found.

A patter of steps.

She strained to hear. Nothing.

Cautiously she rolled to her knees and coiled

into a crouch. She braced herself. She'd throw herself out at him, digging, clawing.

The trunk snapped open, a beam of light smacked her face. His hand closed around her arm and he wrenched her out.

44

He flung her to the ground and she banged against the car as she went down.

He was wearing goggles and held a crossbow. A packet of bolts pricked out of a holster under his shoulder. A breeze riffled his wild hair, a soldier of death dressed in black, bent on destruction and fire and ruin.

'Stand.' His voice was flat.

'Don't do this.' Adrenaline spiked and her mouth dried out.

'I'm giving you to the count of ten. I'll be using the crossbow. Not the gun. More sportsman-like.' He smiled. 'Ten.'

She had seen this phenomenon on a hundred nature shows, a wounded eagle nursed back to health, a falcon, and the gate to the cage lifted, the sudden burst of wind, the explosion of feathers, the silence when the bird disappeared into the sky or the shadowy trees.

In a burst of adrenaline, Grace sprang to her feet and ran.

Ahead of her lay the shadowy ruins of the roundhouse and beyond that, the switching yard. A single light illuminated the WINDLIFT sign, and more than any other thing, that made Grace afraid. The building was empty. No help there. A faint sliver of moon illuminated the rubble of cement berm that had once been a wall. Bristling acacia balled like wire brushes.

'Nine.'

She angled toward the roundhouse, lost her footing and skidded, scattering a wash of pebbles. She wondered if he could see through concrete pillars. She stumbled past a broken, crumbled brick outcropping with a metal rebar poking up.

'Eight.'

She gripped the crumbling edge of a pillar and pulled herself up into the roundhouse. Moonlight angled down through the damaged roof, creating a spidery pattern of shifting shapes.

Faintly, she could hear him still counting, the number now indistinct.

She looked around. She'd seen glittering broken bottles, when she'd driven past it, useless unless she could lure him close enough, and risky in the dark.

She patted along the wall, almost tumbling outside when it ended abruptly in a pile of concrete.

Through the gap, she could see the ghostly forms of boxcars parked on a siding and she had to stop herself from crying out. The sliding door on the fourth boxcar was open, and in the wash of moonlight she saw the painted serial numbers. It was the same boxcar she'd crawled up into earlier with her uncle.

Leaning against the boxcar, Grace saw the dim outline of a man.

She half ran, half stumbled, and took a flying leap out of the roundhouse. She hit the ground hard. The shock rocked up her legs and she took a series of shambling steps to regain her balance.

The wind was picking up. She heard the faint shrill of a train whistle.

She ran toward the silvery boxcars, her ankles and shins stinging with pain. She moved deeper into the yard, creeping around the steel beams, weaving erratically, keeping low to the ground. Her feet slipped on the gravel berm and she stuttered over the tracks and darted around to the other side so that the boxcars themselves stood between her and the roundhouse. She kept running, her body low, head down.

She passed the first boxcar, a high blur of metal. She shot past the gap, glancing toward the opening between the cars, afraid of what she'd find. Only darkness.

She kept running. She passed the second boxcar and then the third and folded herself into the gap between the cars. She bent over gasping, the raw sound of her breathing cutting through the dark. Maybe it was a trick of light, seeing someone. She'd made too much noise not to have been heard. A policeman would have called out to her. Commanded her to stop, ordered her to state her business, so it wasn't a policeman. And a transient would have been as scared as she was. Already melted into shadows. Disappeared.

She wiped her mouth. An owl hooted. She eased herself over the metal knuckle connecting the two boxcars and inched out her head so that she was looking backward toward the round-house. In the shifting light, it looked like a ruined scrap of metal and cement surrounded by sand and stunted palms.

Nothing moved. She jerked her head back and

pressed flat against the boxcar. She had no idea where Stuart was now and that scared her. She strained to hear footsteps, a grating on sand, a breath. There was nothing except the sound of an uneven wind scatting against the rusted boxcars on the edge of the darkened yard.

She was going to have to move, and it was going to have to be now. She calculated the distance to the open door of the boxcar. Grace took a breath, turned toward it, and ran.

It was Johnstone. Leaning against the boxcar in the wavering half-light as if thinking through a serious subject. Strong, solid, wearing the black uniform of a Union Pacific railroad policeman. He stood bent into the boxcar, motionless. Her relief made her angry. Sleeping on the job.

'Johnstone.' She grabbed his shoulder and spun him toward her.

He slid. He landed heavily, his massive shoulder hitting the ground first, followed by his head slamming at an odd angle. A crossbow bolt pierced his throat. The front of his uniform was bright and shiny red.

There was lots of blood and it was still fresh. She screamed.

The moon slid behind a bank of clouds. A section of track glinted and winked out, as if it had been snuffed.

'Grace.'

Stuart made the name sound like a caress. She was exposed, kneeling, Johnstone's body cooling and heavy in her arms.

She was trapped. He was going to kill her and that's how it would end. He pattered around in

379

the darkness, the sound seeming to come from all over, shifting as if he were examining her from all sides, figuring out the best angle, the cleanest kill.

A numbness spread from her lips across her face and her fingers felt clumsy. She shifted her position and the analytical part of her took over.

'How do you think Vonda's going to feel about you when she finds out?'

She risked a quick look down at the body, hunting for the regulation Sam Browne belt. It was gone. Johnstone's gun. The cuffs. The handie talkie two-way radio, all the paraphernalia that could save her. She shifted and felt something in the dirt. A metal lock. A big one. Her hand closed around it.

She realized what had happened. Johnstone and Judith Woodruff, the head of the company, had been signing off on the contents of the boxcar to lock it up when they'd heard the sound of a car.

Judith had made the decision to drive toward it, find out who it was. Maybe they'd been running late. Maybe she trusted Johnstone to finish locking up without her. Maybe she was just exhausted.

But her choice had saved her.

She swallowed the sour taste of fear, wondering if the last sound she'd hear would be the thin whine of a bolt. She wished she knew where he was.

'You didn't have to kill him.' She shifted Johnstone's weight and smoothed her palms down the body. His shirt was slick with blood.

She found the keys in a pants pocket, her fingers moving delicately until she located what she needed.

'You don't know shit.' Stuart's voice was weary and cold. It was coming from a place low to the ground and dead center, and seemed closer by maybe a yard.

Was he creeping up on her? Would he shoot her point-blank, the tip of the weapon exploding inside her? Judging from his voice, he was maybe fifteen yards away now. She shifted to her knees, still holding Johnstone's body.

The clouds split open, exposing him. The night-vision goggles blanked out his eyes. He angled the crossbow down, bounced a foot onto the metal bar to steady the weapon as he guided the bolt into the groove, and yanked the string toward the scope. There was a small, snicking sound as the string caught. He raised the crossbow and found her in the scope. The entire action had taken less than two seconds. He clicked off the safety and eased his finger onto the trigger.

This was the moment when it hit home. Grace had carved out a world with Katie, a world she was going to have to share with Mac, a small, compact orderly world from the outside, but exploding under a microscope when she scratched the surface was a universe teaming with soccer practices, lists undone, melting ice cream left too long in the car, a world of late nights in the lab and early mornings with Katie on the roof huddled in damp, dewy sleeping bags, watching the stars fade and the sky turn into a rosy ball of suffused light.

A world where porpoises jumped, if only on the pages of Katie's pink and orange stationery. A world of light.

She hadn't cared about anything bigger than that, when she'd been called. She wasn't interested in saving the world. She'd only wanted to save what was left of her own. And now she realized they were related.

She saw Katie's face. The light in her eyes. She needed to give Katie a hero to believe in. And more than that, she needed to give herself one.

She yanked Johnstone's car keys from his pocket and came roaring to her feet. She punched the car alarm button. Red lights flashed in the dark. The alarm shrilled. There was just enough light for her to see him, a red strobe washing over his face.

Startled, Stuart jerked his head toward the sound and Grace reared back with the lock in her hand, took aim and let it fly.

The lock was strong, steel, American made, and her aim was good. The lock clipped him on the side of his head and sent him dancing into the yard, still on his feet. He lost his balance and the bolt shot across the yard toward the flashing lights of the car.

Grace scrabbled along the length of the boxcar until she found the first metal rung. She was making small sounds as she climbed, knowing she was giving him a clear shot at her back.

The air changed and she knew she was close; it smelled fetid, sweaty, the air inside a contained space. She flung herself forward into the boxcar and fell to her knees, patting along the grooves until she found the metal bar that had been wedged in to keep the door open.

She yanked the bar free as Stuart shot to his feet and screamed. It was a guttural cry, savage. He jumped, feet high. A ninja posture, legs thrusting, hands curved, the crossbow aimed straight at her. The hairs on her neck rose.

Grace slammed her shoulder into the side of the sliding door, straining to move it, putting everything she had behind it. The metal hinges creaked.

She was pushing hard and she had gravity on her side, but Stuart had madness on his, fueled by rage.

It closed like a sliding door. She said it over and over. Closed like a sliding door, a sliding door. The moon floated free of the clouds.

The last thing she saw was Stuart, the butt of the crossbow wedged into his shoulder. He pulled the trigger. The string snapped. The bolt shot forward.

45

Grace slammed the door shut, pitching the boxcar into inky darkness. Outside, the bolt crunched into the door with such force it sounded as if it were shearing the metal, and Grace instinctively jerked backward. She'd lost the metal bar and she swept her hands over the floor looking for it. Her left heel nudged the bar and she yanked it up into her hand and scrambled back to the door.

She could use the bar as a weapon, striking downward when he jerked open the door, but if she missed in the dark, he'd kill her.

She knew Stuart would be crossing the distance between them in seconds and would try to slide open the door from the outside. She ran her fingers along the groove of the sliding door. She was going to have to do the opposite of what the agents had done. They'd used the metal bar to hold open the door. She would have to use it to seal herself into a tomb.

Outside, muffled feet pounded closer. Her index finger snagged the route of the groove and she followed it. She grasped the metal bar and shoved it down into the groove, jamming the door.

Outside Stuart yanked the door. It shivered and held and she jerked away from the door. She could hear him on the other side breathing.

I've got an extra light on my key chain, you

need it. Johnstone's key chain. She rocked back on her heels, fished out the key chain and found the penlight, stabbing the narrow beam of light along the edge of the door frame.

Stuart rattled the door again and bellowed in rage and she scrabbled away from the door, afraid. The bellow morphed into a howl and abruptly cut off.

She danced the light along the frame of the door, trying to control the quaking in her fingers.

The strength of his rage had jammed the metal bar up under a metal crossbeam in the door and splintered part of the wood.

She was locked in. She wasn't getting out that way. A wave of claustrophobia surged over her. She was shivering. Her teeth clicked. The inside of the boxcar was cold, and she held herself and rocked.

Mac came into her mind, the piercing way he looked at her, his humor, the smell of his skin. It was her own anger and pain that had made her run from him five years before. She had never let herself believe in his goodness, and she realized now, in the stillness of the cold boxcar, how much of her own goodness she'd sacrificed in the process. A loneliness swept over her, and a terror for what was yet to come. She started to cry and clamped off the sound. He couldn't know.

She wondered what he'd try. Fire. Switching the line. Freight trains plowed right through the yard. Stuart must have worked for Windlift long enough to know how to switch tracks and send a train barreling right into the boxcar.

She slid the penlight off the key chain and examined the rest of the keys on it. House key, car key, and a set of sturdy, oversized Baldwin's. Besides keys, Johnstone kept a small canister of pepper spray the size of a tube of lipstick.

It was the best weapon she had, but it was small. She'd only be able to use it once. She carefully worked the spray canister free of the key ring and put it in her shirt pocket. She practiced yanking it out, aiming it, and mock-squeezing the button, going over and over the movements until the actions felt fluid. Satisfied, she tucked the canister into her pocket and picked up the penlight. She played the small beam over the freight stored behind her. In the light's beam, the cargo looked like coffins.

Long arms of fiberglass lay banded and stacked, taking up most of the space. Blades for the wind turbines. Crammed next to them was a wooden crate that came almost to her shoulders, as long as a baby whale. Smaller boxes had been stacked next to it.

Grace waved the penlight in arcs and found the metal ladder, welded to the side of the car, stretching down from the ceiling. It extended only halfway down, but she could reach it if she climbed up the blades. She squeezed past the wooden crate and stepped onto the blades, moving slowly, taking her time. She cautiously transferred her weight to the ladder, aimed the beam of light, and studied the panel above her.

She pressed straight up with the heel of her hand, hard. The metal panel was cold and smooth to the touch. The yard men had done a good job. It was a tight seal. She climbed down and roved the penlight over the inside. She needed to know every inch of the boxcar, its geography.

The metal bands clamping the blades would make a good weapon, but she had no idea how to get them apart. More promising was the crate. She shoved a smaller box over and used it as a step. Nails poked out of the lid a good quarter inch. She went back to the wind turbine blades and shoved the flashlight between two blades, taking her time positioning it. That far away from the crate, the light it gave was dim.

She slipped free an oversize key and jammed it under a nail in the crate lid, rocking the key back and forth, digging it into the wood. The pressure bit into her fingers and she switched hands. She felt the nail pop slightly and switched the key so that the thick side of it stood under the nail head and she could use the length of the key for leverage. The metal bit into the side of her hand and she realized she was bleeding. She kept working. The nail slid free and she put it into her shirt pocket next to the pepper spray.

She repositioned the light. She worked on the easier nails first. She heard a distant train whistle. Her pocket filled with nails and she worried about being able to retrieve the pepper spray if she needed it quickly. She moved the spray to her pants pocket.

She had two sides done now but it was taking too long and she knew it and fresh panic shot through her. Sweat creased her back. She was able now to slide her fingers under the lid and she crouched and lifted the lid, using that leverage to squeeze loose some of the nails. The hard ones she twisted free.

She was working the last side. The nails were popping loose and she wasn't bothering to save them. She could feel the ache in her shoulders and arms as she rocked the lid.

She stopped. Someone was climbing the side of the car.

46

She stared at the roof. His tread was heavy and his boots banged. Something clanged. His voice was soft and insinuating. 'Grace. Can you hear me?'

Her hand stole to her shirt pocket and touched the pepper spray. She transferred it so that it was on top of the nails in her shirt pocket.

'Talk to me, honey. May as well.'

She worked on loosening the lid, attached now only by the last few nails. It came loose in a whine of splintering wood.

'What was that?' He sounded tense but jocular, as though they were having a dinner party and she'd dropped a hot casserole dish in the kitchen while guests waited at the table.

The penlight cast a pale circle onto the crate; everywhere else was darkness. The crate lid was heavy and she moved awkwardly, legs trembling, settling it carefully against the wall in the dark.

'What are you doing down there?'

He'd told her more than he realized.

He couldn't see her. The night-vision goggles were useless through metal. Until he'd removed the roof panel, she still had time to find another weapon. She wasn't going to cower and wait.

She patted her way toward the pale circle of light and pulled the flashlight free. She went back to the crate.

Straw — the kind she used to fill Katie's

Easter basket. She yanked out a handful, exposing a wink of glossy white metal underneath.

'We never had time to talk.' He sounded regretful. 'So I guess this is it. Let me tell you how this is going to work.'

She put the penlight between her teeth and scraped up handfuls of batting, throwing them on the ground. A grating sound rang through the top of the roof, metal on metal, and she flinched. He must have picked up a bolt cutter. That's why he had been gone so long. No, file, thank God. A hasp. He sounded as if he were sawing off a bolt. That would take longer.

How many bolts would he need to crack loose before he could crack open the metal panel?

She dug her hands deep and scooped up armfuls of stuffing, carefully playing the light over what was revealed. She was staring down into the cavity of a turbine. The gears seemed to be a series of huge, interlinking pieces of metal. There had to be something sharp in there she could use.

She wondered if it was just her imagination, or if the light was getting dimmer.

'You know if you try to get out through the door again, I'll pick you off with my crossbow. I'm a little embarrassed by how that's gone down. I'm better than I seem with it, trust me.'

She emptied out as much of the stuffing as she could pull free and then started on one end of the turbine, moving the small light carefully over what was now exposed inside the cavity. A ribbed generator, much like a car's, was connected by a strong shaft to a bigger metal box. Gears. She went more slowly. Rounded edges. Nothing sharp. There was nothing there to save her.

Above her, Stuart sawed in silence. A sharp whine cut the air, followed by a loud metallic click. As if something had been bitten off. The tip of the bolt rained down like metal hail.

'One down. Anything you want to ask, while you can? Time's running out.' The sound of sawing rasped through the air, energetic, faster.

He wanted to talk to her. Fine, she'd use it. She kept pulling straw out of the crate, exposing the shaft of the wind turbine.

'What kind of a whacked-out childhood did you have, to create you?'

'Come on, Grace, you can do better than that.' He sounded amused.

'Must be lonely, being so smart. Who do you talk to, Stuart?'

'I love her. The kid, too. It's a sacrifice, never being able to see them again.'

'Oh, you'll find somebody else.'

'I already have. I have a life completely apart from this, Grace.'

The filing shifted in tone, and the tip of a second long screw clattered down.

'Nice touch. The twisted fingers.'

'Broke both of them in grade school at recess, trying to catch a hardball, Grace. Never healed properly.'

'I don't get it. Help me out here.'

Grace shifted the penlight beam over the gearbox. The circle of light was dimming, growing smaller. The lower half of the turbine was still buried in padding, the gearbox self-contained. She kept the light moving.

He was cutting through the third bolt.

'Really, I want to know,' she said. 'It was brilliant, Stuart, what you did. Modifying the soy. Trying it out on Vonda. Not just Vonda. Yourself. A brave man. A pioneer.'

'To be responsible for killing off an entire race.' His voice was hypnotic. 'Not even Hitler managed that. And see, the beauty is, it will end war, Grace. Just like that. All these politicians. Year after year. All of them promising hope or change or holding the old line. Words. They're just words, Grace. This is change. Powerful. Effective. No going back. Only forward.'

The circle of light contracted, like a faint star being swallowed by a black hole. It was less than the size of her fist now.

She skimmed the light over the rest of the turbine, hunting. A large white shaft poked out the far end of the gearbox and she moved her beam along to where the gearbox flared and connected to an enormous piece of white metal. It was the main shaft, which would lock into the blades.

'Why Riverside U?'

Frenzied sawing and a third screw tip pelted the floor.

'Dying mothers feel the need to get so much off their chests; unnecessary, really, but what's a son to do?' The frenzied sound of his cutting the lock increased.

She jerked her head up, her heart slamming into her chest. Of course.

'Your mother.'

She thought back to the ripped photo that her uncle had showed her, the one that had been taken to the *Desert Sun*. Bartholomew and Jeanne, young, laughing radicals. But there had been another arm in that photo, a slim female arm, and Bartholomew had been staring at whoever that other person was when the photo had been taken.

Tasha. Samantha. Stuart's mother.

'You're Bartholomew's son. That's what you came to tell him. You were his son.'

'The fucker didn't even respond. Stood there dumb-mouthed, as if he hadn't absorbed a word of it. And the next time I saw him, he pretended not to recognize me. I'd come up with this plan, this perfect plan, putting into action all his words, and what did I get?'

Grace wormed the penlight down deep into the socket, shining it back toward the main shaft. The beam caught a dull spark, buried in the cavity of metal. Grace leaned down into the crate, trying to get a better angle.

It was shiny, slippery almost. A baggie.

Not a baggie, exactly. A small pouch, carefully constructed out of a fluid plastic material. She stretched until she could touch it with her finger and it shivered in the light, the way she imagined a silicon breast implant might move. She slid her fingers under it and gently tugged it loose. She held it in her palm. The last of the light flickered and went out.

She stood perfectly still, wondering if she'd actually seen what she thought she had.

Small brown particles in liquid.

Brown soy. The baggie was filled with soy.

Above her on the roof, Stuart shifted position, the sawing reaching a frenzied crescendo.

'No matter how many times you'd walk him through it, he'd never remember it, would he? It never stuck in his head, who you were. So you came up with a plan, the best plan. You played God. And your father wasn't impressed. He was revolted. You were a nobody. Playing God. Not even your father remembered your name.'

'Fuck him! He's a nobody. A nothing! I'm fucking better than God! Smarter! Does God correct injustices? No! All the misery caused in the name of racial superiority. Entire peoples wiped out, or subjugated to unbelievable pain, and for what? I'm the one speaking for the voiceless, the lost. Me. Me.'

She banged her shin into the banded windmill blades and grabbed hold of them to get her bearings. She was going to have to climb them in the dark to get to the ladder. When he cracked open the roof, she needed to be there, waiting.

She dug a toe in between the blades and shifted her weight. She climbed.

Her thoughts were blank, focused on the climb, on trying to balance without falling and then the pieces shifted and she knew.

He'd packed doctored soy into a baggie and inserted it into the middle of the turbine, a small gel-filled baggie that would shred apart the instant the wind turned the blades. Turned the blades and carried the soy out across the air. Floating, sifting in the wind.

Alive.

All it needed was water and sun to take root. Growing like a weed. Exploding across the land. Little pockets of genetic death.

'The girl with the unicorn tattoo. Tammy.'

'You have to understand. Bartholomew — Daddy — had this little group of simpering sycophants — mostly women, of course. Trying to wreak havoc. It was all pretend. Nothing. They grabbed a cargo load of crossbows.'

'And you stole one and used it to kill him.'

'He was a nothing, Grace. A no one. I gave him chances, so many chances.'

'Did you kill Tammy, too?'

The sawing increased. 'Hell, no.'

'Then who did?'

'Who the fuck cares?'

Her hands reached the top of the blades and she crawled up, stretching out her hands, trying to find the ladder. The motion of her hands weaving in wide erratic circles almost made her lose her balance and topple off and she put her hands down to brace herself and found the flat surface of the blade again. She stretched out her hand until she found the boxcar wall. Her knuckles banged into a rung and she carefully turned herself around and grabbed hold of the ladder.

A windmill to each state, each foreign country. Fifty states. Almost sixty foreign countries. Stuart Soderberg had taken fresh soy and sent it out in the windmills across America, one per state, one for each foreign country, each destined for an organic farm where the soy would take root and flourish.

Each windmill carrying death. Fifty new patches of modified soy, from sea to shining sea. America compromised and altered in one terrible instant. And what about the impact on other countries?

Out at night.

Grace closed her eyes against a flash of images: a shivering American Indian reaching for a blanket infected with smallpox; a cattle car pulling to a stop at Auschwitz; Africans dying in chains; and closer in time: skulls piled in a Cambodian killing field; a clearing slippery with blood in the Sudan; a village razed to the ground in Bosnia. If Grace hated those things, then she must also hate this.

She climbed up the ladder. She pressed one hand against the ceiling and felt it give. She reached for the pepper spray. The sawing sound was loud and she yelled through the crack to be heard.

'No wonder he hated you, Stu. What a loser. A nutcase, a zero.'

'Fuck you!'

'I bet your father couldn't stand the sight of you — '

'You don't know shit. Fuck you. I'm done. You had your chance.'

The roof panel cracked off and a blinding light flooded her eyes.

47

Not blinding. Only the night sky, bright compared to the pitch black of the boxcar. Stuart peered down wearing his goggles, crouched on all fours, and Grace came up hard and launched herself at him. She slammed her shoulder into him coming up onto the roof, and it felt as if she'd hit the side of a house in a hang glider and they both went down hard. She sprayed and he jerked back in a boiling vent of pepper, screaming.

A searing pain shot through her eyes and tears streamed. Stuart was a blur, on his back, an insect, feet and hands moving. He yanked off his mask so he could see her. Tears slicked his nostrils. Saliva roped from his mouth.

The red crossing lights blinked and a train shrilled, the sound loud and close. Yellow headlights splashed across the roof. Stuart grunted and rolled to his feet and Grace feverishly dug into her pocket for a nail and the nails burst into the sky and scattered across the roof. He was still crying from the pepper spray and she had a nail in her hand now and she lunged at him and they grappled. He twisted his body and slammed her down. It happened so quickly it took the air out of her, both of them slippery. He yanked her close, his arm gripping her chest, her back to him, and he was twisting her over to the side,

Grace kicking her feet out uselessly, banging her heels on the roof as he dragged her, making inexorable progress.

The Union Pacific train roared past them, a massive wall of metal. Grace banged her head up into his chin and it snapped his head back and she twisted and found his face as if he were a lover.

For a single moment she could feel his heart beating in his neck. She slammed in the nail and raked it down. Blood spurted. She'd been a doctor; she knew exactly where to find the carotid artery. She didn't need sight, only touch. She shoved the nail back the way it had come and he loosened his grip and she rolled away as he staggered to his feet, swinging hard out into space, trying to find her, his blood spraying a fine red mist into the night sky.

Screaming. There must have been screaming. The train reversed itself and gently bumped into the line of boxcars. The motion upset his balance and he lost his footing and backpedaled down the long narrow spine of the boxcar.

The whistle shrilled and the boxcar seemed to come alive in that instant and jerked forward and she slid toward the gaping hole in the roof, hooked a foot in the top of the ladder and held on.

The movement upset Stuart's equilibrium and he took an unsteady step back. His arms flailed.

He teetered, a dark angel.

With a howl of anguish, he fell.

★ ★ ★

The area around the train was roped off with yellow tape and Grace sat in a folding chair as Deputy Coroner Jeff Salzer and his team tidied things up. Jeff zipped up the body in a bag, tagged it with pertinent information, and loaded it into the white coroner's van.

Her eyes were still streaming. She didn't know how much of that was pepper spray and how much was relief at still being alive.

Stuart Soderberg had slipped off the back of the freight car as it started to move. The movement had sheared off his legs and snapped his neck. Along with the injury she inflicted, it had been fast, but ugly. She'd held on to the roof and listened grimly as his moans quickly lapsed into silence.

The boxcars were being linked to the incoming train mechanically, operated from a computer bay inside the engine. It took time before the engineer realized all was not well. Time before the heavy steel and iron freight cars ground to a stop.

The siding was covered with blood and shredded bone.

Stuart had never spoken another word.

She sat trembling and shaky, telling the same story to a blur of detectives, haz-mat crews, the FBI, and Homeland Security. California state ag advisor Frank Waggaman showed up looking strained as he listened to what Grace had to say about what was grown in Vonda and Stuart's greenhouse, and about the wind turbines being sent across the nation and into other countries, each packed with a violent dose of genetic death.

Grace told the same story to a new blue-jacketed Homeland Security man. She left out the part about suspecting Frank.

At some point she heard sobbing, and realized that Judith Woodruff, president of Windlift, was standing on the periphery, her face in her hands.

The wind turbines for the ag convention were being tracked, and each would be met with the same kind of haz-mat team, removing the hidden soy packet and cleaning up the damage. Even if they ultimately weren't destroyed, they'd be held for evidence. All Judith's work was for nothing. A crew had also been dispatched to the greenhouse to tent and contain it.

The boxcar was tented in a heavy haz-mat covering. A team of Homeland Security men hoisted a cannon connected to a rubber hosing and pump.

'They're foaming it,' her uncle explained as he settled on his haunches next to Grace and handed her a cup of coffee. 'They're going to shoot a biofoam up into that tent.'

'Who killed Tammy?'

'Someone in Radical Damage. We're not sure. After she'd planted the soybean rust at Jeanne's tattoo shop, she started to panic. Feel she was in over her head. But the group wouldn't let her go.'

'What was the key to?'

'A locker at the women's gym at school. Tammy kept her diary there. She'd written everything down. How Nate lured her into the group. The target practice in the desert. Tony ran that part of it. Nate worked on the kids who'd

400

perform during the convention. And Andrea imported the natural skin drums laced with anthrax. Sarah was the tag-along. Whatever fell off the desk, she'd catch.'

Grace took a swallow of coffee. For some reason, her uncle had put sugar in it.

'So I'll find out pretty soon, what Vonda did or didn't do.' He looked at the ground. 'Tammy even has in there how they lied to get their anthrax vaccines. They told the clinic they needed them for work. They had jobs at the post office. Now, that right there should have been a flag. There haven't been jobs available at the post office for three years.'

'Good to know if I ever decide to jump ship.'

'We haven't yet found the transient they killed, but Andrea and Nate and their pals are turning on each other like a pack of jackals. We'll know more soon. They were getting ready to leave — all of them — go someplace else.'

'If Andrea and Nate hadn't been arrested in the cargo theft, does that mean they would have tried taking your grandson Sam with them?'

'It occurred to me, too. Turns out that in the group, Andrea's name was Artemis. That's why when Frank Waggaman was dropping off seed in the greenhouse for Vonda and Stuart, he overheard Bartholomew calling Andrea *Miss* and somebody else call her R-T. It was short for Artemis.'

'Greek goddess of the hunt.'

'Another part, too. I looked it up. Artemis was also the goddess of childbirth.' He shifted uneasily in his seat. 'Of painless deaths in childbirth.'

Grace stared at him.

'I think if you hadn't answered that text message that Vonda sent when she was starting labor, there's a good chance Andrea could have tried to take the baby and run with him, right there.'

Grace remembered the frantic attempt by Andrea and Sarah to maneuver Vonda into their car. Grace wondered if she even would have made it to the hospital.

'Sam's beautiful.'

'Yeah.'

'And families come all sorts of ways.'

'Yeah. It was the lie. That's what's hard.'

Her heart seized. 'Yeah. The lie. Is she doing okay?'

'It'll take time. It's hard to bounce back from finding out that your husband isn't who he said he was. That he orchestrated your infertility, that he made it forever impossible to have children with another Caucasian man. Race is a weird thing. And every single one of us on the planet bears the imprint of the wars that have been fought over it, the lives lost. But when it comes right down to it, we all want to be able to live our lives, choose for ourselves.'

'Can't wait to tell Father McDougal you're spouting choice.'

He smiled wearily.

'How extensive was it? The soy damage?'

'He had soy starter kits, Grace, all set to send out. He was targeting private schools, high-end spas. All neatly stacked in the U-Haul with addresses on them. As they went north, he was going to send Vonda into post offices to mail them. That way, if he was caught, she'd be part of it.'

Grace looked away so she wouldn't have to see the rage in her uncle's eyes.

'I have to hand it to Vonda. She kept records of everything. She'd just started selling the bread at the farmer's market and she kept a list of everybody she sold to, so they'll be hearing from us. She was going to expand things after Sam was born. She used the soy for bread she made for her and Stu and their friends.'

'He must have loved it when their friends started miscarrying.'

Her uncle nodded. 'He wrote about it. We found a journal in the van. Dark stuff. Vonda says he's been journaling for years. It probably will give us a beat-by-beat description of how he planned it out.'

He nodded as a haz-mat crew dragged the hose out of the tent. 'The foam kills particulate matter.'

She wondered if particulate matter meant doctored soy, wondering if she'd inhaled some. Didn't seem likely. The baggie in the windmill had been sealed.

But she'd ground up a fragment in the lab when she'd worked with Denise Bustamonte. She must have inhaled some then. Impossible not to. Pete was looking at her as if he could read her mind.

'Too soon to say, of course, what the

individual impact is on people who may or may not have been exposed, but it seems from a quick look at his journal that it was continued exposure that did the trick. Eating it, not inhaling. And not a onetime thing. And of course, every scientist in the plant bio realm will be working on a way to neutralize what Stuart's done.'

'So you think for now, the threat's not that great.'

'I'm not a scientist, Grace, I don't know what's down the road. I saw in the paper the FDA's thinking about okaying the modification of actual animals. You could eat a hamburger someday with part of a mouse in it.'

'Lovely. And not even have the restaurant close down.'

He shifted on his haunches and readjusted his weight. The silence grew. 'Aunt Chel's back. She's with Vonda in the hospital.'

They waited as two haz-mat men in booties and full gear slowly made their way through a fold in the tented enclosure.

'Uncle Pete?'

'Yeah.'

'Are you sorry for what you did to my family?'

He looked at her. 'I thought I was doing the right thing. I was trying to protect you and Andy. The other stuff — yeah. I'm sorry what happened.'

'But are you sorry for what you *did*?'

Her uncle lowered his face and rubbed it with his hands. 'Grace, my own kid's been hit by a bad man. Looking at her little boy is going to be a reminder, for the rest of her life, of what he did to her. My job is to help her in every way I can love that little boy and let him know how much we want him here. How much we need him. And I plan on letting her know the same thing. That's my work.'

He looked at her steadily. 'Whatever work you have to do, get on with it. There's enough hurt and blame and sorrow without going back in time and digging up old ground. And as far as the rest — I see this shit every day of my life. Parents doing the worst things. Selling their kids. Tying up their grandmothers and leaving them in the trunks of cars driven off bridges. Cutting out an eye just for the hell of it. I thought I was doing the right thing. If you want me to rewrite the past, I can't.'

Forgiveness. It was pretty much bullshit, from where she sat, watching the haz-mat team stamping in the fog and dark.

She was tired. 'I don't want to carry this around anymore.'

Something unexpected happened.

His eyes filled. 'Thanks.'

She felt it then, a band loosening in her chest, in her heart. It wasn't about her uncle. It wasn't about who she was now. It was about that small girl in science class, rushing across the room to her crying brother, scared. It was about that girl. Her uncle was right. Taking care of her was Grace's job, and staying angry at her uncle wasn't doing anything to heal that child.

'Can darkness ever be explained?'

Pete stared out over the busy scene in front of

them. 'That's why we're the good guys, Grace. The sentinels at the gates of hell. We don't have to explain it; we just have to stop it.'

He got up, dusted off his pants, and touched her shoulder.

'I'll drive to San Diego later and debrief you there, get a more formal statement.' He hesitated. 'Good job, kid. Now beat it. Go home.'

48

When she got to the 10 she put the windows down. Behind her in the rearview mirror, she caught a glimpse of lights in the darkness behind her. Nobody was on the road in the middle of the night except truckers. She stopped once for coffee at a McDonald's in Oceanside.

The air seemed to grow heavier the closer she got to home. They'd had a run of dry weather, months of it, and everybody was worried about fires. For all its beauty, San Diego was a fragile place.

The sun came up as she made the outskirts of San Diego County. The traffic picked up. She wondered if she had time to go home and take a shower. She didn't want to miss seeing Katie before school. She had things she needed to say. But she didn't want to say those things stinking, with Stuart's blood on her shirt.

She stood under the shower a long time, trying to get the smell of the trip out of her skin, the wounds out of her heart. It was good to wear clean clothes again.

It was almost seven when she pulled into the parking lot of Le Rondelet.

The pink on the water had shifted to silvery gray. A black bank of clouds hovered over the city. Fires could look like that, when they'd been burning, but there was no smell of smoke.

A fisherman in rubber boots came out of the

bait shop across the street, holding a paper bag. A boat and trailer were parked at the curb. He climbed up into the back of the boat and disappeared.

The building had stairwells that ran along the outside of the condos. Her footsteps scraped the metal stairs as she climbed. She hesitated before knocking but the tiredness had caught up, along with the other things. She rapped on the door.

She didn't know what she'd do if he didn't answer, she really didn't. She leaned her forehead into the door. She tried again. This time, she heard something stirring inside. Somebody coming.

'Yes?' His voice was low, guarded.

'It's me.'

He opened the door. He took one look at her and pulled her to him. She buried her face in his robe and he moved her inside.

'What happened?'

She tightened her arms around him. His body was still sleep-warm and his robe was soft and smelled clean.

'I'm sorry.' The pain welled up. She was on her own now. Lost. 'I thought I was doing the right thing, Mac, but I was wrong. I hurt you and I hurt Katie and I hurt myself and I don't know how I can get past that. Make it right.'

'Mama?' Katie walked into the living room, sleepy and digging a finger into her eye. She was a golden color, her skin, her hair.

She stopped. Her nightgown moved around her ankles. 'Mommy.'

Grace dropped to her knees. She opened her

arms and Katie came into them. Grace held her and inhaled, breathing in the sweet sleep scent of her daughter.

'I lied about Daddy.'

Katie tightened her grip, her arms small, and pressed her face into Grace's chest. 'It was mean.'

'It was.'

'How could you do something so mean?'

Katie detached her grip so she was staring into her mother's face. Her dark brown eyes stared fixedly at Grace, eyes wounded, cautious, and it was the cautiousness that broke Grace in two. Katie had never had to be careful around her before and it was Grace's job to make sure Katie never would have to be again.

'Mommy was hurt and I didn't know what else to do. But I wasn't thinking about the right thing. I was thinking about the easy thing. And that was wrong. I was wrong. I'm sorry.'

Katie digested that. 'You'll never do it again, right?'

It was such a small thing to say compared to the monumental wrong Grace had done. She stared soberly at her daughter and saw a flash of years passing, Katie growing long-limbed, growing away. 'No.'

'Okay.' Katie pulled away and yawned. 'Can we have pancakes for breakfast?'

★   ★   ★

Mac walked Katie to school, a tall, big-shouldered man reaching down to hold the hand of a little girl. They'd parked in the back lot at Cabrillo Elementary, and Grace stayed in the car with the windows down and watched them through the windshield. It was almost time for the bell and the walkway teemed with kids with gelled hair and backpacks. The little kids, Katie's age, all had a busy parent pushing them along.

A boy stopped and looked at Mac and back to Katie. 'Who is that guy?' His voice was shrill and carried over the laughter and chatter of the other kids.

Katie looked up at Mac and he smiled.

'That's my daddy.'

★   ★   ★

Mac drove Grace back to her car. He stopped, stared straight ahead, his hands loose on the wheel.

'I've been thinking.' He switched off the engine.

'Me, too.'

He didn't touch her. She wondered if he ever would. A kid on a skateboard shot past.

Finally he said, 'I saw her, and these two things came roaring up out of nowhere. More, but these hit me hard. First, this intense love. You hear about it. You just don't understand it until it's *yours*.' He smiled briefly and Grace could see the pain under it. 'She's so funny.'

'Yeah.'

'Beautiful.'

Grace looked at her hands, willing herself not to cry.

'And the second was anger. So strong, this rage. At you. Even in the hospital, when I was pushing for everything to work, I was starting to feel it. And I never said a word. I kept my mouth shut. For that, I am truly sorry.'

Grace swallowed. She studied the sky, the dark drift of clouds, aware of the pain pulsing through her. She was afraid to breathe, afraid it would hurt.

'What I said in the hospital and that first day in the Bahamas, about trying, even if we're not sure, that's only part of it.'

He glanced toward Le Rondelet. A woman in a business suit pushed open the front door and hurried to her car, talking on her cell.

'The rest — buying this place, hedging my bets, being there for Katie, not knowing how it's going to end, for us — that's true, too.'

A dark green garbage truck creaked slowly into the parking lot and backed up as a man in uniform detached from his perch and trotted forward to guide it toward the bins.

Mac looked at her, his eyes dark with emotion. His voice was low. 'It's over so fast, a life. That's what I was thinking, Grace. There and gone. I remember T. S. Eliot spoke of the future in some poem, and the past, and how they merge only at this moment in time. The *here and now*. So now I'm back to thinking — would it be so bad, staying. Together.'

Her heart twinged. She knew now what she needed to say. 'Yeah. It would.'

If he came to her with no sense of joy, if she settled for that, at some point, whatever dignity and self-respect he had as a man would force him to walk away from her, and when that happened, it would be for good. And Katie would have as a model only two parents who were polite and remote and careful with each other, no map at all, no way in to a country where happiness bubbled between parents, a country Grace feared that without a guide, Katie would never find.

Grace needed to let him go. Let her light-filled daughter go. Into a place she couldn't follow.

She looked out the window again. If the fence at the corner wasn't there, she'd almost be able to see her house. A car cruised by and turned onto Shelter Island Drive.

'I get it, Mac. That's what I came to say. You deserve a chance to get to know her.' A tear slid down her face. 'I've been thinking lately. About forgiveness. What it costs. What I'm *not* willing to sacrifice. You want to hear? It's a short list.'

It felt as if her heart was exploding. As if her breath had stopped.

'Grace.'

The current was hard and fast, a riptide pulling her out to sea, away from everything she loved, far from home.

'Here are the things I will not sacrifice. Katie's laugh. It's gold. It really is. The way she throws her head back and her shoulders rock. Her tender feelings. Her safety and happiness. The importance of teaching her mortal truths. Her need to know her father. And your need — your *right* — to know her — ' She opened her mouth, trying to take a breath and all that came out was a heart-rending cry: 'without me.'

She held up her hands, stopping him from touching her. She licked away a tear.

'No, no, wait, listen. The other day, she took me into the living room and said, *See Mommy, I can make music.* And she ran her bare foot over the heating grate and the grate rang — like chords on a harp. And she had this strong, wide smile on her face. She'd shown me something amazing, just *me*. You deserve that same chance, and if I'm there all the time — '

He reached across the seat and pulled her to him. She held on to him, clung to him. She could feel his heart pounding. He smoothed her hair, carefully, so careful with his touch. She could feel him take a choked breath. 'Thank you.'

She was far from shore now, the edge of the known world growing hazy, indistinct. It was cold where she was, the boat small.

She didn't expect him to speak, and when he did, his voice was uneven. 'We can go nine more rounds with this and keep chewing it or we can just go on.'

She sat with it. Felt it come into her. A cautious warmth. A light.

'Can you do that?'

'Can you stay?' He hesitated. 'I want you to stay.'

It was as if Grace had seen a marker, waving lights, a fire, maybe, people she loved calling her name, guiding her home.

They got out of the car and walked through the parking lot, and as they crossed into the lobby, it began to rain.

Acknowledgements

My life rocks with celestial music, and I thank most the three people who make it out of the air itself: Martha, my brave and tender-hearted daughter, your choices make me proud beyond words; Aaron, my talented and complex son, thanks for the light you bring; and Fred, my guy, who hangs the moon. Thanks, you three, for the songs.

I do believe this house is filled with magic, my four-year-old great-nephew, Daniel White, said to me. And it is. Inside this house, this time, in random rooms: my stepdad, Bruno Johnson, thanks for your encouragement; Carol Landis, for the book about forgiveness; my niece, Dori Altmiller, for the shining piece of glitter I used in my last novel; godmother Kathy Rowley — strong light pours from you — thanks for giving our kids such a perfect model of how to live well; godfather George Palmer, for your tenderness and for driving back the dark; Tony Vittal, for your energy and heart; Judi Vittal, for believing in our friendship even when I drop the ball; Heather Arnett, my friend in the trenches, my friend for life; Linda Molloy, for your goodness; and Caitlin Moreland, Mary Ann Rhode, and Gary Antweiler, who walked in and made my day. And Joanne Newman and Terri Christianson, for the laughter.

This book could not have been written

without help. I thank especially Palm Springs FBI Special Agent Mark Hunter, for your time and the details; police officer Troy Castillo, for showing me how your world works; police evidence technician Sam Pye, for letting me into the clubhouse; Union Pacific Railroad Police Lieutenant Richard Mosley, for the bits about trains and the yard; Riverside County Coroner Sergeant Brent Sechrest, for reminding me that you speak for the dead; forensic document examiner Randy Gibson, for your friendship and for opening doors. Also: Dr Marilyn Carlin, Dr Ned Chambers, UCSD librarian Annelise Sklar, Bill Canales at Full Circle Tattoo, police DNA consultant Zach Gaskin, and Steve Koike of the Monterey County Cooperative. Riff Markowitz is a real person, gracious and dynamic, and the men and women in the Palm Springs Follies defy age, space, and time. Go see them.

Thanks, thanks, and more thanks to my editor, Kelley Ragland, and to the team at St Martin's: Matt Martz, Jessica Rotondi, Hector DeJean, Monica Katz, Karen Richardson, John Morrone, David Rotstein, and Andy Martin, the head of this house; and to Nancy Yost and the gang at Lowenstein-Yost, Zoe Fishman, Natanya Wheeler, Tom Mone, Norman Kurz.

At HarperCollins: Clare Smith, who has championed my work from the start; Essie Cousins, who has been extraordinary in seamlessly picking up the reins; Sophie Goulden, for her good eye and delicate touch; Taressa

Brennan, for the amazing publicity campaign; Mell Vandevelde for her hard work in production; and Leo Nickolls, whose covers are a work of art.

And thanks to you readers. Without you, there would be no magic.

We do hope that you have enjoyed reading this large print book.

Did you know that all of our titles are available for purchase?

We publish a wide range of high quality large print books including:
Romances, Mysteries, Classics
General Fiction
Non Fiction and Westerns

Special interest titles available in large print are:
The Little Oxford Dictionary
Music Book
Song Book
Hymn Book
Service Book

Also available from us courtesy of Oxford University Press:
Young Readers' Dictionary
(large print edition)
Young Readers' Thesaurus
(large print edition)

For further information or a free brochure, please contact us at:
Ulverscroft Large Print Books Ltd.,
The Green, Bradgate Road, Anstey,
Leicester, LE7 7FU, England.
Tel: (00 44) 0116 236 4325
Fax: (00 44) 0116 234 0205

THE TIMER GAME

Susan Arnout Smith

A reluctant CSI detective with the San Diego squad, Grace Descanso is summoned to attend a seemingly routine crime scene. Hours later, two detectives have been brutally murdered and Grace herself is under investigation for shooting the killer. Her daughter Katie is five years old. She's all Grace has got. But when Katie is snatched, Grace is thrown into a nightmare world of timed riddles that she must solve in order to find her daughter before it's too late. She has twenty-four hours before Katie dies. Welcome to the Timer Game . . .

THE STRANGE CASE OF THE COMPOSER AND HIS JUDGE

Patricia Duncker

New Year's Day, 2000. Hunters, in a forest in the Jura, stumble upon a half-circle of dead bodies lying in the snow. A nearby holiday chalet containing children's presents and decorations indicate a seemingly ordinary Christmas. Searching for clues, the judge, Dominique Carpentier and Commissaire Andre Schweigen find a strange leather-bound book, written in mysterious code, containing maps of the stars. The book leads them to the Composer, Friedrich Grosz, who is connected to every one of the dead. And so the pursuit begins. Carpentier and Schweigen are drawn into a world of complex family ties, ancient beliefs and seductive, disturbing music. Carpentier, proud of her ability to expose frauds and charlatans, likes to win — has she met her match in the Composer?

WINTERLAND

Alan Glynn

The worlds of business, politics and crime collide when two men with the same name, from the same family, die on the same night — one death is a gangland murder, the other, apparently, a road accident. Was it a coincidence? That's the official line. But then a family member, Gina Rafferty, starts to look into things and soon finds that she can't accept such a simple version of events. Told repeatedly that she should stop asking questions, she becomes more determined than ever to establish a connection between the two deaths — but in doing so she embarks on a path that will push certain people to their limits . . .

DEAD IN THE WATER

Aline Templeton

The young victim had been pregnant, her body washed up on the rocks. Twenty years on the murder remains unsolved; her father is now dead, and her mother won't talk about what went on all those years ago. Detective Inspector Marjory Fleming is called in to reopen the case that her late father, a policeman, was unable to put to rest. As Fleming digs deeper it becomes clear that her father had struggled to keep secret some of the shameful details around the young girl's death. Can Fleming handle the truth she will unearth, not just about her father, but about herself?

MIDNIGHT FUGUE

Reginald Hill

Gina Wolfe has come to Mid-Yorkshire in search of her missing husband, believed dead. Her fiance, Commander Mick Purdy of the Met, thinks Dalziel should take care of the job. What none of them realize is how events set in motion decades ago will come to a violent head on this otherwise ordinary autumn day. A Welsh tabloid journalist senses the story he's been chasing for years may have finally landed in his lap. A Tory MP's assistant suspects her boss's father has an unsavoury history that could taint his prime ministerial ambitions. The ruthless entrepreneur in question sends out two henchmen to make sure the past stays in the past. And the lethal pair dispatched have awkward secrets of their own.

Please return on or before the latest date above.
You can renew online at *www.kent.gov.uk/libs*
or by telephone 08458 247 200

Smith, Susan Arnaut.
Out at Night

CUSTOMER SERVICE EXCELLENCE

Libraries & Archives

00884\DTP\RN\07.07   LIB 7